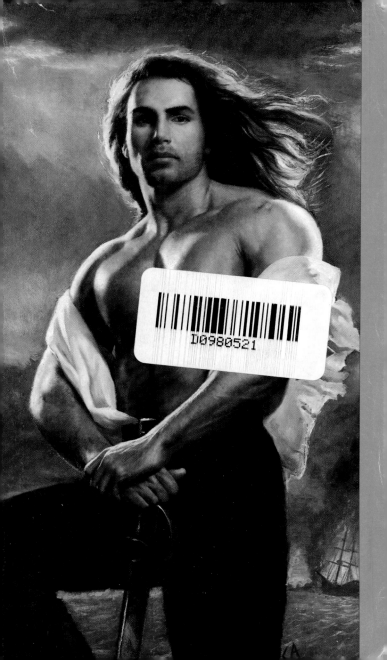

A STOLEN KISS

"Why didn't you say something? Why didn't you show yourself right away?"

"I . . . don't know. I just . . . I don't know. By the time I realized you were there, you were already half naked and—and . . ." She swallowed hard and raised her hand in an unconsciously sensual gesture, pushing aside the edges of her shirt to press cooling fingers against the rapid pulse beating at the base of her throat.

"If—if you would step aside now, Captain, and let me pass, I would be more than happy to give you back your privacy." But instead of stepping aside, he moved forward, keeping her trapped against the gallery windows, cloaking her in the immense shadow of his own frame. "Not just yet, mam'selle."

"Wh-what do you mean?"

"I mean"—his hands came up and he brushed his fingers over the rich abundance of her hair—"not just yet."

She tensed as he caressed the back of her neck. She was more aware than ever of the heavily muscled shoulders, the dark swarm of hair that covered his chest, the molded bands of hard flesh that flexed along his arms every time he asked the slightest motion of them.

Her eyes rose, not enough to have met his, but enough to focus on the half smile that played on his lips.

"I hope you are not thinking of kissing me," she whispered, her throat almost too constricted to squeeze out the words.

UNDER A DESERT MOON

"This has everything a good western should: adventure, murder, mystery, and love. What an unbeatable combination!"
—*Heartland Critiques*

"EXCITING . . . A fast-paced, action-packed story that kept me hanging on every word. Great work, Marsha!"—*Affaire de Coeur*

"EXTRAORDINARY . . . Vivid prose, vibrant descriptions, a delightful cast of characters, fast-paced action and a strong story . . . readers will be spellbound!"—*Romantic Times*

THROUGH A DARK MIST

"All the adventure, rollicking good humor, wildly exciting escapades, cliff-hangers, and, most of all, smoldering sensuality. . . . Once you begin this mesmerizing tale there is no way you will put it down until the very last page."—*Romantic Times*

"Ms. Canham has set quill to bow and struck directly into the heart of every swashbuckling adventure lover's soul. . . . The action doesn't stop until the last paragraph with no questions left unanswered."—*Heartland Critiques*

MARSHA CANHAM

ACROSS A MOONLIT SEA

A Dell Book

Published by
Dell Publishing
a division of
Bantam Doubleday Dell Publishing Group, Inc.
1540 Broadway
New York, New York 10036

ISBN: 0-440-21785-7

Printed in the United States of America

Published simultaneously in Canada

February 1996

10 9 8 7 6 5 4 3 2 1

OPM

I suppose it is time to acknowledge the irreverent group of iconoclasts who comprise the Noake Crescent Revelry Committee: the Griswalds, the Big Souvlaki and Peggy Bundy, the Warden, Ward and June Cleaver, the Rosedale Princess and Tom Terrific, the Commodores, the residents of Fort Noakes, and those unflagging honorary members, Fred and Ethel, Bunky and Rick, Tweety and Sylvester. With a group of neighbors like this, how could I ever run out of material for secondary characters?

Simon Dante narrowed his silvery blue eyes in an attempt to separate the distant galleons from the dancing points of sunlight that reflected off the surface of the water. He saw nothing to make him change his earlier guess. The India guards were small, stubby vessels carrying three masts and a deck bristling with armaments, designed for only one purpose: to discourage raiders and privateers of any nationality from attacking the rich plate fleets that sailed regularly between Spain and the New World. They were usually part of an escort of fifty zabras or more, protecting as few as twenty treasure ships at a time. The fact there were only six surging along at full sail suggested they had become separated from the main body of the fleet they were protecting, probably during the same storm that had battered the *Talon* and *Virago*.

"Three masted," Dante reiterated grimly. "Most likely ten guns apiece, demi-culverins at best, sakers at least. We should have no trouble with them."

"No trouble?" Victor Bloodstone arched a sand-colored eyebrow. "It will be like sailing into a nest of enraged hornets. And in case you haven't noticed, my dear Comte, we are somewhat at a disadvantage—the result, I might also add, of another of your rash decisions, made without any consultation or discussion."

Dante's gaze remained fixed on the horizon for a moment before turning coldly to Bloodstone. It was the kind of stare he normally reserved for scullions and fools, or for very large bugs that made a very sticky mess under his boot, and it did not take but a heartbeat for Bloodstone to interpret the look and flush warmly under the deep bronze of his tan.

Over the past three months it had become blatantly obvious the two men could barely abide each other. Both were brilliant seamen, and equal only to each other as far as nerve and boldness in battle. Both struck terror as well as awe in their crews for having dared to go where none had ventured before, and for coming away with their holds bulging with bars of Spanish gold and silver.

But where Bloodstone was eager to return to England, to bask in the praise and reap the rewards for his success—fully anticipating a knighthood would be in the offing—Dante had no such aspirations. He had already earned more accolades than he could reasonably tolerate. Moreover, the Comte de Tourville was not yet finished with the Spanish. He and the *Virago* would, in fact, have parted ways with Bloodstone a full week earlier had the storm not intervened and forced them to remain together. Now there were six enemy warships bearing down on them—odds neither captain would have hesitated to defy alone had his ship been in prime condition—but they needed each other again if they were to emerge with their ships and their prize intact.

"Very well," Dante said, the huge muscles in his shoulders rippling as he folded his arms across his chest. "My ship is rudderless and leaking like a sieve; yours is storm damaged with a crack in the mainmast and no spare canvas. What do you propose we do?"

Bloodstone pressed his thin lips thinner in an imitation of a smile. "I expect we have little choice but to fight our way past them."

"We have no choice," Dante said flatly. "And we will have to destroy them in order to keep our presence here quiet, at least until we can finish our mission."

"*Your* mission," Bloodstone corrected him succinctly. "Mine is finished. We did what we set out to do, and we did it well enough to set Philip of Spain spinning around on his royal papist heels. Whatever business you now deem to have unfinished is yours alone. I agreed to one raid and one raid only."

Dante's opinion of the Englishman sat on the back of his tongue, souring it like the taste of stale beer. Bloodstone was nephew to Sir Francis Walsingham, the Queen's first counsel and chief advisor. He had sailed with Sir Francis Drake—another arrogant strut of a man—and was reputed to be one of Elizabeth's favorite supper companions. Fawning over popinjays and seducing aging queens did not rank high in Dante's estimation of character qualities, and the sooner he was clear of Bloodstone, the sweeter the air he would breathe.

His cold eyes flicked back to the growing pyramids of sail. "If they have any eyes at all on board, they will have seen the *Virago* by now. The *Talon*, luckily, is still out of view and should remain so until they are almost on us. The wind is behind them and they will keep it to their advantage as long as possible. I propose, therefore"—he looked back at Bloodstone—"to sail the *Virago* across their bows and draw their attention away from this islet. We will engage and hold them long enough for you to bring the *Talon* around and come at them from upwind. We won't have to try very hard to appear to be mortally wounded, and should present a prize too tempting for the bastards to resist."

Bloodstone nodded consideringly. It was an audacious and risky plan, and Dante would undoubtedly draw heavy fire from all six zabras. There were few Spaniards on the Main who did not know the *Virago* by sight, and seeing her wounded and apparently running away in distress would, indeed, attract them like leeches to blood. It would be up to the *Talon* to come to his rescue and blast the Spaniards in a crossfire.

Bloodstone reached up and tugged on a gleaming gold

forelock. He wore rings on all four fingers of both hands, and the jewels glittered as brightly as the sudden avarice in the liquid brown eyes. "My compliments, Captain Dante. It should be like picking ducks off a pond."

Four hours later, with the sun glaring in the westerly sky at eye level, Captain Dante ordered his men into the shrouds. With a temporary patch sealing the gash in the *Virago*'s hull, they had left the shelter of the island and started a run south by southeast and, as Dante had predicted, the India guards had turned, almost as one, and set after him with their noses high and the water sheeting off their hulls in scrolls of blue-white spume. Dante had set his own suit carefully, leaving slack in the square mainsails so they appeared full and straining to catch every ounce of strength and speed from the wind. He had fore and aft maneuverability in the remainder of his sails, but those, too, he kept on an angle not favorable to the *Virago*'s reputation as a flying sea witch.

   Standing on the foredeck, his hair whipping in the breeze like black silk, he passed quiet, steady orders to his helmsman, who knew better than to question why he should make the *Virago* seem erratic and unsteady, when he also knew, even with a jury-rigged rudder, they could have sailed circles around all six of the charging Spaniards and left them reeling in their wake.

   Dante's second-in-command—Geoffrey Pitt—stood amidships, his feet braced wide apart to counter the increasing roll of the deck. His tawny hair was lashed in a tail at his nape and his face, beneath the weathering effects of the sun, was nearly as green as his eyes. He was not a sailor by profession, nor even by choice, and was still battling the galling effects of the week-long storm. But he knew guns and was in charge of the *Virago*'s teeth: ten bronze demi-cannon capable of firing thirty-two-pound lead balls a distance of three hundred yards and more, supplemented by fourteen cast-iron culverins that fed on seventeen-pound shot. There were also the falconets at the bow and stern, long elegant guns of a smaller caliber reserved for special surprises at close range.

Pitt's chief gunner was almost as awesome as the guns he fired. Nearly seven feet tall, black as ebony, the former slave was possibly the only man on board the *Virago* more feared than the captain himself. The Cimaroon's first greeting to the enemy had become traditional. Wearing only a loincloth and a leer of impending pleasure, he climbed barefoot into the shrouds and sent a hot yellow stream of contempt in the direction of the approaching vessels. The men on deck and in the yards cheered, waving their fists and hurling insults even as an answering puff of smoke erupted from the guns of the forerunning galleon.

Although smaller than the *Virago* and not as heavily armed, the galleons had the wind to their advantage, and bearing down like vultures, they formed a fighting crescent and trimmed sail. The ship that had fired the opening salvo commanded the starboard point of the crescent. Seeing that the *Virago* seemed willing—and foolhardy enough—to turn and put up a fight, he pulled arrogantly ahead of the others and opened the attack.

"He thinks we are so bad off, he can take us single handed!" Dante shouted. "Shall we correct his impression, Mister Pitt?"

"Ready on your command, Captain!"

"On my command." Dante nodded and turned to the helmsman. "Bring her hard to larboard and keep her as tight as you can."

"Aye, sir!" The helmsman positioned himself at the makeshift tiller and swore. "I can't say how long this bloody oar will hold, but she has spirit in her yards and she'll take it up with the wind, sure enough."

"Just give me one long, smooth pass, Mister Brighton. She'll take it up with her guns."

"Aye, sir! That she will, sir!"

Dante felt the blood surging through his veins. The Spaniard was closing fast, full sailed and hull up, carving through the iron-gray swells like a cleaver. The *Virago* was still feigning unsteady knees and with only a third of her gunports open, she lured the Spaniard into a show of bravado. The zabra fired another salvo from her two bow guns, one ball spouting harmlessly in the privateer's wake, the other bouncing insolently off her three-foot-thick hull. At less than a quarter mile, Dante could see men on the Spaniard's deck, clustered on the stubby forecastle, fingers pointing at the *Virago* as if they were already arguing over the division of spoils.

His wide, sensuous mouth spread in a slow grin.

"Mister Brighton—"

The helmsman's lips parted, his fist clenched on the tiller.

"—Now! Bring her hard about!"

Tackle clattered and rigging lines sang as cables were loosened and reset to turn the sails. Canvas boomed overhead and the towering masts heeled far out over the rising sea as the *Virago* slewed into the wind, throwing up long plumes of spray in her wake.

"Mister Pitt! Guns away! Open us up and show all of our fine teeth. Fire when ready!"

On deck, Pitt's crews opened the remaining gunports and hauled the cannon into position for firing. Pitt raised his arm, waiting for the initial roll to subside as the *Virago* completed her turn. The Spaniard was directly on their beam, cleanly in the sights of all twelve heavy guns that best haul us in. Keep a square or two aloft for steerage in case a wind does come along."

The order was relayed and almost immediately there were men clambering nimbly up the shrouds and steadying themselves on the yards while others released the tension in the rigging lines and allowed the sails to be reefed and lashed to the spars. It was slower work than normal, for the sails had been well soaked with seawater to swell the canvas and take advantage of any breath of air. They had been becalmed three days now, and aside from the occasional cat's paw that scudded over the surface of the water, they had drifted no more than a league or two in that time.

That was why, when the dawn began to melt away the morning mist, the sight of another ship standing so close at hand had tightened more than a few sphincter muscles. Nearly every one of the *Egret's* crewmen lined the rails; none had moved away over the past hour, few had raised their voices above a whisper. They were still in dangerous waters and without wind to move them, they would be easy pickings for enemy gunners.

The low, thick ceiling of cloud that had hung over them for the same three days had made it near impossible to take any kind of a reading from the sun during the day or from the stars at night. The helmsman's best guess to their position had them stalled square in the middle of Spain's busiest shipping lanes. They were homeward bound, still four weeks out of Plymouth; low on victuals and fresh water, lower still on any inclinations they might have to engage a strange vessel in enemy water. They had heard rumors, before their departure from the Caribbean, that King Philip's plate fleet had cleared Hispaniola two weeks before them. The huge galleons, burdened by the gold and silver mined in Panama and Mexico, would be slower moving than the *Egret*, and it was not inconceivable they could have caught up. Moreover, these plate fleets traveled under heavy escort from India guards whose decks bristled with guns of all sizes and calibers, whose captains had no compunctions about attacking stray ships and collecting English crews to enslave in their galleys.

McCutcheon's concerns were genuine and Spence took his wiry mate's counsel to heart. Spit had been on the sea more years than most ships in the English fleet. What few spikes of hair he had sticking out on his scalp and chin were gray, and if he stood on tiptoes the top of his head might reach Spence's armpit. They had been together nigh on fifteen years, one of the oddest couples on the Main, and known by nearly every merchant and investor in Plymouth for the quality of sugarcane rum they ran up from the Indies.

The *Egret* was armed, as any reasonably minded merchant trader should be, and had seen her fair share of fighting, mostly against Spanish and Portugese privateers who objected to Spence's interference in their trade monopolies. But as any Englishman knew, a man was only as good as the ship he sailed. Both the Spanish and the Portugee had clung to the centuries-old design of square-rigged masts, which meant they could sail only where the wind took them. English vessels were fore-and-aft rigged on all but the main square sail, adding maneuverability in the yards that allowed them to sail circles around more cumbersome galleons, which could only watch and grow dizzy.

The wounded galleon before them was definitely English in design and flew the Cross of St. George on what was left of its topmast, though it was as tattered and charred as her other pennants.

"Below Aulde George, there," Spence said, narrowing his amber eyes to bring the topmast into better focus. "Do ye recognize the pennon?"

"Crimson on black. A stag, or a goat, I make it." Mc-Cutcheon shook his head. "The crest is not familiar to me."

"Aye, well, it *feels* like it should be familiar. At any rate, she's no simple merchant wandered too far from home. She's showin' ten bloody demi-cannon an' fourteen culverins in her main battery as well as falconets and perriers fore an' aft." Spence pointed at the monstrous thirty-two-pounders snug in her waist and added out the side of his mouth, "I'll wager whoever her master is, he's not one to haggle over the price o' trade goods."

"Mayhap she'll have shot to spare an' a tun or two o' powder if her magazine is not underwater." McCutcheon's graveled voice did not betray too much optimism. "Or if she did not use it all gettin' herself in such a condition."

Spence straightened and scratched thoughtfully at the violent red beard that foamed over his chin. It was a cool morning, yet there was a faint sheen of moisture across his brow, glinting off the bald dome of his head. He kept staring at the limp pennant that hung so forlornly in the still air. Something about it was nagging at the back of his mind. Something was making his skin itch and his ballocks tighten—a sure sign of trouble ahead.

"Well, we've no choice but to take a look. An' no harm in passin' by the armory on the way."

"Aye," Spit grumbled, and passed the order over his shoulder. "Cutlasses an' pistols, ten shots apiece. Lewis, Gabinet, Brockman, Hubbard, Mawhinney—" He paused in naming the best musketmen on board and his wizened gaze settled on one particularily expectant face.

The amber eyes of the captain, which more often than not twinkled with mischief and good humor, had not retained their joviality in his offspring. Solemn and serious most times, Beau Spence's eyes were large and fiercely proud and more often than not brought to mind a tigress stalking its prey. Thankfully, neither the captain's ponderous girth nor the shocking red fuzz that dominated his walruslike features had been passed to his daughter. Beau's hair shone with only hints of red in the brightest of sunlight, and then only on the rare occasions she left it unplaited. Most times she kept the rich auburn braid bound as tightly as her doublet, which, though considerably smaller in size than any other garment on board, did a fair job in flattening and smoothing any distractions that might lure a lecherous eye from his work. Moreover, being the only woman on board a ship full of lusty-minded men, she had shown no hesitation or lack of skill in using the razor-sharp dagger she wore strapped about her waist, or—as one poor gelded bastard had discovered—the wickedly thin stiletto she kept sheathed in the cuff of her boot.

There had been some who had balked at the notion of a woman joining the crew of the *Egret*—what soundly superstitious sailor would not? But she knew every plank, spar, and cleat on board. She worked as hard as any of them and ofttimes harder than most, if only to prove she was deserving of their respect. Seven voyages ranging from six months' to a year's duration had more than proven it. It was only the captain who tried to test her patience now and then. Four weeks from home and he was starting to take precautions as if he were suddenly remembering he was her father.

But Spit McCutcheon had no qualms about including her in any venture. She was a dead shot with a pistol and could hold her own with a cutlass against men twice her size. And even if the tiger eyes had not been focused intently on him now, almost daring him to pass her by, he probably would have called her name.

"Aye, Beau. Fetch yourself a cutlass an' join the party.

Have Roald break out some pipes o' water as well; no tellin' what we might find over yonder."

Beau followed the others down to the main deck and waited for the weaponry to be distributed. She buckled a cutlass around her waist and slipped a second belt, strung with powder cartridges and a pouch of lead shot, over her shoulder. A brace of pistols completed her arsenal, tucked securely into the sword belt and adjusted like old friends.

Jonas Spence paid no more heed to his daughter than to anyone else as he raked the small group and pronounced them ready. He led the way to the ship's rail and climbed down the gangway ladder to where four oarsmen were waiting in the jolly boat. He had not troubled to cover his bald head with a hat, but he drew on a pair of leather gloves as the boat pushed away from the hull of the *Egret*.

The captain's gloves were specially made, the left one containing two stuffed fingers to replace the ones he had lost to a misfired musket several years ago. It was a small affectation, wanting to appear whole in front of strangers, and extended to include the wooden calf and foot he had learned to use with only a minor limp to betray the fact his leg was shot away below the knee. Despite the impediments, there was not a tar on board who would not have followed him into hell if he asked it of them. The *Egret* carried a crew of ninety and it was to Spence's credit as a fair and able master, that the same ninety men, give or take a spate, had been with him since his ship had been launched from the dockyards ten years ago.

As the jolly boat came within hailing distance of the unknown ship, the crew's attention was fixed steadfastly on the looming hull. There were still no signs of movement on board, no glimpse of a curious head, no ominous creak of a falconet swiveling on its iron cradle to take aim on the advancing boatmen. There was only the soft rush of water sliding under the keel of the jolly boat, and the faint clinking of two small iron rings that dangled from a broken spar high above the deck.

"Ahoy there! Anyone aboard?"

Spence's booming voice sounded unnaturally loud as it rolled across the gap and echoed off the hull of the wreck.

Eight hands rested over the curved stocks of eight cocked pistols while all eyes continued to stare intently up at the ship. This close, the damage to her superstructure gave clear evidence she had been involved in fierce fighting. Aside from the scars and pocks that marbled her sheathing, there was fully ten feet of clean board below the waterline indicating a fatal leak somewhere in her keel. Another six feet would bring the sea on level with her open gunports, and inboard flooding would finish the job.

Spence signaled the oarsmen to bring them up to the gangway ladder. He was first up the steps, with the grizzled, bone-thin McCutcheon a beat behind. Beau was next to last and made the climb with no difficulty in spite of the perilous tilt of the hull.

The sight awaiting them at the top caused them all to stop in a group inside the gangway hatch. The deck was a wasteland of debris. Planking was torn and blackened from fire, ropes and rigging lines snaked haphazardly across the ruin; the forecastle structure was gone completely, leaving only a gaping black hole in the deck. Barrels and buckets were upturned or on their sides, smashed timbers lay strewn over hatchways, and torn sheets of canvas sail hung limply from the spars overhead. Three crippled cannon rested where they had been blown from their trunions. From under the barrel of one of these smashed cannon a hand and arm protruded, the fingers blackened and frozen in a claw.

A ferocious battle had indeed been waged, not too recently to judge by the lack of staining from blood and ash.

But recently enough to retain the stench of charred wood and decaying bodies.

"Ahoy!" Spence shouted again. "Be there anyone on board alive enough to hear the sound o' my voice? If so, sally forth an' show yerselves without fear o' harm, for we fly the Cross o' St. George an' serve Her Most Royal Majesty, Elizabeth of England."

Something—a boot scraping on wood or a piece of debris carelessly unsettled—startled every pair of eyes in the direction of the bulkhead below the mangled remains of the forecastle. A man emerged from the shadows of the hatchway, too tall to do so without ducking his head. His shirt was torn and filthy, the lacing long gone to some other use so that the edges of cloth hung open to his waist. Both sleeves were gone, baring arms that were carved from slabs of rock-hard muscle, bulging with more than enough power to steady two fully primed and cocked arquebuses on the group at the rail.

He stood with his long legs braced wide apart as if balancing himself against heavily rolling seas. His eyes were piercing even at that distance, so pale a blue as to be almost silver. His hair fell in thick black waves to frame a squared jaw and a wide pillar of a neck, both blunted under a heavy growth of coarse gunmetal stubble. From the deep V of his opened shirt, a similarly dark forest of hair gleamed smooth and silky beneath the linen.

Yet, as formidable as he succeeded in appearing, his skin had an unhealthy waxen cast beneath the bronze tan. His lips were cracked from lack of water, the whites of his eyes were shot with bright red veins. Despite the bulk of muscle that shaped him, his cheeks betrayed a hint of gauntness suggesting he had gone even longer without food than water.

"Who are you?" he rasped. "What ship?"

Spence lifted a hand to signal his men to caution as he took a wary step forward. "My name is Jonas Spence. My ship is the *Egret*. We hail from Plymouth, our home port, an' have been in the Caribbee these past eight months seeking honest trade."

"An honest English merchantman? I count five guns in your starboard battery."

"Aye, an' I count two dozen in yer main, another half score in yer bow an' stern for chasers. Nor have I heard a name for you or yer ship, though I see by yer flags we both claim loyalty to England's queen."

The silver eyes flared with an unaccountable fury for a moment before he answered. "My faith in a man's loyalty is not as secure as it might have been a month ago, Captain Spence. You will forgive me if I feel a need to err in favor of caution."

"Ye're alone here?" Spence asked, scanning the deserted deck.

"If I were, I would have gone mad long before now." He lowered the snouts of both muskets, obviously a signal to the rest of his men, who began stepping forward out of hatchways and from behind piles of debris. There were perhaps fifty in all, though only one, besides the leader, won prolonged stares. He appeared on the deck above them like a thundercloud, tall, black, and massive, naked but for a winding of indigo cloth around his gleaming loins. He held two long, crescent-shaped swords in his hands, the hilts closed in fists the size of small haunches of beef, the fists attached to arms as thick and solid as the stanchions of a bridge.

Seeing where their astonished gazes were fixed, the ebony-haired rogue offered a crooked grin. "His name is Lucifer. He is a Cimaroon—an African chief stolen from Guinea by the Spanish and sent to work as a slave in their gold mines in Mexico. His hatred for the English, who have also robbed his villages and stolen their men and women, is only modestly less than for the Spanish. And since the day I broke him out of his chains some dozen years ago, his only true loyalty is to me, so I would strongly suggest you put your weapons away before the introductions go any further."

Chapter 2

◈

Spence nodded to his men after a moment, then led the way by uncocking his pistol and tucking it back into his belt. He kept a wary eye on the Cimaroon, who remained as still as a statue above them, his wickedly polished blades flaring in the sunlight.

A second man had emerged from the same shadowy hatchway that had concealed his leader. He was not as tall nor nearly as brawny in build, though it could not be said by an honest eye that he suffered for the lack. His hair was light brown, tarnished gold by exposure to the sea and sun. His face was as lean and well defined as the rest of his tautly honed frame; his smile was sheepishly apologetic as he pointed hesitantly to one of the long wooden cylinders slung over Spit McCutcheon's shoulder.

"That would not happen to be fresh water, would it, sir? Most of us have not had the pleasure of licking anything but dew for the past two weeks."

"Aye, it would be that, lad," Spit said, unslinging his pipe and ordering the others to do likewise. "We've plenty more where this comes from, startin' with a full cask in the of the Cimaroon's two scimitars flashed in the sunlight, causing Spence to throw up his hands with a roar.

"Aye, that's enough!" he shouted. "Leave go o' her, ye blackhearted bastard. *Leave go o' her, do ye hear me!*"

Geoffrey Pitt reacted first. He whirled and looked closely at Beau's red and swollen face, then at the front of her doublet where the strain of her frantic efforts to free herself had resulted in the prominent outline of breasts.

"Simon! Simon, for Christ's sakes—it's a woman!"

Dante's eyes screwed down to slits. The veins in his temples and throat were throbbing, the ones in the back of his hand and forearm stood out like blue snakes. He blinked to clear the sweat from his eyes and found himself looking down into a face that was too smooth and flawless to ever know the need for a barber's skills, into hot amber eyes that were blazing with outrage and indignation, but were, beneath the feathery lashes, a woman's eyes.

"What the hell—"

His fingers sprang open and he dropped Beau heavily onto the deck. Gasping, choking for air, she crumpled to her knees and doubled over enough for De Tourville to see the thick auburn braid that hung halfway down her back. If he needed more proof, it came in the form of the shrill, distinctly female voice that began to curse him through coughs and splutters of air.

"Beau! Beau, are ye all right, lass?" Spence shoved past the Cimaroon and crouched awkwardly on one knee. "Slow an' deep. Breathe slow an' deep."

Beau clutched his arm for support and dragged at gulps of air.

The curses were getting stronger, the words more decipherable, and after a minute she glared up and found Dante de Tourville.

"You . . . son of a . . . *bitch*," she gasped. "You . . . *sonofabitch!*"

"Aye," Spence grunted. "Ye're all right."

He pushed to his feet again and glowered at the Frenchman. "It might be she has a sharp tongue in her head at times an' ought not have questioned yer courage so . . . bluntly. But ye had no call to choke her either."

"The captain isn't quite himself—" Pitt began.

"I need no one to make excuses for me," Dante snapped, rounding on his own man. "Nor does the situation warrant one. She spoke out of turn. Maybe she will think twice before doing so again—to me, anyway. In the meantime, Mr. Pitt, we don't have much time. I want as many guns transferred to the *Egret* as we can manage."

"Hold up there," Spence snarled. "She's still my ship an' I've not agreed to take any o' yer bloody guns on board yet."

"You don't have a choice, Captain Spence. And I don't have the time to argue."

"Ye'll damn well make time, by God, or ye'll be arguin' with this!" Spence stepped back and drew his cutlass, but quicker than he could curse, a slash of curved steel sliced across his intentions, the point of the scimitar hooking the hilt of Spence's blade, sending it cartwheeling off into space. The Cimaroon's blade then slid upward, shearing off a thick chunk of wiry red beard as it came to rest across Spence's jugular. At almost the same time the rest of Dante's men drew swords and pistols, effectively halting any move by Spence's group to reach for their weapons.

"I had hoped it would not come to this, Captain," Dante said grimly. "I had hoped you would not force me to take command of your ship."

"Command o' my ship?" A thin red trickle of blood ran down Spence's throat and began soaking into his collar, but the sheer audacity of De Tourville's statement caused the leathery face to break out in a wide, disbelieving grin. "There are near a hundred fully armed men on board the *Egret*. Are ye plannin' to force them as well?"

"I won't have to if they see their captain cooperating."

"Faugh!" Spence snorted disdainfully. "That'll be a cold bloody day in hell! Ye can slit my throat three ways to Sunday an' I'll not give the order to hoist a single sail."

While every man within earshot held his breath and waited, Dante stared at Spence, at the wide slick of blood that streaked his throat and spread across his collar. Something in the fierce, burning topaz of the captain's eyes made Dante look down to where Beau was still crouched on the deck. He took a casual step toward her and used the barrel of his musket to lift her chin, and there was no mistaking the similarity in the bright, hot sparks of amber that flared up at him. His own gaze narrowed in speculation as he glanced back at Spence.

"Such rare coloring," he mused. "Unlikely there should be such an exact match within a thousand miles . . . unless the two were related somehow. She appears to be too young and fresh for a sister. A daughter, perhaps? One with a long, shapely throat more than suitable for slitting in order to ease you of some of your stubbornness."

Spence stiffened perceptibly. But instead of bowing to the implied threat, he allowed a wide, somewhat contemptuous grin to settle across his face as he folded his arms across his barrel chest.

"A clever deduction, Cap'n Dante. And, aye, Beau's my daughter. The sweet fruit o' my loins. Mayhap that's why *she* doesn't take any kinder to threats than I do."

Dante felt a sudden, sharp intrusion of steel next to his skin and his body froze even as his gaze was drawn slowly downward again. Beau's golden eyes were still staring up at

him, but it was her hand that won his full attention, and
more specifically, the stiletto clutched in her fist. The point
had already pierced through his hose and was resting like
a cold sliver of ice across the impressive bulge of his man-
hood. A flick of a slender wrist would reduce that impression considerably.

"We seem to have reached an impasse, Cap'n Dante."
Spence chuckled wryly. "Unless, o' course, ye've no objection to pissin' out a hole in yer belly. She's a fair hand at
carvin', an' blow me dry, but look at them eyes ye were so
admirin' of a minute ago—I'd say she were in a ripe fair
mood to prove it, would ye not agree?"

Dante saw no reason to disagree. Her eyes were large
and wide with an eagerness that sent the point of the blade
nudging deeper into the soft sacs of his flesh.

Geoffrey Pitt held up his hands in a placating gesture.
"Captains—I'm sure we can arrive at some amicable arrangement here, can we not?"

"Not with a blade at my throat," Spence declared flatly.
"Does this ugly black bastard understand English?"

"He does," Pitt replied with a nervous glance at Lucifer.
"Rather well, too, I should warn you."

"Well, then, ye'd best warn *him* if he does not lower his
steel, I'll be breakin' off both his hands an' stuffin' them
down his throat."

The Cimaroon's agate eyes stared at Spence without
blinking. His nostrils flared so wide, the tension produced
a thin purple line around the rims. In the bright sunlight
it could be seen that his face and torso were tattooed with
patterns of lines and dots. The lobes of both ears had holes
in them and the flesh had been stretched to form long,
hanging loops. He was the same height as Spence, roughly
the same weight, though proportioned differently, and

probably could have snapped the one-legged captain in half without raising a bead of sweat.

The only thing he raised now was his lip, curling it back in a bright pink snarl that revealed an enormous rack of shockingly large teeth, all of which had been filed and sharpened into glistening points.

"Lucifer," Pitt urged. "Not now." He glanced worriedly at the stone-faced Dante de Tourville. "Simon—?"

He was still staring down at Beau Spence. Her arm had remained as steady as her gaze and both were causing a visible tightness throughout his body.

"Quite the ferocious little corsair, aren't you, mam'selle?" he asked quietly.

"I have had no cause for complaint."

"You will," he promised softly, and turned to the Cimaroon. "Lucifer, put the blade down."

The Cimaroon obeyed, but not without a final, terse flexing of the huge muscles in his arm. It caused the edge of his scimitar to widen the split in Spence's skin—not enough to threaten the jugular, but sufficiently bloody to leave a warning.

Spence clapped a hand to his neck and glared at the wetness that came away on his glove. "Do ye always treat the men this way who rescue ye, Cap'n Dante?"

"Only if they stand in my way."

Spence frowned uneasily over the flecks of cobalt-blue that had turned the Frenchman's gaze as brittle as glass. "Beau, give the captain some breathin' space."

"Must I, Father?" she murmured.

"Aye, ye must show a little faith sometimes, girl. Sheath yer knife like a good lass. A man can't think clear when he's standin' on his toes."

"Or when he's holding a musket," she added pointedly.

Dante met the long-lashed amber eyes again and almost

smiled with the rush of promisory menace that flowed through his veins. Carefully, he set the arquebus aside, and carefully, he curled his hands into fists by his sides.

Beau, having seen what the Cimaroon did to leave her father a reminder, dragged the point of the knife across tender flesh as she removed it and was gratified to see a thin ribbon of blood color the Frenchman's hose. She tucked the knife back into the cuff of her boot and stood, her eyes still fastened on Dante as she massaged the tenderness in her throat.

Spence cleared his.

"The way I see it, Cap'n, ye've another six, maybe eight hours, topmost, before yer ship goes belly down. If I were you, I'd start talkin' fast. Ye talk *bold* enough, there's a certainty, but if ye want our help, ye'll have to convince me there's a fine enough reason for givin' it."

Simon Dante searched the captain's weathered features with eyes that had lost none of their cold intensity. "I'm genuinely sorry, Captain. If I had an hour to spare, I might be able to convince you we aren't demented fools, but as you already determined, time is of the essence. You say you want a fine enough reason to order your men to help us?" He reached around to the small of his back and, quicker than she could react to avoid it, held a pistol out at arm's length, pressing the nose flush against Beau's temple. "Will this do?"

Chapter 3

Dante exerted just enough force to depress the skin at Beau's temple. His finger was curled around the pistol's serpentine trigger and the look in his eye was the same one Beau had had while she held the knife at his crotch.

"I don't have time for explanations, Captain Spence. When we have transferred the guns safely, I promise you all the explanations will come. For now, I need my guns on board your ship and will do it with or without your help. Your daughter, I am sure, would like to keep the top of her head, so if we have no more little impasses to conquer, I would suggest we reach some kind of an arrangement now."

Beau started to slip her hand down for her dagger but a warm strong grip clamped around her wrist, stopping her.

"Sorry," said Geoffrey Pitt. He had anticipated the move and had come up with surprising stealth behind her. "Not this time."

He removed the dagger from her belt along with her pistols and cutlass, then leaned over to extract the stiletto from her boot. Dante watched, his brow arched in a cynical curve as a third small knife was noticed and taken from the collar at the back of her doublet.

"Any more?"

"You'll find out if you turn your back."

"I'll find out sooner if I have you stripped and searched."

Beau set her teeth and lifted the lower edge of her doublet to remove the blade strapped to her hip.

"A trusting soul, indeed," Dante murmured.

"With good reason, as it turns out," she countered evenly.

He offered a twist of a smile in rebuttal and turned to Spence. "Well, Captain? Do we have your cooperation or not?"

"Ye have my daughter's head under a gun, what choice do I have?"

"None," Dante agreed coldly. "Mr. Pitt will return to the *Egret* with you while you make ready with the winch and cables. Since there is no need for any of the rest of your crew to know our special terms, Lucifer and a few of my men will go along as well, just to make certain everyone works with a smile on his face. Your men can remain here, of course, to help prepare at this end."

Spence glared at him a moment, then looked at Beau.

"She will stay with me, naturally."

"Ye touch a hair on her head—" Spence warned softly.

"I'll not touch anything," Dante insisted. "So long as she behaves."

"Father—do I have your permission to slice out his liver if I get the chance?" Beau asked with casual disregard for the pistol denting her temple.

"That probably would not qualify as behaving," Pitt muttered at the back of her neck. She ignored his sarcasm—ignored him completely, in fact—and waited expectantly for her father's reply.

It was Dante who gave her the answer.

"Lucifer will be keeping your father as close company as I will be keeping you. My liver goes, his liver goes; simple as that. Mr. Pitt—?"

"Aye, on my way." He tucked Beau's pistols into his own belt as he passed. "Without a wind, we'll have to tow the ships close enough together to hook on grappling lines."

Dante nodded. "In the meantime, I'll set the men to work dismantling the guns and carriages. You"—he nodded in Spit McCutcheon's direction—"do you know your way around cannon?"

"Enough to blow ye off the edge o' the earth if I had ye in my sights."

"Good. You're in charge of the dismantling."

Spit thrust his tongue into his cheek and folded his arms across his chest.

De Tourville sighed. "Captain Spence?"

"Do it, Spit," Spence ordered, his eyes narrowed. "He's right—there's no harm in takin' on valuable cargo."

McCutcheon glared for as long as it took him to lean forward and project a wad of phlegm onto the deck, missing Dante's boot by the width of a nose hair.

"There is shot and powder—if the saltwater hasn't ruined it—below in the magazines. It will have to be transferred as well. And did you say you had a cask of fresh water on the jolly boat?"

"I did," Spence said through a snarl.

"I'm sure it will be much appreciated for the hot work ahead. Mistress Spence, if you would care to come with me, I will see about clearing my cabin of logs and charts."

The invitation was peremptory. Beau was given little

choice but to accompany the pirate wolf as he wrapped his fingers around her upper arm and guided her to the after hatchway. While they were still in sunlight, she glanced back over her shoulder, catching her father's eye a step before he disappeared through the gangway hatch. He was flanked by Pitt and the Cimaroon, neither one allowing him the opportunity to convey a strategy to her, if indeed he had devised one yet.

"You won't get away with this," she declared savagely. "My father has friends in England. He has friends in Court who will not tolerate an act of blatant piracy against one of their own kind."

"Well, the next time I am supping with Bess, I shall be sure to inquire who they are. Watch your head, the ceiling has caved in in places."

She was shoved through the hatchway and found herself smothered almost immediately by the dark, musty haze. No light penetrated the gloom save for the few slivers that showed through cracks in the splintered timbers. Half the steps on the ladderway were broken or missing altogether and she would have stumbled on the unfamiliar footing if the iron fingers had not remained around her arm.

The stench of old smoke was cloying in the narrow passageway. Dante ordered her straight, then to the left through an arched doorway and she was as relieved to leave the gloom behind as she was the smell of decay and death.

The captain's great cabin was as cluttered and strewn with wreckage as the rest of the ship, yet there was evidence to suggest it had once been grandly appointed. There were carved oak panels on the walls with brass fittings and candle sconces. One entire wall had once been lined with wire-fronted bookcases, the shelves filled with books bound in leather and embossed in gold. Most of the volumes lay scattered across the floor; some were stacked in piles where a path had been cleared around the massive gumwood desk.

Spanning the full width of the cabin, canted inward to follow the shape of the ship's stern, were the gallery windows. Most of the hundreds of small diamond-shaped panes had been shattered, and over everything—floor, chairs, shelves, walls—there lay a fine white coat of glistening glass dust. Only on the desk had there appeared to be any effort made to keep the surface clean, and then only because the top was littered with charts, maps, navigational instruments, and writing materials. A solid gold replica of a galleon in full sail was being used as a paperweight to hold down a sheaf of documents badly stained by smoke and saltwater.

There was no bed. A scorched heap of twisted planks indicated where it must have been, and to judge by the size of the empty space, it had been considerably larger than the functional cots on board the *Egret*.

"There," Dante said, pointing to a large ladder-back chair. "Sit."

Beau stood where she was and planted her hands on her hips. "You may have been able to convince my father you would have killed me if he didn't obey you. But I doubt very much if you would kill *him* with quite as little compunction, so you will excuse me if I don't quake in fear each time you bark."

Dante walked around behind his desk and glanced up at her from beneath the black slash of his brows. "You're probably right. I wouldn't kill him over such a trivial annoyance as you refusing to do as you're told. But it might make me angry enough to break off his kneecap. Or smash his good ankle. He already walks with a limp and I suppose it is possible for a captain to go to sea with two crippled limbs . . . but I have never seen it done, have you?"

Beau opened her mouth. She shut it again. And sat.

Dante's mouth curved at the corner as he set the pistol on his desk and eased his big body into his own chair. He had some difficulty keeping the relief off his face as he was able to take the weight off his wounded leg; even more so as he stretched it out in front of him.

Beau allowed herself a brief glance at the bandaged calf, sincerely hoping it was festered and crawling with maggots. She focused on his face again and had the same wish, embellishing it with slashes and open sores, runny pustules, and loose, rattling teeth. It gave her some comfort to feel the presence of the thin, finger-sized knife concealed at the small of her back, and to know that if he did, indeed, lower his guard for a second, she would make short work of his mocking smile.

In the meantime she took advantage of his discomfort, staring at him calmly and steadfastly with what her father called her "smotheration eye."

For a legend, she decided, he was sorely lacking in appeal. His face could have been hewn out of rock for all the character it boasted. It was, in fact, dark and foreboding, more suited to a devil or a satyr than a man who frequented Court and rubbed toes with nobility. It was true he had the high, smooth brow of an aristocrat but the effect was blunted by the thick black waves of his hair. Trimmed by an uncaring hand, it curled in uneven lengths over the collar of his shirt and blew about his temples and throat as if he stood in a perpetual wind. And something she had not noticed until now: in one of his earlobes he wore a gold loop, a common enough adornment for seafaring men who did it to ensure they always had the price of a decent burial—or a tall cask of ale. Yet on a man of Dante de Tourville's supposedly exalted stature, it seemed a cheap and tawdry affectation. Aside from being a titled lord, did he not also boast at being one of the most successful privateers on the Main?

It was said even Sir Francis Drake had begun to look over his shoulder, fearing the pirate wolf's exploits were beginning to surpass his own. And while Drake had the Queen's ear, he was also short and squat and bowlegged; no match for a villain who exuded virility. If it was true Simon Dante enjoyed private suppers with the Queen—private enough to call her Bess!—then nothing he did or said to a mere merchant trader would earn more than a perfunctory reprimand.

Beau's attention shifted to the broad chest, the long, muscular arms, the strong, square-tipped hands that had already shocked her with their power and savagery. He was a beast in his prime and Beau had encountered enough of them, most so full of their own potency they could not fathom how anyone could resist falling under their spell and into their beds.

Beau could resist. She was under no fainthearted delusions as to what someone like Dante de Tourville wanted from a woman, or, once he had it, how quickly he would deem her soiled and dispensable goods. Beau had learned that unpleasant lesson the hard way, having had a man fill her eyes with stars and her body with pleasure, only to discover he preferred to take a virgin to his marriage bed and have a wife who simpered and fawned over his every whim, who fainted at the mere mention of blood, and who would never dare challenge his opinions—whether she had the wit to understand them or not.

Beau, on the other hand, was her father's daughter. Having lost her mother's influence at an early age, she had been raised by a man full of blasphemies who called a fool a fool to his face and damned the consequences. Spence had honestly tried to settle her with a spinster aunt who had, in turn, tried to instill the rigid values of young womanhood on her recalcitrant charge. But the first time the *Egret* had set sail without her, Beau had stood in the parlor, wired into a farthingale and stiff velvet skirts, shouting such obscenities, her poor beleaguered aunt had swooned into a dead faint.

The second time he had sailed, she had stolen a single-masted skiff and followed, battling the strong currents and errant winds of the English Channel on her own, catching him three days later, half dead from fatigue but stubbornly refusing to be turned around and sent home. The crew had been amused. Spence had been enraged enough to order her into the tops, determined to break her spirit by making her stand watch in stormy weather until she begged to be relieved. Beau had remained there, lashed to a trestletree for seven days and nights, and in the end it had been her father's guilt that begged her to come down.

That was eight years ago and she had been a member of the crew ever since. During that time she had dined with pirates and lords, kept company with princes as well as scoundrels, and not once had she met a man who could melt her resolves or cause her a lingering moment's worth of regret for the course she had chosen. And except for that one brief lapse—a lapse she now credited as a necessary learning experience—she had not fallen into anyone's bed or under the spell of any man's charm, however roguish, virile, or darkly handsome he might be.

Thus she stared at the pirate wolf, part of her responding in an odd, ticklish way to the fact that they were alone in his cabin; that he was easily twice, if not three times, her size; and that it was doubtful a threat against touching a single hair on her head would dissuade him from touching anything else he wanted.

Another part of her was admittedly curious to know

what he was thinking as he sat there returning her calm, casual appraisal with an equally detached reserve.

As it happened, Dante was thinking she was rather small for the rigors of shipboard life, even if she served as cook's mate or cabin boy. Her waist was a trifling thing, easily spanned by two large hands. Her arm, when he had held it to guide her belowdecks, had been taut enough to suggest she possessed more supple strength than the average woman of her size and build, yet nothing so ungainly as muscular. She did indeed possess a long, slender neck. One that led to an equally long, slender body. Breasts? Aye, she had them. Round, firm little expressions of her femininity thrusting against the confines of her doublet. Probably too small to give a hungry man more than a taste.

Her face was the true paradox. Standing in the shadows of the bulkhead, he had carefully appraised each member of Jonas Spence's boarding party and not one had set off any alarms or seemed to be anything other than what he appeared to be. He retrieved their images one by one but could recall nothing that should have forewarned him. She had struck him as a slim dark-haired boy who stood shifting his weight slightly from one foot to the other, probably due to the extravagant armory of weapons he had strapped about himself.

She was seated across from him now. There seemed to be a similar restlessness in her body, though there were no overt movements he could detect. The air surrounding her was a haze of dust motes suspended in the heat of the light streaming through the gallery windows, sparkling just enough to mock him for having failed to see what seemed so obvious now.

She was no raving beauty. Her complexion was too dark for one thing, tanned beyond any hope of redemption from rice powders or milk washes. Yet the warm honey glow paid perfect compliment to the long auburn lashes and dark wing-shaped eyebrows that might have looked too bold on a more toneless palette. Her hair was gathered back into a single glossy braid, the color as rich and deep as roasted chestnuts. Her mouth was far too sulky for his liking, but he could imagine how a softly formed word—if she could manage one—would send a shiver down a desperate man's spine. The nose was delicate, the cheeks almost too smooth to believe they could bear exposure to harsh elements of the weather. And her eyes. They were cat's eyes, molten gold, dangerously obstinate, dangerously defiant. . . .

Just plain dangerous.

They did not relent by so much as a flicker—an odd enough sensation to deal with, especially since most females of his acquaintance normally avoided looking directly at anything above the level of his chin, regardless how brazen or uninhibited they might be. Geoffrey claimed it was his own fault, that he looked at women the same way a hawk looked at its prey. But that was only because Geoffry Pitt tended to fall in love at the first flutter of an eyelash.

Dante preferred his freedom, guarded it like a crown jewel. Women were fine in their place—preferably beneath him with their backs arched and their limbs wrapped tightly around his thighs—but he had no room for encumbrances in his life, no desire for any more shackles or chains of any kind, especially if they came burdened by emotion.

Her eyes commanded his attention again. Lush amber-gold, flecked with every subtle shade between green and brown, they were as bright as polished gemstones. And direct enough to cause an unsettling tightness in his groin. They were not the eyes of a virgin, for they held no fear. Neither were they the eyes of an experienced courtesan, for there was no hint of an invitation in their depths. Again he found himself comparing her to other women he had encountered, recalling none who could provoke, anger, challenge, and temptation all at the same time.

He wondered what she looked like naked.

Dante blinked first, breaking contact.

It was a singularly unfamiliar experience, knowing the wench was able to break his concentration. She still had not looked away, flaunting, it seemed, her ability to keep his level of irritation high enough to be a distraction.

He decided the best way to defuse her was to ignore her.

He lifted the golden ship—his *Virago*—and started collecting up the letters and documents beneath. Most were written in Spanish, some bore official seals and ribbons and flamboyant signatures belonging to governors and dignitaries in the New World. Dante spoke six languages fluently, including Spanish, and had translated most of the papers into his own bold script. Some were important, some not. Some went into great and boring detail about crops and harvests, weather conditions, even the hell of living with swarms of bloodsucking insects that attacked day and night in the jungles. Other documents, of more interest to a seafaring gentleman of private enterprise, concerned the staggering amounts of gold and silver that would be shipped to Lisbon with the next flota. These so-called plate fleets were tempting to raiders of all nationalities because of the enormous quantity of gold stolen from temples and villages throughout Mexico and Panama, most of it already hammered into plates and large sun medallions.

All of the papers, letters, and documents had been in the treasure house at Veracruz awaiting the ships that would carry the correspondence home to Spain. Pitt had snatched them up almost as an afterthought, speculating there was always something of some interest to someone who cared to know the state of affairs in Spanish-held territories. What he hadn't counted on was finding something that would irrevocably alter the course of their destiny.

Dante glanced up. The wench was still staring.

"If you want to make yourself useful," he said irritably, "you can start rolling these charts and stacking them in a chest."

"I have absolutely no desire to make myself useful, Captain Dante." She arched her brows in surprise that he would even think so. "In fact, I shall strive to be as useless to you as possible for as long as possible."

"You are already that, mam'selle," he countered evenly.

"Then we have nothing more to discuss."

He looked at her, hard. "I am not happy with the way this has turned out. I have no quarrel with your father or his crew, nor do I have any nefarious designs on your ship."

She merely stared back, her face a study in abject contempt.

He drummed his long fingers silently on the top of the desk. "Your father mentioned you have been at sea for eight months." When she neither confirmed nor denied it, he asked, "Should I assume this was your first voyage?"

"Why would you assume that?"

"Your hands are too soft, for one thing, your skin is too fresh: You don't exactly have the look of a weathered tar about you."

"For your information, I have been at sea since I was twelve," she snapped.

"A whole year?" He cocked his head in mock surprise. "I am impressed."

"*Eight* years, thank you very much."

From the instant sparks that had flared in her eyes, he guessed he had touched upon a tender subject. She had obviously met his brand of sarcasm before, both about her choice of lifestyle and the fact that she did, indeed, have the smooth, round face of a youthling—when she wasn't scowling, that is.

His brief victory did not taste as sweet as it should have, for his reaction was stalled somewhere between satisfaction and grudging admiration. Eight years was a long time. The sea offered no easy life and was merciless to anyone who showed the slightest weakness.

Beau was no better off. He angered her, irritated her, made her furious with his smug arrogance, but he was also an enigma. He was, after all, Simon Dante, an aristocrat, a member of the nobility with vast estates in England as well as France. He had spent the last half of his—what? thirty years? plaguing the Spanish shipping lines. For his most recent outlandish adventure he admitted to having raided Veracruz, and had fought a pitched battle with six Spanish galleons—a feat of daring and courage that normally would have had her perched on the edge of her chair, hanging on his every word.

She couldn't ask him about any of it, of course. She couldn't even look interested.

So she looked instead at the clutter of books littering the floor. "You can read," she said, inflecting her voice with the same patronizing tones he had used. "I'm impressed."

His long fingers ceased their drumming. The golden cat's eyes were scanning the volumes haphazardly when they came to a sudden stop at one in particular. They widened slightly and an exquisite tension seemed to ripple the length of her body. He tried to follow her gaze to the book that had so riveted her attention, but when she saw what he was about she turned her head and let the mask of indifference settle over her features again.

"If you have seen something you want, by all means help yourself. They will only end up on the bottom of the ocean."

"What I want"—her eyes shot back—"is to return to the *Egret*."

"And so you shall," he said solicitously. "Just as soon as all these charts and maps are rolled and packed away in a chest."

Beau surged to her feet, abruptly enough to send Dante's hand an inch or so in the direction of the pistol.

"Where is the damned chest?" she demanded.

His hand relaxed—rather, it flattened in an attempt to appear as though the movement had been unintentional, not that either one of them was fooled.

"Behind you. Empty the clothing out of the big one and stow as much of this paperwork in it as you can. My ship, too, if you please," he added, his voice softening unexpectedly as he ran a hand lovingly over the gold replica of the *Virago*. "Perhaps if one survives, the other will not be forgotten too soon."

"It is a . . . beautiful ship," she was compelled to admit.

"The *Virago* was a beautiful ship," he said, all but to himself. "Quick and keen, sleek as a nymph. She was the ideal companion—loyal, trustworthy, brave beyond measure in heart and soul, with a fiery temper that could set any foe running before the wind. She did not deserve"— he glanced around the wreckage in the cabin and sighed— "this."

"You said you were set upon by six Spaniards and sank them all. I could not think of a more fitting end, if it were my ship."

"She did us proud against the Spanish, aye. But it was an Englishman who betrayed her."

"You were betrayed? An *Englishman* told the Spanish where to find you?"

His eyes narrowed against the memory and for a moment, the rage and fury that darkened his face was potent enough for Beau, standing half a dozen paces away, to feel its heat. She saw the subtle shifting in the color of his eyes as they went from being a pale, smoldering gray to searing blue and she remembered seeing the same extraordinary change a split second before he had grabbed at her throat. With an effort Beau forced herself to breathe, aware she had filled her lungs, so as to preempt another strike.

"Captain—?"

"Behind you," he said, cracking his words like kindling. "The big chest. Quicker done, quicker away. That is what you want, is it not?"

Beau felt a measure of her own anger leak back into her cheeks, dusting them a soft pink. He had been betrayed. Fine. It perhaps explained his lack of willingness to place his trust in strangers. But it did not excuse his behavior in turning around and betraying Jonas Spence, who had done nothing more malicious to the crew of the *Virago* than offer them fresh water and rescue.

She turned on her heel and strode across the cabin, kicking bits of debris out of the way as she went. She muttered one of her father's favorite blasphemies under her breath, then repeated it with more substance when she knelt beside the leather chest and flung open the strapped lid.

For almost a full minute she stared, her anger gradually receding and giving way to surprise. The sea chest was brimming with women's clothes. Skirts, bodices, petticoats . . . even delicate chemises made of cloth so sheer, it was almost transparent. She plucked one, embroidered with silk floss and threads of pure gold, off the shimmering pile and

let the fabric slide through her hand, noting it was like
letting water glide over her skin and puddle in her lap. She
could hardly imagine wearing anything half so fine and
fragile, and wondered at the kind of woman who would.
Surely the smallest flaw, the tiniest freckle, would shine
through. A question more pertinent to character would be
to wonder what kind of man sought out such things, much
less carried them halfway across the world to present to
whom? A wife? A mistress?

Conscious of that very man seated across the room from
her, Beau started removing bundles of garments and setting
them on the floor beside her. When the chest was almost
emptied, she saw something else that made her movements
slow, then come to a complete halt. Tucked into one corner, nestled in a bed of silk stockings, was a silver jewel
casket. The top was rounded, the base was supported on
four small clawed feet; the style and filigree work was
French in design, a fact not entirely betrayed by the De
Tourville wolfhound and fleur-de-lis engraved on the lid.

Beau stole a glance over her shoulder, but Dante had
seemingly forgotten her. He was staring out the broken
gallery windows, motionless and expressionless, his raven
hair tinted blue by the hazy light.

Beau lifted the casket out of the chest and rested it on
her bent knees. She flicked the tiny hasp with the edge of
her thumbnail and raised the lid slowly, half expecting serpents to spill out onto her lap. There were no serpents, but
there was a large gold salamander, easily the length of her
hand and as fat around as two fingers. The golden beast
had two cabochon rubies for eyes and a glittering row of
pyramid-cut diamonds winding down its spine. Its four rep-
tilian feet were splayed possessively over a bed of loose
gems—pearls, tourmalines, emeralds, and diamonds—most
of them uncut and unset, but all of a size and quality that

caused a small thrill of heat to unfurl at the base of Beau's spine.

"Why, Mistress Spence, can that be the sinful gleam of avarice I see shining in your eyes?" His voice was deep and soft and very near and Beau did not have to turn around to confirm he was standing right behind her. She could *feel* him there, looming extremely large above her, and the small flutter of heat became a disturbing downpour.

She snapped the lid closed. "I presume you want this to come with you?"

"Actually, I had forgotten about it." A large, well-callused hand reached over her shoulder and took the casket. "I'm surprised it was missed in the search."

"Your ship was searched? By whom?"

He either ignored or chose not to acknowledge the question, and after a few tinkling sounds of a finger raking through the stones, he handed it back.

"As I said, if you see something you want, help yourself."

"What if I say I want the whole box?" she asked sardonically.

"Then it's yours. If I recall correctly there are some topazes in there that, when cut and polished, should about match the color of your eyes."

The entire exchange had been so out of character, Beau came instantly alert for a trap. She drew a deep breath and pushed to her feet, rounding on him with another healthy dose of Spence's epithets ready on the tip of her tongue.

They died without a squeak when she found herself standing so close to Dante, she felt the brush of his linen shirt as he pulled the hem free of his belt and shrugged it up and over his big shoulders.

The sheer scope of muscle laid bare before her took her breath away along with her intentions. His arms were sculpted out of marble, smooth and hard-surfaced. His shoulders had deep indentations where the top of his breastbone met the column of his neck. A thick, luxuriant mat of black hair covered his chest, whorling down to a silky cable's width over his belly. A finer coating of ebony hair covered his forearms, and above the elbow the tracery of veins stood out on the bronzed surface, flexing with each movement of his hands.

The scent coming off his flesh was that of sun and sea and male arrogance. She should have known. She should have seen it coming.

"What do you think you are doing?" she asked with quiet intensity.

Dante's eyes lingered a moment on the pout of her mouth. It had been shocked out of its usual insolence and as he watched, the flush came back into her cheeks, the color blooming softly on the sculpted crests, then flowing downward to stain the slender length of her throat. He knew he had struck another sensitive chord, physical in origin, and he wondered, for all her acid tongue and bravado, how many times she had been faced with a similar threat for which she had no defense. She was bolder than the average woman, stronger than the average woman, but she was still no match for a man who had gone several months without sheathing himself in the velvet heat of a woman's flesh.

He lowered his hands with deliberate slowness to the buckle of his belt. "What does it look like I'm doing?"

Chapter 4

Dante unbuckled his belt and slung it over his shoulder.

"It has been so long since I have felt the need to appear presentable, you will have to forgive the error. I thought this was the chest that held my spare shirts and breeches, but I see I was mistaken. Ahh. There it is."

He moved past her, releasing her from the heat of his gaze. Beau felt it as almost a tangible loss and suffered a mild rush of light-headedness as he walked away. The blood was humming through her veins. Her belly, which had been in the process of melting down to her knees, required a concentrated effort to retrieve and she had almost succeeded when she turned to glare after him . . . and saw his back.

It was a mass of lines and welts and crisscrossing scars. They were not fresh, for most of the lines had been incorporated back into the muscle and were as tanned and weathered as the rest of him. But some had been severe enough, deep enough, to cut through to the bone and no amount of time would ever smooth them or render them less visible.

Beau had witnessed floggings before. It was the accepted means of keeping discipline on a ship. Five strokes with the cat-o'-nine was her father's usual limit, but rarely delivered with enough heart to split the skin.

Simon Dante, Comte de Tourville, had been subjected to ten, twenty times that many strokes, laid on by a vicious hand that had known no mercy whatsoever.

What in God's name did a man do to earn a hundred lashes of the cat?

While she pondered the question, Dante opened the second chest and pushed a few garments impatiently from side to side until he found the ones he sought. The shirt he drew over his shoulders was white as snow, cut full with long, loose sleeves gathered at the wrists and edged in open cutwork. The collar was more of a ruffle, made to extend over the edge of a doublet, but he ignored the lacing in front and let it hang open over the vast darkness of his chest while he rummaged for other articles.

When his hands went to his waist and began peeling his hose down over his lean hips, Beau instinctively averted her eyes. She heard the dull thud of his boots striking the floor and a sharp, half-formed curse when he disturbed the bandages on his calf. The briefest, smallest peep sidelong gave her a glimpse of naked, muscular legs and taut buttocks. A longer, more contemplative look was directed toward the scrolled wheel-lock pistol he had left lying on top of the desk.

Dante was bent over, unwinding the layers of filthy bandages. His back was to the desk and although he was a pace or two closer to it than she was, he would be hobbled by his leg and hampered by the unraveling strips of linen.

Beau sent her tongue slicking across her lips to moisten them.

With her lower lip clamped securely between her teeth, she made a dash for the desk, snatching the pistol off the piles of documents and aiming it at Dante de Tourville before he had fully spun around.

The gun was heavier than she had expected, the stock inlaid with ivory and mother-of-pearl. The lock and escutcheon plate were brass overlaid with gold filigree, the pyrite holder was shaped like a dragon's head with the body curling down in an S to form the trigger. The spanner key was in the cocked position, meaning the spring was fully wound and the slightest pressure on the serpentine trigger would release the wheel, showering sparks into the firing pan, thus igniting the powder and charge.

Dante's initial surprise over her quickness mellowed into cool curiosity as he straightened and stared into the long, gleaming barrel.

"Well," he said quietly. "You do have a knack for creating impasses, don't you?"

"I see no impasse here, Captain. I have the gun. You have about two seconds to pull on a pair of breeches and walk ahead of me to the door."

Dante folded his arms across his chest. "And if I don't?"

"You can die as you are. It matters not to me."

The silver eyes looked bemused. "And once we are through the door—what then?"

"Then . . . you call your dogs off my father's ship, and if you are extremely lucky, depending on Captain Spence's mood, we may leave you another barrel or two of water before we sail away."

"You would leave us here to sink?"

"Gladly."

His gaze smoldered thoughtfully for much longer than

the ordained two seconds before the fine creases at the corners deepened and the wide, sensuous mouth flattened into a wolfish grin.

"So. You have killed men before, have you, mam'selle? Standing face to face, close enough to feel the splatter of hot blood on your skin?"

Beau took an involuntary step back but kept the gun aimed squarely in the middle of the broad chest. "I do what I have to do, Captain Dante, even if—as you say—it is not my original intention."

"No," he mused. "Your original intention was to castrate me."

She glanced down out of reflex and although the hem of his shirt covered him to midthigh, the light from the gallery windows was beside him, giving substance to the shadows beneath. He was, she was shocked to see, impressively large all over.

"Put the gun down, Mistress Spence," he ordered softly. "Before I get truly angry."

She adjusted her grip, using both hands to balance the heavy weapon. "Find yourself a pair of breeches, Captain, before *I* get truly angry."

"I might like to see that."

"I don't think you would."

"Why not? What happens? Do you spit and hiss like a hellcat?"

"Come a step closer and you will find out," she promised.

He took the step, measured carefully against the darkening flush in her cheeks.

"I will shoot," she declared evenly.

He shook his head slowly. "I don't think you will."

Beau sucked a breath between her teeth and cursed it

free as he took another step. She jerked the gun downward, switching her aim from his chest to the uninjured leg.

"Maybe I won't kill you. Maybe I will just shoot out one of your knees."

Dante stopped and pursed his lips consideringly. Soft, ominous flecks of cobalt were beginning to shimmer in his eyes but he only broadened his grin and took another step forward. "Remind me not to make any more brilliant suggestions in your presence."

"Captain—!"

He took another step and Beau's finger tightened on the trigger. She pulled it until the mainspring released, causing the wheel to spin against the piece of iron pyrite and create a small burst of sparks. Another part of the lock worked a brass coverplate, pushing it aside to expose the powder pan to sparks, but where there should have been a deafening explosion of gunpowder and a violent recoil from the discharging shot, there was only a loud rasp and a small puff of acrid smoke.

Dante halted again.

"By Christ," he exclaimed with genuine surprise. "I didn't think you would do it. I took the precaution of removing the prime, of course, but I truly did not think you would do it!"

Beau gaped at the gun, then cursed and threw it disgustedly at the dark, grinning face before she darted for the door. He caught her with effortless ease, hooking one long arm around her waist, and clamping a hand over her mouth to cut off the scream of outrage. She felt herself lifted and crushed back against the wall of muscle. She kicked and flayed and tried to scratch at his hands, his eyes, his ears, but he only swore and upended her, swinging her dizzily around and slamming her down hard on the top of the desk, unmindful of the flurry of papers and letters her thrashings scattered to the floor. As she writhed like a fury, the breath driven out of her lungs, he leaned over her, restricting her movements with the weight of his body.

"Stop it," he hissed. "Stop it right now, before I—"

Her hand, raking the top of the desk, closed around the gold replica of the *Virago* and she swung it hard and fast, missing his temple and eye by the slightest of miscalculations.

He cursed again and grabbed her wrist with his free hand, grabbed the ship, and twisted it roughly out of her grip before wrenching both of her hands above her head and pinning them flat on the bed of papers. Her legs were swinging over the edge of the desk, and while she wriggled and squirmed to gain a good, clean kick, Dante was able to wedge his hips firmly and forcefully between her thighs.

Her body bucked against the pressure, her scream was a muffled combination of rage and pain as his weight all but crushed the breath and fight out of her. Her eyes were squeezed tightly shut, her chest was rising and falling as if she had just swum across half the ocean. Her arms, her legs, were trembling, the latter so painfully close to being broken off at the hips, she had no choice but to keep them still and tense beneath him.

"Now, then," he muttered roughly, "if I lift my hand away from your mouth, are you going to make me regret it?"

Her eyes sliced up at his, burning with a thousand gilt-edged threats, all of which vowed immeasurable regret.

"Take as long as you like to decide. I'm quite comfortable myself," he added, shifting his hips, forcing her legs to bend even wider to accommodate him. "Although I cannot promise how comfortable you will be in a minute or two when your breeches start to annoy me."

Beau's eyes widened. There was no mistaking his meaning; she could feel the heat of his flesh where it pressed into the juncture of her thighs and it was nowhere near as deceptively soft as the threat in his voice, nowhere near as indifferent as the lazy threat in his eyes.

She tried one last time to squirm free, to dislodge him, but he only chastened her with a slow smile and pressed closer, making her aware of the swelling expansion of his flesh as it responded to her futile efforts.

Shocked that there was any more of him to expand, her body went completely still beneath him. Her breath came faster, the pounding in her blood became distinct enough that he could feel her heart hammering in her chest and see her panic throbbing through the small veins in her temple.

"Was it something I said?" he asked with a wolfish grin. "Or something you might like me to do?"

His face was so close, all she could see was the black slash of his eyebrows, the splash of ebony hair flung forward over his brow and cheeks, and the amused mockery in his eyes. She closed her own for a moment and when she opened them again, they blazed with such fiery contempt, he almost laughed out loud.

"I gather we understand each other?"

She managed a jerky nod and he cautiously eased the pressure from her mouth. He did not remove his hand completely, choosing instead to rest it across her throat in such a way as to lock her head flat and firm on the desk, not allowing her the luxury to turn either way or avoid the further confrontation in his eyes.

"I say again, mam'selle. Quite the ferocious little corsair. Ferocious, warm, and surprisingly tempting," he added, shifting his hips slightly for emphasis. "I don't suppose I could interest you in a small skirmish of another nature?"

She swallowed and he could feel the movement of her throat muscles beneath his hand.

"Get off of me," she rasped.

"Ah. Mam'selle declines," he said softly. *"Pour le moment."*

"Get . . . off . . . of me!"

He watched her mouth shape the words and savored the echo of them as they vibrated down his spine. He had made the proposition in jest, yet his flesh was betraying the fact she *was* soft and warm and extremely tempting. And that there were other needs besides food and water he had gone too long without.

"If I do, I want your word—your blood oath—that you will not try any more of your foolish tricks."

"My word?" she spat. "My blood oath? How do you know you can trust it?"

"Because you are going to trust me when I give you *my* word, and *my* oath, mam'selle"—he lowered his head, lowered his mouth until the heat of it renewed the flush of warmth in her cheeks—"if you ever . . . *ever* draw another weapon *of any kind* on me, I will bind you hand and foot to the shrouds and flay your backside into bloody strips. And that"—he molded his fingers more poignantly around the arch of her throat—"only after I have sliced out your tongue and fed it to the sharks."

She swallowed again and her lips parted, trembling as much from the force he was exerting on her throat as from the cool promise mirrored in the silver-blue of his eyes.

"Your word, mam'selle?"

She tried forming the words twice before there was any substance to her answer. Her face felt as if it were on fire. Her hands were curled into fists, cold as ice, and her limbs were aching from the strain of trying to keep him at bay.

"You have it," she whispered. "You have my word."

"No tricks?"

"No tricks."

He allowed a crooked smile to underline the warning in his finger as he lifted his hand from her throat and traced a smooth line along the curve of her lower lip. His other hand released her wrists and he was struck by another image as he straightened: that of her lying exactly as she was now atop the clutter of papers and charts, naked, with her hair unbound and spread like dark silk beneath her.

His flesh jumped noticeably and he had to suppose, after being at sea so long and having come so close to death, anything female, supple, and breathing would have had the same effect. A purely reflexive response, comparable to a thirsty man's reaction upon stumbling into a pool of fresh water.

He left her to struggle upright on her own and walked back to the sea chest. He found a pair of relatively clean hose and, testing his sanity along with Beau's word of honor, finished dressing with his back to her. He did not bother rebandaging his calf and barely glanced at the raw wound before pulling on his boots. The pain helped to clear his head and distract his body, and after thrusting his arms through the sleeves of a leather doublet, he rebuckled his belt, raked his hands through his hair, and was all business again.

Beau had used the same time to gather her faltering wits about her once more. Her body still seethed with the impression of his, her skin was stretched so tight in places, she wanted to scratch herself to ease the tension. Her breasts in particular were as prickly as pincushions. Her thighs ached from being nearly split asunder, and the bridge of flesh between felt oddly hot and runny, as if the sensation of melting she had felt earlier had not all been in her imagination.

"I'm going up on deck," Dante said casually, eyeing her from across the cabin. "Feel free to join me when you have finished here."

He stepped out into the passageway, ducking his head to clear the low lintel, but only moved a pace or two into the gloom before stopping and cocking his head back to listen.

He did not have long to wait. The sound of Beau's curse and the smashing of a brass candlestick hurled at the door assured him her temper had not been permanently suppressed. Why it should make him smile, though, he had no idea.

Chapter 5

The *Virago* managed to stave off the pull of the sea for another ten hours. Although it was a fierce race against time and nature, the crews, working together, winched six of the monstrous demi-cannon on board the *Egret*. The added weight—nearly twelve tons—settled the hull half a strake deeper in the water, but under Pitt's guidance, balance was maintained and would even afford steadier handling in rough seas. A quantity of powder and shot was salvaged as well, though the stores had been badly depleted in the fight with the India guards. There were few personal items worth rescuing, most having been lost to the bilges and damaged by salt water. One large white mouser—Clarence—adamantly refused to leave his hidey-hole and it took an hour-long search by Pitt and two others to flush him out. When he emerged, his fur more black than white, he refused to be carried, but strutted, his back arched and claws extended in disdain, along one of the grappling lines that spanned the two ships.

Including the cat, there were forty-one survivors removed from the *Virago*. When the guns were shifted and

warnings issued that it would be unsafe to remain aboard
her much longer, they filed slowly across the wide planks
and, to a man, remained by the *Egret's* rails, their faces
taut, their bodies rigid, as they watched Pitt and Dante
make a final search through the wreckage on deck. It was
Simon Dante, with his ship groaning and trembling beneath him, who climbed the shrouds to the top of the
broken mainmast and removed her flags. Carrying them in
his clenched fist, with his limp more pronounced and the
pain graying his face, he was the last to make the crossing.
Pitt ordered the cables cut, and under the faint stirrings of
a breeze, he called for enough sail in the tops to ease the
Egret slowly away.

The sun was setting behind the *Virago*, painting her
ruined and battered hull in gold. The blaze spread across
the surface of the ocean and fanned orange and red across
the sky. One by one the eyes of the men turned away from
the sea and focused on the solitary figure standing on the
afterdeck, his hands gripping the rail, his profile etched
against the crimson sky as he watched his ship die.

Even Spence, who had fed off his anger most of the
afternoon, mellowed somewhat, respecting the pain of a
fellow captain forced to watch the last bit of shadowy hull
slide beneath the whispering sea.

"One clean shot, Father," Beau murmured, standing at
Spence's side. "I could pick him off from here with one
clean shot."

"Aye, I'm sure ye could, lass. An' I'll keep the thought
in mind if I don't hear any answers I like."

"You're going to let him talk his way out of this?"

"I'll admit I'm curious to hear what he has to say. A
man o' Dante de Tourville's reputation simply does not
behave like a petty thief unless he has a damned good
reason."

"He has stolen your ship!" Beau hissed, wary of Pitt and the Cimaroon standing half a deck away. "He has forcibly taken command and stolen your ship! It is hardly petty thievery!"

"He hasn't stolen it very far yet," Spence remarked dryly. "Nor will he so as long as we outnumber him two to one."

Spit McCutcheon came up beside them, swabbing his face and neck with a large square of red linen. There were lanterns and cressets burning amidships where the men still worked in the thickening darkness.

"I can take naught away from them brutes," he said, hooking a gnarled thumb over his shoulder. "Finest bronze bastards I've seen in my day or any other. No more'n a year or two out o' the foundry, but well seasoned an' not a crack or split showin'. They'll fetch a damned pretty price in Plymouth; he weren't pullin' your nose on that count."

Spence grunted, allowing the cannon might be a valuable commodity, but it did not explain their hellfire importance.

"I . . . er, been watchin' an' listenin' to some o' those *Virago* men, like ye asked," Spit said, lowering his voice. "Damnedest thing I ever saw. Most o' them should have been happy just to have their bellies filled an' a sound deck beneath them. But to a man they've put their backs into the work, restin' only when our men rest, askin' no favors an' takin' no more'n a fair share o' water an' victuals. An' all the while, it's 'Aye, sir,' 'No, sir,' 'Begging pardon, sir.' 'Tisn't natural. Got my skin crawlin' worse than if I'd got a passel o' maggots nestin' under my codpiece."

He spat over the side of the ship and swabbed his face again, muttering under his breath as he walked back to where a crew was struggling to seat the last of the bronze monsters in its wooden carriage. The foremast had been sheered of sail and put to use as a hoist. With timber creaking and yards straining, ten men on cables hauled and grunted over the huge barrel of the gun while half a dozen more pushed and prodded with tackle and pikes to swing it up and over its cradle of ten-inch square beams. The carpenter, Thomas Moone, had cut a new port in the hull and was affixing the last hinge and length of bracing tackle when the hoist lines were slackened and the full weight of the gun settled into its carriage.

The *Egret* heeled slightly, riding a low swell on the sea. Someone had neglected to wedge chocks under the wheels of the gun carriage and the two-ton monster started to roll forward with the motion of the deck. Thomas Moone heard the warning shouts and the ominous rumble of wooden wheels, and turned in time to see the great black hole of the muzzle lunging toward his face.

He tried to jump out of the way but his foot snagged on a cable and he went sprawling flat on the deck, his leg sandwiched between the muzzle and the raw edge of the gunport. His scream brought Simon Dante to the rail of the afterdeck. Not bothering to seek the ladder, he vaulted over the top and landed heavily on the main deck, barely stopping to register the pain from his injured leg. Two long strides brought him to the side of the gun at the same time as Jonas Spence, who grabbed the nearest cable and shouted orders to the men to take up the slack on the tackle. One of the large wheels had split under the weight and the gun would not move. Dante, his muscles bulging with the strain, thrust a steel pike beneath the barrel of the cannon and put all of his strength into levering the cannon long enough for Spit and Geoffrey Pitt to drag Moone clear of the port. A split second later the steel pike snapped, the wheel shattered, and the cannon slid forward, stopping only when it was wedged fast in the gunport.

Spit looked from the gun, to Moone's bruised but intact leg, then to Dante and the broken pike. He found Spence next, giving him a pointed *I-told-you-it-weren't-natural* glare.

Simon Dante, meanwhile, had slumped down beside the gun carriage, his face streaming sweat, his hands trembling where they were squeezed around the bloom of fresh red blood staining his hose.

"Simon?" Pitt dropped onto one knee beside him.

Dante shook his head and spoke through a gleaming rack of tightly clenched teeth. "It's nothing. It will pass."

Spence pushed his way around to the side of the gun. "What is it? What's amiss?"

"His leg," Pitt said. "The stubborn bastard insists there's nothing wrong with it, but in two weeks, it should have healed by now. Have you a barber or anyone with doctoring skills on board?"

"Cook knows how to set bones an' lance boils." Spence nodded. "An' we've a sailmaker who turns a fair stitch with needle an' thread."

"It's just a bloody cut," Dante insisted. "Jostled one too many times."

"It isn't *just* a cut," Beau said quietly, stepping out from behind the bulk of her father. "I saw it earlier when he unwrapped it and there is far too much swelling and bruising for just a cut."

"Save my soul," Dante spat through the sheen of sweat glistening on his face, "and tell me you are neither the cook nor the sailmaker."

Beau looked amused for the first time. "Your soul is safe, Captain. Not even a starving man would eat my cooking, and I stitch more holes in my fingers than I do in canvas."

"Pray alleviate my ignorance and tell me what you *do* do on board this ship."

Beau's eyes glowed the same smoky amber as the nearby lantern as she squatted down beside him, her elbows propped on her bent knees. "I doubt such a simple measure would remedy such a vast shortfall. Besides which, it is your limb in immediate danger from your ignorance. A simpleton would have had the sense to swallow his pride and seek help for it."

Quicker than it took a protest to form on his tongue, she drew her stiletto and put the tip to the bloodied hose, slicing a long enough opening in the wool to part the edges and expose the wound on his calf. The slash was as long as her hand, the surrounding flesh was shiny from the swelling, mottled red and blue. There was evidence it had scabbed over and split open a time or two, but it did not take a physic's eye or nose to detect the source of the oozing white pus that was draining along with the thready rivulets of blood.

"There must be something lodged in there," Beau said, prodding the angry swelling with the point of her knife. "No wonder it hasn't healed properly."

"Whatever it is, can you get it out?" Pitt asked.

Beau straightened. "I am not a doctor. And if it has been in there for two weeks, it may have to be cut out."

"The alternative is infection and gangrene."

Spence shifted uncomfortably. "Aye, so it is."

Dante's head rolled and he focused on Pitt's face with a scowl made even more menacing by the black bearding. "You do it. Or Lucifer. Don't even *think* . . . of giving the wench the pleasure of cutting me."

Beau arched an eyebrow. Without waiting for anyone's decision—or permission—she dipped her knife to the wound, dug until the point found something solid, then pried it out with a quick jerk of her wrist.

Dante roared and Pitt swore. Spence jumped forward to

pin the captain's shoulders to the gun carriage, while Pitt grabbed his wrists to keep him from lunging at Beau. She, quite calmly, held up her knife, displaying a four-inch-long sliver of oak impaled on the tip.

"Christ Jesus," Dante spat. "You enjoyed that, didn't you?"

"No," she replied. "But I *am* going to enjoy this."

She flicked the bloodied sliver to the deck and bent over the wound again. There was fresh blood welling to fill the hole in the muscle, and with a few efficient strokes she cut away the old scabbing and squeezed the swollen flesh until the pustules were all drained and the blood ran clear red. Spit held a lantern over her head while she worked. Thomas Moone, despite his tender leg, fetched a pannikin of vinegar to wash away the purulence, and Spence, being more practical by nature, ordered someone to fetch a stone crock from his cabin along with a couple of pewter cups.

When the crock came, he used his teeth to remove the wax bung and filled one of the cups to the brim.

"Wrap yer lips around this, Cap'n Dante. Yer gut will burn so fierce, ye won't even remember ye have a leg. All at once now, mind. Don't waste time dippin' yer tongue or ye might regret it before ye start."

Dante's long fingers curled around the cup and Beau met his eyes briefly, suspecting it was her throat he regretted he could not be squeezing instead.

The knife flashed again and Dante tossed back the full measure of amber liquid. Spence, who had filled himself a cup as well, smacked his lips with relish as the liquid fireball plummeted into his belly. Dante had to suck at a breath and steady himself until the shock of the flames receded. But Spence had been right; he paid no heed to what Beau was doing to his leg, he cared only if he had a throat and gullet left at the end of the burn.

Spence chuckled inwardly and asked, with all the innocence of a babe, "Care for another?"

"If I were you," Dante rasped, "I would be trying to find some way to throw me and my men overboard. I doubt I would be tending wounds and offering to share a draft of rumbullion . . . unless of course it was poisoned."

"The thought crossed my mind, lad, believe me. But in this case, 'twould be a waste o' good Indies Gold to sour it with poison."

"So it would," Dante agreed, holding out his cup for a refill. "God's teeth, but it does have a keen bite to it."

"Brewed by the brown-skinned heathens on Tortuga who drink the stuff like water an' only have to piss on a piece o' wood to start a fire."

Dante drained the second measure and let his head fall back on the support of the wheel. His gaze strayed down to Beau, caught as she was in the glow of the lantern light. Over the course of the long afternoon and evening, a fine mist of hair had escaped the restrictive confines of her braid, framing her face in a soft reddish halo. She had removed her doublet sometime during the day, betraying softer, fuller breasts than Dante had originally envisioned. Her shirt was laced tight to her throat, but he could see where curves and indents formed impressions beneath the cloth, and where the plump, firm strain of young flesh stretched the cloth flat.

"I suppose you drink this like water as well?" he asked dryly.

"I don't gasp and wheeze like a child when I do," she said brusquely, and finished binding his calf snugly with a wide strip of cloth.

He grinned unexpectedly and reached for the crock himself, filling his cup and handing it to Beau. Without wavering her gaze by so much as an eyelash, she took the cup and swallowed the contents, displaying the same hearty degree of appreciation Spence had.

Jonas chuckled aloud this time. "That's my little black swan. Sooner pluck her own eyeballs out with a dull stick than refuse a challenge."

"Why does it not surprise me?" Dante murmured.

"No reason it should," Spence agreed, "unless ye're a poorer judge o' character than I make ye out to be."

De Tourville offered up a faint smile. His leg was throbbing dully but the outpouring of sweat had stopped along with the tremors in his hands and arms. The rum had warmed his belly considerably and he had no great urge to move or retreat from the cooling night air. He could have slept then and there quite happily and left the explanations to the morning—or to Geoffrey Pitt—but he knew the captain of the *Egret* deserved better.

"Is there somewhere we can go and talk in private?" he asked Jonas.

"My cabin. If it's still my cabin, that is."

"It is your cabin, sir. Your cabin and your ship, and you have my heartfelt apologies if I made it seem any other way. Mister Pitt will join us, if you have no objection, and your navigator, if he can be spared. We lost our pilot and most of our instruments in the storm that blew us to hell and gone; with the fighting and the drift and the heavy cloud cover we could be within hailing distance of Cathay and I'd not know it."

"We've been plagued by the same cloud cover, but near as we can fix it, we are a week south o' the Canaries, thereabouts. Another three after that, with luck, an' we'll be home."

Dante nodded consideringly, deliberately avoiding the glance Pitt shot his way. He did not refuse the hand his first mate offered to help him up, however, and after testing his weight on the wounded leg, he found the pain vastly diminished. He still swayed unsteadily on his feet. Fatigue and two cups of Indies Gold on an empty stomach put his head into such a spin, when he squinted upward and tried to focus on the darkness overhead, he saw two north stars twinkling brightly off the bow.

Jonas started to lead the way along the deck toward the stern of the ship. "Beau—will ye not see if Cook has aught in the way o' hot victuals in the stewpot? Bring along a biscuit or two as well; a man can think an' talk better when he isn't listenin' to his belly rub on his ribs."

Beau planted her hands on her hips and glared mutinously after her father. "I'm not an errand boy either," she muttered, watching with hot, flashing eyes as the three men ducked through the after hatch. Her last glimpse was of Dante's flowing white shirt as he lagged behind, favoring the newly bandaged leg.

"And a gracious 'you're welcome' to you too," she snorted.

Chapter 6

Beau was still grousing as she descended the shallow ladder into the area beneath the forecastle where the cook held rein over the ship's stores. He was a bellicose man, lean as a whip, ugly as a wart, with the unparalleled talent of being able to pass wind upon request. Beau's query for food won a resounding demonstration of his skill, followed by a hand waved sullenly in the direction of the huge iron cauldron. Assuming it meant help yourself, she did. There was a thick miasma of rice and beans bubbling sluggishly in the kettle, some of which she ladled into a large wooden bowl. Two thick slabs of boiled, salted fish were tossed onto a tin platter along with a handful of rock-hard biscuits and a wedge of yellow cheese.

With the crumbs of one hastily devoured biscuit clinging to her lower lip, Beau threaded her way back to the stern, choosing to take a path belowdecks rather than crossing above. The air was dank and smelled of too many sweaty bodies cramped together in too close quarters. Hammocks were slung between every beam and board, many of them already occupied by men of both crews who had worked hard throughout the day. Most of them would be up again before dawn, engaged in normal ships routine.

A small, clear section perhaps six foot square was devoid of any hanging canvas cocoons and it was there, around an upturned barrel, that a dozen or so men who were not slated for the early watch gathered to whittle and trade stories. A shielded lantern hung over their heads, swaying with the motion of the ship. Some chewed on knots of leather or sucked on hoarded sticks of sugarcane that had been left out in the sun long enough to ferment the juices.

Most of the twelve were from the *Egret* and tugged a forelock respectfully as Beau passed by. One offered her a strip of cane, which she accepted and popped into her mouth, chewing and sucking the stringy pulp to release the sweet, strong liquor.

Two of the men were off the *Virago* and watched her with curious eyes and slack mouths.

"She don't belong to nobody," she overheard one of the men whisper in response to a muffled question. "And if ye know what's best, ye'll forget ye askt."

The narrow passage leading to the captain's great cabin was dark, but Beau knew it as well as she knew the back of her hand. She ducked for the low beams and veered once to avoid clipping her hip on the ladder rail, a second time to maneuver around a barrel of water.

Where there was usually one large cabin spanning the breadth of the ship's stern and occupying most of the area beneath the raised aftercastle, on the *Egret* there were two. It was Spence's only concession to Beau's sex, that she have somewhere private to sleep and tend to her "woman's things." Thus the great cabin had been partitioned into two slightly unequal halves, with two separate doors and a wall of oak planking between. Spence's was the larger of the two, overstuffed with furniture as stout and well sea-

soned as the man who used it. A wide, square berth filled
one corner, a desk and a wire-fronted cabinet were
crammed into the other. The door to the gallery—a two-
foot-wide balcony that stretched across the stern—was lo-
cated in Beau's half, leaving that much more room for the
captain's sea chests and piles of assorted clutter that filled
every spare inch of space. A large five-spoked wheel with
simple brass lamps hung suspended from an overhead beam,
spilling a pool of pale light over the top of a much-abused
dining table and four sturdy chairs.

Spence, Simon Dante, and Geoffrey Pitt were seated at
the table, a fresh jar of rum between them. Beau's approach
had been silent and no one looked up or noticed her standing in the darkness of the companionway, the platter balanced in her hands.

"Not near as fancy as yer *Virago*, I warrant," Spence was
saying. "But then I'm not a fancy man an' it suits me just
fine. Beau has the other half—fer her own safety, if ye
know what I mean. Not that she wouldn't sling herself in
a hammock alongside the rest o' the crew, given her druth-
ers. Aye, an' if it meets yer needs, Cap'n, ye can put up in
her berth for the journey home. Beau won't mind."

Out in the corridor Beau's mouth fell open.

"I'll stay with my men. I don't want to put anyone out
of their bed."

"Nonsense. There's a perfectly good sail closet Beau can
make proper cozy. An' *I'm* not wantin' to be known as the
man who slung Dante de Tourville in a canvas sack atween
two beams."

Dante gave the red-bearded ship's master a curious look.
"A few hours ago you would have gladly slung me in a
noose."

Spence shrugged. "That were a few hours ago. Since

then I've come to think ye're an honorable bastard despite yer lapse o' manners."

Pitt grinned over the rim of his cup. "He's actually fairly well housebroken when he isn't chewing nails and spitting fire."

Spence guffawed. "Aye, I figured as much when he didn't rape my daughter when he had the chance—likely the provocation as well."

"Was she disappointed?" Dante asked dryly.

"Only that yer gun did not fire. She thought it a dirty trick to blow out the prime."

"Lucky for me I did or she would have blown out my gizzard."

"Lucky fer ye she did not carve it out anyroad. She probably had more blades on her," he added matter-of-factly. "Even stripped naked an' searched ten ways to Sunday, she would have had one hid somewheres."

"I'll keep it in mind."

"Just keep it in yer breeches, Cap'n," Spence said with a not-so-jovial smile. "I've yet to see a man take somethin' from her she did not want to give. Just like her mother, rest her soul. Regular hellcat when her fur was ruffled. Gave me this"—he tilted his chin and lifted a hoary handful of red fuzz out of the way to reveal a six-inch-long scar running down the side of his windpipe—"on our weddin' night, an' this"—he pulled open the V of his shirt to display another badge of honor high on his shoulder—"the day she told me she were with child."

"Her way of celebrating happy occasions?"

Spence chuckled again. "She were Portugee. A rare dark-eyed Gipsy with hot blood an' mischief in her soul. I took her off a ship we raided an' wed her the same night; she took offense we did not stand before a priest, so she did not consider us married. When she found she was with child, she could scarce bear the shame an' forced me, at gunpoint, to seek out a Catholic sermoner. The gun went off, accidentallike, an' she wept fer two days thinkin' she'd killed me. When she judged I would live, she packed me into a cart an' propped me in front of a priest anyway." He paused and smiled wistfully at the memory. "Only wench I knew could give a man the sweetest taste o' heaven one minute an' the hottest bite o' hell the next. Have ye a wife o' yer own?"

"I had one. Once." Dante said flatly. "But she was out of my life a long time ago and we are both happier for it."

Spence chuckled. "Not a pleasurable experience, I gather?"

"No more pleasurable than falling into a pit full of snakes."

"Now ye sound just like my Beau. Claims she wants no part o' a husband, nor o' any man who would pull her away from the sea."

"Who put her here in the first place?"

Spence snorted. "She put herself."

He assumed his companions' cups were as empty as his and refilled all three before setting aside the crock and taking a slow, leisurely scratch at his armpit. "Aye, so now I can tell ye all about what put my Isabeau on board the *Egret* . . . if ye need more time to decide if ye can trust me . . . or ye can tell me what killed yer ship."

Pitt and Dante exchanged a glance. Pitt's shrug was almost imperceptible and Dante lowered the cup from his lips, swallowing carefully.

"Greed, Captain Spence. I warrant it was greed and cowardice that killed my ship."

Spence's beard shifted over a thoughtful grimace. "When we heard about the raid on Veracruz, we also heard there were two ships sailed away, stuffed beam to bilges with gold."

Dante nodded. "When the venture was first conceived, I knew it would need two ships. The risk was enormous, as you can appreciate, but the prize was worth ten times what a single vessel could hope to earn on a dozen voyages. The Queen herself put forward the candidate. She assured me he was . . . cut of good cloth."

Spence grunted. "Even the strongest canvas comes with flaws, lad. Some with great gapin' holes."

"Aye, well, you can be sure Victor Bloodstone will have a great gaping hole in him ere I'm finished."

"Bloodstone? Walsingham's bastard?"

"He prefers the term *nephew*, but aye. One and the same."

"Last I heard, he were the new darling o' the Court, the prettiest face to amuse the Queen."

"Indeed, he has a pretty face and Elizabeth likes to surround herself with beauty in the hopes it might be contagious. He also knows how to sail a ship, damn his soul; I can't fault him for lack of skill or experience. It was the only reason I agreed to take Bloodstone on, and in the beginning he did not disappoint. We sailed for Veracruz like two hungry wolves stalking fresh meat." He hesitated and stared blankly out the darkened gallery windows. "Do you know the Spanish harbor at all?"

Spence shifted in his seat, obviously not wanting to appear ignorant, but at the same time not wanting to admit he had never risked so deep a foray into Spanish waters. Veracruz was a terminus for the mule trains that carried gold and silver out of the mountains of Mexico. It had confidently been declared by the Spanish to be out of reach and impregnable to any foreign sail, as heavily fortified as any madman would expect a treasure depot to be.

"At any rate," Dante continued, talking now to his rum, "thanks to Lucifer, we knew of a secluded bay on the Island of Sacrifices, not five leagues from Veracruz. It was big enough to hide two ships and easily within striking distance of the harbor. We each carried the framework for several pinnaces in our holds on the voyage down, and when we reached the inlet, it was a small matter to assemble the vessels and launch our tiny fleet on a surprise nighttime raid.

"No one expected us. No one raised an alarm, for we looked like harmless fishing boats. We landed a mile or so up the coast and went overland into Veracruz; eighty men in all, and each came away with as many bars of gold as he could load onto a mule. Christ, the cocky bastards even left the stables unguarded.

"By morning, of course, all hell broke loose, for we had not exactly been tidy with the bodies at the treasure house. As luck would have it, however, a squall blew up and delayed their pursuit by a full two days—plenty of time for two nimble wolves to slink away and use those same winds to blow us clear across the Caribbean. We were successful too. We broke into open sea and were more than halfway home before misfortune struck. A gale, the likes of which I had not seen in twenty years, swept us along like spindrift for seven days and nights. It battered the *Virago* so badly, she ended up on a reef with a hole in her hull wide enough to swim through.

"Our first thought was to find someplace safe where we could haul her over and make repairs. We were as yet unsure of where we were but the lookouts spied a small island and we made for it, hoping for time to make repairs. Once there, we lightened the *Virago*'s burden by off-loading our weight of gold bars along with every spare barrel and crate we carried—including most of our food and fresh water.

We had the cables attached and the men on shore to careen her when we saw sails on the horizon." He stopped and snorted at some terrible irony, which he shared a moment later with Spence. "They were bloody zabras. Six India guards unluckily driven off course by the same storm that ripped at us."

"Blow my ballocks," Spence muttered. "What did ye do?"

"The only thing we could do: We stood and fought. The *Virago* was wounded, aye, but we had Bloodstone at our back; we should have taken them in a trice. He was to remain out of sight behind the island while we drew fire and led the zabras away. The intention was to catch them with their eyes looking forward, not back, and while the *Talon* bore some damage to her mainmast, she still had full steerage and an equally full battery of guns to call upon."

Dante's voice grew brittle and a tremor appeared in the hand that gripped the pewter cup.

"The zabras took the bait, as we expected they would, and came on, all six of them bristling with their own importance. We sallied forth to meet them, feigning we were in worse straits than we were, knowing that Victor Bloodstone, courtier to the Queen, nephew of Elizabeth's chief counsel, would be running out from behind the island with all guns blazing." He paused and tossed the considerable contents of the cup down his throat. "He ran, all right. Bearing due north and east the last glimpse we had of him, with every square inch of canvas warped into the wind. He ran and just left us there, one against six, knowing full well that this time *we* were the fresh, bleeding meat, and the Spaniards were the stalking wolves."

Dante's throat was beginning to roughen from the spirits, but the blazing blue eyes remained fixed and burning on the pewter cup. "My brave, brave *Virago*," he whispered.

"She took them. Sank four and sent the other two limp pricks off, dragging their sails behind them. There were sixty of us left at the end of the day . . . sixty out of one hundred and thirty men, fighting on decks that ran red with their own blood. When we returned to the island to lick our wounds, everything was gone. All of it: the gold, the silver, even the barrels of food and water. And what they could not load on board the *Talon*, they smashed and threw into the sea. The wounded," Dante finished on a savage hiss of fury, "did not stand a chance."

He fell silent and Pitt took up the remainder of the story. "We patched the *Virago* as best we could and rigged enough sail to catch the prevailing winds, not knowing whether or not the two zabras managed to limp into a nearby port to relay our identity and position. The ship was too badly damaged and the crew too weak to have held off another attack . . . which might explain, although not excuse, our extreme caution and lack of manners this morning when we saw you sliding out of the mist."

Spence nodded pensively. He was dumbfounded, and more than a little outraged himself at the treachery perpetrated on the crew of the *Virago*. There were unwritten laws, codes of honor among seafarers as sacred and unbreakable as the laws of God. First among others was never to abandon a sister ship in distress, and De Tourville, though half French himself, had sailed the *Virago* under English colors with a mostly English crew. He was a privateer and an adventurer. To be sure, some even called him an opportunist and a pirate, but he was also a respected member of the elite group of sea hawks whose skill and daring on the high seas was the only thing standing in the way of Spain's complete dominance of the oceans as well as the New World.

While publicly commiserating with the King of Spain

over the losses suffered at the hands of the sea hawks, behind closed doors Elizabeth not only encouraged her privateers to plunder and raid the rich treasure ships that sailed between Panama and Lisbon, she was the largest single investor in many of their planned expeditions. There had been rumors flooding England for over a year now that King Philip was at the end of his patience over Elizabeth's feigned innocence. Her fledgling navy of merchant marauders was costing Spain staggering losses in shipping and prestige, and there were stories of an enormous fleet of galleons being amassed in Spanish harbors, a great armada of warships being built to carry an army of conquest across the English Channel.

It was no time to hear of open treachery and cowardice among the English ranks. Elizabeth would need all her best captains, her fastest and deadliest ships, to counter any threat Spain might present.

This was not to say all the sea hawks were friends. Most were bitter rivals who would no sooner reveal their plans and destinations to a fellow privateer than they would voluntarily report the full value of their plunder to the Crown. Even Jonas Spence had his secret compartments and false walls, though both were sadly empty at the moment. Nor was he above a little larceny or piracy if the acts were warranted. But to abandon a sister ship? Or to tuck his tail and run for safety while someone else fought to the death? He had not lost two fingers and half a leg because he went out of his way to avoid confrontations.

"Blow me," he muttered again. "I can well see why ye'd be wantin' to chase after the fellow. An' with more guns than a mere merchant trader would have to offer."

Dante shook his head, causing his earring to glitter in the lamplight. "He has more than a two-week start on us. Even burdened as he is, I have come to believe over the past few hours, it would be sheer foolhardiness to think we could catch him.

Spence's brow pleated over a frown but it was Beau, still looking on in silence from the doorway, who felt her spine prickle at the implication that the *Egret* was too slow and unrefined to merit the pirate wolf's respect.

"I would have you know, sir," she said, striding briskly into the pool of brighter light, "with a fair wind in our sheets we can run at fifteen knots and better." She dropped the platter without ceremony on the table and leaned forward on the heels of her hands. "We have sailed from Plymouth to the Tortugas in under six weeks. I doubt even your *Virago* could have outrun us."

Dante glowered while Pitt stepped quickly into the breach. "You must have had an excellent navigator and pilot."

"We did," she said evenly, turning to meet the smiling green eyes. "Me."

The smile was startled off Pitt's mouth. "You?"

Spence settled his weight back in his chair, balancing precariously on the two hind legs while he folded his arms across his chest. "Best damned pilot I ever had at the helm. Hell, she once took us through Magellan's Straits in a storm. An' her charts? Ye'll see none their equal. If anyone can run us up the arse o' yer rogue captain, it's my Isabeau."

"A woman," Dante muttered, still disbelieving, "at the helm of a ship? Has the world gone mad?"

Beau glared at him. "Only the small portion with you in it."

"Well, regardless," Pitt interjected quickly, "it does work to our advantage that we know precisely where Bloodstone is going."

"To London, ye mean."

"To London." Pitt nodded. "He'll waste no time boasting his prowess to the Queen and her counsel, likely taking all the credit for the venture in the same voice he uses to mourn the loss of Simon Dante."

"Aye, an' he'll do it all with yer gold in his pockets."

"My gold," Dante agreed, finally tearing his gaze away from Beau. "Which could be half yours if you brought me within striking distance of the cowardly bastard."

"Half?" The tiny glands under Spence's tongue squirted with more than casual interest. And, looking at the hard gleam in Dante's eyes, he saw no reason to doubt the man would, indeed, pay the price gladly. The *Talon* would be doubly burdened and moving slower than a snail, taking longer routes around known lanes of shipping in order to avoid being set upon by scavengers. Two weeks of plodding could be made up in a few days of spirited sailing with the wind in their teeth.

"Beau?"

She looked at her father, amazed he was even considering the possibility. "What if the zabras did make it back to a Spanish port? What if there are a dozen ships out there right now hunting for a wounded privateer?"

Spence pursed his lips and had to acknowledge the threat. The Spanish coast was less than two hundred leagues off the starboard beam, and if they had indeed sent out hunters . . .

Something else the Frenchman had said caused Spence to frown and turn to Dante again. "Ye said yer mission was not yet finished after ye left Veracruz. What more were ye plannin' to do?"

Dante drew a deep breath and avoided catching Pitt's eye. "We were planning to make a small detour past the harbor at Cadiz."

Spence's chair thumped forward and he shook his head

as if to clear water from his ears. "Cadiz? Did ye just say *Cadiz?*"

Dante smile grimly. "That was the same response Bloodstone gave me. He wanted no part of it, either, and was planning to separate from us once we veered east."

"Why, by God's grace, would ye want to veer anywhere near Cadiz and risk the charred toes and crimping irons of Philip's Inquisitors?"

"Pitt," Dante said on a rum-laced sigh.

"Pitt?"

"A damned efficient fellow. Too efficient at times. While most of my men were busy picking the treasure house at Veracruz clean of anything that glittered, Pitt was bending over a packet of letters and documents waiting to be included in the next flota to Spain. He thought they might provide the Queen and her councillors some interesting reading."

Dante held out his cup for another splash of rum. "As you must know yourself, over the past year, every ship that leaves an English port sails under orders to keep their eyes and ears open. Although Drake and the other sea hawks have been warning Elizabeth to prepare for an invasion from Spain, without any real proof of Philip's plottings, she cannot justify emptying the treasury to build more warships. She is stubbornly determined to find some way to negotiate a lasting peace, despite every logical sense and argument telling her she should be adding to England's pitifully small navy, not tying their hands behind their backs."

Spence felt a chill run down his spine. "Are ye sayin' ye have such proof?"

"I have more than rumor and gossip. I have letters from the governors of Panama and Mexico applauding the King on his choice of Don Alvaro de Bazan, Marquis of Santa

Cruz, to *lead the invasion fleet*. I have documents that read like a list of supplies and provisions the governors will be able to provide, as well as an estimate of a million ducats' worth of gold that will be available *before spring* to pay for the army. Of course, he may have to amend that estimate somewhat now, but there are other lists, other provisions promised in such quantities as would suggest the rumors we have been hearing are all true. Philip is preparing for war."

"And you were planning to stop him by sailing into Cadiz and spitting in his eye?" Beau asked wryly.

"I was planning only to sail past the harbor and see for myself what strength he has hidden there. Cadiz was mentioned prominently in nearly every document, as was Cantabrico and Lisbon. Frankly, I have no idea where Cantabrico is, and Lisbon is too well protected, the harbor being enclosed and well fortified. Cadiz, on the other hand, is far enough south and too deep in Spanish waters for them to even dream of an Englishman sailing down their throat."

"No more probable than an Englishman sailing into Veracruz and making a withdrawal from the King's treasure house?"

Dante actually smiled up into the amber tiger eyes. "Exactly so."

Spence grumbled deep in his chest. "Still an' all, do ye not know what they do when they catch an Englishman, or do ye just not have any particular love fer yer nether parts? It's torture, lad, with hot irons and wooden racks and red-hot faggots thrust up yer arse; all done in the name o' Catholic purification. Afterwards, if ye survive, it's into a galleass with ye, chained to an oar till ye die or the ship sinks."

"I am well aware of the fate of captured crews, Captain,

but I am also well aware of the fate that awaits England if Spain has a thousand ships to send against us."

Spence had no retort and Dante's gaze traveled beyond the rim of his cup, lifting to Beau's stubbornly set chin and firm, bow-shaped lips.

"I thought you relished a good challenge, mam'selle?"

"If it is a sane and sound one, I usually do."

"Of course," he mused, "if you are simply not up to it . . . ?"

"You obviously weren't."

Dante scraped to his feet, looking for all the world as if he ached to have his hands around Beau's throat again.

"You have a singularly sharp tongue on you, mam'selle, and you seem bent on testing its edge on my patience."

"You have a singularly sharp arrogance about you, m'sieur, and you seem to think that because you are who you are and you have been so grievously maligned, it gives you the right to treat others with contempt and disregard."

"Only those who deserve it," he snapped. "You seem to have conveniently forgotten you held a knife to my vitals and threatened to blow a hole through my chest. Such refined behavior warranted a little disregard, in my opinion."

"*You* seem to have forgotten you held a pistol to my head first and threatened me with rape. Hardly an honorable accounting of yourself."

"It was hardly an enthusiastic threat," he countered evenly, his gaze sliding down the tautly held length of her body. "Or delivered with much conviction."

"Scarcely any conviction at all, Captain. I have encountered more *substantial* threats from boys."

"I'm sure you have. Youths and weanlings, no doubt, who find the dirt under your nails most appealing."

Beau's cheeks flushed crimson and he started to raise his

cup in a salute to his own wit. He never quite completed the maneuver, for the cup slipped out of his fingers and splashed the remaining drops of rum down the front of his shirt. Dante blinked and stared at the splatters for a moment, his face contorted with surprise and not a little shock as he started to pitch forward, his legs turning to jelly beneath him.

Spence caught him up under one arm. Beau, who was closer than Pitt and reacted instinctively, propped him by the other.

"Indies Gold," Jonas said, wobbling none too steadily on his own feet. "Knocks yer ballocks down to yer toes if yer not used to it—or if ye haven't had any solid food in yer belly."

"I'm sure he will thank you for the excuses," Beau muttered, struggling to hold her balance under the weight of the muscular shoulder and arm. "If not the swollen head and rancid tongue he'll have come morning."

"Now, daughter—Christ, he's a heavy bastard—show some Christian charity. Ye heard all he said, did ye not? Fer all his bluster, he's a brave man. An' ye know yerself t'would be a worthy challenge to see if we could catch up with the cowardly whoreson bastard."

Beau glared at her father and could see he had already absolved Dante de Tourville of any blame for his churlish behavior.

"You might call it brave to face six ships alone," she pointed out. "I would call it reckless and foolhardy. As for chasing after Victor Bloodstone . . ."

Dante's dark head swung loosely around, seeking her voice. His face was hanging between his shoulders, level with her chest, and as he opened his mouth it pressed against the soft cushion of her breast.

"A woman at the helm of a ship," he muttered. "Another at the helm of England's destiny. What next, I wonder. Petticoats in the yardarms and breeches in the kitchen?"

Beau cursed and jerked away, leaving Geoffrey Pitt to scramble and catch his captain before both Dante and Jonas Spence found themselves in a heap on the floor.

"You'd best get this drunken lout to bed before he feels my knife on his vitals again," she directed Pitt crisply. "And tell him from me that he is to touch nothing—*absolutely nothing*—in my cabin or when I do run him up Bloodstone's arse, it will be from the spout of one of his own damned cannon."

"I . . . will be most happy to convey your message."

"You may convey this as well," she said, throwing the blur of steel that was her stiletto, embedding the point in the tabletop. "Unless my eyes deceive me, there are creatures in his beard and in his hair. They had best not find their way into my bed or belongings, or I will come for him myself and scrape him bald. What is more, there is a bar of lye soap on the gallery ledge. You might consider using it yourself, Mister Pitt, unless you share your captain's affection for his own filth."

"Er . . . not at all, Mistress Spence. But in Simon's defense it must be said we were hardly concerned with cleanliness."

She planted her hands on her hips and glowered. "I am not anyone's mistress, Mister Pitt. On board this ship, I am just Beau. Or Mister Spence, if your tongue has trouble with simpler things."

"The simpler the better," he avowed, refusing to take offense at her tone. "For I would indeed have trouble addressing you as Mister."

Beau cocked an eyebrow warily, wondering if he was mocking her or if he was truly so magnificent a fool as to think a charming smile and twinkling green eyes would make him seem less of an ogre than his black-souled captain.

Mocking, she decided, and with a parting curse she scowled her way out of the cabin.

Balancing Dante on one shoulder and carrying a lit taper in his free hand, Pitt shuffled into the dark cabin next door. He propped De Tourville against the wall and searched out a lantern, glancing around as he did so, wary of disturbing the slightest mote of dust. Not that there appeared to be any to disturb. The cabin was neat and clean, devoid of the mustiness and clutter that warmed the atmosphere in Spence's cabin. The walls were bare planking, the berth was high and narrow and looked as comfortable as a coffin. Most of the free space was taken up by a large chart table positioned to catch the best light from the gallery windows. There was a storage bin holding rolled charts and maps, a bookcase neatly stacked with volumes held in place with leather strapping, a sea chest, and a small desk weighted down under various navigational instruments.

Dante's eyes opened a slit. He was not entirely drunk, which Pitt had already deduced, but neither was he completely without a strong whirling sensation in his head.

"You have that disapproving look in your eye again," he said to Pitt.

"It was a cheap way to end an argument. Were you afraid she was winning?"

Dante swore and rubbed his temples. "I was not in the mood to justify myself to a woman."

"No? You seemed to be in the mood for something. Your tongue was sharper than I've seen it in a long time."

"I said nothing she did not deserve."

"Mmmm. Just enough to stir her blood into helping you

chase Victor Bloodstone to ground. Do you think she can do it? Do you really think she can pilot this ship?"

"If she can't, she'll find herself accidentally fallen over the side one dark night."

"Your usual subtle solution," Pitt remarked dryly. "Of course you could always try something a little less drastic and work some of your immeasurable charm on her."

"To what end, pray?"

"Well, she is a female and soft in all the right places."

"I have no desire to bed a she-cat."

"When did your tastes become so refined? Unless you have suffered some holy revelation, you are normally content to bed everything that walks and breathes."

Dante glared at Pitt, then the door. "Haven't you a canvas sling waiting for you somewhere?"

Pitt grinned, nonplussed. He acknowledged his dismissal with a tug on a tawny forelock, then set the stiletto on the desk in plain view. "I presume you would prefer to slit your own throat rather than tempt someone else to do it?"

Dante snarled and looked for something handy to throw, but Pitt was already gone, his laughter muffled by the closing door.

Chapter 7

Dante de Tourville slept, unmoving, for almost seventy-two hours. He slept through a heavy squall, replete with thunder and lightning. He slept through the crash of several dozen tin plates that flew out of Cook's arms when he was startled by the sight of Clarence the cat leaping out at him from a dark corner of the passageway just outside the door of the cabin.

What finally brought Dante awake, and grudgingly so, was the soft sound of a footstep moving stealthily across the cabin floor. That and the aromatic vapors rising off a platter laden with hot broth, a large slab of boiled fish, and the ship's staple, beans and rice. The finely chiseled nostrils flared and the long black lashes shivered open. He suffered a few moments of disorientation before he remembered where he was, that he was not just imagining a real berth beneath him and a cabin not smashed to utter chaos around him.

He judged it to be sometime in the late afternoon, for the room was flooded with harsh beams of sunlight. The gallery windows were mullioned, each palm-sized diamond framed in lead and flaring with points of brilliant light that seared the back of Dante's eyeballs like burning sulphur. He closed them almost immediately, not all the way, allowing himself a narrow slit through which to see who or what had disturbed him.

It was a who and he had to blink again, not believing what his eyes were seeing. It was the girl, standing at the chart table, frowning over some calculations while she casually munched on portions of the meal intended for the occupant of the cabin. In her other hand she held a square of rough toweling that she was using to dry her newly washed hair.

Dante did not move or do anything to betray the fact he was awake. Instead, he took the opportunity to study Beau Spence while her guard was down. Her hair was longer than the braid implied. Full and thick with natural waves, it spread in a dark auburn mass halfway down her back. With the light pouring through the windows behind her, the driest curls glistened with threads of gold and red, forming a soft halo around her head. Her face was dominated by the large, expressive eyes and a mouth that never should have known a coarse phrase or a sullen scowl. The light was also strong enough to betray the slender body beneath the oversized shirt and breeches. Some vague memory of feeling one of those pert breasts pillowed against his mouth brought a crooked smile to his lips and a faint surge of hot blood through his veins.

She glanced up from the chart table and Dante closed his eyes. He was at a distinct disadvantage with the light blinding him. He also had a wad of blankets tangled around his ankles—the only part of him not naked and open to full disclosure.

"So, Captain Dante, your man did not take me at my word," she murmured, advancing slowly toward the bed.

"You loll about for three days in my cabin, in my bed, and no one thought to delouse you."

She wiped the crumbs and grease off her hand and tossed the toweling aside. Passing by the desk, she picked up the stiletto she had given to Pitt, along with the oblong whetstone, and began slowly honing the edge of the blade to razor sharpness.

Dante saw the blot of her shadow crowding over him and it took a commendable effort on his part not to open his eyes or visibly brace himself for what might come next. He recalled Pitt's words, that he might prefer to slit his own throat than tempt someone else to do it. Beau Spence would be the last one he would trust his jugular to, but he forced his breathing to remain slow and shallow, forced his hands to remain flat on his belly and not clenched by his sides.

At the same time the soft drift of freshly washed hair piqued his senses. Because he dared not open his eyes, he was left staring inwardly at the unwanted picture that had impressed itself on his brain the first day—the one of her lying naked across the top of his desk, her hair spread in glossy disarray beneath them, her body arching to receive him, her amber eyes full of flame and fire, heavy lidded with passion.

The sound of the knife scraping over the whetstone rescued him from the dangerous abyss of his imagination and he risked opening one eye a sliver. She was just standing there, her hand moving by rote to sharpen the already wickedly keen edge of the blade while her gaze roved freely over the immodest sprawl of his body. Dante was not particularily vain about the breadth of his shoulders or the well-thewed musculature of his arms and legs; the sea was a demanding mistress, tolerating neither fools nor weaklings lightly. His lack of vanity did not necessarily include other parts of his anatomy, which he knew to be as formidable in size and substance as the rest of him, and it amused him to think of the little pirate wench fainting into a heap by the bed.

The grinding stopped and Dante saw Beau drag her eyes up to her own arm, where she tested the keenness of the blade's edge on a patch of her own fine hairs. Far from fainting, she set the whetstone aside and advanced toward the bed again, her brow creased in a frown of concentration.

She leaned forward and Dante tensed his muscles as he felt the edge of the knife press beneath the crest of his cheekbone. A slow, steady descent scraped a clean path through the heavy black bearding, a second widened the path to his ear.

She stopped to clean the blade just as one silvery-blue eye slitted open. "I trust you are not just throwing that on the floor. I have been given quite specific orders not to make a mess in here."

Beau nearly dropped the knife as she jerked back. "Christ Jesus! How long have you been awake?"

"Long enough," he answered vaguely, and lifted a hand to wipe a smear of grease off her chin. "Did you enjoy my meal?"

She drew further back, out of reach of his long arm. "It is a crime to let good food go to waste. You have already slept your way through enough meals to fatten ten men."

Dante pushed himself up onto his elbows. "Did I hear you say I have been asleep for three days?"

"Two full days and an hour or so shy of the third," she obliged, glancing out the windows. "The sun is almost touching the horizon now."

"Three days," he muttered, massaging his temple with

a thumb and forefinger. "*Merde!* My head feels as if it has a thousand drummers inside."

"No small surprise, considering what you drank as your last meal."

He glared up at her. "How are the rest of my men?"

"They are well-fed and well-rested."

"And Lucifer? He has not killed anyone yet?"

"Is he likely to do so?"

"His moods can be . . . somewhat unpredictable."

"Between being with Mister Pitt during the day and sleeping across your door at night, he seems to be well-enough behaved. He does not talk much, does he?"

"He does not talk at all since the Spaniards cut out his tongue." He ran his fingers through his hair, then down onto the cleanly shaved stripe on his jaw. "Did it not occur to you to ask if I wanted a bare chin?"

"If you didn't, you should have scrubbed out the vermin before you collapsed in my bed."

He grinned carelessly. "Since you started the job, would you care to finish it?"

She glanced sidelong at the faint stirring in his groin. "No, thank you. You appear to be enjoying the attention too much."

Still grinning, he reached down and drew the blankets up over his hips. "Forgive me if I have insulted your sensibilities."

Bright tiger eyes flickered back to his face and he had to admit she was a lovely creature with her hair curling damply around her face and her cheeks dusted a soft pink.

"Do not flatter yourself into thinking you have anything I have not seen a hundred times before."

"Flattery was the last thing on my mind," he assured her.

"Oh? Dare I guess what was the first?"

"It would probably disappoint you to know it was food. And a stoup of water to remove the dry rot from my throat."

"Cook sent ale."

"I would prefer water . . . if you wouldn't mind."

She released another huff of exasperation and went out into the corridor, returning a few moments later with a wooden ladle brimming with water.

Dante was sitting on the edge of the bed, his long legs hanging over the side, the blanket draped across his loins. He accepted the ladle graciously and drained it in a few deep swallows, savoring the coolness and the taste despite the fact it bore the woody taint of oak from the barrel.

Beau watched him drink, watched the movement of his throat as he swallowed. Her gaze drifted down to the broad, well-muscled shoulders and arms, then across the luxuriant mat of hair that covered his chest. She skipped deliberately over the area covered by the blanket, although what lay concealed beneath was warmly impressed on her mind.

"Cook has changed the bandages on your leg twice. The wound seems to be healing well."

Dante glanced at his calf and gave his foot and ankle a turn. "Aye, it feels markedly better. I thank you."

Casually awarded, his gratitude deepened the stain in her cheeks.

She cleared her throat. "The captain will want to know you are awake; I should go and find him."

"Wait," Dante said sharply, putting aside the ladle. She reacted warily to the tone of command in his voice, and remembering Pitt's suggestion, he softened his expression and attempted a look of disarming humility.

"I know we started out on the wrong footing," he said, "but you must understand I was at the point of desperation and not in possession of my full senses."

Beau narrowed her eyes, thinking he looked like Clarence the cat after he had been caught stealing fish off the cook's plate.

"My only thought at the time was for the safety of my men and for salvaging what we could from the *Virago*."

"My father boarded your ship in good faith. His only thought at the time was to rescue you and your men before your ship sank. Even now he has ordered our stores of food and water be given freely to your crew, though we suffer shortages ourselves."

Dante gritted his teeth but kept smiling. "I have already apologized to your father and attempted to explain—"

She cut him off. "Would an apology and explanation from Victor Bloodstone serve to cool *your* anger?"

"We are hardly guilty of the same crimes."

"No? We found your ship foundering and on the verge of sinking and my father's only crime was showing concern for any possible survivors. Yet you threatened him with killing me, you took command of his ship and crew and forced both to accept the unwanted burden of your heavy guns. You have turned the *Egret* from an honest trading vessel into a warship and dispatched her on a hunt for another warship with no thought to the consequences."

"The consequences are that you will be better able to defend yourselves in hostile situations."

"Our situation will become hostile only if we succeed in finding the *Talon*. Or if we are found by another vessel and your presence here on board is discovered."

Muscles folded over powerful muscles as he crossed his arms. "Would it ease your mind if I promise to throw myself overboard should the latter occur?"

"There is no need for such promises, Captain. I shall do it myself if I think the safety of the *Egret*, her captain, or crew is compromised."

"All by yourself?" he asked with an easy smile.

"I am stronger than I look, sir. Better men than you have discovered it to be so, to their disappointment and loss."

"And what about your disappointment?"

"Mine?"

"Yours . . . that they were not strong enough to match you."

Without warning, Dante rose from the bed. The blanket fell to the floor, but he paid it no heed as he stalked forward the two long strides it took to bring him directly in front of her. Not knowing what to expect, she tried to stumble back, but her retreat was blocked by the chart table. She raised the stiletto instinctively. Dante was anticipating the move and managed to grasp her wrist, twisting it sharply enough to startle the knife out of her fingers.

He raked his hands into the damp thickness of her hair and forcibly tilted her head up, and, after supplementing his challenge with a mocking grin, lowered his mouth, brutally crushing her lips beneath his.

Beau was outraged. Her body burned with anger, her senses exploded with a corresponding fury. Her hands were trapped against the marble-hard surface of his chest and she tried to push herself free, but it was like trying to push against a stone wall. She opened her mouth to scream a curse, but he only took advantage and filled it with his tongue, thrusting with hard, deep strokes that were as shocking as they were enraging. His grip was firm, his hands twined tightly through her hair. His mouth was brutal and possessive, chasing after each cry, each attempt to twist away from the forced intimacy.

Only when *he* chose to end it was she able to wrench herself free. When she straightened and faced him again, it was with the gleaming threat of another smaller, thicker blade grasped firmly in her hand.

"You son of a bitch!" Crimson faced, she rubbed her mouth with the back of her hand, removing the wetness. "How dare you!"

"I dared," he said calmly, "because you challenged me to."

"I . . . *did not!*"

"You most certainly did. With those big brassy eyes and that lovely, luscious pout of a mouth. Perhaps you weren't aware it was a challenge, or perhaps you are simply accustomed to men who find your stubbornness and rudeness intimidating. But only a fool would misread it as anything else." His gaze fell to the knife and his voice became a lazy drawl of menace. "What's more, I would suggest you put that away before I mistake it for a challenge of another sort—or have you forgotten my promise if you ever drew another weapon on me?"

"I have not forgotten," she said tautly, quivering with fresh outrage. "Nor have I forgotten you are not a man bound by conscience or burdened by an overabundance of honor."

"You are forgetting patience," he added succinctly. "Of which I am quickly running short."

Beau ignored the warning flecks of blue smoldering in his eyes and turned angrily to gather the charts she had initially come to retrieve. He watched, a vein throbbing noticeably in his temple as she circled behind the table to collect her brushes and pots of ink.

"I'll have someone tell the captain you're awake," she said crisply, and headed for the door.

"Isabeau!"

She stopped and glowered back over her shoulder. "I

have not given you permission to call me that. My name is Beau. Just plain Beau."

His eyes took in the soft cloud of her hair, the kiss-swollen lips, and the two hardened nubs that crowned her breasts and pushed impudently against her shirt.

"If I have discovered nothing else, *Isabeau*," he said quietly, "I have discovered you are anything but plain."

"Just as I have discovered, Captain Dante, that you are no different from any other bandy-legged rooster, so impressed with what you have between your legs, you expect every woman on earth to be sweating and panting to have at it. Well, I am loath to disappoint, but I have *seen* better"—she cast a disdainful glance down his thighs—"and *had* better without becoming the smallest part damp across the brow. And if you ever . . . *ever* dare to touch me again, I will fillet you in such small pieces, the sharks will have to search the entire ocean to find a solid mouthful!"

With fury snapping in her eyes, she whirled and exited the cabin, giving the door a resounding slam behind her.

Chapter 8

────────⟋⟍────────

With the weather clear and a brisk north-by-northeast wind blowing steady, the *Egret* made good time through the remainder of the week, skimming over the waves like a frisky foal. The survivors of the *Virago* had been understandably withdrawn the first few days and preferred their own company, but as their health returned, so, too, did their spirits. Most, like their captain, vowed certain death to the master and crew of the *Talon* if and when they caught them, and when all the treacherous details became known to the crew of the *Egret*, it stirred equally strong sentiments in every quarter. To abandon any ship in distress was to do the unthinkable. To leave so famous a ship as the *Virago* and her crew as sacrifice to Spanish predators put every man's blood to the boil and had more pairs of eyes than those belonging to the lookouts scouring the distant horizons for sight of the fleeing vessel.

Dante de Tourville had appeared on deck to the cheers of his own men and those of the *Egret*. Spence was there to greet him and celebrate his recovery with a cask of rumbullion, inviting both crews to toast the brave memory of the *Virago* and her daring forays against the papist plague. The pirate wolf had been harassing the Spanish Main for the past decade and there were a good many adventures to recount. It became a pattern of sorts after that, for the men to set their work aside for a time each day and gather on the main deck to share a tot of brandy or ale and listen to the adventures of the *Virago*. Some had the *Egret's* crew poised on the edges of their seats, their eyes round as medallions; others had them clutching their sides and rolling with laughter.

"You would think he walked on water," Beau remarked dryly after a particularly loud outburst of ribald humor.

"Who?" Spit McCutcheon stood beside her on the forecastle deck looking down over the daily gathering.

"The valiant Captain Dante, who else? Is there some other icon on board with a halo and crown of thorns on his head?"

She turned away from the rail and leaned over her charts again. The sea was relatively smooth and she had been able to take a fair reading of their latitude from the astrolabe. It was a simple instrument used to measure the altitude of the sun or a particular star. It consisted of a large graduated ring of brass fitted with a sighting rule that pivoted at the center of the ring. Suspended vertically by the thumb, the rule turned about on its axis so that the sun could be aligned and the altitude read off the ring. It was less than accurate in heavy seas off the deck of a rolling ship, but in smooth waters with little heaving, it fixed approximate latitudes and, to an experienced navigator, an estimate of leagues traveled and those yet to come before reaching port.

Beau's working charts were divided into grids drawn over rough sketches of the oceans and continents; a series of small *x*'s marked their progress against the readings she took off the astrolabe and the last sightings of known landmarks. It was with a twinge of satisfaction she studied her figures now and added another small *x* a good deal north and west of the Canaries.

Five days into the chase, they had covered roughly ten degrees of latitude.

"Almost two hundred leagues," she said, smiling up at Spit.

He only grunted, distracted for the moment by the sight of a white streak of fur racing down the main deck, followed in hot pursuit by the axe-wielding Cook. When they disappeared from sight, his attention wandered back to the cask of ale that had just been unbunged, prompting him to hitch up his breeches and run a dry tongue across his lips.

"I'd say that were cause to join the celebrations, then."

Her smile tightened, then faded on a sigh. "Go ahead, if you like. I can take the helm and finish out your watch."

"Aye, an' yer father would tail me out for shirkin' my duties."

"Considering he is in the midst of the crowd, I doubt he could justify punishing anyone for laxity."

"Still an' all, I were lashed once. It wasn't a treat I'd like to share again. Five strokes, I had, an' it left me raw enough to feel I were layin' on a bed o' red-hot coals."

Beau thought of the marks crossing Dante's back; it must have been like a foretaste of hell.

Spit peered slyly in her direction. "Cap'n Dante, now, he took his shirt off the other day an' set one o' the younger lads to pukin' his biscuits over the side o' the ship. Aye, it were just lucky for him the wind was blowin' in his favor."

"I have seen the marks." Beau pursed her lips thoughtfully. "I wonder what a man has to do to earn so many lashes with the cat?"

He snorted. "On some ships? Might as well ask what a whore has to do to get laid."

Beau glanced sidelong at the gunnery chief. "I'm sure I don't know the answer to that, either, Spit. Why don't you enlighten me?"

The crusty old tar looked embarrassed—for all of two seconds. "Warrant it ain't up to me to be enlightenin' ye on the whys an' wherefores o' somethin' like that, lass. Warrant ye should be lookin' for someone with a stouter heart an' a stiffer pole than mine to be givin' ye lessons."

"Too old and withered to instruct me, are you?"

"Too old to handle yer father's fists, more's the like. Now, enough o' yer heathen talk—tease a poor man's pride, for shame. Why don't we both slink on down an' catch a dram or two?"

Beau stared over the rail a moment, then shook her head. "There should be at least one sound and sober head on board."

Spit scratched at the white bristles on his jaw and crooked a rheumy eye in her direction. "Ye don't seem to hold an overly high opinion of 'is lordship."

Beau shrugged. "I hold no opinion of him whatsoever."

"An' here I figured ye to be one o' the first in line to listen to the exploits of the *Virago*. Ye were always crowdin' the edge o' the quay whenever Drake put into port."

Beau looked at Spit in shock. "Surely you do not compare this—this displaced Frenchman to our own Sir Francis Drake? You, who did not even recognize his ship or his pennon when you first saw it?"

Spit grumbled and scratched harder. "I recognized it well enough afterwards. It were just . . . in the heat of the moment, it temporarily deserted me."

"There could be an inferno of flame and smoke surrounding the *Golden Hind* and no one would fail to recognize her. Neither would they need to gather around a capstan to hear tales of Sir Francis Drake's adventures. What schoolboy does not know he was the first Englishman to sail his ship around the world? The first—and only one—to sack San Domingo and Cartagena—*two* of Spain's best defended cities in the Indies—not to mention being the first to cross Panama on foot and stand where he could see both the Atlantic and the Pacifica at the same time! You dare compare *him* to an arrogant, ill-mannered French bull rogue who cannot even steer his ship through a gale!"

Sometime during Beau's diatribe, Spit's eyes had widened out of their creases and tried to direct Beau's to a point over her shoulder. They flicked again now, with a more meaningful intensity, and Beau whirled around, the question dying on her lips when she saw Simon Dante lounging casually against the rail, his arms crossed over his chest, his mouth curved into a smile. It was impossible he could have missed a word she'd said, for the argentine eyes were dancing with amusement.

Beau had been adroit in avoiding the company of the pirate wolf over the past few days, managing always to be at one end of the ship if he was at the other. Mealtimes were a challenge, for Spence insisted his daughter share his table with Dante and Pitt. But she had been able to rise to the occasion by changing her watches and inventing plausible reasons to be at the helm.

Seeing him from a distance did not prepare her for a face-to-face meeting. His jaw was clean shaven, revealing a sharp and angular profile that would have put the noblest aristocrat to shame. His mouth, clear of the concealing black fur, proved to be wide and generous in shape, blatantly sensual, easily provoking memories of their audacity. His hair gleamed like polished ebony under the sunlight and fell in thick, silky waves to his shoulders. There were still faint smudges under his lower lashes, but they only emphasized the startling color of his eyes and lent him a more dangerous air, as if he preferred to stay always in the shadows while he observed the rest of the world.

"So. Sir Francis is one of your heroes, is he? Chaste and untainted by his own fame?"

"He does not require a round of free ale for men to appreciate his deeds."

Spit started to chuckle and covered it with a cough. Dante looked his way and nodded an affable enough greeting, although he kept staring, kept smiling, until McCutcheon cleared his throat with a nervous rattle and excused himself under the guise of checking the set of the topsails.

Beau stood her ground. It was one thing to effect an avoidance of the man; quite another to give the appearance of being frightened off.

De Tourville uncrossed his arms and walked over to the table where her charts were spread. He examined the topmost sheet with its rough scrawls and hasty figurings, then lifted it out of the way to study the more detailed, beautifully painted map beneath. Beau, like most ship's navigators, was an accomplished artist, recording by means of sketches and paintings what a particular coastline or island might look like from the sea. With no other means of recording what they saw on their voyages, and verbal descriptions unreliable at best, these paintings and maps, often displayed in cartographers' windows, were the only means some people had of envisioning the world beyond London's city gates.

"Your work?" He touched a long, tapered finger to the painting and added, "It betrays the favor of a woman's hand, but with an authority I would not have expected."

"Why? Because I *am* a woman?"

He glanced up and grinned. "Because I would not have

guessed there to be enough patience in you to sit overlong with a single-haired brush just to show the probable variance of shore currents."

An odd look came over his face and before she had a chance to respond to his mockery, he stared back down, not at the painting so much as at the precisely rendered depiction of a swan in the lower corner. The first day, her father had referred to her as his little black swan, but the significance of the endearment came clear to him only now.

"You," he said sharply, his eyes sparking with genuine astonishment. "You are *the* Black Swan?" He looked down again, cursing his own lack of perception, for he had seen some of the other charts in her cabin and not made the connection. It was some small consolation to know that few of the other sea hawks would have guessed the Black Swan to be a woman, for her charts and maps were highly sought after and graced the cabins of many famous ships. He had himself been outbid on a chart of the Azores, the shoals depicted with such an expert eye, he had looked closer to see if there were fish in the water.

He would be damned if he told her that, of course, but he allowed some grudging interest in her training.

"Where did you apprentice?"

"I didn't. I used to copy maps from Father's study. He had a copy of *Theatrum Orbis*—"

"—*Terrarum*," he finished for her. "Are you saying you learned how to do this from copying paintings out of a book? No one stood over your shoulder to guide your hand? No one taught you the techniques and methods?"

Beau's cheeks were warming uncomfortably. "No. I had no time for such frippery."

"Frippery," he mused, and looked down again. "In that case, 'tis a pity no one thought to salvage some of the master charts off the *Virago*. Many of them were works of art, painted by the hands of Mercator and Wagenaer. You could have made good use of such . . . frippery—not that I can see much room for improvement."

Beau experienced another rush of discomfort. "As it happens . . ."

"Yes?"

The silver-blue eyes were penetratingly direct and they stalled the response in her throat long enough for her to suffer a distinct, warming flutter in the pit of her stomach.

"I—I did see them crushed beneath a pile of books on the floor, and I thought . . ."

The blue flecks danced with an odd light. "And you thought it would be a waste to leave them behind?"

"Well, it would have. And you did tell me I could take anything I wanted."

"I did indeed. But I rather thought you had your sights set on the jewels."

She squared her shoulders. "I have no need for jewels. The maps were more valuable to me, and I took them. I did not *steal* them, however. There was heavy damage to some and I was intending to repair them, and perhaps copy them, before giving them back to you."

His attention, which had begun to stray rather disarmingly over her hair, the slender arch of her throat, the bloom of color in her cheeks, focused intently on her eyes again. "How very honorable of you . . . Beau. I, too, would have placed a higher value on the charts than I would on a cask of jewels, although it would be my pleasure to make you a gift of them anyway. Both the charts and the jewels."

"I told you, I have no need for jewels."

"Then I shall give them to your father, as payment for his hospitality."

Standing so close, she was more aware than ever of his

imposing height and of the shocking breadth of his shoulders. He wore the billowing white shirt, still unlaced and left carelessly open over the solid bronzed expanse of his chest. His hose were clean and made of wool woven to so fine a fit, they looked as if they had been painted on, and it did not require much strain to her imagination to remember how he had appeared naked and sprawled on her bed. The sight of his powerful physique had struck her with the chill of speechlessness then; his nearness was having the same effect now, and she took a precautionary step back, making it seem as casual as she could.

"Have you no one of your own who would appreciate such a gift? A wife? Children? Family?"

Dante regarded her warily for a moment, wondering if she was genuinely ignorant or just attempting to pry. There were times he did not think there was a soul alive in all of England or France who did not know about his personal life. About his wife. About the parade of lovers she had taken to amuse her while he was away at sea.

"I had an older brother," he said at length. "But Giles died before he could have any heirs of his own to pass on the family name and fortune. It was an unfortunate turn of fate, for he was much better suited to assume the titles and responsibilites. As for a wife . . . I had one once, when I was young and stupid and too blinded by my own ignorance to see that all she wanted *was* the family titles and responsibilities. And perhaps a warm body in her bed now and then . . . though God forbid that warm body should necessarily be the *same* warm body each time. No, mam'selle, I am as you see me. Accountable to no one but myself and quite content to remain this way."

It was not difficult to understand how the staid, socially regimented life of a nobleman could stifle a man like Simon

Dante, although it was somewhat more difficult to imagine a woman tossing him out of her bed for another.

The abruptness of the thought startled Beau and she reddened slightly. "So . . . you are content living the life of a pirate?"

Dante gave his shoulders a careless shrug. "I am content living a life that is my own, being accountable to no one. I sincerely tried being the Comte de Tourville for a while but it gave me very little pleasure. Even now, I have a flock of gray-cloaked bankers and managers who chase after me constantly with crates of documents, letters, and ledgers to approve or disapprove—it drives the account-keepers apoplectic when I am away at sea for any great length of time. But for the most part they are all dry, cold men who do not understand the soul of an adventurer, and I think they are quite content to serve me from a distance.

"It was much the same for my wife. She managed to spend my money well enough, and act the part of regal chatelaine to an excess of praise, but for all her charm and beauty—and I will admit she was an exquisite creature— she had no soul whatsoever."

"Surely you must have felt affection for her at one time?"

More than a hint of cynicism crept into the thin smile that curved his lips. "Why would you suppose that? Marriages, especially those for whom the proper bloodlines are considered paramount to all else, are never based on affection, *ma pauvre innocente*. They are based on greed and power and ambition. God save the man who expects love, passion, and loyalty."

He sounded bitter enough to refute his own words and Beau suspected he must have loved his wife very much indeed. So much so, he had not yet recovered from her betrayal and used his anger against her as a weapon against others. Or a shield. He was, in fact, proving to have many shields and cloaks. He had the demeanor of an aristocrat when he wanted to call on it, the character of a pirate when he needed to use it, and a body that emanated a dangerous combination of elegance and savagery—a combination that sent warning chills up and down her spine even as he tilted his head to one side, trying to read her thoughts.

"And you, mam'selle? Have you no regrets for a path not taken? What brings you to this point, this place in time? Why are you not swathed in satins and silks, sipping chocolate from tiny porcelain cups, and discussing the newest court scandal?"

Beau grimaced. "Court scandals have never interested me. And one can hardly climb rigging and set sails in a skirt and farthingale."

His eyes gleamed with shared amusement and he let his gaze drift downward, seeming to measure every curve and indentation of her body, lingering so long in places, Beau could have sworn it was his hands, not his eyes, causing her skin to react so alarmingly.

"No," he mused. "I suppose one could not. But my question had to do with why you were here climbing rigging and setting sails in the first place, You have no brothers, no sisters? No . . . husband, or expectations thereof?"

"It is doubtful a husband would be content to sit at home by the hearth fire while I sailed away to sea."

"That would depend a great deal on the husband, would it not? Have you given any stout-hearted lads a fair chance?"

"I have no use or need for a husband," she insisted. "Therefore no use or need to give any of them a chance."

"Them? So there have been candidates willing to attempt a breach in that formidable armor you wear?"

Beau looked down at her hands. She had no idea how the conversation had turned to such things and even less idea why she was tolerating any of it. Or him, for that matter, and she turned her attention back to her charts.

"There is only my father and myself . . . and the *Egret*," she said crisply. "And we are quite happy to keep it that way. Now, if you don't mind, Captain, I have work to do. You will have to excuse me."

"We seem to making good speed," he observed, ignoring her request.

"You sound surprised."

He brought his gaze back from the horizon and weighed the depth of pride tightening her features against his own dislike of making apologies to anyone, deserving or not.

"Forgive me if I have misjudged the character of your ship," he said. "It was, perhaps, a judgment made in haste."

The tiger eyes were waiting expectantly, but he only nodded at the astrolabe and added, "You have taken your noon reading? I would be more than pleased to assist."

"Spit has already done so, but . . . thank you anyway."

"He seems like an efficient fellow, despite his rather brusque habit of speaking precisely what is on his mind."

"You find honesty disconcerting?"

"Not in the least. Just unusual in that there appear to be a large percentage of forthright-speaking members among your crew."

"My father is rarely so arrogant as to assume he has absolute knowledge of all things," she said, choosing her words with the same care he had shown. "Most times, he encourages his crew to say what is on their minds, thus avoiding sullenness and dissent."

"An admirable policy. Does it hold true in battle?"

She looked him straight in the eye. "I said most times, Captain. In battle there is no discussion, no room for arrogance or dissent. The men follow Spence's orders without question or hesitation or they know they have earned themselves a dozen or so lashes of the cat."

The muscles in Dante's jaw clenched noticeably. He knew the taunt was deliberate and his eyes gleamed at her boldness. "In my case," he said quietly, "it was not my arrogance that won me my stripes, but my misfortune in serving on a ship whose captain was too cowardly to give any orders at all, and surrendered, without firing a single shot, to a Spanish raider. Those of us who survived the trials of the auto-da-fé—a warm little gathering hosted by members of the Holy Inquisition—were then sentenced to serve out the rest of our lives chained to the oars of a galleass."

"You were a galley slave?" she asked, startled.

"For nearly seven months. Lashings were part of the daily routine, whether we were sullen or not."

"I'm . . . sorry. I did not mean to pry."

"Yes you did. You just didn't do it very well. In future, if you want to ask me something, just ask."

He turned and was about to leave the deck when Beau blurted, "Very well: How did you escape?"

He stopped and took a moment to reset the rigid line of his jaw. When he glanced back, it looked, at first, as if he were going to take off her head instead of answering, but then he saw the cool defiance in her eyes and had cause to remind himself again that she was not a woman easily subjugated by authority. A challenge given was a challenge accepted, however minor.

"As it happened, the captain-general of the galleass was cruel and incompetent and not very well liked by his officers. One of the younger ones, on board for his first voyage, dared to challenge the harshness of some of the punishments we received and, for his trouble, spent a week chained to the oar beside me."

"You befriended him?"

"Hell, no. He was weak and foolish; when he wasn't weeping like a child, he was praying incessantly for our salvation. I hated the bastard as much at the end of the week as I had at the beginning and probably more so because I knew, for all his bawling and keening, he would get to see sunlight again, whereas all I could expect was death and rats—with death being preferable. I must have conveyed my wishes in some way, for they began to use me to demonstrate the proper method of applying the lash to cause the most pain. The same foolish young officer crept below one night, hoping to convert me to the One True Faith while there was still time to save my soul. The man beside me was able to hook an arm around his throat and choke him, and we used his crucifix to break the lock on our chains. A dozen or so of us managed to fight our way up on deck and jump over the side. Luckily we were passing close enough to an island to swim for it, but because I was in pretty bad shape, Lucifer had to haul me on his back most of the way."

"Lucifer?"

"Aye." A black eyebrow arched sardonically. "He is really a very likable fellow, once you get to know him."

"Lucifer? Likable? He spends most of his days terrorizing everyone on board."

"He is leery of strangers, leery of their motives. He had a family, a wife and three sons, all of whom died beside him, slaving in the mines of Mexico."

Beau chewed her lip. "And Mister Pitt? He seems another odd sort to be sailing the high seas—especially since he does not appear to enjoy the sea all that much."

Dante offered a wry grin. "You should see him in heavy weather."

"I have. You slept like a babe through it; he turned as green as grass and hung over the rail for two days."

"Ahh, yes, but put a gun in his hands, the bigger the better, and he has no equal on this earth. He designed those demis, cast the bronze himself, and trained my crews to give me three shots per minute, rough seas or smooth." He grinned suddenly. "But if you think Pitt and Lucifer are odd, it is a pity you never met our helmsman, Ivory Brighton. He lost his eye to a misfired musket and replaced it with a ball carved from an elephant tusk. He also had two thumbs on his left hand and a nose so long and hooked, he could scratch the tip with his bottom teeth."

Beau almost smiled. "Admirable qualities. I'm sure I will regret not making his acquaintance until the day I die."

"I know he would regret not making yours, for I'm sure he would have thought it impossible for a woman to hold a ship this size on a steady course, let alone throw her into a heated pursuit."

"Much like his captain?"

"Much like his captain," Dante admitted, his silver eyes gleaming.

Beau felt her skin warming again and drew a shallow breath. "My mother used to tell me the only things truly impossible are the things you are too afraid to try."

"Was she the one who encouraged you to come to sea?"

"She did nothing to *discourage* me, although she did insist I go to school and learn how to deport myself like a lady."

While Dante struggled to hold his laughter in check, Beau planted her hands on her hips and glared at him.

"You find the notion amusing?"

"Not amusing; perhaps just . . . difficult to envision at this precise moment."

"It did not seem to put too much strain on your imagination when you laid me flat on your desk, or when you kissed me the other morning."

The gray eyes narrowed; then, with a disconcerting abruptness, he threw back his head and laughed. It was a deep, lusty sound and made several of the crew on the deck below turn and stare.

"Ah, mam'selle, you are indeed refreshing." He shook his head and raked a hand through the glossy black mane of his hair. "Your suspicions are etched on your face as precisely as the currents on your magnificently painted maps. May I set your mind at ease somewhat by saying my interests in any of our conversations, past and yet to come, are completely without any motive other than that of trying to get to know your crew and ship a little better. I have absolutely no interest in prying your legs apart if, *alors*, you were willing or not. While I will confess you inspire a certain amount of curiosity—which I have already admitted— I doubt very much your preference for boots and doublet over silk underpinnings and satin skirts would be enough to drive me to extremes of wild, irrepressible lust. As it happens, I still prefer my women soft, seductive, and eager to do more with their mouths than scowl all the time."

Beau's flush grew hot enough to become painful. "I am relieved to hear it, Captain. Does this mean I will not be excessively plagued with your company in the days and weeks to come?"

"It means I will save you the trouble of having to scurry from one end of the ship to the other every time you see me on deck. Moreover, I apologize wholeheartedly now for distracting you from your work." He offered an exaggerated bow. "I came to ask only if you might be interested in joining the rest of your crew below. Pitt was about to give them a lesson in firing the thirty pounders and your father suggested it might be of some interest to you as well. But since you are so busy with your paints . . ." He shrugged and started back toward the ladderway.

Beau clamped her jaw tight against the urge to hurl the vilest epithet she could think of at his broad back. He knew damned well she was as interested as any other crewman on board, just as he knew she would have put aside her paints in a snap. But she did not stop him and he did not look back as he descended to the main deck and strode into the midst of the gathered men. The lure of the demicannon was a sore temptation to have to pit against her own pride, but she would stand before a smoking muzzle and let the shot blast straight through her heart before she would give the arrogant Captain Simon Dante, Comte de Tourville, the satisfaction of seeing her run after him like a beggar.

He *was* arrogant. And far too sure of himself for her liking. Just the way he cocked his head and smiled with such self-serving belligerence proved he did not think anyone on board this ship to be his equal, or even worthy of his consideration. Most infuriating of all was the patronizing, amused manner with which he regarded her position on board the *Egret.* It made her fervently wish for a glimpse of sails on the horizon.

And, whether it was because she wished for it so hard, or because the booming thunder of the huge guns had rolled to the edge of the horizon and attracted other searching eyes, it was less than an hour later that the watchman sounded an alert from his perch high in the tops.

"Sails, Captain! Sails off the larboard bow!"

Chapter 9

"Well, she's a Spaniard, no mistake," Spence pronounced.

"Six hundred tons or more, to judge by the size of her." Dante stood on the deck beside Jonas Spence, his hand raised to shield his eyes against the glare of the sun. "I make out two tiers of guns, probably perriers and quarter cannon—impressive, but only if they get within decent range."

The swift excitement that had brought him to the rail had waned somewhat when it became clear the ship they had sighted on the westerly horizon, running parallel to them, was not the *Talon*. It was therefore with a more critical and practical eye that he continued, pointing disgustedly at the huge silhouette, dominated fore and aft by castellated superstructures. "They pile up six storeys worth of fancy cabins all gilt and mahogany, filled with furniture as fine as any king's courtesan ever graced, and expect to draw more than eight knots from the wind. Even the balconies on the stern galleries are painted with gold and carved by the same men who fashion their cathedrals and churches.

"At the same time, they have to keep them as deep and broad as possible in the belly to hold the several tons of cargo as well as the three or four hundred soldiers they ferry around. Another hundred or so sailors are needed to crew her and the same again to man the guns, for God forbid any among them should know how to do two jobs. The soldiers sit with their hands warming their cockles until the sailors bring them into grappling range. By then the gunners are spent and have to take their leisure while their fancy conquistadores wave swords and slash throats in the name of the Catholic Christ. Stupidity, if you ask me. Sheer mindless stupidity."

"Aye. We could circle her half a dozen times," Spence snorted derisively, "before she could even line her guns on us."

"We have a fair wind behind us," Dante mused, almost to himself. "How much speed do you think we could put into the sheets?"

Spence turned to his left and frowned at Simon Dante. "Fifteen. Eighteen if we mount extra canvas on the tops an' fores—an' if the ship's in the mood."

The pale blue eyes narrowed. "What would it take to get her in the mood?"

Spence arched his brows. "A bitch the size o' that one comin' over the horizon will surely do it. We'll be able to outrun her without raisin' a sweat."

"Assuming you were of a mind to outrun her," Dante said quietly.

Spence stared at him for a moment, then glanced at the approaching galleon. "Ye're not suggestin' we could go up against her alone?"

"The *Virago* went up against six of them alone—not as

large as that bitch, to be sure, but daunting nonetheless. Had she been sound or had we a fellow captain with a spine sturdier than Victor Bloodstone, we would have sunk the lot on the first pass. You can see for yourself, she's slow and wallowing. Slower than usual and wallowing more because of a full hold than because of a few fancy cabins. You said your bays were unhappily emptier than you like to see them. Would it improve your humor to see them filled with crates of Spanish ducats?"

"Spanish ducats?" Spence's tone changed instantly. "Ye think she's carryin' treasure?"

"I think—calling on some measure of experience in such things—she is not out here for a pleasure cruise. If it is true the King of Spain is building an invasion fleet, he will no longer be able to afford the luxury of having his full flota of treasure ships linger in Panama until all their holds are filled. My guess is, as soon as three or four galleons are loaded, they are sent on their way back to Lisbon, with only a small escort, relying on their size and firepower to frighten off any mad-minded freebooters. This one has obviously become separated from the flock by some means or another."

"At least ye've used the right term to describe yerself," Spit grumbled, mindful of keeping Spence's bulk between them as a shield. "Only a madman would take on a ship four times his size."

Spence was still mulling over Dante's opinion of Victor Bloodstone's spine. "I've ten guns. She has"—he lifted an enormous, hairy paw of a hand and smoothed it over his bald pate—"thirty or more!"

"You're forgetting my demi-cannon. You can pepper her from three hundred yards out while our papist friends can only spit vitriol past eighty. What's more, double shot my bronze beauties with incendiaries and you'll have the Spaniard's sails down and her decks burning by the second pass."

"There wouldn't be somethin' more in this, would there? Like sailin' home to England with a bloody big prize in tow so ye could thumb yer nose at the Queen's counsellor's nephew?"

Dante's face hardened. "I have already told you my quarrel with Victor Bloodstone is my own."

"Aye, an' it's a quarrel ye'll not have a penny's worth chance o' resolvin' at sea if we take time out to shake our fists at yon Spaniard."

"With no insult to your ship or crew, the chances of catching him in open water were slim at best. That being the case, the decision is yours whether you sail home with a few tuns of Indies Gold . . . or with your flags raised and your guns blazing to call the guild merchants to the quay."

Spence locked the younger man's gaze with his own until his eyes began to burn. The lure of Spanish bullion was surely tempting, but they were outmanned, outgunned . . .

"Spit?"

The wiry little man grumbled and scratched savagely at the spikes of hair that grew across the back of his head. "I think ye'd be madder than a Bedlam inmate if ye tried to take on a lumberin' Goliath the likes o' that out there. She'll chew us up an' spit us out like fodder."

Spence squinted into the sunlight. "Mad, eh? Jaysus an' all the saints be damned, but I'd piss blood to have a little taste o' madness about now. How are we for shot an' powder?"

Spit swore under his breath and glared at Simon Dante. "We've plenty o' both to have ye pissin' blood, if that's yer pleasure."

"It might well be. Beau!"

She was right behind him. "Aye, sir?"

"Do ye think it would be possible to take us on a few turns around that comely Spanish sow?"

The first shadow of hesitation flickered in Dante's eyes as he glanced her way and Beau could see the doubt, the stirrings of an objection, even as she stared him down through her reply. "The wind is steady from the west. The seas are moderate, the horizon clear in all directions. Aye, sir. I can give you as many passes as you need, as close or as wide as you order them."

"And *spines*?" Spence shouted over his shoulder. "Do they stand sturdy enough, do ye think?"

An eager cheer of approval went up from the crew. Those close enough to have overheard the conversation on the forecastle had been relaying it word for word to those behind and their excitement was almost palpable. After five days of being regaled with the bold adventures of the *Virago,* if Simon Dante said the Spaniard carried gold and if he thought the risk worth taking, who were they to stand in the way of a possible fortune?

"Clear the decks, then," Spence roared. "Gunners, ready yer stores. Helmsman, set every square o' canvas she'll carry an' bring me alongside her beam at three hundred yards, not a lick less."

"Aye, sir!"

"Six hundred bloody tons," Spence muttered as chaos erupted around him. "I hope ye're right about this, Cap'n Dante. I've no desire to set my teeth against the bite o' an Inquisitor's crimpin' iron."

The pirate wolf grinned. "Your permission for Pitt and me to take charge of the demis, Captain?"

"Aye. Ye have it. Take what lads o' mine ye might need on the tackle if some o' yer own are still shy on strength."

"Never on courage, though, as you will see."

"Make those monsters spit fire, lad; that will be worth all an' more to see."

Within fifteen minutes the *Egret* had changed her course to intercept and raced with her nose held high under a swollen pyramid of sail. Her decks were cleared for action. The gunports were opened, the lashings taken off the muzzles of the culverins, and sturdy breeching tackle attached. Buckets of sand and ash were spread on the planking for added traction, barrels of seawater were hauled on board and set between the guns in case of fire. Sponges, crowbars, linstocks, and handspikes were laid alongside the gun carriages; the wooden wheels were given an extra smear of grease, and the trolleys were stacked high with iron shot in varying weights and calibers.

The Spaniard, within the next quarter hour, had been identified by her silhouette and fittings as the *San Pedro de Marcos*, indeed a treasure ship, and one that had likely been in the small fleet that had cleared Hispaniola a fortnight before the *Egret*.

The captain-general of the *San Pedro* had equal time to prepare, for there was no way to misread the *Egret*'s intentions, though it was doubtful he would know the identity of the merchantman beyond the Cross of St. George she flew. With predictable insolence, and being nowhere within range, the *San Pedro* fired the first shot, its main purpose being, Spence declared in a contemptuous bellow, to frighten them away. He ordered a temporary course change, one that presented his broadside for a brief snub, then gave the helm back to Beau, who tacked efficiently into the wind again. Someone on board the Spanish galleon must have recognized the insult for what it was— either that or he realized the *Egret* was not going to be so easily discouraged—and ordered another volley, this time

a full salvo from both tiers of guns, fired almost simultaneously so that the leviathan was lost for a moment behind
a dense cloud of smoke.

The *Egret* streaked within five hundred yards, then four.
A second full salvo and a third followed the first, all of the
shots falling well shy of any real threat, and by twos and
threes the grins began to break out on board the English
merchantman. The biggest grin by far came on the face of
the Cimaroon, who startled everyone around him by leaping nimbly up onto the deck rail, flinging his loincloth
aside, and sending a long stream of yellow liquid in the
direction of the Spaniard.

Spence ordered the gunners to open fire at three hundred yards. Geoffrey Pitt's crew scored the first direct hit,
albeit a harmless one, bouncing an iron ball off the *San
Pedro*'s two-foot-thick outer hull. His succeeding shots, and
those of his other gunners, were more accurate and far
more deadly, blasting away sails and yards and the men
who balanced there precariously awaiting orders from their
helm. Standing off at what must have seemed a preposter-
ous distance from the startled Spaniard, Pitt's crews split
rails and smashed through the ornately gilded stern galleries.

They maintained a steady barrage, firing as quickly and
as smoothly as the guns could be swabbed and reloaded.
Clouds of smoke and flame erupted continuously from the
long black row of muzzles, cloaking the lower deck in a
thick, impenetrable fog of choking cordite. Sweat streamed
from the bodies of the men who lifted and rammed the
thirty-pound shot into the smoking muzzles. A shout had
them jumping back from the anticipated recoil and cov-
ering their ears against the tremendous roar of each explosion. Another shout had them leaping forward and
swarming over the gun again, feeding a powder cartridge

down the barrel, packing down the shot and wadding, then grunting against the winch lines to reseat the carriage in front of the gunport. More black powder was poured down the touch hole and ignited, and the macabre dance began again.

Beau's throat soon grew raw from the smoke and heat, from shouting orders to the men who worked the miles of rigging, setting the sails to her directions. By the time they made their fourth pass around the Spaniard, each one as tight and clean as if executed with a brush stroke, her nerves had settled, although her blood still roared with the excitement, the thrill of battle. The treasure ship was so sluggish and heavy, she seemed to be standing still while the *Egret* swooped and carved furrows in the sea around her. They were returning fire, but for every shot that chanced off the *Egret's* hull or decking, the *San Pedro de Marcos* suffered thirty or more in return.

The afterdeck was Spence's domain and he ruled it with thunderous authority, ordering tighter circles on each pass, allowing the gunners on the smaller culverins to join in and pour round after round of mercilessly destructive shot down the Spaniard's throat. She was a magnificent example of Spain's finest, with gold figureheads and ornate carvings on all her decks. Regal beauty though she was, Spence's armaments made short work of her fancy trimmings and scrolled grotesques. The rows of diamond-paned windows across her stern galleries were reduced to powder, exploding in founts of shattered glass. The sails were shredded, the rigging slashed in so many places, the yards swung loose in their braces. Two of the masts took direct hits and were cracked off midway down the stems. They hung over the side of the ship, dragging their sodden sails and lines in the water, further hampering the ability of her helm to respond.

Dante's demi-cannon were impressive, wreaking most of the damage on the *San Pedro*'s sails while well out of range of the Andalusian guns. De Tourville and Lucifer labored side by side on one of the cannon, both men working as hard as the rest of the gun crew. Dante was stripped to the waist like the common seamen, trading off blisters and cuts from flying splinters against the more dangerous threat from the clouds of live sparks and burning cinders. His chest was a gleaming wall of muscle, rippling under the strain of loading shot and hauling winch lines. His hair was tied back with a leather thong, his face streaked with sweat and as blackened by smoke as Lucifer's was by nature.

Geoffrey Pitt stalked the rows of guns like a panther, thundering as loud as the cannon if he saw a line too slack or a flambeau hovering too carelessly close to a bucket of loose powder. The crew of the *Egret* had become accustomed to his amiable and cheerful presence on board their ship; they had to adjust their perceptions accordingly as he turned into a green-eyed devil in battle. But they responded each time he pounded them on the back for encouragement, and they grinned as broadly as he did each time one of their shots tore down rigging or sail. Even Spit McCutcheon, whose bony nose had been put out of joint watching the demis outshine his culverins, was seen to roar and leap with approval a time or two and he began to look to Pitt and watch for his signal that they might send the next volley arcing out across the water in unison.

The Spanish galleon staggered under the assault. She had been caught completely off guard by the *Egret*'s size and audacity. The haughty, armor-clad hidalgos paced atop the tall forecastle in frustration, their polished breastplates winking through the smoke, their plumed helmets bobbing up and down as they shouted useless commands to their crews. Sailors and soldiers alike were helpless to do more than watch as the *Egret*'s guns turned the open and unprotected decks into a bloody slaughterhouse.

As the *Egret* closed her deadly circle the returning fire came closer to the mark, but the shots were solid and easy enough for a man to avoid by tracking the high-pitched whistle. Unlike Pitt's little innovations. He began to fill hollow shells with combustibles, rusty nails, and sharp iron filings. They flew in silent, lethal arcs across the water, exploding on the enemy deck with a decimating spray of slivered metal and smoldering faggots. Fires began to break out on the *San Pedro*'s shattered decks, turning the entire length of the ship into an inferno of thick, boiling clouds of black smoke shot through with columns of orange flame. On every gust of wind they could hear the screams of the soldiers and crewmen, for a shipboard fire was dreaded even more than sinking in shark-infested waters.

Dante's earlier misgivings were replaced by genuine admiration each time he looked through the smoke and spouting water and saw that the distance between the two ships had not varied by more than the length of a knife throw despite the increasingly choppy waves. The *Egret*'s motion was becoming more unstable as she rocked against the swells and the spine-juddering recoils, but they had the wind to their advantage, blowing sharp and steady, and a helmsman who was relentlessly efficient at presenting the *Egret*'s best broadside to her enemy.

Spence's daughter was good, as much as it galled him to admit it. Damned good. She was guiding the helm with a sure, deft touch and the *Egret* was responding like a lover, thrusting and withdrawing, thrusting and withdrawing, at her pleasure. More than once Dante found himself staring at the slender figure on the afterdeck. She worked the tiller with a young, muscle-bound crewman named Billy Cuthbert, and even though her arms surely had to be tiring from holding the rudder in such a tight pattern for so long, she did not take more than a few minutes' break at a time. Her shirt was soaked in sweat and her cheeks wore two red blazes from her exertions . . . yet Dante suspected she would have to fall over in a dead faint before she would relinquish the helm.

The *Egret* was a damned fine ship as well and Dante was envious of the baldheaded walrus who was her master. She was stout hearted and fast as lightning, capering through the waves with a headstrong grace that reminded him all too painfully of his sylphlike *Virago*. He regretted he was not the one passing orders to the helm, for there were some tricks, some clever maneuvers, he was certain the *Egret* could execute that might bring a quicker end to the Spaniard's stubbornness.

The thought had barely left his head when he felt the incline of the deck shift beneath his feet. His crew had just fired the demi-cannon and it took a moment for the echo of the explosions to fade and for the cloud of hot, roiling smoke and sparks to clear. When it did, Dante looked up sharply at the groaning of spars and snapping of canvas sheets overhead. On a signal from the helm all the sails had been backed and the yards swung about in their braces. A quick look over the rail confirmed what the sudden shift implied: The *Egret* had taken a stunningly sharp turn, almost skidding sidelong through the swells, and was refitting her canvas to sweep her in a new direction.

In a few minutes they were once more running with the wind in their teeth, heading straight at the *San Pedro*. As a target the *Egret* would pose a nearly impossible challenge to the inept gunners on board the Spanish galleon; as a threat, she was at a temporary disadvantage herself, able to bring only her forward bow chasers into play until Spence gave the order to shear away and present a broadside. Since it was almost the exact maneuver Dante himself had been thinking about, he clenched a fist in a show of support and cast a broad grin up at the captain. Spence, in turn, executed a courtier's bow to acknowledge the pirate wolf's praise, and was still partly off balance when the iron ball screamed through the sails overhead and struck the afterdeck.

A younger man with two good legs and several stone less weight around his girth might have been able to spring clear and come up laughing.

As it was, Spence jerked to one side, and instead of taking off his head, the ball struck the lower half of his leg. It tore away everything below his knee, and sent Jonas spinning sideways against the mast, with his hairless skull cracking as loud as a gunshot against the solid white pine.

Dante dropped the iron shot he had been holding and was in motion before Spence's body sagged to the deck. He mounted the ladder in two bounding strides and caught the massive shoulders under the arms, propping him against the trunk of the mast even as Beau skidded onto her knees beside them.

"Father! Father!" she cried.

"God deliver me from the sin o' fornication," Spence gasped, clutching at the sheets of blood that poured from the deep gash in his head. "Have the bastards killed me?"

"No." Beau wilted briefly under the weight of her relief. "But your head nearly killed the mast."

She ripped the sleeve from her shirt and used it to bind her father's wound. Dante, meanwhile, was gaping down at the shredded flaps of Spence's breeches, at a wound that *should* have been spouting gouts of blood but was only leaking a few feeble drops where the leather leg brace had been torn away.

He looked up at Spence's face, then over at the shattered remains of the wooden limb crushed against the rail.

"You didn't know?" Beau asked with some surprise.

"I . . . merely thought he had a limp."

Beau grinned. "How profoundly observant of you, Captain Dante."

The impish smile produced a startling change on her face and Dante found himself completely unsettled by it. Soft brown brows arched above eyes that had the luster of burnished gold; supple pink lips were gracefully curved, unexpectedly sensual. She had shed the thickly padded doublet and her breasts pushed against the linen as if trying to burst through . . . indeed, where she had ripped the seam of her sleeve, the whiteness of her flesh shone like a hidden pearl.

Billy Cuthbert shouted for their attention. His face was contorted with strain as he leaned against the tiller, trying to hold it steady. "Is the captain all right?"

"He has cracked his head hard enough to cross his eyes," Beau said, tying off the makeshift bandage. "But otherwise he will probably live."

"Good. Because we have a problem here that might require his attention."

Beau cursed and sprang to her feet. Dante was a beat behind and did not need to see the sudden, appalling drain of color from her face to know that in the brief few minutes they had taken to tend Jonas Spence, the *Egret* had come well within the range of the *San Pedro's* guns.

Within range and still streaking toward her like a hawk diving on its prey.

Dante looked at Beau, then swore his way through a quick decision as he whirled and strode to the rail. "Mister Pitt! Mister McCutcheon! Double-shot every gun and be prepared to fire on my signal!"

The gnarled face of Spit McCutcheon turned hesitantly to Beau. At the same time, several of the Spaniard's shots found their range and smashed through the bow rails, spraying fragments of timber on the heads of the men in the waist of the ship. More ripped through the canvas overhead, bringing down the skysail and sending lines hissing through the air like snakes.

"Do it, Spit," Beau ordered. "Do as he says!"

"Aye, sir! *Double up, lads!*"

"I need five men up here on cables!" Dante shouted. "*Now!* Lucifer—!"

The Cimaroon emerged from the debris on the run and jumped up to the afterdeck without troubling himself to use the ladder. A curt order from Dante put him on the tiller anchoring the heavy cables at intervals along the thick oak arm, passing the ends to the other men who had responded to Dante's call.

"Beau—" Dante whirled again. "On my command, put everything you have on the rudder. She'll fight you at this speed, but you have to hold her. Can you do it?"

"We're moving too fast! You'll tear her apart!"

He shook his head. "She's strong, she'll hold! If we try to slow her down, we'll only stay under the Spaniard's guns longer and if we shear away now"—he ducked as another barrage of exploding wood splinters and rubble narrowly missed him—"they'll be able to hit us with everything they have."

"What are you going to do?"

"*We* . . . are going to surprise the hell out of them," he said with a predator's grin.

They were coming up fast on the *San Pedro*, close enough now to clearly see the Spanish officers in their shiny breast-plates and feathered helmets moving along the decks, ordering their gunners to bear down on the approaching ship. Their efforts were finding some success as a burning spar crashed onto the *Egret's* gundeck, crushing one man and sweeping another, screaming, through a new gap in the rail.

McCutcheon and Pitt encouraged their gunners with a calmness that might have been applied to a training drill, not the fiery maelstrom erupting around them. When both batteries were loaded and ready, the men looked up at Simon Dante, their faces white and streaming sweat, and nodded.

Dante repeated the gesture and raised his hand in Beau's direction, watching her, watching the fast-approaching galleon, watching the shocked reaction on board the Spaniard as the crew scattered in panic, expecting the *Egret* to ram them bow-on. Dante waited to the last possible second, judging the tack with the likeliest amount of clearance before he brought his arm slashing down.

"*Now!*" He shouted savagely. "*Bring her hard to starboard, now!*"

At a distance of barely fifty yards the *Egret* started to carve a deep blue swath in the sea as she turned into a parallel course with the galleon. Because of her comparative size she looked more like a mongrel running into the shadow of a stallion, but Dante had gauged her speed, her roll, the swell of the sea, and when his arm came down a second time to release his gunners, the bite she took out of the monstrous ship was both devastating and crippling in its effect. The thunderous volley was delivered almost as a single shot and exploded with such a vengeance on the enemy deck, there was a corresponding explosion of planking, timbers, and bodies on board the galleon. Screams and smaller blasts followed as stores of powder were struck and ignited. McCutcheon's crews were able to fire a second murderous barrage, then a third and a fourth, before the *Egret* started to peel away. By then the galleon was enveloped in a thick black boil of smoke that left scrolling plumes in the sky behind her.

"Captain!"

Beau's scream did not allow Dante time to celebrate the success of his maneuver. She was sprawled on her backside, as were Lucifer, Billy Cuthbert, and the other four men who had been putting their backs into holding the rudder. The arm of the tiller had snapped under the incalculable strain and sent them all into a crushed heap against the rail. Suddenly free of tension, the rudder swung loose, guided by momentum and motion, breaking out of the tight turn and plunging instead toward a sure collison with the wide stern end of the galleon.

Lucifer staggered to his feet, shaking a spray of blood droplets off his hand. Beau was struggling to her knees as Dante ran past and snatched her upright by the scruff of her shirt. Her lip was split and the palms of both hands were raw from rope burns, but she gathered up the cables and ran after the two men to the broken stub of the tiller. Lucifer twined the rope around the oak, then coiled it once around his body and pulled, while Dante and Beau plied every last ounce of their strength to pushing on the opposite side. The rope gouged deeply into the Cimaroon's flesh and he let loose a bloodcurdling roar, one that had the veins popping in his neck and his eyes rolling back so that only the whites showed.

Dante's every muscle and sinew bulged across his back and arms. His long legs were braced back on the deck and his head was dropped between his shoulders; he did not have to look to see if their exertions were having any effect, they would all know well enough in the next few seconds.

The sound of cold, rushing water filled their ears. An

ominous black shadow swept over their heads as the *Egret* passed so close to the Spaniard, they could feel the heat of her fires belching out the broken gallery windows, so close the end of an English yard snagged on the tangle of Spanish rigging overhead and was brought screaming around in its fittings, ripping cables and cleats free as it twisted around the mast. A massive, almost human groan rose from the *Egret*'s belly as she squeezed past the galleon, her planks and boards shuddering with the friction as she cut through the turbulence of the *San Pedro*'s wake. When she was clear, and bursting into sunlight again, the groaning was deafened by the cheers of the men as they threw their arms in the air and whooped in triumph.

While Lucifer eased some slack into the cable, Beau collapsed in disbelief against the broken spar.

"Did we do it?" she gasped. "Did we really do it?"

Dante, grinning, did not answer her with words. Instead, he reached down and took her face between his hands, kissing her hard and full on the lips.

Chapter 10

⟨————⟩

Within fifteen minutes the *San Pedro de Marcos* brought down her flags. To the last there were sporadic shots fired in anger and frustration at the *Egret*, but with masts and sails in ruin and gundecks in chaos, it was only a matter of time before the captain-general signaled an end to the fighting. Almost immediately, the *Egret*'s jolly boat was lowered and filled with armed crewmen who, under the bristling command of Spit McCutcheon, crossed to the Spaniard and issued the terms for surrender.

During the interim the carpenter on board the *Egret* jury-rigged a temporary new arm for the tiller. Dante ordered the mainsails reefed and kept aloft just enough canvas for steerage as he maneuvered the ship around the galleon, waiting for the Spaniards to douse their fires and make preparations to be boarded. He kept the gun crews and arquebusiers at their posts but otherwise ordered the decks to be cleared of debris, damaged sails to be cut away, and critical repairs made. The wounded were helped below, where Cook was already red to the elbows, hard at work with his saws and cauterizing irons. Amazingly enough, there were only five dead and fewer than a dozen with serious wounds. Those with blisters, cuts, and scrapes tended each other or themselves, making light of their trifling injuries in lieu of the excitement of winning such a resounding victory.

Jonas Spence had had his scalp stitched closed but was too befuddled to retain a lucid thought for more than a minute or two; he had been moved below to his cabin. Lucifer had earned a crushed rib through his exertions but refused to be attended by a ship's cook. He archly conveyed by hand signals that he could easily cure himself if he had a severed chicken foot, but since there were no fowls on board, he made do with the limb of a gull that had been unlucky enough to be caught in the exchange of fire.

Dante de Tourville similarly disdained any suggestion of having his cuts and scrapes seen to. There were far more pressing matters to concern him, like breaking out muskets and pikes for the boarding parties, readying the grappling lines, clearing space in the holds for whatever plunder might soon be coming onboard. While he was undeniably pleased at the *Egret*'s performance, he was also markedly disappointed at the amount of damage the *San Pedro* had sustained. Although it was indeed a lumbering sow, it was one of Spain's finest and could have presented quite a sight being sailed into an English port as prize. As it stood now, the hulk would be lucky to stay afloat as far as the Spanish coast—providing it could even raise enough canvas to catch the wind.

Billy Cuthbert brought him a bucket of seawater and a scrap of lye soap to make himself presentable before going on board the Spaniard. The bulk of the fighting over, it would now become a battle of wits, with the Spanish captain-general expressing indignation and outrage over an open act of piracy, issuing dire warnings of reprisals, revenge, and outright war should any of his cargo be appropriated. Dante had heard it all before, too many times for it to have much effect on anything but his temper. The bastard had surrendered. His ship and all its contents were forfeit. It was as simple as that. If he wanted to debate the issue, Dante would gladly reshot his guns.

In the calm that followed the battle, Dante had to admit, if only to himself, just how remarkable a feat they had accomplished. Had it not been for the *Egret's* spirit and her captain's slight madness, a victory over such a Goliath should not have been so swift or easy. Not just the *Egret*, but her entire crew had spirit and guts, and Dante found himself staring back at the afterdeck, his soul aching over the loss of the *Virago*, once again envying Jonas Spence his fine ship and crew.

One crew member in particular, he conceded with a wry smile.

Dante ran his hands through the blue-black waves of his hair, shaking a spray of water droplets free. He took his shirt from Billy and shrugged it over his big shoulders, then stood easy while the shorter man climbed atop a capstan and helped him into his doublet and sword belt. There was still a thin pall of smoke drifting over the decks of the *Egret*, cloaking the sun, making it appear small and pale in a colorless sky. Dante had to narrow his eyes to identify the figure he saw standing by the afterdeck rail, and, confirming it was Beau Spence, he thanked Cuthbert and made his way along the deck toward the stern, weaving a path through and around the men who were recovered enough to speculate excitedly among themselves over what plunder might be waiting for them on board the Spaniard.

The lion's share, they knew, would go to the captain, who had financed the voyage himself and owed nothing to investors. The remainder would be divided among the crewmen, and if it was a very rich prize, they would all be sailing home to England wealthy men.

When Dante mounted the ladder to the afterdeck, he saw Beau's head turn slightly to acknowledge his arrival.

"I have dispatched a man below to check on your father, but I do not hold much hope of his being able to savor his victory just yet."

She offered up a weary imitation of a smile and looked out over the rail again. "I am not even sure I have enough energy left to savor it. I think . . . if I had a bed beneath me right now, I could sleep until we reached Plymouth."

Dante surprised himself with a thought of what *he* might want to do if she had a bed beneath her right now. The sun was behind them, bathing her head and shoulders in a golden light. Despite the dust coating her hair, it gleamed a rich auburn and the floating wisps betrayed a stubborn tendency to cling in soft, feminine curls against her temples and throat. Her one bare arm seemed at once too slender and exposed and he wanted to remove his own leather doublet and offer her the protection of its warmth.

"I also came to apologize," he said after another long moment.

She turned and gave him an odd look. "What could you possibly have done that requires an apology? You saved the day, Captain Dante. You saved the ship, saved the crew, won the battle."

"I should not have taken command so . . . arbitrarily."

She frowned, as if the thought of anyone else taking command had not occurred to her, especially the thought that it might have been her place to do so. "Perhaps not," she said consideringly, "but I am thankful you did. This was . . . not my first fight, you understand, but . . . it would have been my first command, and . . . I do not know if I could have handled it. I have always had my father behind me, you see, and . . . well . . ." She paused and caught her lower lip between her teeth. "I just never gave a thought to what we would do or what it would be like without him. Foolish of me . . . I suppose."

Her voice trailed away and Dante moved to the rail beside her.

"You have no reason to doubt yourself or your skills. In fact, I would offer a confession freely, mam'selle: Despite your father's confidence in your abilities, I did not believe a woman's place was at the helm of a ship going into battle."

She smiled wryly and averted her eyes. "You made your belief quite obvious, Captain. You looked as though you had a gull's egg stuck in your throat."

"Aye, maybe so. But"—he tucked a finger beneath her chin, forcing her to turn and look at him—"I swallowed it quickly enough when I saw the way you handled yourself and this ship. I did not find you lacking in either skill or nerve."

The praise was as honest and sincere as the smoky light that came into his eyes, and Beau felt an oddly satisfying flush of pride wash through her. She *had* done a good job. She *had* kept a level head even after weathering the shot that had almost blown Jonas Spence into the sea. She just hadn't expected to hear it from a man who regularily executed such feats and would likely have kept a helmsman beside him who would act on his orders without hesitation or fault.

"Perhaps I should have been more cautious with an unfamiliar ship," he admitted, reading the concern in her eyes. "I did not know if the *Egret*'s beam was sound enough to take the strain and should have heeded your warning."

"If you had," she said evenly, "we would likely not be

standing here waiting for the signal to board a treasure ship."

Their eyes remained locked together a moment longer, a moment wherein his touch became almost a caress under her chin, and the urge to take her in his arms and hold her washed through him like a slow fire.

"Mam'selle," he murmured, "since it appears I cannot win you over with immeasurable amounts of flattery, might I try with my limited knowledge of physicking?"

A small frown knitted her brows together and did not ease until she followed his gaze down to where her hands rested on the deck rail. Both palms were burned from the coarse jute cables; the heel of the left was scraped enough to be leaking blood.

" 'Tis nothing," she said quickly, trying to put them out of sight. He was even quicker, however, in reaching down and capturing her wrists.

"Nothing a simpleton would not have the sense to seek help for," he quoted wryly, "until they become infected and you find you cannot bend your hands or touch anything through the pain. Can you move them at all? Make a fist?"

"Of course I can," she said, and showed him. The discomfort was minor, but he insisted on leading her over to a bucket of seawater and plunging her hands in the brine.

He kept a firm hold on her wrists, fighting her shock as well as her stubbornness as he did so. He held them long enough to weather the stream of curses that started off as strong as the stinging in her palms and faded, after a time, to disgruntled mutters.

"Better?"

"I was better before."

"I'll have Lucifer blend up one of his special decoctions to rub into them tonight. It will make your hands a little rough for dancing, but the skin will heal faster."

She was not the least amused by his attempted wit and her eyes flashed upward. Dante grinned handsomely and although he did see the faint hint of a blush glow through the grime on her cheeks, she did not falter or look away in discomfort. It was rare enough to find a man willing to meet and hold his gaze for more than a few seconds without faltering. With women he was more accustomed to admiring the sweep of their lashes and wondering what it was about his feet that could possibly hold their interest for such long stretches at a time. Unless of course, it was their intent to seduce him, which he did not, for the smallest instant, believe was anywhere in Beau Spence's repertoire of tricks.

He was, in fact, becoming convinced she had no tricks at all. If she had a thought, she either spoke it aloud or wore it brazenly on her face. And those eyes, by Christ. They were starting to get under his skin, distinctly affecting the way the blood flowed through his veins.

"What are you staring at?"

He met the challenge in her voice with a crooked smile. "You," he said simply. Then to cover himself, he added in a more matter-of-fact tone, "Your mouth, actually. You have a rather nasty cut on the corner."

The moist, pink tip of her tongue came out to find it and Dante was thankful it was still daylight and there were men working all around them.

"Because if you were thinking of kissing me again," she warned, "I have my filletting knife handy."

He covered his bemusement with a frown. "The thought had not even entered my mind. I am intrigued, however, to know why you would suppose it would."

"Because it obviously entered your mind a few minutes ago."

"It did?" His frown deepened.

"Right over there," she charged, indicating the tiller, "—after we cleared the galleon."

"Ahh." His brow cleared and his mouth curved upward at one corner. "*That* kiss. Surely you do not take offense at a harmless little peck on the cheek."

"It was not a peck, it was a kiss. Nor was it on the cheek; it was squarely on the mouth."

"A matter of poor aim, I promise you. And it was not a real kiss, not by any measure. It was more an expression of relief, or gratitude, like a handshake. Or a snapping of the fingers to show approval. Or a cheer of 'huzzah' to show enthusiasm."

"It was a kiss," she maintained flatly. "And the devil will explain you the difference if you ever dare to do it again."

"If I ever dare do it again, I promise I will take greater pains to show *you* the difference between a peck of friendship and a kiss. And speaking of the devil," he said, "our Spanish friends will be expecting to see Satan himself stalk through the gangway."

"Then they will not be disappointed when they see you," she retorted.

"What I meant was, your father would have met their every expectation, but since he is in no condition to go anywhere—"

"You think the honor should fall to you?"

He sighed and lifted one of her hands out of the water, inspecting the palm closely for embedded rope fibers. "As opposed to you? Yes, I do."

"Another outpouring of confidence in my abilities?" she asked sourly.

He saw a piece of cloth lying nearby and tore off a strip to bind around her hand. "Have you ever negotiated for prize monies before?"

It took a moment for the answer to grate through her teeth. "No."

"Are you at all familiar with the order of command and authority on board a Spanish treasure ship?"

"I cannot say I have ever cared."

"Well, you should, if only to save you from insulting the wrong man. The feathered peacocks you see in their velvets and armor are the hidalgos—nobles and sons of nobles who were likely given command of the ship in return for some favor they have done the King. They know very little, if anything, about the actual sailing of a ship, but they like to strut about the decks, brandishing their swords and wishing death upon all the heretics of the world.

"Helping them drink wine, pray, and count their gold ducats are the priests, who know even less about currents and weather gauges, but who strut right alongside the captain-general, exhorting him to follow God's counsel rather than the advice of any of the real sailors on board. One of the reasons I encouraged your father to attack was because the hidalgos and priests would be in such a sweat trying to outmaneuver each other and dazzle their captain-general with their brilliance, the sailors on board—well down in the ranks of authority and the only men who would know what their vessel was capable of doing—would be standing there with their hands tied, unable to act without orders, unable to mount any kind of defense whether it was tactically sound or not. The captain in charge of these sailors would have to watch his men being blown to hell while listening to the priests vow they were all going to glory in the righteous service of their most Catholic king."

Beau's eyes widened in surprise. "You sound as if you feel sorry for them. You pound hell out of them, destroy their ship, force their surrender . . . and now you feel *sorry* for them?"

Dante ignored her sarcasm. "The captain, were he to believe he had been defeated by a woman, would probably reach for the nearest sword and throw himself on it. The captain-general, on the other hand, would be too appalled to even deign to address you, and even if he did, whatever he said would be so insulting or so patronizing, I would likely be angered into killing him."

"You . . . would kill a man for me?" she asked haltingly.

"I would kill any man who insulted a member of my crew, wouldn't you?"

She lowered her lashes quickly. "Of course. Of course I would."

Dante finished bandaging the first hand and drew the second out of the water, bathing it with enough gentleness to send her lip curling between her teeth and a spray of gooseflesh rippling down her arms. She could not fathom what it was about the man that made her skin hot and her throat close like a trap every time he offered a glib compliment. The fact he was standing so close, touching her, made it even worse. Her chest was constricted so tightly, she was forced to breathe through her mouth. Her blood was pounding through her temples and her feet were rooted to the spot like sticks simply because he was showing concern for her wounds, tending them himself.

She searched his face for an answer, studying the rugged squareness of his jaw, the bold straight line of his nose, the pale blue-gray of his eyes. It was indeed absurd for a man to have eyes like that, with lashes so long and thick, they lay on his cheek like silk crescents when they were lowered. And when they were raised, as they were now, the very blackness of them made his eyes dominate his face in such a way, she could not have looked away had she wanted to. She should have been mortified that he caught her inspecting him so closely and she would have been, she supposed, if her senses had not suddenly deserted her completely.

She had only had one lover—Nate Hawethorne—in all her twenty years. The son of an earl, he had paid Spence handsomely for the opportunity to sail on the *Egret* during one of her voyages to the Indies. He had been looking for adventure and excitement, and his enthusiasm for the romance of the sea had been contagious. Beau had lost her virginity on a beach in the Azores, and while she had felt warm and trembly when they were in each other's arms, it was not what she would have called an earth-shattering experience. It was . . . warm and trembly, with a lot of sweat and stickiness to clean up afterward—mostly his.

A single glance from Simon Dante roused far more stunning responses in her body, disturbing in their intensity, unsettling in their discovery.

"Would you care to try it again?"

Beau was startled. "Try what?"

"Making a fist with your hand."

She curled her fingers over her palm and although the linen strips hampered her movements, there was definitely less pain.

"Better?"

She nodded mutely.

"Good enough to defend yourself if you have to?"

She nodded again, this time with a faint crease between her eyebrows. "Are you expecting treachery on board the Spaniard?"

"I always expect treachery. In this case I am almost sure of it. You may or may not have noticed, but the *San Pedro* is no ordinary treasure ship. I did not see it myself until we were fairly close, but look to the mizzen top—*merde*, it's gone. Someone must have worked fast to remove it."

"Remove what?"

"A small gold pennant, mounted on the mast just beneath the captain-general's flag. It means a member of the King's court is on board, probably acting as an ambassador, returning from the Indies or Panama."

"Is that important?"

"It could be. Ambassadors carry papers, documents intended for the King's eyes only."

"I thought you already had documents; the ones you took from Veracruz."

"They are important, and revealing to be sure, but easily interpreted as nothing more than export manifests. Royal communiqués, sealed for the King's eyes only, would surely prove interesting reading to a queen's eyes, especially if she was searching for ways to defend her country against an invasion." He paused and seemed to debate something for a moment before he added, "And there might be another benefit to having a member of the royal family on board."

"To ensure our safe passage to England?" Beau guessed.

Dante's eyes kindled warmly. "You are going to have to stop doing that, you know."

"Doing what?"

"Being so quick with your tongue and your wit."

"You prefer a woman to be slow and dull?"

"Not at all. But perhaps just a little kinder to a . . . what was it now? An arrogant, ill-mannered French bull rogue?"

Beau's eyes, which grew as large and bright as medallions, remained steadfast on Dante's face as the heat rose up her neck, darkening the honeyed tan of her complexion. For the first time he noticed a fine spray of freckles glowing across the bridge of her nose.

"When I said that, I . . . did not know you were listening."

"Would it have stopped you from saying it?"

She considered the smile he gave her before she smiled herself, openly and frankly. "No. Probably not."

Her smile, and the total change it wrought in her face took him by surprise again. Beneath the grime and soot and blood smudging her skin and clothes, she still managed to look fresh and far too vulnerable to be so well acquainted with the stench and violence of battle. And those eyes, God love him. They would be his downfall yet. Sparkling like new-minted gold, lashed with strands of pure silk, they were infinitely more desirable to behold with pleasure creasing their corners rather than contempt or anger . . . and he was not altogether certain he liked this unsubtle shift in his perceptions. Despite Pitt's advice he would feel much safer if he continued to regard her as a doublet-clad, knife-wielding hellion who fought any suggestion of an underlying softness.

He brushed the pad of his thumb gently over the cut on her lip, wiping off the small smear of blood, then took what he hoped was a casual step back.

"Spit is calling for the grappling lines," he said, indicating the sudden flurry of hooks, ropes, and planks being readied by the *Egret*'s rails. "I guess it means we have ourselves a prize."

Beau followed his gaze, startled to see they had come within hailing distance of the smoking Spaniard. She had left Billy Cuthbert at the helm and he was gently easing the *Egret* alongside the treasure ship, awed, no doubt, by the sheer size and towering magnitude of what they had accomplished.

"I should help Billy," she began.

"Billy is doing fine. You should go below and try to restore some of that ferocity I so admired the first time I saw you."

Beau followed his gaze again and saw where the tear in

her shirt had widened over the sleeveless gap, revealing more than a comfortable amount of soft, sloping flesh over her breast.

She caught up the torn flap and a second flood of heat darkened her skin but Dante was already moving away, descending the ladder to the main deck, looking every inch the pirate wolf with his sword and pistols glittering as he shouted orders for the men to stand ready by the lines.

Chapter 11

When the two ships were within a dozen yards of each other the grappling lines were launched across the gap, the metal hooks biting into the rails and planking of the *San Pedro*, tethering the galleons together. Most of the fires on board the Spaniard had been doused, but there were still clouds of hissing steam and smoke rising from the debris on deck. The Spanish officers were clustered below the forecastle, rigid in their humiliation. Spit McCutcheon and his men had herded all the able-bodied seamen and soldiers together in the stern and were keeping watchful, wary eyes on them as well as on the large pile of weaponry—swords, muskets, pikes, and arquebuses that had been collected on the main deck.

The captain-general identified himself with suitable pomp as Don Alonzo de Valdez, a Knight of Santiago, Marquis of Niebla, twelfth Señor and fifth Marquis of Moncada. He had spent the last four years in the service of his most revered king, Philip II of Spain, and it was, he declared in a high-pitched voice, trembling with outrage, a blatant act of piracy to have attacked them. Moreover, it was an overt act of war against a country whose king was, at that very moment, engaged in serious negotiations with England's monarch for a lasting peace.

Dante de Tourville claimed formal possession of the prize ship. He ignored Moncada's initial outburst and strode purposefully onto the main deck, his eyes moving intently side to side, bow to stern, absorbing everything from the smashed superstructures to the torn and sagging rigging.

Geoffrey Pitt, Beau Spence, and a large complement of smartly armed men flanked Dante as he assessed the extent of damages to the galleon, all of them trying to look as nonchalant as their ebony-haired leader, but none quite managing to keep his excitement in check. Dante was no stranger to laying claim to captured vessels, but for most of the crew of the *Egret*, this was their first foray onto the deck of a surrendered Spanish treasure ship.

If the *Egret* had seemed dwarfed beside the huge, castellated monster, her crew members felt like urchins stumbling uninvited into a rich man's drawing room. The rails around the decks, the trim scrolled around the bulkheads, the lavish designs that formed the molding around the doors, hatchways, and portals, were coated in gold leaf. The whole of her high stern, the panels and rails of the quarter galleries, were a solid mass of beautiful carving, all of it painted crimson and gold and resembling a church tabernacle. Remnants of a large silk canopy hung over the foredeck with shreds of the exquisitely embroidered fabric snagged around the golden crowns that surmounted the two enormous stern lanterns.

Equally impressive in appearance were the Spanish officers, garbed in silver breastplates worn over velvet doublets and slashed satin balloon breeches. There were twenty in all, ranging in age and stature from the captain-general to his adjutants, obviously all wealthy hidalgos unaccustomed to defeat at any level, let alone at the hands of English heretics. Half a dozen priests swathed in red robes and capes stood in a cluster behind their captain-general, their hands clasped around ivory crucifixes, their eyes blazing with religious fervor. Standing in the rear, lowest in rank, was the captain in charge of the sailors. His helmet was gone, leaving his hair standing upright in sweaty spikes; his plain white shirt was stained from the filth of battle, his breastplate dented and dulled by smoke. He kept his eyes focused straight ahead, fixed on some nameless point on the horizon, refusing to so much as acknowledge the presence of the tall privateer on his gundeck.

Deciding it was too big an audience, Dante removed himself and Lucifer, along with Beau, Pitt, and McCutcheon to the massive great cabin of the *San Pedro*, inviting Moncada and two of his officers to join them there and vent any complaints he might have.

For an hour the incensed captain-general vented.

Dante de Tourville, sitting in the shambles of the great cabin, propped his long legs on the grandly carved oak desk and steepled his hands together under his chin. He listened to Moncada's shrill denuciations, barely interrupting except to signal Spit to pour more wine. Spit had found several jewel-encrusted goblets in the debris that littered the cabin, and a tall flagon of Madeira wine, which he both served and drank enthusiastically at each crook of Dante's long, tapered finger.

Pitt, who as usual had managed to set aside his motion sickness during the heat of battle, lounged against a wall of the cabin, his arms folded across his chest as much to help keep his stomach in place as to try to appear casual. Beau, on the other hand, appeared to be vastly amused watching Dante deflect the flecks of spittle and acid vitriol that flew from Moncada's lips. She knew her father would not have handled the situation half so well, for Jonas Spence was man of flamboyant blasphemies and great courage, but he was no diplomat. He was quite happy to take what he wanted at the end of a sword, but close him into a room with too many words and he grew impatient with his own shortcomings.

Lucifer hung back in the shadows of the doorway, his eyes fixed on the three Spaniards, the coal-black centers burning like brands. Every now and then he would caress the silver hilts of his scimitars, earning stares and nervous twitches from the two hidalgos.

Their leader, the fifth Marquis of Moncada, was a rotund strut of a man with a face like a boil of dough stretched too thin over spidery red veins. He had small, dark eyes set so close together, they seemed to touch at the bridge, and he had made a feeble attempt to hide a weak chin under an abram beard trimmed to a perfect point. He spoke in faultless, unbroken English, a deliberate counterpoint to Dante's initial address delivered in equally flawless Castilian.

The two other officers were, by contrast, tall and lean, handsome men with short, curly hair and liquid brown eyes that flicked nervously from face to face.

"Blatant piracy!" Moncada was screaming. "And at a time when you English should be doing everything in your power to convince my king and country you are not ruled by thieves and bloodthirsty heretics."

"Bloodthirsty," Dante mused, speaking more out of boredom than a need to defend anyone's habits. "An interesting turn of phrase coming from a people who advocate the use of torture and mutilation in the name of their faith."

"The devil can be a difficult entity to eradicate, and his stain must be scorched off the face of the earth, as must all heretics who worship him! Like you, señor," he added, lashing the air with an accusing finger. "*¡Picarón!*"

"Me?" A pirate, señor? I am but a humble merchant trying to go about my lawful trade."

Moncada snarled and leaned forward, slamming his fist on the desk. "You attacked my ship without cause!"

Lucifer bared his filed teeth and started forward with a growl, but Dante stopped him, then spread his hands in a gesture of innocence. "If you will recall, señor, you fired the first shot. We were only defending ourselves."

"Defending? *Defending?*"

"Aye, and now we intend only to take a fair measure of compensation for our trouble and for the damage your guns have wrought on our ship. We sail these waters with no intent to commit acts of war. You can see for yourself, we travel with women"—he waved a hand airily in Beau's direction—"and old men."

Spit McCutcheon gave a toothless smile on cue. It was enough to send another flush of red fury spreading down Moncada's face and throat, and another spray of venom across the desk.

"You do not fight like simple merchants! Nor do you *look* like a simple merchant, señor. You give your name as Jonas Spence and you may believe that I will remember it. I will remember your name, your face, your ship, and I will pray hourly for the pleasure of crossing your path again one day!"

"The pleasure will be all mine," Dante assured him. "For now, however, you may please us all by giving my quartermaster a copy of your cargo manifests so that he might be saved the trouble of having to search the entire ship plank by plank."

Moncada glared at McCutcheon. "Rot in hell, señor. And you may trouble yourself until that hell freezes, for we will none of us lift a finger to assist you in this profane act of thievery."

Spit scratched at his jaw and curled his lips at the corners. "Well, now, I'm pricked to have to disappoint ye, but I won't be rottin' anywheres just yet. I already seen me a storeroom bulgin' with bales o' spices; another filled with wood crates heavy as a whore's arse an' stamped with the mint seal o' the governor o' Mexico. Onliest thing profane is our holds might not be big enough to carry it all away. We'll surely try, o' course, Cap'n," he added, winking at Dante. "We'll surely try."

Dante crooked his head to indicate McCutcheon could go and begin an inventory of the treasure, then turned back to address Moncada.

"We will also want a list of your passengers, Señor Marquis. Unless I am mistaken, you have a rather important guest on board."

Moncada waved a hand dismissively. "I have many sons of nobles on board, and they are all important guests."

Dante exchanged a significant glance with Geoffrey Pitt, who reached inside the front closure of his doublet and withdrew a long, gold silk pennant.

Moncada's ferret eyes widened a moment before glistening in Dante's direction. "You would dare violate the sanctity of a member of the King's court?"

"In case you had not noticed, I would dare a great deal. And unless you would care to have your own sanctity violated"—he slowly withdrew one of the brass inlaid wheellock pistols from his belt and set it down on the desk in front of him—"it would be in your best interest if you voluntarily produced him."

"It is an affront to His Most Catholic Majesty, Defender of the Faith, Suppressor of Heresy, by the Grace of God King of Spain—"

Dante sighed, anticipating all sixty-five of the King's titles were about to sprout forth. He picked up the pistol, cocked the spanner key, and squeezed the serpentine trigger. The powder in the pan ignited, causing an almost simultaneous explosion as the lead ball was discharged and shot past the captain-general's shoulder, tearing a harmless stripe through the rich velvet sleeve of his doublet. The two Spanish officers recoiled from the sound of the exploding shot; the fifth Marquis of Moncada screamed, clutched his shoulder, and promptly fainted.

Dante, waiting until the puff of smoke cleared, swung his long legs off the corner of the desk and leaned forward to peer at the unconscious Spaniard. He cocked an eyebrow and glanced sidelong at Pitt and Beau.

"Damn my soul, but my aim must be off today. I was actually trying for the lamp behind him."

The two hidalgos turned and gaped at the lamp, easily eight feet to the left of where the captain-general had been standing.

"Gentlemen"—Dante drew their owlish attention back to where he was removing the second pistol from his belt—"would either of you care to assist us in this matter or would you prefer I practice my marksmanship again?"

For a long moment neither of them moved. Only when Dante thumbed the spanner key did one of the officers stiffen and look straight into the silvered eyes for the first time. "His Majesty's niece, Doña Maria Antonia Piacenza, Duchess of Navarre, travels aboard the *San Pedro de Marcos* under the protection of God and the King of Spain. To even attempt to desecrate this holy coverture would be a sacrilege against the Heavenly Father and all of mankind."

"We have no desire to desecrate anyone," Dante assured him blandly. "In fact, I am most anxious for you to escort a couple of my men to her quarters now so that they may guarantee her personal safety." He glanced at Pitt and Lucifer. "Gentlemen?"

Pitt nodded and Lucifer stepped out of the shadows, his scimitars glinting in the dull wash of light.

The Spaniard hesitated, but since his captain-general was still prone on the floor, he had no choice but to lead the two Englishmen out of the cabin.

When they were gone, Dante aimed the barrel of the pistol at the second officer. "We can both save ourselves a great deal of time and energy if you will show me where the captain-general keeps his logs and manifests."

The young man's face glistened with sweat, but to his credit he remained rigidly silent. Dante sighed and caressed the brass trigger with his forefinger. It was Beau who reached forward and touched Dante's arm, murmuring a cautious "Wait."

She had seen the smallest flicker of movement in the Spaniard's liquid brown eyes and she followed it now to the pair of cabinets behind her. Being set against a solid wall they had, for the most part, avoided sustaining the damage suffered by the rest of the cabin. The squatter of the two cabinets held the goblets and bottles Spit had availed himself of; the taller and more ornately carved had wide arched doors that, when she swung them open, unfolded to present a religious triptych, the central panel depicting a two-foot-tall rendering of Christ on the cross. A small compartment beneath held gold reliquaries that contained holy artifacts; an altar below that was covered with a cloth woven of fine linen, exquisitely embroidered along the edges and hem with gold silk thread.

Beau was about to dismiss the find and close the arched doors again when her foot scuffed the hem of the altar cloth, scraping on wood beneath. She parted the edges of linen and turned slightly to throw a grin over her shoulder at Simon Dante. Hidden by the cloth were two more doors, both securely locked.

Dante returned her grin and addressed the Spaniard again. "I don't suppose you know where the keys are kept?"

"Keys," Beau scoffed, and dropped down on one knee. She produced her stiletto and worked the tip in the lock, rewarded a few seconds later by the sound of the catch springing free.

"Have you any other talents I should know about?" Dante asked, lifting his eyebrow.

She met the silver-blue eyes briefly before she turned and opened the two unresisting doors. The chair creaked as Dante leaned forward to look over her shoulder, and she heard him swear in a soft, deep voice.

Inside the cabinet were the leather-bound logs and manifests, a large gold and jewel–encrusted box stamped with the marquis's family crest, and, not the least of all, multiple stacks of beribboned documents and letters, all bearing official seals meant only to be broken by the hands of King Philip of Spain.

"*Voilà*, mam'selle," he murmured. "*Le vrai trésor.*"

Beau started to turn, to remind him that Jonas Spence would likely not be talking French, but the chastisement died on her lips when she saw that the Marquis of Moncada had pulled himself to his feet and had already retrieved one of two small pistols he had concealed beneath his breastplate. He had the gun raised and cocked, the barrel aimed at Dante's broad back, and it was instinct rather than any sensible thought that made Beau fling herself forward, knocking Dante to one side just as the powder exploded in the firing pan. The shot barely missed its primary target, streaking past Dante's ear close enough to startle his gold earring before it struck Beau's temple and sent her crashing back against the open cabinet door.

Chapter 12

Geoffrey Pitt did not hear the first shot, nor the second. He and Lucifer had descended through five of the six levels of cabins contained in the massive aftercastle of the galleon. Each level boasted cabins as lavish and ornate as suited the wealthy young hidalgos whose privilege it was to serve aboard the *San Pedro*. With few exceptions most of those on the upper three tiers were in ruin, for the gilded stern rails and glittering array of gallery windows had been hotly contested by the *Egret*'s gunners. Panes from the stained glass lights lay in shards on the floor; the contents of bookcases, shelves, cabinets, and chests were strewn as far as the corridors. Furniture was broken, curtains and tapestries blown off the walls and windows. Here and there, fresh stains on the planking indicated someone had been unfortunate enough to have been standing in the way of flying glass.

Shattered though it all was, the opulence was staggering. Furnishings were upholstered in embroidered brocades. Thick wool carpets covered the floors, and scores of solid silver sconces and candelabra provided the light in the companionways and on the tables. On one level a massive dining table stretched from one side of the ship to the other, laid in fine white linen and, to judge by the debris scattered beneath it, set with solid gold plate in anticipation of a meal. On another, situated low enough in the hull to have avoided heavy damage, the cabins were decorated by an obviously feminine hand; furnishings were delicate and frilled with satin ruffs, the bed was an ornate four poster draped in tiers of fine netting that made it seem to be suspended in a frothy white cloud.

Geoffrey Pitt, observing all this as he followed in the wake of the Spanish officer, approached the last cabin on the tier and stepped around a door that had been knocked off its hinges. The quarters had been transformed into a salon as elaborate and comfortable as any in a grand palace. He had to duck his head to clear the lintel, and when he straightened he saw the four occupants of the salon huddled together against the far wall.

The Spaniard stopped short as well. His eyes jumped from one pale, shocked face to the next, their accusing stares, combined with his own mortification over the purpose of his visit, causing him to blanche the color of ashes.

One of the women was clearly the matron. She was older and stouter than the rest, with a face as harsh as a winter wind and a forthright bosom that protruded like the prow of a ship. She boasted a comely moustache for a woman and in moments of high tension—like this one—it glistened with dewy droplets of sweat. Two others were dressed similarly in modestly high-necked bodices and skirts that were rich enough to suit their exalted stations as companions to the King's niece. The fourth member of the group was situated protectively to the rear, her wide, startlingly blue eyes focused on the men who stood in the doorway.

Pitt, the son of a common foundry worker, had not an ounce of aristocratic blood—however diluted through past generations of droit du seigneur—flowing through his veins. His adventures and close friendship with Dante de Tourville had almost allowed him to forget his past as an ironmonger's son who always stank of metal filings and sweat, and he had worked hard to adopt the manners of his betters. He had learned to read and write, to use his wit and quick intelligence to talk, charm, bluff his way out of almost any situation.

But there were times nothing could keep him from feeling like a coal-blackened urchin born alongside the barrel of a cannon—and this was one of them.

Doña Maria Antonia Piacenza was simply the most beautiful creature he had ever seen. She was as petite and fragile as the first buds of spring. Her hair was dark, not quite black, not quite brown; her face was heart shaped and pale as cream, the skin so delicate and smooth as to be all but translucent. Her eyes were like pieces of the sky, large and wide and solemn, and started a sliding sensation in his chest and belly that had nothing to do with the motion of the ship.

The blue of her eyes was perfectly matched in her gown, cut with a low, square neckline that showed just a hint of the rose-dust silk chemise beneath. Already exquisitely tiny, her waist was further reduced to nothing by the sweepingly deep V of the bodice where it met the exaggerated flare of the farthingale. From her shoulders descended a conch, a sheer, gauzelike veil of such fine material, it was all but invisible. Nervousness had made her gather the edges of the floor-length veil around her shoulders and hold them like a shield over the tender young half moons of her breasts. Her hands shook so badly, the tremors caused the transparent fabric to shimmer and quake.

The Spaniard seem to find his tongue and bowed stiffly, offering his most abject apologies for disturbing them in so brusque a fashion. The English dogs, he added in rapidly whispered Spanish, had already shot the most revered Don Alonzo de Moncada and he was certain they would have no scruples shooting any or all of them, despite assurances given that no harm would befall the royal ward.

"Why has he come here?" the younger of the two maids snarled. "What does he want?"

The second one, with her brown eyes glittering speculatively, took a long, slow perusal of Pitt's broad shoulders and lean waist. She was as petite as the duchess, with a face that could have launched a thousand ships—in the opposite direction. Her shrewish, harpy features became even more pinched as she stared boldly at the bulge of Pitt's codpiece and whispered something in the duchess's ear.

Whatever the confidence, it made Doña Maria turn as pale as her veil. The first maid, whose eyes and mouth grew rounded and wet, stared at her more wordly-wise companion in horror.

"It is true, you innocent turd," the latter whispered haughtily. "It is what these English dogs do and what they expect *you* to do to them in return."

Having overheard the waiting-woman's crude observation, the bulwark-breasted duenna flared her nostrils and flew across the room, her wide skirts belling behind her, and planted herself in front of Pitt.

"How dare you vilify the air with your presence here! Who are you to threaten the welfare of Doña Maria Antonia Piacenza, Duchess of Navarre?"

"My name is Geoffrey Pitt. Our ship is the *Egret*, her master is Captain Jonas Spence. I assure you we pose no threat to anyone's welfare."

The duenna knotted her fist and thrust a sausagelike finger under Pitt's nose. "You attacked our ship! You shot and killed our captain-general! You barge uninvited into my little quail's chamber and stand there panting and sweating like a stallion eager to rut ... yet you say you pose no threat!"

Pitt looked down at the angry duenna with some surprise. "You are English?"

The bosom lifted and heaved proudly forward. "To my eternal shame at this moment, yes. I am indeed English. I am also Catholic and have vowed never to return to that heretic country until the legitimate queen and heir, Mary Stuart, is released from prison and restored to her rightful place on the throne!"

Pitt frowned. "Since she has already been in prison nineteen years, you may have a long wait."

"Blasphemer! Heretic! Murderer! *Pirate!*"

Pitt offered a wry smile and repeated his captain's words. "The *San Pedro* fired the first shot, it therefore attacked us. As to the charge of murder, your vaunted captain-general *fainted* without suffering so much as a scratch to his person. If I have shattered royal protocol by not knocking on a door that is no longer there ... I do offer my humblest apologies, but"—he looked over the duenna's head and, trying to temper the fear shining in the duchess's eyes, in her own language added, "I swear on my honor and on my life we have no intentions of ravaging anyone. My captain has dispatched me to offer his personal protection, and to this I add my own blood oath that no harm, however slight, will come to Doña Maria Antonia Piacenza."

The duchess held his gaze a moment and blushed so beautifully and so noticeably, the harpy took her scoldingly by the shoulder and turned her around.

"Indeed." The duenna snorted derisively. "Why should we believe you?"

Pitt's green eyes descended again. "You don't have to, of course, but you might find the alternatives somewhat less appealing."

Something, a twinkle in Pitt's eyes or a faint movement in the shadowy corridor behind him, drew the duenna's attention to where Lucifer stood, the expanse of his gleaming, bulging black torso and limbs broken only by the scanty width of his loincloth and the twin scimitars tucked into the folds. Her jaw sagged and she sucked in such a horrified mouthful of air, the shock of it sent her eyes rolling back in her head and her body teetering on her heels.

Pitt managed to catch her before she slumped to the floor and was in the act of passing half the burden onto the Spanish officer when Billy Cuthbert skidded to a breathless halt outside the door.

"Spit says you're to go back to the great cabin, sir!" he gasped at Pitt. "There have been shots fired and the captain's dead!"

Pitt's response was delayed a split second before he shoved the duenna into the Spaniard's hands. He shouted at Billy and Lucifer to stay where they were, to let no one in or out of the cabin until he returned. He drew his pistol and raced out into the companionway, taking the steps topside two at time.

Beau returned to consciousness slowly. Her limbs felt weighted, her whole body felt as if it had been submerged in some heavy liquid that would not let her rise to the surface. Sounds were distant and muffled. Someone was talking—to her, she thought—but the words were garbled and distorted, making no sense at all. She tried to turn her head and open her eyes but a dull throb of pain caught her unawares and she grasped instead at the solid wall of muscle that was holding her and tried to bury herself deeper into the warmth.

"Isabeau? Isabeau, it's all right. It's over."

She knew that voice. It was not her father's, but she knew that husky, deep voice. And something told her she knew whose arms were holding her and whose fingers were smoothing gently over her cheek and throat, trying to coax her back into the light.

"Isabeau, can you hear me?"

She groaned and nodded her head.

"It's me, Simon, and you're all right. You're safe."

"Wh-what hap-pened?" she gasped.

"You were shot, *mon enfant*. Moncada was attempting to play the hero and waited until I had my back turned, then . . ." He stroked her hair, her cheek, her throat again. "It was meant for me. I guess everyone's aim was off today."

"Y-your shot was deliberate," she said weakly.

"Indeed it was. The second time too."

"The second time?"

She lifted her head, wincing and shivering again as a stab of pain sliced through her. She could not see much beyond the breadth of Dante's shoulder, for he was on the floor beside her and held her cradled in his lap. What she could see were two booted feet sticking out from the corner of the desk—Moncada's booted feet, lying lax and motionless.

She looked up into Simon Dante's face. "You shot him?"

"He did not leave me much choice."

She blinked, but found the silver-blue of his eyes too intense to bear and looked instead at the strong, gunmetal jaw.

"You're bleeding," she whispered.

Dante followed her gaze and reached up, touching his earlobe. The shot had passed so close, the gold loop he wore had torn a wider hole in the pulpy flesh.

"You are bleeding as well," he pointed out. "All over yourself *and* me."

Beau lowered her gaze reluctantly from his wide, sensual lips and saw the blood spattered extravagantly down his shirt. Even as she stared, she could feel a warm, wet trickle starting down from her temple again. She tried to squirm up-right but Dante urged her head back onto his shoulder.

"Luckily it's just a crease, and luckily your head is as hard as your father's, but I wouldn't recommend acting with too much haste just yet."

Beau was still too dizzy to argue. The pain was fading, or she was starting to control it better, and she could hear men shouting and footsteps hurrying along the corridor. A few seconds later, Geoffrey Pitt burst into the cabin.

"Billy said there were shots. He said the *captain* was dead, and I just assumed . . . Christ Jesus! He doesn't have a head."

"He lost it in a moment of carelessness," Dante said dryly. He adjusted Beau's weight in his arms and rose unaided to his feet "I was about to take Beau back to the *Egret*."

Pitt stared at all the blood. "Is she all right?"

"She will be; it's just a scratch." He paused and Beau could feel the strong cords in his neck shift as he looked down. "Damn little fool threw herself in front of a shot meant for me."

"Damn little fool," Pitt agreed, tucking his pistol back into his belt. "Saved your life, did she?"

Dante scowled. "Did you manage to find the duchess?"

Pitt nodded. "She's hardly more than a child and terrified half out of her wits. She has two maids with her and a draconian matron, but . . . I would not want to see her frightened more than she is already. Unfortunately, there was only Lucifer and Billy to leave with them, so if you have everything under control here—which it seems you do—I would like to get back."

"When you do"—Dante tilted his head to indicate the concealed cabinet—"have Billy bring all of these papers over to the *Egret*."

"Charts," Beau murmured.

"What?"

"Charts. Maps. Have him search the pilot's cabin"—she lifted her head again—" or better yet, let me do it. A ship of this size and importance is bound to have accurate charts of every current and shoal along the Spanish coastline. If we are bound for war with Spain, the Queen's Navy might find such things invaluable."

Dante stared down at her, disgusted at himself for not having thought of it first. "You are absolutely right . . . of course. But you'll not be searching for anything yet. At least not until you can walk a steady line."

"I can walk . . . if you will put me down."

"You think so?"

"I know so."

He lowered her feet without further comment, though he kept an arm circled loosely around her waist.

Beau staggered a moment before she found her balance. A bright stab of pain sent her head on a wild spin, causing the walls, the floor, the furnishings, to slide back and forth with sickening irregularity. She put out a hand to steady herself and it met with Dante's chest. Luckily, she'd had nothing to eat all day or there would have been more than just her blood on the privateer's shirt.

Dante grunted and the next thing she knew she was scooped up into his arms again and was being carried out the door and up into the daylight. A film of thin clouds and lingering smoke was obscuring the sun, but there were still two to three hours of natural light in which to work. The deck of the galleon was swarming with activity and some of the men stopped as Dante passed. Word had already spread through the ranks concerning what had happened in the captain-general's cabin and several—including Spit McCutcheon—crowded the gangway to see for themselves that Beau was not seriously harmed.

After they crossed to the *Egret* by way of a steeply canted bridge of long, wide planks, Dante took her directly to her cabin. He sat her on the edge of the bed and, seeing the look on her face, stripped out of his bloodied shirt and donned another from the meager supply that had been salvaged from the *Virago*. He then fetched a basin of water and bathed the red from Beau's cheek and throat, dabbing gently at the musket crease and reaffirming it to be hardly more than a cut.

"Are you certain you are not a physician?" she asked sardonically.

"No, but if you keep on as you're going," he said, glancing down at her hand, which was still bandaged from earlier in the day, "I may have to become one."

"I have been eight months on this voyage without so much as a bee sting," she remarked crossly. "You come aboard and look what befalls me."

"Look what might have befallen you had the shot struck an inch to the left. You would have lost an eye, mam'selle, and more than likely we would have been denied the pleasure of your company for the journey home."

She made the effort to raise her lashes, which she had kept firmly shut while he bathed and dressed her wound. "If I hadn't moved at all, it would be *your* company we would be despairing."

"I won't even ask why you did it," he murmured.

She bowed her head. "Even if you did, I probably would not have an answer."

"You know"—he tucked a finger under her chin and tipped her face upward, struck once again by the unsettling combination of tangle-haired urchin and soft-lipped vixen—"if I were Moorish, you would now own my life until such time as I could repay you in kind by saving you from mortal danger."

"You are not Moorish," she pointed out.

"No. But I find myself in your debt nonetheless. And I always repay my debts."

Beau smiled crookedly. "Is that why you look like you have a mouthful of hot peppers? Because you find yourself indebted to a mere woman for saving your life?"

He released her chin, thankful she interpreted his discomfort as harboring a mouthful of hot peppers rather than a craving for something else.

"I do not consider myself indebted to a woman," he said carefully. "Did you not say yourself—and most emphatically—that on board this ship you were just a part of the crew, no more, no less?"

The outward nature of Beau's smile did not change, though inwardly she chided herself for having almost fallen into the trap. Such concern. Such solicitude. Fool that she was, she had almost succumbed to the oozing charm, the easy smiles, the soft, husky timbre of his voice. She had even almost succumbed to the heated lure of his body. Cradled in those powerful arms with the beat of his heart just beneath her hand, she had felt swamped by the heat and sheer animalism of him. All the time he bathed her wound she could not look up, could not move for the cool, prickling thrills that showered through her body. Her belly had turned to mush and her breasts had grown so taut and sensitive, the slightest breath chafed them raw against her shirt.

"You are absolutely right, Captain," she said evenly. "I should have said a mere *lackey*. And as such, you would therefore owe me nothing, since such action as I took to save your life would have been expected of any loyal member of a ship's crew."

He scowled. "That wasn't exactly what I meant."

"But it is exactly the truth."

Dante's hands actually curled by his sides in an effort to supress the urge to take her by the shoulders and shake

her. He was saved by the arrival of Billy Cuthbert, who
came into the cabin with an armload of papers and documents taken from the *San Pedro*. A young, strapping lad of
eighteen years, he seemed to possess unflagging strength
and exuberance, neither of which amused either Beau or
Dante at that particular moment.

" 'Nother load as big as this one," he reckoned. "Then
two or three trips to the navigator's cabin. Took me a quick
look, I did, and blink me if there ain't a whole library o'
maps and charts to choose from."

"Perhaps I should go back with him," Beau said, starting
to climb down off the bed. "He won't know what to look
for."

"I will," Dante said, reaching out his hand to stop her. "If
you're up to it, and you want to make yourself useful, go next
door and calm your father. He's been hollering for attention
the past hour, I'm told. Or you might even try getting some
rest; you were dead on your feet two hours ago."

"I'll rest when you do, Captain," she said firmly. "And
when the rest of the crew, equally dead on their feet, get a
chance to close their eyes. For now, yes, I will go to my father. I suppose he should be told he has just killed the captain of the *San Pedro de Marcos*." She took a few steps toward
the door, then halted and looked back. "May I ask you
something before I go?"

His hesitation was barely perceptible. "You may indeed."

"When we first went on board, why did you give your
name as Jonas Spence? For the taking of so rich a prize, I
would have thought you would have wanted the credit for
yourself."

"I gave my name as Jonas Spence because he deserved
the credit, not me. By this time next week, all of Spain
will be burning him in effigy, cursing his brilliance and
audacity as a sea hawk. Priests will be lauding him as the

Devil Incarnate, a Heretic Scourge upon the Holy Faith, and his crew not only deserving of God's wrath but the wrath of every God-fearing Christian on both sides of the Ocean Sea."

Dante caught Billy's wide grin and winked.

"I don't suppose it had anything to do with you not wanting word of your resurrection from the dead to reach England before you do."

His mouth thinned with sudden irritation. "Can I do nothing right in your eyes? Can I do nothing without rousing suspicions of an ulterior motive? Must you always look for the worm in the wood?"

"If it is there, yes. I would prefer to know a beam is sound and trustworthy beneath me before I put my faith into walking upon it."

He raised one eyebrow as though amused, but she could see a muscle jump in the tautness of his jaw.

"Then we have something in common at last, mam'selle, for I trust no one, put my faith in nothing, and walk nowhere without checking the shadows at my back."

Chapter 13

———◆———

"**Y**e look befuddled, daughter. Is yer head painin' ye?"

Beau had been preoccupied, pulling at a frayed edge of the bandage still wrapped around her hand. At her father's querulous prompting she touched the cut on her temple and although it was tender, she could not say in any honesty that it was the source of her sullen mood. She was bone weary, and that did not add an excess of charm. If not for the stupid, pigheaded statement she had made to Dante de Tourville, she would have crawled into her miserable little sail closet hours ago.

The seemingly tireless Frenchman had returned to the *San Pedro* and, the last she'd heard, was supervising the transfer of cargo from one vessel to the other. It was not unusual for a treasure ship of that size to take a week or more to load; Dante wanted the bulk of the plunder transferred by noon the next day. With the drastic difference in the sizes of the ships—and the fact that it took nearly two hundred men just to work the sails and rigging of the huge Spanish galleon—it would not be possible to either sail or tow the vessel as far as England, and so Dante had ordered only the richest cargo be selected and stowed in the *Egret*'s holds. To that end Spit burst periodically through Jonas's door waving a new list of "selections" under his nose. And Spence, with a bandage wrapped askew around his head, propped in his bed like a one-legged king, toasted each new addition to the *Egret*'s manifests with a fresh goblet of prime Madeira wine.

Twice he had ventured up on deck, enlisting the aid of several stout crewmen to carry him. But there was nothing he could do to make himself useful and nowhere he could go without a crutch or an arm to help him, and in truth, he was enjoying all the attention he was receiving in his cabin.

Among the more toastworthy items Spit's men removed from the *San Pedro* were barrels packed with gold plate, candlesticks, cutlery, crucifixes, gold and silver coins. One large chest was crammed full of ropes made of gold links— one hundred and fifty-three chains in all, with loops as thick as a man's finger. There were two thousand bars of solid gold bullion and four thousand of silver, all stamped with the official seal of the treasure house in Panama. Of no lesser importance were the thirty tuns of Madeira wine, twenty of cocoa beans, and assorted numbers of indigo and island spices.

From the personal items of the officers and soldiers were swords made from fine Toledo steel, their hilts crusted with gold and precious stones. Even the plain, unadorned cutlasses were of superior quality and would have brought a tasty price from the London merchants, but these were considered of little value now and tossed overboard with the casual aplomb of men drunk on excess.

For treasure of a different sort, there were casks of salted beef, bacon, and rice; wheels of cheese and earthenware crocks of olives. A squealing platoon of pigs and sheep had been herded across the planks and there was already excited talk of a celebratory feast planned for the morrow.

"Fasten yer lovely eyes on this; it'll shake the sleep out o' yer bones," Spence said, swinging a pendant hypnotically before her. Suspended in the crux of the chain was a pearl the size of a hen's egg, the surface gleaming like a candle through frost.

"I'm told she likes pearls, our Queen Bess does. Drapes herself in ropes o' them, even pins them in her hair. D'ye think she'll like this? This an' the other trinkets I've set aside so far?"

With a benevolence kindled by the warming effects of the wine, Spence had declared his intentions to send, along with the jewels, the most exquisitely wrought sword, a selection of the finest plate, and the sheerest bolt of silk as gifts to his most royal sovereign.

"I think she will find a warm spot in her heart for all you send her. Warm enough to forgive you your rashness in turning your trade from simple merchantman to hell-raising pirate."

Spence looked over and a slow, wide smile parted the red froth of his beard. "A Heretic Scourge on the Holy Faith? Is that truly what he called me?"

"Truly." Beau nodded. "Along with the Devil Incarnate—which we knew already."

Spence chuckled heartily. "I don't mind sayin', lass, twixt you, me, an' the lanterns, this devil near fouled his breeks when he saw the size o' that sow up close. God's truth, I could die tomorrow an' never know a prouder moment. Lift yer cup, girl, an' toast the best bloody damn ship an' crew on the Ocean Sea!"

Beau echoed his words and tipped her cup as unsparingly as Spence did, though she managed to drain hers without spilling any down her chin, and she finished without a loud, raucous growl of enthusiasm.

"Damn their zealot hearts anyway, but one thing ye cannot fault the Spanish for is their Madeira. Red as blood, sweet as sin; lies like a slip o' crimson velvet on the tongue." He saw Beau's smirk and rubbed the stump of his leg with a pained look on his face. "Aye, an' great medicinal qualities too. Almost makes a man forget *the incompetence o' some men on board this ship who would rather count their coins than carve their captain a new limb so he could get up out o' this infernal bed!*"

His shout echoed down an empty corridor, as he expected it would, and he grinned his way through another oath as he shoved the bandage back up over his ear. He shoved it too high and the ugly gash, swollen and mottled, stitched with thick black threads, caught the light.

"We do make a fine pair," Beau said, touching her own temple again.

"Do we not, though," he agreed with a chuff of laughter. "Aye, an' if yer mother were here, she'd say 'twas lucky we got cracked on the heads, for it's the hardest part o' both o' us."

Perched against a small mountain of canvas, bemoaning the inconvenience of having to wait on the carpenter's pleasure, Beau supposed her father did not want to think of how truly lucky he had been today. A step slower and he could as easily have had the other leg shot out from under him. She remembered all too well the night he had been brought home in a two-wheeled cart, straight off the ship, his flesh burning with fever, the stump of his leg a bloody, festering mess. The doctor had not given him much hope of living through the night and Beau, only ten years old at the time, had refused to move from his side through the night, the next day, the next night, and two full weeks after that. She had made her decision then and there that if he survived, she was not going to stand on shore and watch him sail away again. Not without her.

Beau pulled at the threads of her bandage again.

"Do ye remember her at all, lass?" Spence inquired softly, seeing the melancholy expression creep over his daughter's face again.

"Mother? I remember everything. The way she looked, the way she smelled—like cinnamon, all the time."

"Aye. I used to liken her to sunlight, hot an' clean, an' bright as flame. Why she ever stayed with the likes o' me, I'll never know."

"The way I have heard you tell it, she had little choice in the matter."

"Only because I knew she were the one I wanted. Knew it the minute she flashed them hot eyes at me an' told me she wanted me too."

"You knew because of the way she *looked* at you?"

"Well, that an' a few other things." The bandage on his head slipped down and he nudged it back in place with the stub of his finger. "She had this funny way o' always makin' my skin feel two sizes too small for my body, an'—an' my hair—when I had it, that is—stand up on end like I pricked my finger on lightnin'." He cocked an eyebrow. "There wouldn't be a particular reason yer askin', now, would there?"

"No. No particular reason."

Spence pushed himself up on one elbow. "Ye'd tell me if that Dante fellow were pesterin' ye, wouldn't ye?"

"He isn't pestering me, and, yes, I would most certainly tell you if he was."

"Is it that ye *want* him to pester ye an' he'll have no part of it? I'll skewer his gizzards just as deep for the insult."

"No! No, it isn't anything like that at all, it's just . . ."

"Just what, daughter? Spit it out!"

Their amber eyes met through the glow of the overhead lamp. They kept few secrets from each other. Beau had spoken to him openly and freely when she had lost her virginity and with whom she had done the deed. Conversely, she knew all of his mistresses and his favorite whores and exactly what it was about them that made them his favorites.

"It's just that . . . there are times he makes me so angry I feel like I could explode. And others . . ."

"Aye? Others?"

"Others . . . when he doesn't make me angry at all, but I feel like I could explode anyway."

Spence pursed his lips and gave her a long, contemplative look from the top of her head to the scuffed toes of her boots. "Mayhap yer doublet's too tight."

Beau, who had not realized she had been holding her breath, released it on a curse that was not as casual as Spence was expecting, and he recanted immediately.

"Bah, I'm sorry, lass. 'Tis the drink an' all. Ye know I'm not good at givin' advice on such things. For a man it's different. He sees somethin' he wants, he takes his ease an' walks away with a clear head in the mornin'. For a lass, well, what kind o' father tells his daughter to go an' scratch the itch if she's got it?"

"The itch?"

"The itch, lass, the itch." He waved a flustered hand in the approximate vicinity of his crotch and scowled. "Ye're not a virgin, for pity's sake, ye must know what I mean. An' don't go puffin' yerself up like a peahen tryin' to deny it. He's not the ugliest bastard on this earth, an' neither are you, an' if he makes ye feel like ye're wantin' to come out o' yer clothes all the time, well then, ye've got the itch for him, plain an' simple."

Beau stared and Spence glowered an addendum. "As long as that's all it is, is an itch. Ye wouldn't be expectin' anythin' more from him, would ye?"

Beau's mouth sagged open to reply, but she was cut short.

"Because he's had one wife already he couldn't tame, an' I doubt he'd be lookin' for another. Ye knew he was married, did ye not?"

She found her voice and her indignation. "Yes, I knew, and I wasn't—"

"Did ye also know she whelped two bastards on him while he was away at sea?"

"No," she admitted softly. "I didn't."

"Aye, well, it's not the kind o' thing a man like him would talk about too freely, nor is it the kind o' thing he would forget or forgive too soon. Seems she got caught twice with her legs too wide an' her belly too full an' tried to tell him they were his. He knew they weren't, bein' as how he were away at sea both times. With the first, I heard he forgave her an' even offered to give the brat his name. With the second, he disowned the lot, petitioned the court for a divorce, an' took himself off to sea nearly two years before he ventured back home. It's likely he'd keep himself well away from any more graspin' females for fear o' bein' duped again—just like you carve a man's liver out if he smiles at ye, all on account o' what that nob-licking Nate Hawethorne did to ye."

"I am hardly a grasping female," she said with a flush of resentment. "And Nate Hawethorne is not the only reason I keep to myself."

"Maybe not. But he's the best excuse ye can think of in a pinch. God above, girl, ye can't judge all men by the measure o' Nate Hawethorne. He was a bastard an' led ye by the nose, promisin' ye all manner o' things he had no intentions o' givin' ye. Use him to take yer soundings an' ye'll dry up like a piece o' salted fish."

"Are you telling me I should keep the door to my cabin open all the time?"

"No, I am not!" He surged forward, pointing a stubbed finger at her. "I'm not tellin' ye in any shape or form to go out an' jump on every man who waves his nethers at ye, for I'll not have any daughter o' mine called whore!" He bristled himself back against his prop of cushions and glared. "But I am sayin' it's a hard life ye've chosen for yerself an' sometimes ye just have to take yer pleasure where ye can find it. Bah!" He dropped his chin to his chest and swirled the last dregs of his wine around his cup. "Yer mother would have my ballocks for earrings for tellin' ye such things, but it pains me sometimes—as I know it would pain her—to see ye so afeard o' the very thing that gave her one o' the greatest pleasures in life."

"I'm not afraid," she protested weakly.

"Ye are! An' I blame myself for not takin' ye back to yer aunt Mavis an' tyin' ye hand an' foot to the newel post when I should have! Look at this—" He waved a hand around the cluttered cabin. "What kind o' life is this for a young wench?"

Another minute, Beau feared, and he would be weeping into his cup. She jumped to her feet and crossed to the side of the bed, bringing the bottle of wine with her as she did.

"It is the only kind I want," she insisted. "And if you have any thoughts of leaving me behind with Aunt Mavis . . . *ever* . . . you *will* be wearing your ballocks for earrings!"

"Bah!" he said again, giving the snort less conviction this time. He held out his cup, however, and chided her soundly when she would have filled it only halfway.

"I'll have to fetch another bottle."

"Fetch it, then," he grumbled, "ere a body dies o' thirst."

Spit had thoughtfully brought half a dozen on his last visit and Beau took out her knife, about to peel off the wax seal, when she looked up and saw Simon Dante standing in the doorway.

He was just standing there, with several rolled charts tucked under his arm and a large wooden crate balanced in his hands. The shirt he had changed into earlier was black, and with the dark hose, the dark boots, the dark richness of his hair, he had simply blended in with the shadows. Nothing in his expression indicated he had been there long enough to overhear any part of their conversation, but all the same, Beau felt an airless tickle pass across the nape of her neck, like the filament from a spider's web.

"Come in, come in, come in," Spence urged, having noticed Dante the same time as Beau. "Fetch up a cup an' join us."

"Actually"—Dante grinned and stepped into the brighter circle of light—"it was cups I was bringing you."

He set the heavy crate on Spence's desk and started lifting out goblets, all solid gold with jewels encrusted around the stems and bowls. Spence's eyes bulged when he was handed one embedded with diamonds and sapphires as big as his thumbnail, then another studded with rubies, tourmalines, and topaz.

"I thought, if you were toasting your victory, you should have the proper vessels to do it with."

Spence beamed and sent his plain silver cup clattering onto the floor. "Daughter, have yer hands frozen on the bottle? Crack it open an' bring it here. How goes it topside?"

"The lads are putting their backs to it. We should be well fixed by morning."

"How well fixed?" Spence asked, narrowing his eyes.

"A rough estimate? Sixty thousand. Possibly as much as a fourth more, depending on what the gold and silver will fetch in London."

Spence's jaw sagged and he did not seem to notice or care as the bandage on his head dropped down over his eye.

"Sixty thousand . . . ducats?" Beau asked breathlessly.

Dante held up a goblet and gauged the depth of the fire glinting off the gemstones against the sparks kindling in Beau's eyes, and handed it to her. "I read ducats off manifests, but I think in terms of good English pounds."

"Sixty thousand pounds," Jonas whispered.

"Enough to gild your *Egret* in gold if you want." Dante laughed.

"Sixty thousand," Spence muttered. "Why, that would be—roughly—thirty thousand for me, an' thirty for the rest o' the crew, including you an' yers, o' course," he added, snapping his head around to Dante, "—for all fought equally hard an' are equally deservin' o' shares."

Dante raised his goblet to acknowledge the compliment as well as Spence's generosity. Seeing that the bottle was now indeed frozen in Beau's hands, Dante lifted it gently away and poured a brimming measure in all of their cups.

"To the *Egret*," he said, "and her fearless crew!"

"To the *Egret*!" Spence roared, spilling as much Madeira down his beard as he did down his throat. "An' to the good grace an' common madness o' Simon Dante, Comte de Tourville, bastard Frenchman, pirate wolf, an' . . . have I forgotten aught o' yer titles, my lord?"

"Admitted heretic and free-rover," Dante supplied with a smile.

"Oh, aye, aye. Well, we're all of us heretics in the eyes o' the foamin' papists, are we not? An' though we may rot in hell for our earthly sins, while we're here, we'll bloody well enjoy them!"

Beau shared the toast and felt her head take a delicious twirl toward weightlessness.

"Where, by Christ's tailfeathers, are McCutcheon an' Pitt an' that other black devil o' yours?" Spence demanded. "It was a good part their skill on the guns won us this day, they should be here to share it."

"Lucifer is standing guard over the Spanish crew—God save them—and McCutcheon could not be dragged from the cargo holds if you wrapped a hundredweight of chain around his ankles. Mister Pitt is, I'm afraid, in love again, so I doubt we'll see him tonight either."

"Eh?" Spence sputtered a mouthful of wine down his chin. "Did ye say . . . in love?"

"The little Spanish duchess is quite a rare beauty, and if there is one thing Pitt cannot resist, it is a *ravissante* dark-haired, blue-eyed young innocent who speaks in waif-like whispers and flutters her lashes like butterfly wings. He was smitten the instant he saw her and I doubt he'll be much good to either one of us over the next few days."

"You're still planning to bring her to England with us?" Beau asked.

"The duchess *and* her little silk pennant. A day after the *San Pedro* makes port, every Spaniard worth his salt will be after us. A hostage against safe passage would not go amiss, here at sea as well as at home."

"At home? Why would we need a hostage at home?"

"Have you forgotten the prize ship Drake towed into port two years ago? The spider king screamed piracy and demanded the ship be returned and El Draque brought before a Spanish tribunal to answer for his crimes. Coincidentally, the ship was also carrying a member of the royal family, whose safe return to Seville was all that saved Bess and Sir Francis from a lengthy diplomatic battle. In this case, we not only have your sorry hide to bargain for, but mine as well."

The wine was fogging Spence's thinking. "Yours?"

"Veracruz," Beau supplied dryly. "And Victor Bloodstone. Do you think, Captain Dante, a youthling duchess and a few Spanish documents will placate the Queen when you declare Walsingham's nephew a thief and run him through? Think you Bloodstone has not already paid her handsomely from his profits and told his uncle all there was to tell about what you found in the documents at Veracruz?"

Dante's eyes narrowed. "I can assure you the Queen will claim the first bloody thrust once she is apprised of how he came to sail so gloriously up the River Thames, his holds bulging with *my* silver and gold. She abhors treachery in her Court almost as much as she abhors the thought of marriage and having to share her crown with a man.

"As for Walsingham, he takes pride in his web of spies and puts great store in the accuracy of the information he receives from his hundreds of little moles. No doubt Victor *has* already dazzled his uncle and the Queen both, by reporting the contents of the letters we took from Veracruz, but since I was the only one with any skill in translating, he would only have been able to base his reports on what I shared with him."

"Which was not the complete truth," she surmised with grudging admiration.

" 'It is the nature of every man to err, but only the fool who perseveres in error,' " he quoted. "Cicero, I believe. At any rate, I made an error once in trusting someone completely and paid for my mistake dearly."

Beau saw the muscle shiver in his cheek again and she recalled what Spence had said about his wife.

"But what if it isn't enough?" she asked quietly. "What if a duchess and a few documents are not enough to convince the Queen that the death you plan for Bloodstone is not simply a vengeful, cold-blooded murder?"

"If it isn't, I suppose I shall have to pray the executioner's blade is sharp when it kisses my neck, for I plan to kill the bastard anyway."

Beau found herself staring into eyes that were as cold as ice and she felt a shiver down her spine. Impossible though she would have thought it, the gleam intensified and a moment later, he was grinning. "On the other hand, I may have found just what we both need to keep our necks and our prize monies intact."

He drained his cup and set it on the desk, then reached for one of the thickly rolled charts he had brought to the cabin with him. He unrolled the sheets—there were three—and weighted the corners with gold goblets. Beau craned her neck slightly to see over the shadows, a needless exercise as Dante was quick to beckon her over anyway.

"Philip of Spain has been bragging," he said, stepping aside to give her a full view.

Beau looked down and for a few moments it was not exactly clear what she was seeing. Ships, certainly. A painted forest of masts and great gilded sterns lying regally at anchor in some unidentifed port.

Seeing her frown, Dante slid a blunt-ended finger across the bottom of the vellum, drawing her eye to the artist's signature. The name meant nothing to her, but the date beside it was very specific.

"This is . . . April, is it not?" she said hesitantly. "Unless . . ."

"No, you haven't been at sea that long, and neither have I."

He moved two of the goblets he was using as weights and let the top painting curl back into a roll. There was another beneath, of more masts, more ships in a much larger harbor, and again she read the script, aloud this time.

"*Maius—May—anno* 1587."

"The first port I am not familiar with, but this one"—the pewter eyes glanced from Beau to Spence—"is Cadiz."

"Cadiz?" Jonas queried. "Why the devil—?"

"The King is showing off his fleet preparations," Beau said in awe. "He is showing off his armada."

Dante grinned again. "I told you, you were going to have stop doing that: being so clever."

"But . . ." She looked down at the paintings. "How can you be certain these are accurate depictions? How can you be certain it isn't just braggadocio and wishful thinking?"

Dante gazed at her a moment, then ran the tip of his finger along the soft auburn wisps of hair that curled against her neck.

"I know because of these. They're standing on end. And because of these—" He reached into the crate again and withdrew a thin sheaf of papers. They had been heavily waxed and sealed with the imprint of the King's ambassador in Veracruz. With fresh wine shimmering in his cup, he pulled a chair under the lamplight and began skimming the pages, translating from the Spanish as he read small excerpts that might interest his audience.

" 'Like hawks they came out of nowhere, struck, and flew away again in the night, with Satan himself blowing in their wings. We are told the attack was led by the French dog,' " He paused in his reading and scowled. "Dog? When was I demoted from a wolf to a dog? At any rate, '. . . the attack was led by the French dog De Tourville, with some measurable success, which, I regret to inform Your Most Royal Highness, bears a loss to the treasury of some five hundred thousand ducats.' " Dante stopped again. "The thieving rogue. It was no more than four, by God, although he has put the reward for my head up to fifteen thousand ducats. Five thousand more and I'll be worth as much as your hero, Sir Francis Drake."

"Fifteen thousand is tempting enough," she said wryly. "Believe me."

He swallowed a mouthful of wine and lifted the papers again. "Then there is this."

"What?"

"I don't quite know; it's in code."

"Then how do you know it's important?"

"Why else would it be in code?"

Beau resisted the urge to curse and instead snatched a sheet of paper out of his hand and scanned it quickly. "It looks like perfectly innocent writing to me."

"You read Spanish?"

"I can read charts and currents, and *this*"—she stabbed a finger at the document—"looks like nothing more ominous than weather reports."

"Which is precisely what they are. Weather reports, harvest predictions, wind movements . . ."

"How dreadfully foreboding."

He took another sip of wine and lounged back in the chair. The black silk of his shirt trapped small puddles of yellow light from overhead and made him look as if he had been gilded. Beau, who could still feel the line his finger had drawn on her neck, tried very hard not to notice how his shirts never quite seemed to be laced to the throat. She failed miserably and found herself staring at the muscular V of his chest with its dark, smooth mat of hair, so lush and thick, it made her want to bury her hands in it.

"Before we reached Veracruz," he was saying, "we had occasion to prime our guns on a Spaniard just off Barbados. There were dispatches on board from the King to Diego Flores, the governor of Panama. They were also filled with weather reports and harvest predictions and I did not think too much of it at the time . . . until Victor Bloodstone"— he spat out the name with, if it was possible, more venom than before—"advised me, through knowledge of his uncle's dealings with spies and so forth, that Philip of Spain has a penchant for putting all of his important correspondence in code."

"Harvests and such?" Jonas guessed, wanting back into the conversation.

Dante nodded. "I've a dozen like this in the papers we took from Veracruz, and there are twice as many more on the *San Pedro*. I had nothing much to do while we drifted at sea for two weeks, so most of mine are translated. If there is a code there, I have not found it yet. A fresh pair of eyes might help, though, if you had someone on board who could read Spanish and perhaps see something I missed."

"Spit," Beau said.

Dante's dark head came around again with a frown. "I fail to see how that would help."

"Spit McCutcheon," she explained on an exasperated sigh. "He reads and writes Spanish. Latin as well. He was a church cleric at one time."

"A minister of the Lord?"

"Try his patience sometime and you will have him spouting psalms."

"From the pulpit to a gunport is still an interesting leap for the imagination to take."

"So is the one from a French chateau to the deck of a pirate ship."

A smile was startled into his eyes, and a moment later

it turned into quiet laughter, directed as much at himself as at anything she had said.

"*Touché*, mam'selle. Rarely have I been called a pompous goat with such delicious finesse."

Spence laughed as well and clapped his hand to his thigh to call for another toast. "Paintings be damned! Spain be damned! Philip an' all his blatherin' papists be damned! Come here, the pair o' ye, an' take my hand. Captain! Ye already know what I think o 'yer skill on the seas; there's naught I could say to add to it, save that I was honored to share a deck with ye today. An', Beau! I'm not forgettin' I've got the finest damned helmsman a sailor could ever want guidin' the keel! I'm that proud o' ye, Isabeau Daria Spence. Proud enough to burst the heart clear out o' my chest!"

Beau stared stupidly at her hand as Spence took it and sandwiched it with Dante's between his own huge paws. She felt a thrill of light-headedness and pride, being praised by the father she loved above all else and toasted by a man who regularily scorned danger and cast his destiny to the wind.

Her gaze drifted upward to Dante de Tourville. He'd asked her what had brought her to this point in her life, if she had any regrets that she was not sitting by a hearth wearing silk frocks and sipping chocolate out of tiny porcelain cups.

For the past eight years she had been sipping life and living adventures those safe at home could not even imagine. She'd had salt spray, not rice powder, dusted on her cheeks, and instead of sitting cozy by a fire, she had climbed to the top of the mainmast and gazed out across a moonlit sea, standing close enough to the heavens to reach out and snatch at a handful of stars. Was there anything anywhere half as beautiful as a molten sea at sunrise or half as intoxicating as the smell of a spice-laden breeze off a tropical island? She had swum in the crystal-blue waters off Tortuga, and she had chipped ice off a floe near Greenland. She had made friends with Indians in the New World and enemies with gunners on board Spanish galleons. She had shared the camaraderie and the danger, the excitement as well as the fear.

And she had been kissed, for whatever reason, by a pirate wolf who would not have passed her a second look had she been sipping chocolate beside the Queen.

A round of laughter intruded on the magic of the moment and she realized, with an odd sense of detachment, that Jonas was no longer holding her hand in Dante's; it was staying there of its own accord. The long, tapered fingers were closed lightly around hers, cradling her in the warmth of his palm, caressing her with an intimacy that sent a fierce rush of heat spiraling through her body. Her breasts blossomed with it, her belly shimmered with it, and her blood raced until the heat became as intoxicating as the wine.

She was aware Dante's eyes had not left her face, but she resisted the compelling urge to meet them. The penetrating silver-blue was always dangerous, never more so than now as they challenged her to acknowledge something he already suspected: that she wasn't as strong as she pretended to be, wasn't as independent, as sure of herself, as indifferent to the feelings she tried so hard to guard against revealing. He could see that Spence's praise had set her emotions in a turmoil; was he wondering how deep and how far that turmoil extended?

Beau withdrew her hand and curled it tightly by her side. Jonas was offering another toast to God knew what and calling for a fresh bottle of wine.

"No more for me," she said quickly. "My head is already spinning in circles. I think I will bid you both good-night."

Jonas belched, his nose red as paint, and tried to focus on Beau's face. "Are the watches set an' armed? We're twenty feet from an enemy ship an' we'd not want to be caught with our cods open an' our pissers hangin' out."

It took a second or two for Beau to redirect her thoughts, to concentrate on something as practical as watches and the safety of the ship and crew, but she was thankful for the cold, hard sense required to form an answer. "Lewis has the deck until midnight, then Hubbard, and Simmonds for the ghost watch, all with full crews."

"Aye." The bald head wobbled slightly on its barrel neck. "Keen eyes on all o' them. We can sleep sound tonight."

She risked another glance at Dante, but he had moved out of the circle of light and had his back turned while he opened another bottle of wine.

"Good night, Captain Dante."

"Dormez-vous bien, Isabeau, et revez du plaisir."

Chapter 14

Sleep well, he had told her, and dream of pleasure.
Beau closed the door to her father's cabin behind her and stood in the gloom of the companionway, hearing the echo of Dante's parting words in her head.

Dream of pleasure?

An innocent phrase or another subtle mockery?

A round of male laughter drew her eyes down to the narrow slice of light fanning out from the crack beneath the door and she wondered what they would be dreaming about this night. Probably the pleasure of going to war with Spain.

While it was true Sir Francis Drake and others had been warning the Queen for many months of a building frenzy in Spanish ports, it was also true—and the dilemma of any sovereign who did not want to venture into a war unless all avenues of negotiation were exhausted—that Elizabeth could not squander the money of her overtaxed subjects to build a navy on rumor and speculation alone. If Dante had found proof of Spain's intentions, then war was inevitable and the Queen would need all of her loyal

merchantmen and privateers to defend England's shores
from invasion. That included the *Egret,* and the sooner
home, the better.

Beau looked along the corridor to her own door. There
was another weak sliver of light spilling out the bottom,
and she supposed Billy had transferred the rest of the maps
and charts from the Spanish galleon. She needed her own
charts for the morning and it was probably best to find
them now instead of stumbling about with a thick head at
dawn.

It seemed odd somehow to hesitate on the threshold of
her own cabin, to feel like a trespasser when most of the
belongings inside were hers. Perhaps it was just the sight
of the shirt Dante had cast off earlier, still crumpled in a
heap in the corner, or the faint scent of sunshine and
leather that lingered behind, that was making her skittish.
Even more likely, she could blame the wine and the talk
of itching and scratching for making her skin prickle and
her throat aware of every breath she took.

A single candle flickered inside its glass lamp on the
chart table. There was brighter moonlight streaming
through the slanted windows, and drawn by the thought
of a fresh breath of air, she crossed to the gallery door and
slipped outside onto the narrow balcony.

To starboard the looming hull of the *San Pedro* blocked
the horizon. The *Egret* was anchored off her stern quarter,
riding lightly on the gentle swells, kept at a secure distance
by the grappling lines. She could hear banging and sawing
on the decks above; she could smell pitch and smoke and
the metallic scent of spent gunpowder. She would have
liked to cross the gallery and have a closer look at the
humbled goliath anchored beside them, but to do so she
would have to pass the windows on Spence's side of the

ship and unless she ducked down like a thief, they would think she was spying on them.

She walked instead to the larboard side, where the moon glistened close to the horizon and poured a molten river of rippling silver toward the *Egret*. An earlier mass of clouds scudded away to the east, glowing blue-white on their underbellies. The brightness of the moon had washed most of the smaller stars out of the sky, but there were enough winking in the darkness to bring Beau's elbows down on the rail and her chin into the cradle of her hands.

Would she rather have rigid buckram corsets and wire farthingales? Or crow-faced matrons telling her how to wear her hair or chiding her if a freckle appeared on her nose? Not likely.

A frown brought her chin up again and she pulled the bunched linen strips off her hand. The palm was still tender, but luckily she'd had enough calluses to absorb the worst of the rope burns. And probably enough wine to dull whatever sensations were left.

She tossed the bandages overboard and, on a further restless urging, unplaited her hair from the constricting tightness of the braid. Careful not to waken the crease on her temple, she gave her scalp a few good scratches, easing the tension a hundredfold. She stared down at the inky blackness of the water twenty feet below and wished she'd found time earlier for more than just a perfunctory wash to rid herself of the heat and grime of battle. A long, slow, hot bath would be comparable to heaven right now. A hot bath, an oiled rub, and a soft, deep featherbed.

Beau's head jerked upright and her eyes popped open. She had a hammock in a sail closet waiting for her. Moving reluctantly away from the rail, she started back for the door.

She was not quite there when she saw movement inside

the cabin and froze. Simon Dante was closing the outer
door to the companionway; a heartbeat later he was putting
toe to heel and scraping off his boots, kicking them aside
with the relish of a man unhappy with restrictions of any
kind. The thongs on his shirt were already loose and dangling. In less time than it took for a gasp to leave Beau's
lips, his belt was unfastened and flung to the floor and the
black silk shirt was pulled up and over his head.

Shocked and too stricken to move, she watched him
extend his arms wide and give a mighty yawn. He clasped
his hands behind his neck and stretched the bulging biceps,
then bent his torso from one side to the other, his muscles
rippling in the candlelight, his hair falling in waves over
each shoulder as he moved. Unlacing his hands, he reached
straight up, easily curling them over the top of a ceiling
beam. He arched forward, stretching his chest and belly,
then back until he was clinging by his fingertips and balancing on his heels.

The wound on Beau's temple throbbed once with the
sudden rush of blood to her head. Her cheeks were burning,
her throat was dry, and she tried frantically to think of a
way to escape the gallery without being seen.

She turned her head ever so slightly, knowing the
moonlight was behind her, outlining her silhouette. When
she looked back again, he was bending over his sea chest,
fishing out a stoppered bottle. He opened it with his teeth
and poured some of its contents into his hand; a few seconds later, the strong scent of camphor oil drifted out the
door.

Beau could not have moved if she'd wanted to. She
watched him rub a gleaming film of oil into the powerful
display of muscles along his arms, massaging it into the
squared bulk of his shoulders, his neck, into his ribs and
chest, and as far around on his back as he could reach. She

watched him knead each muscle and work each sinew and by the time he was finished, standing in the light like a burnished war god, Beau's limbs were weak. Her belly was a moving, liquid mass of heat. Her own skin, she could swear, had shrunk two sizes too small and threatened to burst at the slightest movement.

A fresh, sharp whiff of camphor restored a measure of her senses. She *had* to get off the gallery—but how? There was only one door leading inside and even if she could muster the nerve to walk boldly through it, what possible explanation could she give for having waited so long to do it?

There were more than enough hand- and footholds to climb to the upper deck, and it was the mistake she made, lifting her head to locate the first carved groove, that alerted Dante to the dark outline of an intruder on the gallery.

Beau had the advantage of the candlelight to show her the startled look on his face as he spied her through the diamond grid of the windowpanes. He had the advantage of long legs and quick reflexes to carry him through the door and out onto the narrow gallery before she could put a foot to the rails and reach for the first handhold.

Strong hands, rough hands, grabbed her around the middle and dragged her back, slamming her hard against the canted hull of the ship.

"You!" he gasped. "By all that's holy—*what the devil are you doing out here?* You could have been killed, sneaking around in the dark like this, you little fool, or have you forgotten there is an enemy ship anchored beside us with several hundred angry men just aching to swim across and slit our throats?"

Beau looked down and saw the glitter of a knife in his hand. "I . . . haven't forgotten. And I wasn't sneaking. I

came to get my charts for the morning and—and then I
wanted a breath of air, and—and—it *is* my cabin, you
know. I am not accustomed to having someone else in it,
or to asking someone else's permission to go inside."

Dante's eyes lost some of their murderous intent and he
relaxed enough to put away the dagger. "Why didn't you
say something? Why didn't you show yourself right away?"

"I . . . don't know. I just . . . I don't know. By the time
I realized you were there, you were already half naked
and—and . . ." She swallowed hard and raised her hand in
an unconsciously sensual gesture, pushing aside the edges
of her shirt to press cooling fingers against the rapid pulse
beating at the base of her throat.

"If—if you would step aside now, Captain, and let me
pass, I would be more than happy to give you back your
privacy."

But instead of stepping aside, he moved forward, keeping her trapped against the gallery windows, cloaking her
in the immense shadow of his own frame. "Not just yet,
mam'selle."

"Wh-what do you mean?"

"I mean"—his hands came up and he brushed his fingers
over the rich abundance of her hair—"not just yet."

She tensed as he caressed the back of her neck. She was
more aware than ever of the heavily muscled shoulders, the
dark swarm of hair that covered his chest, the molded
bands of hard flesh that flexed along his arms every time
he asked the slightest motion of them.

Her eyes rose, not enough to have met his, but enough
to focus on the halfsmile that played on his lips.

"I hope you are not thinking of kissing me," she whispered, her throat almost too constricted to squeeze out the
words.

He grinned and studied her through narrowed eyes. "I think it only a fair exchange for watching me strip naked."

"You're . . . not naked," she pointed out.

"Let us not split hairs, *ma petite*. You have already seen all there is of me to see, whereas I . . . I remain somewhat in ignorance, relying only on my imagination. Granted, I have a good one, but I confess I am intrigued to know what you keep so carefully guarded behind your belts and buckles. Here, for instance——" His fingers nudged aside the collar of her shirt and touched on the smooth white slope of her shoulder. "And here," he murmured, sending that same impudent finger over the folds of her shirt, tracing the swell of her breast.

Beau blushed to the point of numbness. The heat that had all but paralyzed her earlier was spreading downward, fanning through her body with unsettling precision, as if he knew just what to touch and how to touch it to render her immobile. She was also aware of the negligent power in those hands—hands that could easily take what they wanted without her cooperation or assent.

At the moment they were taking the knife out of her belt, another out of the concealed sheath she wore on her hip; they were traveling lower and skimming down her leg to the cuff of her boot.

"Wh-what are you doing?"

"Following your father's advice."

Startled, she looked up into his face.

"He warned me to search you ten ways to Sunday, and even then, not to turn my back on you."

Beau opened her mouth to protest, but his lips were on her temple, on her cheek, they were seeking out the soft pink shell of her ear. His hands had not stopped moving, stroking and smoothing over her arms, her waist, her hips. Her heart was pounding, she was certain he could hear it.

Surely he could feel it, for his body was crowded warmly against her, pressing her back against the gallery ledge. And his mouth—God save her, his mouth was exploring the crook of her neck, roving at leisure, his tongue swirling hot, moist patterns on her skin.

"Christ Jesus," she gasped, "if you're going to kiss me, can you not just do it and be done?"

The words were no sooner out of her mouth when his lips covered hers, claiming them with a rough imperiousness that chastized her for her impatience. Yet his own was no less compelling and he chased her gasp inside her mouth, filling it with his tongue, shocking her with an intrusion that reverberated to the soles of her feet.

His hands raked into her hair and would not let her move or twist away to avoid the plundering boldness. His lips were hungry and demanding, moving hot and sure over hers, ravaging them with a fierce insistence that left her weak and reeling with confusion. She wasn't enjoying it. She wasn't! Yet she was trembling, quaking everywhere. Her hands, pinned against his chest, began to feel more restrained than trapped and longed to be set free to roam the wide expanse of swarthy muscle.

Dante lowered a hand to the small of her back and urged her forward against the growing hardness of his body, introducing her to yet another shattering sensation. When she offered no objection, when she met this new boldness with a soft, ragged moan, he angled her head back and sent his mouth down to plunder the curve of her throat again, finding and laying seige to the tenderest of nerve endings.

"Isabeau, Isabeau," he murmured, shifting his hands, his body, his intentions. "I knew there must be a softer side to you. Softer. Sweeter. Tantalizing."

Beau's eyes shivered open. His hands were creeping up beneath her shirt and the impossibly long, solid shaft of his phallus was pressing into her thighs, into flesh that was suddenly alive with raw, liquefying sensations.

"Stop," she gasped weakly. "Please . . ."

"Why?" His voice was thick and husky, muffled against her throat. "Why are you so afraid of admitting you are a woman with a woman's desires, a woman's needs?"

"A woman's needs," she cried, shuddering as his thumbs caressed the round underside of her breasts. "You mean your needs, don't you?"

"I was hoping, for tonight anyway, they might be one and the same thing."

"I don't need you," she insisted on a broken whisper.

His hands descended. They shaped themselves to her buttocks and drew her against him, savagely enough that they both gave a little groan. "But you *want* me. Almost . . . and God damn my soul for admitting it—almost as much as I want you."

"No," she gasped. "No."

Resisting the urge to call her a liar, he slanted his mouth more forcefully over hers. He ran his tongue across the velvety smoothness until a soft cry parted her lips again and he thrust deeply, possessively, inside. The tension snapped back into her neck but he was ready for it. He held her firmly, closely, snugly, against his body, letting her know the games were over, letting her know exactly what effect the rumbullion, the moonlight, the scent of her skin, was having on him.

Yet none of those things was as potentially devastating as the silky warmth of her mouth. He had not expected anything half as arousing nor a fraction so seductive as the sound of the tiny, stifled moans that came on each swirling incursion of his tongue. He had not expected himself to come half out of his skin, imagining other areas of her body that would be as smooth and silky, as hot and wet, as lush and sensitive to his every move. Raw, sexual heat flamed his senses and made him probe even deeper, made him turn his mouth this way and that so there was no part of her left unexplored, untouched.

"Please," she gasped. "Wait! Stop. . . ."

He surely hadn't expected to feel himself respond to her half-whispered pleas, or to stand away, or to put an arm's length of distance between them.

What he saw caused his jaw to clamp and his body to ache with unbelievable pressure. Her hair was a tumble of luminous waves trapping the moonlight—softer, fuller, more luxurient than his silk-starved hands could expect to resist. Her shirt was pulled taut over her breasts, emphasising their proud, upthrust shape and the small, rounded beads of her arousal. The thought of stripping away that shirt, of taking those small, firm beads into his mouth and suckling them until she groaned from the pleasure nearly brought a flush of sweat across his brow. And her eyes, damn them. Her eyes. There was a wildness in them that defied him to try his hand at taming her, yet there was also a soft shimmer of uncertainty, a vulnerability that almost caused the last of his senses to desert him.

She was shaking. But so was he.

"If this isn't what you want," he said hoarsely, "you'd best get the hell out of here . . . and you don't have much time to do so."

Beau's lashes were almost too heavy to lift, but lift them she did, and was not surprised to find the smoldering argentine eyes waiting for her. Waiting to tell her how foolish she would be to underestimate his dark desires. There were no promises there, no hint even of an obligation that would go beyond the next clear thought. There was only the moment they were in right now, only an offer of heat and sin and pleasure beyond her wildest dreams.

She reached out her hand—it was more of an instinctive gesture than anything else, intending to do . . . what? Apologize? Attempt to explain again an error foolishly made?

Instead, it turned into a kind of wondrous journey, a shy exploration of forbidden territory, as her fingertips encountered the oil-slicked surface of his forearm. When her hand did not instantly erupt in flame and cinder, it was with some fascination she laid it flat and skimmed it over the silky furring of dark hairs, sliding upward to the crease of his elbow, then higher onto the solid bulge of hard muscle. The residue of oil had left his skin as smooth as satin and her hand seemed to glide of its own accord to his shoulder and across the sculpted plateau of his upper chest.

A small frown bade her explore further, and she combed her fingers lightly through the wealth of sworling hairs, spreading them wide and laying them flat again to feel all of him, all the splendor of the hard-surfaced flesh that had been tormenting her thoughts since she had first seen him on the deck of the *Virago.*

A second, tentative hand joined the first and she found the dark discs of his nipples, surprised to feel them roused and pebbled hard on their surrounding island of soft velvet. She had wanted to touch all this male heat earlier, to run her fingers through the dark fur, to explore the vast, uncharted planes of her imagination, but she had thought it all out of her reach.

It was not out of reach now, and with an exquisitely shivered breath she lifted her eyes to his and wondered what other transgressions might be permitted.

"Whatever you decide," he warned her softly, "know that I will not be able to stop again."

Fine wisps of her hair, ruffled by a passing breeze, floated across her cheek and throat, brushing over her lips, clinging to the faint moisture left by her breath.

"I will . . . likely . . . not want you to," she whispered.

Dante felt every word ripple across the nape of his neck. Her voice was low, quivering with the effort to sound calm and detached, but laced with enough tension to send tendrils of shock coursing down his spine. Desire pooled hot and heavy in his loins, and he reclaimed some of the distance he had put between them. He sank his fingers into the tousled pelt of her hair and drew her forward. He tilted her face up to his and for a long moment just held her that way, their mouths a breathless gasp apart, waiting until he could count the heartbeats in her eyes before he kissed her.

It was a savage, relentless kiss, one that invaded her mouth, filled it, and molded it to his own with a fierce passion. His lips were merciless, his tongue ravaging, but instead of frightening her or shocking her, it brought her crushing into his arms. It sent her hands curling up and around his broad shoulders, it brought her body straining eagerly against his, riding the hardness of his thighs with an urgency that sent one of his hands down to cradle her bottom and pull her roughly against him.

He lifted her away from the awkward canting of the gallery windows and propped her on the oak rail, wedging himself boldly between her thighs, nearly gasping himself as their two heated centers came together. Beau's hands pushed into the thick, shaggy mane of his hair and kept his mouth fastened to hers even as he began to search out the bindings of her shirt. Impatience made his efforts clumsy and he tore the garment down the front seam; tore it and tugged it free of her belt with a throaty growl as he dispensed with yet another hidden knife. Belt, shirt, and knife were cast into the inky blackness of the sea twenty feet below, the splash lost among the other night sounds.

His eyes, glowing like pewter in the moonlight, registered their surprise and their pleasure. Her breasts were small but perfectly shaped to fill the cup of his hand, lush enough to draw a groan of appreciation from his throat as he bowed his head and drew the puckered flesh into his mouth. The stunning intimacy was too much to bear in silence and a strained plea came from her throat, begging him not to stop but to pull her deeper into the heat and wetness. Partially supported by the rail, partially supported by the enormous bulge of his erection, she flung her head back and let the moonlight bathe her bare shoulders, let it silver the rippling power of his broad back and show her where his mouth worked so skillfully, so determinedly to turn her into a shivering, shuddering mass of pleasure.

His hands, clamped rigidly around her waist, began to tremble with the force of his own aroused passions, and with another smothered oath Dante lifted her into his arms again, snarling a soft threat into her mouth that kept her limbs wrapped tightly around his waist. He carried her inside the cabin and directly to the bed, each step increasing the friction and the urgency between them.

A moment, no more, was all he wasted tearing aside the last flimsy barriers of their clothing before she was lying naked beneath him. He was poised between her thighs, hard and thick and pulsing with eagerness, and then he was inside her, breeching the last of her doubts with the swift, invasive heat of his body. Her lips parted around a gasp—a gasp that was startled into a soundless cry of disbelief and awe as he filled her, filled her, filled her so full and taut and deep, she had no time to brace herself as the first wave of pleasure swept through her, shattering all perceptions of pleasure that had gone before.

He thrust again and again, and the heat was so fierce, the sensations so shockingly explicit, she clutched at the rigid muscles of his arms. But they were still slick with oil and her hands skidded down to his hips, holding him fast, arching feverishly into one rich torrent of pleasure after another.

Dante's body echoed her every spasm. She was supple and hot, unbelievably sleek and greedy, pulling him deeper and deeper into the tightening fist of her sex. He was not surprised to find he had awakened a fiery passion within her; he *was* surprised by the intensity of the heat pouring into his own loins, by the helpless urgency fueling his every thrust. The taunts, the challenges, the game of cat and mouse he had played, had been deliberate. He had played it because he was a man and he had gone without a woman too long, and he had played it only for the pleasure of stalking something wild and untamable and bringing it to ground beneath him. He had not expected to want more than a swift, perfunctory release. He had not expected to *feel* more. And yet he did. He was trembling like a loose sheet of canvas; his bound and reinforced edges were unraveling, fraying more and more with each startled cry that broke from her lips.

An ache he had not felt in too many years to recall began to govern each stroke, each gust of ragged air torn from his throat. He wanted to feel her wrapping herself around him, he wanted to see her flushed with passion, racked with pleasure. He wanted to take her to the highest peaks of ecstasy and beyond, and he wanted to share that ecstasy with her, soak himself in it, drown himself in it.

His heart thundered in his chest, his blood pounded in his veins, and he could hear her name whispered over and over on his lips. He could feel his body gathering in upon itself, channeling all the heat, the power, the feverish hunger, into nothing more noble than the savage rise and fall of his hips.

As Beau arched up beneath him, he threw his head back and braced himself on outstretched arms, stiffening, shuddering in the throes of an orgasm so bright and brilliant, it was all he could do to keep from roaring his pleasure out loud. As it was, he was helpless to hold the smallest part of himself back as he spent himself in a white-hot and seemingly endless climax within her.

Beau was melting. Trembling. Quivering like a silk pennant on a shiver of wind. Dante's solid presence was still inside her, thudding against dewy folds of flesh that had gone slack and buttery with shock. Her hands were still grasped to his hips and her legs were locked tightly around his. His breath was warm against her throat, his body was heavy and damp and, where it was wedged between her thighs, as reluctant as she was to relinquish the gentle rocking motions that were bringing them slowly back to reality.

A final satiated groan brought him to a languid halt. He was all chest and arms and rock-hard thighs and he must have felt her trying to shift slightly beneath him, for he lifted his head out of the crook of her shoulder and thoughtfully transferred some of his weight onto his elbows.

Sometime between being outside and coming inside, the candle had died and there was only moonlight bathing their features. His face was a mixture of pale light and shadow, mostly the latter because of his hair, which had become as wild and tangled as her own.

"Well," he murmured, and then just "Well," again.

Beau searched for something equally profound to say, but her tongue seemed to have become too clumsy to do more than keep company with her teeth. Her hair was spread across the bedding, and her legs—one was wedged against the cabin wall and the other had nowhere to go but off the side of the bed—felt chafed and tenderly abused along the inner thighs. A movement out of the corner of her eye caught her attention and she turned her head slightly—with Dante following the motion—to see a pair of hose snagged on the corner of the chart table where he had tossed them.

Reading the consternation in her eyes, Dante bent his head down and nibbled gently at the corners of her mouth. "You will have to forgive me, mam'selle, if I was a tad overeager. It has been a long time and my . . . manners . . . may have been somewhat lacking."

"You tore my shirt," she said, frowning. "And threw it overboard."

"It was worth the price of a replacement," he murmured, running his lips along her chin and down the supple length of her throat.

"A belt and a knife as well."

"I'll buy you a dozen more. For that matter, you are a wealthy young woman now, you can afford to buy your own and to throw them overboard after each time you wear them."

Beau let her senses track the progress of his mouth as he nuzzled her temple, her cheek, the tight, damp curls that lay below her ear. A smile curved her lips and for one mad, irrational moment, she wanted to thank him, for he had done his best and she had survived, emerged with all of her faculties intact. She could breathe, think, react, reason. She could regain control again.

The moment passed and the smile became an open-mouthed sigh. His lips were around her breast, grazing impudently on her nipple.

"Are you not . . . the least bit sleepy, Captain?" she asked dreamily.

"Truthfully?" He paused and warmed her skin with a slow roll of his tongue. "No. Are you?"

Beau contemplated her answer while she watched his mouth take a meandering course from one pinkened nipple to the other. If anything, she felt remarkably exhilarated, even though seconds ago she could have sworn every muscle and bone in her body had melted away to nothing.

His tongue made a final, wet revolution before his dark head came up and he gazed thoughtfully at the lushness of her mouth.

"Because if you are"—his hands twined around the silky ribbons of her hair and the heat of his body pressed forward, stretching and swelling within her—"I am afraid you are going to have to tolerate my ill manners again. And possibly again after that."

Beau's great golden eyes shimmered up at him. Her hands skimmed lightly around the strong column of his neck and threaded themselves with equal conviction into the glossy black mane. "Father would say good manners are required only at the Queen's table."

"Your father is a wise man."

"Yes," she whispered. "I know."

Part Two

The Wind
Commands Us

Chapter 15

⚬—⎯⎯⎯⎯—⚬

The grappling lines between the *Egret* and the *San Pedro de Marcos* were cast off two hours after sunrise. There was plenty more cargo in the holds of the Spanish galleon, valuable cargo that would have brought a small fortune with the London merchants. But there was simply no room left onboard the *Egret*. They had already made one hard decision to dump the weightier bars of silver overboard rather than leave it on the *San Pedro* to benefit the Spanish king. After the gold was loaded, what little storage space that remained was saved for the lighter, more exotic, and therefore more profitable bales of pepper and cloves.

Jonas Spence had already been on deck when the sunrise spread orange and pink clouds across the horizon. Spit had come to fetch him when the last available cranny had been stuffed and sealed. Crews had been working all through the night on repairs; and with their holds bulging, their next priority was to put as much open sea between the two ships as possible.

With the Marquis de Moncada dead, command of the *San Pedro* had fallen to the next senior officer, one of the two who had been in on the original discussions of surrender in the captain-general's great cabin. His name was Recalde, and he had been standing less than a pace from Moncada when Dante's shot had torn away most of the Spaniard's face. He would not soon forget the name of either Jonas Spence—as Dante had given it—or the *Egret*.

Spence had been carried on deck to supervise the ungrappling. Thomas Moone had still not fashioned a new limb, and as the irascible captain was already bleary eyed and thick tongued, there were few men brave enough to venture onto the foredeck where their bullish captain hobbled along the rail roaring orders until his face was as red as his beard.

Used to her father's temper, Beau appeared on deck ten or fifteen minutes after Jonas but preferred the company of Billy Cuthbert and her charts. It would be her job to plot the course least likely to be intercepted by any ships sent to hunt them down, not to mention the many predators from England, Portugal, or France who regularly stalked the sea lanes looking for easy prey. Dante's guns would act as somewhat of a deterrent, as would the obvious signs of a battle hard fought and won. Even so, Beau would have preferred a little heavy weather and stronger winds to hasten them on their way.

Before the confrontation with the Spaniard she had estimated they were three weeks out of Plymouth, but that was also before adding several tons of plunder to their ballast. Their speed would suffer, as would their maneuverability; there would be a detectably heavy difference in the way the *Egret* responded to orders from the helm. But she was fixed with a new arm for the tiller, stouter and stronger than the first, and a crew determined to reach the shores of England with their newfound wealth intact.

The last transfer between the *San Pedro* and the *Egret* may not have been the most valuable in terms of monetary compensation, but to some on board the English galleon, Doña Maria Antonia Piacenza's presence was as comforting as Dante's demi-cannon. She crossed the ladeboard with only her duenna and Geoffrey Pitt as escorts. Her two other maids had, for lack of any comfortable quarters to house them, been left behind. She was permitted to bring only three of the twenty-three leather trunks that held her personal possessions and, for her protection, was assigned hastily cleaned and reconfigured quarters opposite the captain's great cabin. Beau's tiny sail locker and the weapons armory were consolidated into one cabin and refurbished with a bed, a washstand, and Persian carpets taken from the *San Pedro*.

It was one of the few times Beau's head came up from her charts. She stood by the after rail and watched as Geoffrey Pitt led the tiny duchess across the planks, one gingerly taken step after another. She was bundled head to toe in a hooded velvet cape, with only a suggestion of huge frightened eyes and a pale face peeping out from the circle of fur trim. Her gloved hand was clutched to Pitt's arm as if it were a lifeline. Equally dainty satin-slippered feet stepped down onto the deck of the *Egret* with all the confidence of a bird fluttering to its doom.

Dante had said Pitt was smitten by her beauty, so it was no surprise to see him acting so protectively and attentively. It was surprising, however, to see some of the weathered tars doff their caps and stare, with their mouths gawped open and their normally lewd and ribald catcalls choked back into their throats as the Duchess of Navarre passed.

As chance would have it, she had to pass directly under where Beau was standing in order to make way to her cabin. The large eyes, darting every which way in trepidation, looked up and, for a moment, registered shock at seeing another woman on board. The hood slipped back and the creamy white, heart-shaped face was exposed. And if all the sweetness, innocence, and virginal naïveté were not cloying enough, a traitorous breeze pushed aside the edges of the duchess's cape and revealed a gown of polished lavender silk beneath. The hem was decorated a foot or more with a banding of elaborate gold tracery; the overskirt was parted almost to the waist and pinned back to display the elegantly brocaded petticoat of dark, rich rose. Around her neck she wore a crucifix, the cross positioned directly over her heart; around the impossibly narrow span of her waist, she wore a long, jeweled belt, the ends falling in a cascade of rippling gold links.

Beau looked down at her own dull hose, shirt, and doublet, none of which could be called perfectly clean or perfectly whole. Her hair was once again pulled back and fettered in a braid, leaving nothing to camouflage the large blue bruise on her forehead or the scabbed crease that ran into her scalp. Her hands, where they rested on the rail, were tanned and weather-roughened, the nails chipped and stained. The palms, at least, were minus a few layers of calluses, but the rope burns had left them as red as if she had dipped them in crushed berries. Her mouth was probably no better off, having been suckled and kissed for the better part of the night. Her chin and throat were tender as well, chafed by an irreverent jaw stubbled blue-black with coarse hairs.

As for the rest of her body . . . *dainty, delicate,* and *virginal* were hardly the words she would use to describe how she felt. Despite the fact that Dante had spent an inordinate amount of time massaging each muscle, each square inch of skin, with his scented oil, she was aching and tender in places that brought a blaze of hot color to her cheeks just thinking about them.

And where was he, anyway?

He had not been in the cabin when she had groaned herself out of bed at dawn. He had not been on the foredeck with Spence or on the main deck to greet Pitt and his delicate little duchess, although she imagined the pretense of his being the captain of the *Egret* had ended the moment the ladeboard planks had been withdrawn from the *San Pedro*.

"Good morning."

Beau jumped an inch or so out of her skin and whirled around. He was standing behind her, dressed in a clean white shirt and tight black hose, looking as fresh and roguish as if he had slept another three-day stretch. He had shaved and bound the waves of his hair back with a leather thong. The ends of each strand glistened with water, suggesting he had just emerged from the sea.

"Good morning," she said, and hastened back to her charts.

"To everyone's good fortune it looks like we will be under way several hours ahead of schedule."

It was more of an observation than a question and she barely gave it a glance by way of acknowledgment.

"Pitt and his princess are on board, I see. Rather a lovely little thing, is she not? Like a rosebud with dew on the petals, so fresh, she fairly begs for a man's protection. Poor Pitt. He'll likely be stammering like a schoolboy before the week's out."

Beau slapped down her charcoal stick and straightened. "Was there something specific you wanted, Captain? I have readings to take and a course to plot. If you are so taken by her *freshness*, why don't you go below and enjoy a closer look?"

If either her rebuke or her mood surprised him, he gave no sign. In fact, the only response he offered was through his eyes, and what Beau saw there made her catch her breath and hold it. He was subtly telling her what she knew already, that she looked thoroughly and utterly debauched, that she could lace her doublet twice as tight and he would still know what lay beneath, that she could scrub her skin raw with lye soap and he would still be able to detect the scent of camphor and musk. That she could pepper her every word with brimstone and cordite and he would still be able to hear the echo of her begging gasps.

"No," he said quietly. "There is nothing specific I want. Not at the moment, anyway."

"Then please"—she released her pent-up breath in a soft gust—"leave me to my work."

The smoky, silvery eyes narrowed. "It's a small ship, Isabeau. You won't be able to hide behind your work forever."

"I can try."

He held her gaze a moment longer, then gave a small bow. The roguish smile was still playing about his lips as he turned and descended the ladderway. Beau watched him, she could not help herself. He moved like a big, graceful cat, a sleek panther with the air of lazy indifference that came from being well fed and content. And why should he not look so satisfied? He had spent the night doing exactly as he pleased with her and, true to his warning, had not stopped again to ask her permission . . . for anything.

No specific needs at the moment? Did that mean he expected something at a later time? Tonight, perhaps? Did he expect her to go to him again for a lusty repeat of what had happened last night?

Beau's skin shivered at the thought but she resolutely pushed the notion, even the possibility, as far to the back of her mind as she could. She had weakened once, but that was all. That was the end. She could blame her lapse on the excitement of their victory over the *San Pedro*, the amount of wine she had consumed, her exhaustion, her inability to fight her own curiosity any longer . . . or the itch, as her father had so artfully put it.

All these things could explain a single lapse, but to do it again? To go willing and sober into his arms would put more than just the swagger of satisfaction in his gait. It would put her at his mercy, reduce her once more to a mere female in his eyes . . . and in the eyes of every other man on board the *Egret*.

She looked slowly around the deck, but could see no one staring at her or pointing and murmuring behind raised hands. But they would. If they knew she had succumbed to the Comte de Tourville's sexual prowess, she would lose all of the hard-won credibility she had gained over the years. One clumsy tumble from a capstan was all it took for years of finely balanced work in the rigging to be forgotten.

She could not let that happen. She would not.

It took nearly four hours before the *San Pedro de Marcos* was reduced to a speck on the horizon. During that time a goodly portion of the *Egret*'s crew were sent to their berths to catch up on some much-needed sleep, while those who seemed to thrive on nerve alone continued to work on repairs. Most of the spare canvas had gone into the yards, leaving the damaged, torn, and scorched sheets to be patched and reinforced. Men sat on overturned barrels much as at a quilting bee, stitching and cutting, swapping versions of their own involvement in the battle. Damaged ropes and cables were spliced, the guns were reamed and their carriages greased. Spit McCutcheon had thriftily retrieved most of their spent shot from the wreckage of the Spaniard's deck, plus helping himself to powder and fuses from the galleon's stores so they would not be lacking in firepower should they attract the eye of any cruising vultures.

Cook was in his glory. He now had rations to spare and spent most of the day happily at work over his cauldrons. Two large pigs were slaughtered and the meat set to roast over a long metal trough filled with scraps of wood and broken timbers. At various times during the day men gathered to stare, their mouths watering, their palms sweating, their bellies rumbling in a chorus of expectation. At mealtime every man's pannikin was filled to the brim. Chins and hands dripped with grease, and the jeers that had been challenging Cook's slowness all day long were replaced by the sound of chewing, drinking, and belching in robust contentment.

Spence called for a barrel of ale and ordered twice the normal measure for each tar. With his head still bandaged and the bottom of his hose knotted over empty air, he sat in the midst of his crew, drinking, eating, cheering, as heartily as the others each time a fresh platter of carved meat was passed from the trough.

Even Clarence the cat had no need to resort to skulduggery. He sat by Cook's heels, his tail snaking back and forth across the planking, his face upturned and his eyes bright, waiting patiently to catch the thick, meaty scraps that fell his way.

Beau deliberately chose to take a seat with the common seamen. Spence arched an eyebrow in her direction, indicating an empty place reserved beside him, but she only shrugged and smiled and raised her cup in a silent salute. Dante sat on the other side of Spence and Lucifer sat cross-legged on the deck beside him. It made for one of many uncomfortable moments during the meal when Beau looked over to find the Cimaroon's eyes fixed upon her. She recalled, later, that he usually slept across Dante's door at night, and if so, had likely heard more than snoring coming from inside the cabin last evening.

Pitt had made a brief appearance carrying two fine porcelain dinner plates, but his tawny head disappeared quickly belowdecks again as soon as they were filled. The duchess was still in shock and too sick at heart to leave her cabin, thus Pitt had assigned himself her personal guard and messenger.

Eventually, a long and mighty belch from Spence marked the end of the revelry. Fresh watches were sent up into the tops with orders to report so much as a farting bird on the horizon. The coals in the trough were doused in a billowing cloud of steam and the residuals spaded carefully overboard. By habit the men contributed their bones and scraps back into a soup pot, knowing full well that one day's excess could mean another day's lack.

They finished out the first full day under sail without incident. The wind picked up in late afternoon and the seas roughened, but Beau was happy with the way the *Egret* responded. She took the galleon through a few tacking maneuvers to test her seams—one of which brought Geoffrey Pitt stumbling up onto the deck again, pale as ash and taut around the mouth—and was satisfied the ship could handle herself with courage and spirit if need be. When the blue of the sky began to leech into pinks and grays, Beau took a fix from the first star that appeared and gave orders to the new helmsman who arrived to take the watch. She rolled her charts under her arm but instead of venturing anywhere near the cabins in the stern, she found an empty hammock in the darkest corner of the crew's quarters, curled herself into a blissful ball, and slept.

Sometime during the night two large shadows made their way through and around the maze of hanging, swaying cocoons. Billy Cuthbert led the way, his hand cupped around the weak flame of a taper, and when he found the one that held Beau, he stood aside and let Simon Dante pass in front. The Frenchman lifted her carefully into his arms and the two men retraced their steps, parting company with a whispered thanks on the starlit deck.

Dante made his way alone into the stern cabin and deposited his sleeping bundle on her own bed. His hand may have lingered a moment longer than was necessary on the chestnut lock of hair that had curled forward on her cheek, but whatever thoughts or cravings that may have passed through his mind were dismissed before they could take hold. He pulled a blanket up to her chin, doused the guttering candle, and closed the door quietly behind him as he left.

Chapter 16

⚜

The *Egret* made good time on her journey north. She managed to avoid notice most of the time; sails were spotted twice on the horizon, too far to do more than identify one suit as belonging to a Frenchman, the other English. Neither paid the *Egret* more attention than it took to read her silhouette and dismiss her as being of little importance.

Spence was fully mobile again. Thomas Moone carved him a new limb, though not as elaborate as the last with its shaped calf and solid foot. A stout peg was the best he could do, he declared, until they reached England and found a good, solid piece of Norfolk pine.

Carrying forty extra crewmen, the quarters on board were cramped and free space extremely limited. Privacy, normally only a word thrown out in jest at the best of times, was nonexistent. The men ate, slept, and tended to their bodily functions in groups, sometimes crowds, and if not for the weight of the gold and treasure in the *Egret*'s holds, tempers would likely have flared along with the squalls that blew with seasonal frequency. One in partic-

ular, striking on the tenth day of April, had strong enough
teeth to rip the mainsail and send a yard slamming into
the back of a sailor's skull, splitting it open like a melon.

On clear days the men still gathered on the gundeck and
swapped stories. Once in a while Spence would join them,
but conspicuous by his absence was Dante de Tourville. He
spent most of the daylight hours poring over the salvaged
letters and documents from the Spanish ship, searching for
the key to the King's code. They were all translated to the
best of his abilities but if there was a key, he could not find
it. Spit McCutcheon's limited knowledge of Spanish
proved to be just that. He knew how to ask a whore the
price of a tup and how to barter for food and ale, but the refined Castilian spoken and written by the King and his
governors left the quartermaster scratching his spiky gray
stubble and scowling over the plague of the nobility.

Lucifer's rib, with or without the chicken foot, appeared
to heal with miraculous speed. He was the only one who
commanded a wide private space at least once each day
while he practiced with his twin scimitars. The men would
fan well back or swarm like ants into the shrouds and rigging, hanging by hooked arms and legs while they watched
the enormous black man move gracefully around his
cleared circle of deck, blades flashing and slashing at invisible foes.

After a few days of watching, one brave lad ventured
into the circle, his new Spanish cutlass glinting dully in
the sunlight. Lucifer's eyes narrowed warily for as long as
it took the man to wipe the sweat off his palms and challenge the Cimaroon to a friendly match. The men who
had put their mate up to it called out their wagers, and
soon it looked as if there might be a new afternoon diversion. The unfortunate challenger had no hope of putting
his blade anywhere near Lucifer and the Cimaroon became

so frustrated himself at the boy's ineptness, he started giving him instructions. From then on, at various times of the day, Lucifer's gleaming ebony body could be seen leading a dozen or so men at a time through the intricate steps and arm movements that made him seem so invincible.

Different groups drilled on the heavy guns. Geoffrey Pitt and Dante supervised these exercises until McCutcheon became almost as proficient, whereupon the task of honing the crew fell on his willing shoulders. As for Beau, she became as wily as Clarence the cat at avoiding Simon Dante. Whenever he was on deck, she managed to be elsewhere, and after the first few days he did not even trouble himself to look for her. The only times she could not make herself entirely invisible were those when Spence insisted on having everyone present for an evening meal. Then she would seat herself at the opposite end of the long trestle table, uncomfortably trying to ignore the hot and cold flushes that skittered along her spine each time Dante spoke or laughed, or just raked back his hair with impatient fingers.

These were the same scarce times when Pitt and the Duchess of Navarre could sit in relatively close proximity without the bulk of the duenna intruding. These, too, were the times when Mistress Agnes Frosthip, who had started out guarding her charge with the tenacity of a fighting cock, seemed less concerned at the glances the pair exchanged than she was at the frequency with which her wine goblet was filled. As the days and leagues were swept swiftly behind them and it became clear that neither the burly captain nor the crew had any rapinous intentions toward her little lamb, the duenna even appeared to mellow somewhat, and to preen her moustache into a smile whenever Jonas Spence offered up an amusing anecdote.

Geoffrey Pitt was, as Dante predicted, quite hopelessly

taken by the petite duchess. His eyes shone like polished jade whenever they were set upon her; his hands suffered from a nervous tremor whenever their arms accidentally brushed or whenever the sky-blue eyes risked a glance into his. Because of Agnes Frosthip the two were rarely left alone, but those few moments, stolen here and there, were enough to suggest to Pitt that Doña Maria Antonia Piacenza did not really mind him finding ways to distract the duenna.

"You were very wicked, señor," the duchess whispered, drawing her cape closer around her neck to ward off the cool night breezes. "Señora Frosthip will have a very large head in the morning but a very short temper."

Pitt acknowledged his guilt with a wry chuckle. Throughout the meal he had kept the duenna's goblet brimming and now, with Spence's conspiratorial help, had earned a waved dismissal and permission to escort Doña Maria Piacenza around the deck for a last breath of fresh air before she retired.

"If she so much as raises her voice to scold you, simply tell me and I will toss her overboard."

The duchess looked startled, then eased somewhat when she saw his wide, handsome smile. "You tease with me, Señor Pitt. It is unkind, since my English is not so very good."

"Your English is excellent and a credit to the señora. But yes, it was unkind of me to tease you."

She accepted his compliment and his apology with a shy little half-smile and Pitt's heartbeat stammered in his chest. She had turned her face into the soft amber glow of the stern riding lantern, and every sweet translucent curve was brushed with a pale shimmer of gold light. His belly, his chest, his arms, ached with the need just to reach out and touch her, to run the backs of his fingers along her cheek to see if her skin was anywhere near as warm and smooth as he imagined it to be. He ached to see, just once, the timid, fearful wariness washed from her eyes, and to see her look at him with nothing but trust . . . and love.

It was true: Pitt loved women and fell in love with nearly every beautiful woman who crossed his path. It was his one weakness and Dante mocked him mercilessly about it, saying that he could never just bed a woman and part with a fond farewell come daylight. He had to take her to heart, to woo her and win her and regard each act of lovemaking as if it was a commitment of the soul.

More than just his soul was in his eyes, lodged in his throat, knotted in his belly now as he looked at the alabaster perfection of Doña Maria Antonia Piacenza. These were no ordinary knots either, they were deep and penetrated to the core, and ached with the hopelessness of knowing this was not just another cavalier infatuation. She was the niece of the King of Spain and he was the son of an ironmonger. Who she was, her lineage, her royal bloodlines, only made it that much more excruciating to know he could never have her even if he reformed his ways, abandoned the renegade life he led, vowed everlasting obedience, even took up the Catholic cross. . . .

He could love her but he could never touch her.

A frisson of shock ran up his arm as he realized he *was* touching her. His hand was on the rail and the edge of her cloak was brushing up against it. She was looking out over the vast black emptiness of the sea and so could not see the expression on his face as he gazed down and caressed the tiny patch of cloth with his thumb and forefinger.

"Señor"—she was suddenly there again, her face upturned to his, her eyes wide and dark and filmed with moisture—"do you believe in heaven and hell?"

The question took him aback and he had to swallow hard before an answer stumbled off his tongue. "I . . . suppose I do. I mean, I must."

"But you are not certain."

"Of course I'm certain. I mean, if there wasn't any such thing as heaven or hell . . . there would be nothing to separate good from evil. There would be no rules to follow, no reason not to kill, cheat, steal, lie." He paused and twisted his mouth into a wry smile. "No hope of redemption for sinners like me."

"Are you a very bad sinner, señor?" she asked in her breathy whisper.

Pitt gave more weight to the question than he normally might have done, partly because of the solemn expression on her face, partly because, in his twenty-nine years, he had not given it much thought before. Surely, he had done his share of cheating, scheming, and lying; it was a necessary evil in order to avoid spending the rest of his life molding iron over a peat fire. He had done his share of killing as well; it went hand in hand with the life he had chosen. But he had never deliberately betrayed the trust of another man, never raised a hand against a woman or child, never kicked a dog or slit a man's throat for the sheer sport of it.

"Not as bad as some," he said finally. "Possibly worse than others. But I sleep well at night, and know many men who call me friend."

"Including your Capitán Dante and Capitán Spence?" Her lashes fluttered down to shield her eyes. "They helped you tonight, did they not?"

Pitt cleared his throat. "Helped me?"

"Distract the señora."

He had the good sense not to deny it, and the better

sense not to say anything at all while she struggled through whatever dilemma was putting a small frown on her brow.

"You all seem so . . . kind. And far more honorable than I was told to expect in an Englishman. My . . . maid . . . warned us before we were taken from the *San Pedro* . . . that both the señora and I would probably be raped by every member of the crew before the first sun fell."

"Your maid frightened you needlessly," Pitt assured her. "You have nothing—and no one—to fear on board this ship."

"She—she also said England is a pit of snakes and vipers; heretics who sacrifice children and drink the blood of their victims. She said it is a cold, dark place of pestilence and sickness where the sun never shines and terrible storms ravage the land all year round."

"We have a fair share of rain, but—"

"She says the rain is God's tears and that He despairs of ever saving England from the hands of heretics and devil-worshippers. She also says there is no beauty in England, no beauty in the people who live there." Her lashes lifted and the stunningly clear blue eyes roved over the tawny gold waves of his hair, the handsome planes of his face, the solid breadth of his shoulders, before she continued. "She says the people are small and twisted, that they stink of sin and corruption. That to touch one, to—to lie with one, can only breed more corruption in the womb and condemn the immortal soul to everlasting hellfire."

"She said all that, did she? Words of comfort to cheer you on your journey?"

"I . . . had never seen an Englishman before," she confessed shyly, her eyes finding his again. "Only the señora, who told me once she used to be the most beautiful woman in her village."

"Had she been enjoying too much Madeira at the time?" Pitt asked with a frown.

The duchess tilted her face higher into the light and smiled in a way that sent Pitt's heart into his throat. "I believe she must have been, for you are not the smallest part ugly. Or frightening. And you smell . . . quite wonderful."

Pitt's tongue suddenly felt as dry and matted as a skein of uncombed wool. All of his wit and most of his senses deserted him, and he could think of nothing either charming or amusing to say in return. He could only think of what he would forfeit at that particularly desperate moment—an arm, a leg, all his teeth, his ears, his toes—just to kiss her bow-shaped mouth one time.

The moment faded along with her smile. "What do you think will happen to me when we come to England? Will I be . . . sent to prison?"

"Good God, no. You will be treated with all the courtesy and respect due a royal visitor. Judging by what your maid has told you about England, I can only imagine the stories you have heard about our Queen, but I promise you, none of them are true."

"She is not thin and old and does not have hair the color of unripe cherries?"

"Her Majesty is slender, and mature, and her hair is . . . er, reddish, yes, but would pale to inconsequence beside Captain Spence's beard."

"She does not hang priests and burn those who follow the Catholic faith?"

"She . . . discourages them from practicing openly, but the fires, I am afraid, belong to your own Court of Inquisition."

A fine crease of a frown reappeared. "And she has not

kept her only sister locked away in a prison cell for nineteen years?"

"Mary Stuart is her half sister and has plotted ceaselessly to assassinate Elizabeth and take the throne by force. She had the throne of Scotland and could not keep it through all her wild affairs and schemings. Our Queen has tried on numerous occasions to effect a reconciliation, only to uncover yet another plot, another attempt to steal the throne, another assassin lurking in the shadows. Would your King react any differently to someone who repeatedly committed outright acts of treason?"

"I do not know how our King would react, I am only—" She stopped and bit her lip, consigning her face to the shadows again. "I am not privy to Court discussions."

It was not the first time Doña Maria had taken refuge behind the innocence and ignorance of her position. Many times, in fact, when the discussions over the meal table became heated—which they often did with Spence, Dante, and Beau expressing their opinions as freely as flowing water—the duchess would grow visibly pale and cringe in apprehension of any attempt to draw her into the conversation. Pitt supposed it was because she had been raised in a convent and groomed to do nothing more than marry into a rich alliance. Nonetheless, she was a sharp contrast to someone like Beau Spence, who spoke her mind with a frankness and authority that brought to mind a not too distant parallel with England's own queen.

But then everything about Doña Maria Piacenza was a sharp contrast to Beau Spence. And while Pitt had come to admire the captain's daughter for her intelligence and wit—not to mention her skill at the helm of a ship—he was not about to discount the appeal of a woman whose unfounded fears and vulnerability struck at the very soul of chivalry.

It was true she had been taken as a hostage to ensure safe passage home, but political hostages were taken frequently, on both sides of the Channel, and exchanged on a regular, almost amicable basis. The more valuable the hostage, the quicker the exchange.

Pitt looked down at the duchess's hands again, which were now worrying the elaborate lacing on the cuff of her sleeve. They were slender, delicate hands, devoid of the sort of gaudy jewelry most nobles liked to wear to flaunt their wealth. Her only adornment was a plain gold circlet, molded at one end to the shape of a tiny hand, the other an equally tiny heart, the two twined together to close the circlet.

Was she married? Was the ring worn to signify her heart belonged to another?

"Maria," he murmured, easing closer and placing his hands on her shoulders, "Maria, I don't want to squander what little time we have together debating politics or—"

The duchess reacted as much to the familiar use of her name as she did to the warmth of his hands and body pressing against hers. She recoiled sideways and spun fully into the light, her hands flying up to rest against the base of her white throat.

Pitt acknowledged both infractions at once. "I'm sorry. I'm so sorry, Doña Maria, I did not mean any disrespect—"

"We can have no time together, señor. I should not have come out here alone with you tonight; I must not be alone with you again." She turned and ran along the deck and was swallowed into the shadows of the hatchway before Geoffrey Pitt could uproot his feet to follow. He caught the merest glimpse of the hem of her cloak as she dashed into her cabin, but he was too late to earn more than the sound of the door slamming in his face.

He leaned his hands on the rough surface of the wood,

fisting them against the urge to open it and force his way inside. Behind him the door to Spence's cabin was open, spilling a wide shaft of bright light into the companionway. The slamming of the duchess's door had caused a notice-able break in the conversation, and he heard the scraping of a chair as Agnes Frosthip hurriedly excused herself.

Pitt stared at the closed door a moment longer, then pushed himself away. He crossed paths with the duenna but ignored her glowering expression with the same tense indifference he ignored the eyebrow Dante raised askance. He returned to his seat and snatched up the bottle of wine, splashing a healthy draft in his cup before glaring at Dante, Beau, and Spence to resume whatever discussion they had been having before he interrupted.

In actual fact, with the duenna present, they had not been discussing anything remotely interesting to either Beau or Simon Dante and while both had been trying to find some excuse to end the evening, both had been wary of the look in Spence's eye warning them against leaving him alone with Agnes Frosthip. But now Pitt was back and Frosthip was gone, although there appeared to be no significant in-crease in pleasure at the exchange of one surly face for another.

Spence thumped his goblet on the table. "Damned if I haven't dried out my mouth tryin' to keep that codface from going on an' on about herself an' her fine life in Spain. If we were any closer to the coast, I'd gladly mount a sail on her arse an' let her swim for it."

"I think she has warmed to you, Father," Beau sug-gested. "Perhaps she was trying to impress you."

"Impress me?" The red fuzz of his beard gaped open. "God's liver, girl. I'd sooner risk splinters from a pine knot as poke anythin' she has to offer. Aye, Cap'n, an' ye've been a dread good help fer a man worth near as much as Francis bloody Drake. Could ye not have jumped in a time or two an' dazzled the drone with some o' yer wit an' charm?"

"Neither my wit nor my charm seems to hold any merit these days," Dante answered glibly, toying with a bead of moisture on the rim of his goblet.

"Aye, well, no wonder at that, broodin' all the blessed day long over them papers. Plymouth is still two weeks away by my reckonin', plenty o' time to work out a code . . . if it's there."

"It's there," Dante said evenly. "I just haven't seen it."

"Aye, well, I've got better things to mull on. For one, I've a hold full o' treasure to make the rest o' my days as easy as easy can be. For another, I've got a comely widow woman on New Street who should be watchin' the port every day about now, waitin' for me to drop anchor. Broad as a beam she is, but strong enough to squeeze me till my eyes roll back in my head. An' no teeth. Not a one. Doesn't waste a breath or a beat on idle prattle. Not like this one—" He crooked a thumb at the duenna's empty chair. "Like as not, a man would have to stuff her mouth with flannel to keep her from talkin' him to death."

Grinning at his own humor, Spence glanced at Beau, who was shredding a sliver of wood she had gouged out of the table, then at Dante, who was still chasing beads of sweat down the side of his goblet. Pitt was staring at his hands as if he wanted to crush the heavy gold cup between them.

"Cap'n . . . have ye no heart's desire waitin' fer ye on yer return? An' I don't mean yer business with Bloodstone, or the Queen, or the Queen's counsel. Is there naught . . . by tradition . . . ye normally do on yer first night home in port?"

Dante pursed his lips and raised his dark head. His eyes flicked barely perceptibly over to Beau before he smiled at Spence. "My heart's desire, if I must name one, would be a fat, tender haunch of beef swimming in gravy, pillowed on a bed of biscuits so soft and thick and slippery with butter, I won't have to chew. Aye, and another platter of onions roasted in garlic and mustard, served alongside a charred capon drowning in its own juices. And a pie. A gooseberry pie as high as my arm, with a crisp sugar crust and half a spadeful of clotted cream." He sipped at his wine and flared his nostrils as if the scents were saturating his senses as he spoke. "After that, if I still had any desires, I would consider my options over a tall tankard of stout English ale."

Jonas, whose mouth had gone slack during the recitation, firmed it up with an effort and raised his goblet in a sincere toast. "Cap'n . . . ye're a bastard after my own heart. An' blow my soul, I'd be honored to share that repast with ye; that an' aught else ye can think of twixt here an' Plymouth. Ye'll stay with us there, o' course, for as long as ye please. Beau an' I, we've only humble lodgings compared to what ye must be used to, but it's a roof an' a bed, an' a place to soak the salt off yer skin afore ye get on about yer business."

Dante vaguely noted the small choking sound Beau made in her throat. "I thank you for the invitation, Jonas, but my . . . business . . . won't allow me to dally overlong in Plymouth. Especially not if too many men recognize my face."

"Aye, aye. Ye'll not be wantin' Bloodstone to hear your name too loudly, at least until ye know which way the wind is blowin'. Hell an' all, if it helps ye stay dead awhile longer, I'll gladly take all the credit for the *San Pedro*. 'Tis the least I can do," he beamed broadly, "for one o' the brotherhood."

"You put me in your debt again," Dante said genially.

"Bah! Just put a drop more wine in everyone's cup, that'll be payment enough."

Beau abandoned the shredded splinter and stood. "Since you appear to be safe from attack now, Father, I think I will bid you all good-night."

She left, promising to check the watch, and went up on deck, breathing deep to remove the smell of stale food and candle wax from her lungs. The wind was blowing briskly from the east and she imagined she could taste and smell the olive groves of Spain where they grew five hundred miles off the starboard beam. Another day or two and they would be past the northernmost tip of the country and running parallel to the Bay of Biscay. With luck they would clear the Channel in another two weeks and be dropping anchor in Plymouth Sound.

As if to challenge any doubts she might have, the *Egret* leapt in one graceful bound after another across the swells. The night was moonless, the sky a black velvet canvas with uncountable millions of stars painted in a wide swath overhead. Billy Cuthbert had the helm and Beau could see at a glance that the sails were perfectly set to take the best advantage of the wind. The ship was moving fast, throwing an appreciable feather of white water off her bows. Even as Beau watched, the foresails were trimmed and those on the main and mizzen were slowly turned and reset, fluttering like great bat wings until they took the wind and strained forward again.

Beau nodded to herself in silent approval. Billy had joined the crew of the *Egret* four years ago, a gangly, sullen orphan with no ship's skills and bruised to the bone from an indentured life with a tavern keeper. He had clubbed the taverner on the head after taking one beating too many and stowed away, thinking he had killed the brute. Billy was eighteen now and a fine seaman, quick to learn and even quicker to smile, especially when Beau was nearby. She knew—the entire crew knew—he was smitten with her, but she had never given it any thought or credence before. And although there was only two years' difference in their ages, she considered herself so much older and worldly wise, she could not imagine ever looking at someone with such puppyish longing in her eyes.

Plagued by restlessness she turned from the rail and swung herself into the main shrouds. She started climbing, finding the ratlines with her hands and feet, passing the huge ghostly curl of the main course, then the smaller topgallant and royal. Set higher still was the small moonraker, aptly named for anyone with the nerve to perch on the trestletree just beneath it. The sail itself was reefed tonight, probably because Cuthbert had deemed it unnecessary, and Beau found herself clinging tightly to the mast to ride out the more pronounced pitch caused by the ship's motion.

She hailed the crewman who stood watch in the crow's nest on the foremast and relieved him. It was not an uncommon thing for Beau to do, and with two hours, more or less, remaining until the next watch change, she waved off his thanks as he descended to his hammock below.

Seated snugly on the trestletree, forty feet above the deck, there was nothing above her but the sky and stars, no sound other than the wind humming through the sails and the distant rush of water beneath the keel. The vast belling of the sails obscured everything below except for the bright, curling tails of spume that scrolled out in the *Egret's* wake. It was her favorite place on board, her private place, where she came to think or worry away from prying eyes.

Unfortunately these days, it was more difficult to get the image of someone else's eyes out of her head. The starlight was bright enough to reflect off the surface of the water, silver in places, light blue off the crest of waves: the exact color of Simon Dante's eyes. She had seen them glancing at her throughout the evening, throughout each evening they endured in the close confines of Spence's cabin. Sometimes she thought she saw understanding in their depths, sometimes mockery, other times simple anger. Her own mind had been in a turmoil since she had spent that single night of bliss locked fast in his arms. Every night since, she had swung restlessly in her hammock replaying each kiss, each caress, a hundred times.

It was worse sitting at the table, inevitably drawing unfavorable comparisons with the doe-eyed Duchess of Navarre. It was a certainty Beau did not know how to flutter her eyelashes so demurely—blinking rapidly only made her dizzy. She knew how to strap herself into a corset and padded bumroll; she even knew how to walk in a wheeled farthingale without getting her toes hooked in the loops, for all the good it did her. But she couldn't breathe in the contraptions and she couldn't sit any length of time without turning blue, and she certainly could not abide a stiff and scratchy neck ruff strangling her throat, obstructing the path of food from her plate to her mouth.

Nate Hawethorne had expected all that and more to be endured by the woman he married. He expected refined social graces and a woman who would demur to his every opinion on any subject, right or wrong. More to the point, there were several generations of pure, aristocratic blood flowing through his veins. Far too pure and aristocratic ever to mix with the dull red offerings of the daughter of a one-legged merchant. The night Hawethorne had made that abundantly clear was also the night Beau had realized most men only wanted one thing from a woman and once they had it, they sloughed them off without a thought or care.

De Tourville's blood ran even bluer. He had chateaus in France, estates in England, even a small duchy in Portugal if the rumors were to believed. All that on top of a healthy mistrust for women. To even *think* he wanted more than a pleasant diversion was ludicrous.

Even if she were willing to trade in her breeches for skirts and petticoats—which she was not—or willing to give up the sea for a life of luxury in some drafty old chateau—which she most definitely was not—or to trim her ways to suit the behavior of a respectable young lady—a pox on any such notion!—men like Dante and Hawethorne would still run as quickly as they could in the opposite direction. She was an oddity. A misfit.

An amusing diversion, nothing more.

"Listen to me," she muttered, gazing out over the immense, bleak beauty of the empty sea. "Just listen to me. As if it matters what he thinks of me. As if any of it matters at all. He had his fun and you had yours, now leave it at that. Just leave it!"

She gave the mast an angry slap just as the *Egret* took a sweeping dip. She made a grab for the reefing tackle too late to do more than feel it slither through her fingers. Her balance lost, she slid off the trestletree and fell headfirst, plunging past the upper royal and the topgallant, skidding off the taut canvas too quickly to snag a buntline and slow her descent.

The topsails, rigged to catch the westerly wind, were at a sharp angle to the main course, which was fixed and square, and she hit the wide upper yard squarely on her belly, driving the air out of her lungs with hardly more than a hollow *whoomfph*. Her foot hooked a line and she jerked to a halt, but she was hanging upside down with the air knocked out of her, disoriented with the stars at her feet and the sea overhead. The line, only twisted around her ankle, began to loosen as her weight depressed the sail. She thought she might have screamed but the sail belled forward again, smothering her face in canvas.

Chapter 17

Simon Dante wandered out onto the deck to relieve himself and remained at the rail, letting the breeze brush back his hair and fill the loose folds of his shirt. He braced his hands on the wood and let his head hang between his shoulders, cursing his own foolhardiness even as he wondered what hidey-hole Beau had taken herself off to tonight. He could, he supposed, hope against hope she was waiting for him in her cabin, but what point was to be gained in making a bigger fool of himself than he had already? She hadn't been there any night this past week. She was avoiding him as she would a festering boil.

In a way, he was glad. It had given him time to clear his head and focus on the course that lay before him. She had distracted him. Unsettled him. He had been full of rage and fury, bristling with a desire for revenge when he had come on board the *Egret*. Isabeau Spence had lured him back into a world of softness and sexual heat, her body had lured him into its silky folds and he had lost himself there. He had not offered anything and she had not demanded anything beyond that one night. She did not want anything from him now, not even conversation, so it seemed, and that should have suited him just fine.

So why was he unable to concentrate on anything for any length of time without closing his eyes and seeing her body stretched out pale and luminous in the moonlight? Why was he not able to look at her without his usual detachment, or fall asleep at night without first spending time staring into the darkness, craving the soft sound of her breath against his throat?

And why was he standing on a chilled, windy deck, hoping to pace Beau Spence out of his system?

He still could not rationalize his attraction to her. She was coarse and ill bred—a snobbish thought, to be sure, but one that was as ingrained as the manners and mannerisms that kept him from becoming anything but the Comte de Tourville, regardless of how hard he tried to avoid his titles and responsibilities. His former wife had been the ideal, suitable match; a dazzling beauty with impeccable social graces and a blinding ambition that would have left any man gasping in her wake. He had indeed been dazzled and blinded, and she had left him gasping at the coldness and treachery that flowed through her veins. She had made him cynical and mistrustful, wary of ever surrendering his soul to any woman again.

And yet, Isabeau Spence was not like any woman he had encountered before. If she had a thought she spoke it or wore it openly on her face. She was fiercely independent and fiercely possessive of her freedom, and he doubted there was any man alive who could tame her completely . . . or want to tame her completely.

He felt like a cat trapped in a cage, and he wished for stronger winds that might blow them to England's shores sooner. The quicker he was off the *Egret* and away from the temptation of those golden tiger eyes, the quicker he could return to a more comfortable state of indifference. A drunken, senseless night at a brothel was what he needed. What both he and Pitt needed to clear their heads and shake them back to reality.

Dante stroked a hand along the cold bronze body of one of the demi-cannon. A glance at where the lines from the topsails were dogged told him the set without having to search the darkness above, and it was purely force of habit that made him glance up. After all, it wasn't his ship, wasn't his course to order, wasn't his place to challenge the bearing of the wind. . . .

At first he saw nothing but the pale bloom of canvas interrupting the tableau of stars and night sky. But then he caught sight of the figure of a man dangling down, swinging against the mainsail, one foot tangled around the clew lines, the other crabbing as frantically as his arms were windmilling to grasp hold of something more secure.

The scream was brief and muffled, leaving the distinct impression of the owner's identity trembling on the air, and Dante was in the shrouds, climbing, before the sounds of the wind and the sea had completely absorbed it. He reached the stout upper yard and crossed it with hardly any thought to his own footing or balance.

"Beau? Beau! Hold fast, I'm almost there!"

"M-my—my foot is slipping!"

Anchoring himself to the mast with one arm he slid down and straddled the yardarm, reaching down, lunging for a fistful of her clothing just as the wind relented and the sail slackened. Her foot slipped free and she screamed again, a short, panicked cry that was bitten off when she felt the pressure tighten on her doublet.

"Grab my arm! Reach up and grab my arm!"

Beau managed to clutch at his sleeve. A powerful surge of strength tautened the muscles as he hauled her upward and she felt herself upended and lifted over the yardarm so that she sat straddling it with the mast at her back and the bulk of his chest in front.

Dante released her doublet in exchange for a more secure hold around her waist. "Are you all right? Are you hurt?"

A rapid shaking of her head was the only answer she could muster.

"You're sure? You haven't broken or twisted anything?"

She hesitated and he could see her turning her ankles, testing her knees and hips. She shook her head again and leaned forward, burying her face in the crook of his shoulder.

He let go of a lengthy sigh and waited for the pounding in his chest to abate. "Should I even ask what you were doing up here?"

"I . . . come here all the time," she replied, her words muffled against his throat. "To think."

"To . . . think?"

"To *think*! Sometimes I just need to get away from everybody and everything and *think*. Is that so terrible? So hard to understand?"

"No, but on a night like this, do you not *think* you could have found someplace a little less venturous? And where the devil is the watch?"

"I relieved him."

"You—?" He swore under his breath again. "If this were my ship, and you were one of my crew, I don't give a damn how good or valuable you are, I would—"

She lifted her head, lifted her eyes slowly to his, and he was startled to see a bright film shimmering along her lashes, starting to swell at the corners.

"—I would give you the thrashing of your life," he said gently, "for risking your neck like this."

"I told you," she whispered. "I have never so much as cut my hand or . . . stubbed my toe . . . until you came on board."

"Forgive me," he murmured, "if I have brought this ill fortune down upon you."

He reached up and tucked a wisp of hair behind her ear, then urged her head back onto his shoulder again. "Go ahead. You can cry if you want to, I promise I will not tell a soul."

"There is nothing to tell, because I never cry! *Never!*"

"Forgive me again," he said softly, stroking his hand down her hair. "It must have been a trick of the light."

"Stop that."

"Stop what?"

"That."

He stopped stroking her hair and moved his hand away. "This?"

She took a small breath. "No, not that."

He put his hand back.

"Stop l-laughing at me."

"I swear I am not."

"You are," she insisted. "You're *always* laughing at me. You laughed when you found out I was a woman, and again when you were told I was the ship's pilot. You found it amusing when I tried to shoot you on the *Virago* and you did not take me the least bit seriously when I said I would fillet you into tiny pieces if you kissed me. And in the cabin that night—" Her head came off his shoulder and not only her eyes, but her cheeks, were suspiciously damp.

"Yes? In the cabin that night?"

"You were laughing at my ignorance," she whispered. "I know you were."

Perhaps it was because of the bad fright she had just experienced, or perhaps it was the starlight playing with his powers of perception, but when she looked at him, her guard was down and the full measure of her vulnerability was suddenly, unwittingly, revealed in her eyes. The ship still pitched side to side, sliding forward and rearing back as it carved through each new swell, and he was forced to keep one hand grasped around a mast brace, the other clamped securely around Beau's waist, but he could and did draw her even closer than she had managed to insist herself.

"No, mam'selle," he said slowly. "If I was laughing at anyone's ignorance, it was my own. Believe me, Isabeau . . . it was my own."

A small huff of air escaped her lips, and while it might have shaped the word *liar*, he did not contest the charge with more words. The stars shifted dizzily overhead and the wind snatched at locks of his hair, blowing it forward so that when he dragged her mouth up to his, silky black strands were trapped between them.

She scarcely noticed. Or cared. He was kissing her, that was all that mattered, and she flung her arms around his neck, kissing him back with a desire that bordered on desperation.

They broke apart, both gasping quick, shallow breaths, both staring at one another as if expecting some form of rejection. When none was forthcoming, they melted together again, open mouthed and open eyed, holding one another hostage until the tremors in their bodies threatened to rival the tremors coursing through the mast.

He tried to draw her closer and cursed at the impossibility. He tried to appease himself by devouring her with kisses, thinking it would do until he could get them down out of the rigging and he could devour her in other ways. His hand did not have as much faith and went beneath her doublet instead, unfastening the belt that held her hose snug around her waist. He gave the wool a fierce tug, tearing the seam open from waist to crotch, and, with his mouth slanting more determinedly over any effort to protest, he slid his fingers deftly through the gap.

She was sleek and slippery, and he stroked deep into the heated folds of her flesh, groaning when he felt how hot she was, how tight, how soft and wet and quick she was to respond to the intrusion. The first shivering volley of pleasure was starting to tighten all the grasping little muscles even as her hands clutched at his shoulders and her head shook side to side in denial. Spasms drenched her with more heat and it was not enough, suddenly, just to hear her crying out his name in disbelieving whispers. He withdrew his fingers and made a similarily accommodating gap in his own clothing, then, with her body still quivering with shock, with pleasure, he hooked her legs over his thighs and lifted her onto his lap.

"You're mad," she gasped. "We'll both fall."

"Not if you hold on," he snarled savagely, "and trust me."

Beau spared a glance for the deck, still thirty feet below, and then she spared nothing, for the solid shaft of his flesh was furrowing up inside her, so hard and thick and unyielding, she had no choice but to lock her arms around his shoulders and trust his madness. Both of his hands were braced on the mast now, his feet were stirruped through lines of rigging. Every muscle and sinew in his arms and across his back stiffened as he pushed up into her clinging heat and a primitive sound broke from his throat.

The ship took a frisky leap through a deep trough and one of his feet slipped, leaving him scrambling a moment to balance himself and his precious burden on a yardarm no wider around than a tree trunk.

"Wait," he commanded desperately. "Wait. Hold yourself there, or I swear—"

Beau was panting lightly against his neck, her body paralyzed, not from fear but from the almost inconceivable depth of his penetration.

"You might be right," he admitted raggedly. "This is mad. I can't move. I can't . . . do anything. And I don't want to hurt you."

"You are not hurting me," she assured him on the outward escape of another breath. "And you don't have to move. You don't have to do anything at all."

To prove it, she arched her back and let the ship's motion press her hips forward, swallowing him to the hilt. They both groaned, then groaned again when the *Egret* rocked back and the pressure eased.

"Don't . . . do that again," he warned softly. "Or I will explode."

"I . . . can't help it," she cried, half laughing, half sobbing, as the *Egret* plunged again. The rocking motion, less pronounced on deck, was magnified by the weight and pull of the sails, by the rush of the wind, and the vibrations that shook the stem of the mast. Each giddy swoop brought him deeper and deeper inside her until it seemed he might touch her heart.

Dante's arms were shaking, his teeth were clenched tight enough to make his jaw ache, but there was nothing he could do. His body tensed and his flesh reared, and his pleasure did indeed explode with a stunning lack of finesse. Beau felt the throb of each scalding burst and bit down hard on his shoulder to keep from crying out, to keep from screaming as the waves of ecstasy began to sweep through her with an equally fierce and unrelenting mercilessness.

"It occurs to me," he said some time later, his voice hoarse and muffled against her throat, "we might both need rescuing."

Beau shuddered softly and burrowed closer to the massive bulk of his chest. The conflagrant waves of heat had passed but not the pleasure. If anything it remained steady and threatening, sending small spirals of warm thrills along her spine and through her limbs.

"We should try standing up," he suggested gently.

She opened her eyes and debated the question from the point of if she *wanted* to stand up.

"I don't think I can," she whispered. "I don't even think I can move."

Dante risked unclamping a hand from the mast ring and found her chin, forcing her to look up at him. Her eyes were glazed and heavy-lidded. Her mouth was deliciously puffed and moist but he refrained from kissing her, suspecting if he did they might never find the strength to untangle themselves and climb safely down the rigging. Even now the motion of the *Egret* was working its mischief again, making him aware of the sleek, molten friction where their bodies were still joined.

"We'll make a pretty sight when the watch changes."

Beau frowned and leaned forward, silencing his common sense with her lips. His tongue was too gallant to refuse her invitation and she welcomed him into her mouth with a languid sigh, running all ten fingers up into his hair and refusing to let him go until he'd been properly rebuked.

He groaned but still he eased her reluctantly away. She resisted halfheartedly for another moment, then let him lift her off his thighs and settle her back on the yardarm. They were both embarrassingly wet, although he seemed to regard the evidence of their expended passions with somewhat less mortification than she.

"*Mon petit corsaire féroce,*" he mused.

"What?"

"My fierce little corsair. Only you could have inspired me to such desperate measures."

"So you admit it. You *are* mad." She glanced at the belling sail below them. "On a yardarm, for pity's sake. We could have both ended up in the sea." She looked to her rumpled and torn clothing and sighed. "It would not hurt to learn a little restraint."

"Me?" His dark brows shot up. "I have been showing remarkable restraint this past week. You cannot know the number of times I have been tempted to haul you out of your miserable hammock again and— By the way, you never thanked me."

"For what?"

"For letting you enjoy a good night's sleep . . . alone . . . in your own bed."

Distracted momentarily by the shape of his mouth and the intriguing way he used it to fashion words, she gazed up into his eyes and wondered if she should feel cheated or guilty.

"So . . . why did you do it?"

"For one thing, you were dead tired. For another . . . I did not intend to force something on you that you didn't really want. I foolishly thought—like the arrogant bastard you believe me to be—I would wait until you came to me."

"I did not come to you tonight," she pointed out quietly.

"Not by design, no. But neither did you push me away. Or refuse me my madness. And after tonight, whether I come to you or you come to me, it will make little difference in the end."

A gust of wind caused Beau to turn her head and look out over the vastness of the sea. It defied all logic to be straddling a yardarm thirty feet above the gundeck of a moving ship, her thighs slick, her body runny and warm, her sex pouting, quivering for more. It defied every shred of common sense and judgment to even let there be an 'after tonight' . . . yet what could she do? Where could she go to hide from him? The *Egret* was a small ship and she was an even smaller fool.

"Surely you know . . . this cannot possibly last beyond the first step we take on English soil."

There was a very noticeable hesitation before he said, "England is more than two weeks away. We could grow quite bored with each other in that time—gallery balconies and swaying yards aside."

She rested her head against the mast, feeling suddenly trapped in the narrow space between his outstretched arms. "And if we become bored with each other before then?"

He shrugged blithely. "Then it's you to your solitary hammock and me to my solitary bed."

"And on to a civil parting on the quayside in Plymouth?" she added dryly.

"It will be so civil, mam'selle, the angels will weep." He laughed at her expression and pulled himself up so that he was standing on the yardarm. He adjusted his clothes, then reached a hand down to help her to her feet, and on an impulse drew her against his chest, holding her there long enough for her to feel the hardness rising in his body again.

"But for now, *ma petite*, and for the next two weeks, we'll make them weep over other things, shall we?"

Chapter 18

Over the course of the next three days not a moment passed that Beau would have described as boring, occupied as she was with the normal, if somewhat nerve-wracking, routines of guiding an overburdened galleon through seasonable squalls and strong currents.

The evening meals continued to be a trial, more for Spence than anyone else, once it was deemed a certainty that Agnes Frosthip had set her sights on him; she even appeared at the dinner table with her moustache shaved off, a clear indication to everyone but Jonas that he was a doomed man. As the duenna's attention turned more and more to Spence, it lapsed even further toward her royal charge. Had the duchess been willing, Pitt's stolen moments could have become outright theft of virtue for all her chaperone seemed to notice. It was Doña Maria, however, who took care never to be caught alone again with the handsome master gunner, although it was obvious to anyone with half a wit—which excluded Pitt by this point—that he would not have had to resort to theft; she would gladly have given him anything he cared to take.

Beau continued to excuse herself early from the evening meals, wanting nothing either by word or gesture to put more of a suspicious gleam in her father's eye than was already there. To her credit she managed not to blush whenever Dante glanced her way, which he did with reckless frequency and with more suggested intimacy than she would have preferred. Conversely, at other times, it was a struggle for her to keep from staring openly at his starkly sensual countenance, especially if the light caught his smile a certain way, or his hands moved in a manner that brought to mind the treacherous skill of those long, deft fingers.

She took to pacing out her frustrations on the gallery balcony during the politic quarter hour before Dante joined her. Sometimes they talked. Sometimes they argued. Always it depended on the mood Beau had worked herself into, whether she had accepted what they did together as casual and finite and a pleasurable way to pass the nights . . . or if she was convinced it was foolish, reckless, callous, and predatory on his part, senseless and potentially destructive on hers.

Either way they ended up naked and breathless in a tangle of sweat-slicked arms and legs, with Beau telling herself it was the last time. It had to be the last time. He was becoming too powerful an intoxicant in her blood, drugging her with his passion, draining her with his prowess and potency. It simply wasn't fair.

Once. Once only she had managed to escape the cabin before his eyes, his hands, his mouth, had lured her into the realm of sensual decadence. She managed to stay away too . . . long enough to wonder why he had not come after her. To wonder if he was, indeed, growing bored.

She had returned to the cabin on some lame excuse and found him bent over his infernal documents again, his handsome face awash in candlelight. His expression had been cool enough to suggest indifference, but his eyes had betrayed too much relief for either one of them to waste effort on words. She had gone to him and he had taken her as he had wanted to take her that first day, sprawled naked on a bed of scattered papers, her hair spread in a wild spill of auburn beneath them.

The morning of the fourth day, she woke when dawn was nothing more than a hint of pearl-gray seeping over the horizon. Dante was actually asleep beside her, a rarity she had come to appreciate in the short time she'd had a chance to study his habits. It was as if he begrudged wasting even that much time, letting life go by without being in absolute control, absolute command.

Not wanting to disturb him, she eased herself out from beneath his arm and padded barefoot to the chair, groping through the gloom for an identifiable garment in the pile that had been so hastily discarded. Her shirt, she was not suprised to discover, was ripped into two halves, drawing a muffled curse from her lips. Dante's was beside it and she pulled it over her head, losing herself briefly in the voluminous folds. She went out onto the gallery and leaned on the rail, letting the wind comb through the tangles in her hair. From the sound of the wash and the height of the wake curling out behind them, she guessed their speed to be between eight and ten knots; the faint sound of a bell overhead tolled the fifth hour of the morning.

She sighed and cupped her chin in her hands. The soft, indistinct light that hung over the far edge of the sea was spreading in gauzy strips, lightening to pinks and golds and grays. Soon the sea would become a vast, shimmering puddle of bronze and the wash would glitter with the first pinpoints of sunlight.

There was a chill in the air and she closed her eyes to

savor the crispness. Her skin rippled with a spray of goose-flesh but before she could hug her arms and chafe some heat through the cool linen of Dante's shirt, a pair of large, warm hands slid around her waist and invited her to share the heat of his body.

"I thought you were asleep," she murmured.

"Mmm." He nuzzled aside a tousle of curls and pressed his lips to the nape of her neck. "Come back inside and wake me properly."

Desire stirred along her spine, spreading outward like a slow, rolling wave. After three nights of avid explorations of each other's body, she would have expected to have at least grown more immune to the timbre of his voice, but even that small measure of control had deserted her. The low, throaty vibrations were as tempting as sin itself and she found herself shifting slightly in his arms, inviting his hands to cup her full, swollen breasts.

"I am surprised *you* aren't still asleep," he murmured against the curve of her spine.

"I . . . wanted to watch the sunrise."

"Really? I would rather watch you rise all flushed and pink beneath me."

"I rose quite enough last night," she said through the catch in her voice, "thank you very much."

He laughed softly and his hands slid downward. They met over her belly, then continued lower, pressing into the juncture of her thighs, pulling her even closer to his chest. As cool as the air was, his big body was as hot as a brazier. His skin was heated velvet, the muscles smooth and hard, burnished as bronze as the sea in the growing light. He loomed extremely large behind her and she felt as she always did: too short, too small, too inadequate, to accommodate all that massive power and strength.

Yet she knew it wasn't true. She fit him as a glove fit a hand, snug and sleek and tight.

"You're thinking of something other than sunrises," he mused. "I can tell."

His fingers seduced her through the linen and another ribbon of heat unfurled within her, coiling between her thighs, slithering past flesh that had become far too knowledgeable in such a short time. It was shameless, that's what it was. It was shameless and brazen and . . .

"There," she whispered, "please."

Dante smiled against her nape and snatched up the hem of the shirt she was wearing. A hard-muscled leg urged her thighs apart, wide enough for him to slide his partly aroused flesh into the warmth. Beau cursed softly at this new torment, this new wickedness to add to his repertoire. His fingers were still dancing and stroking, now his flesh was stretching and expanding, vying for equal attention.

Beau leaned forward at his murmured urging and he curled an arm around her waist, holding her firmly against him. He probed the lush, pearly folds, not quite deep enough to penetrate, but teasingly enough to send her head bowing forward on a shiver.

"I have the morning watch," she groaned.

"It's hours away yet."

She sucked in a quick breath and shuddered as his big body stretched and throbbed and taunted her with a brief, swiftly retracted thrust.

"You are taking shameful advantage of my position, Captain," she whispered.

Dante's hands encircled her breasts, finding the nipples peaked into hard beads. He kneaded them, caressed them, gently chafed them, until she was pushing back against him with wriggling impatience.

"If I am, you have only yourself to blame. Standing here,

robed in my shirt, with those long, luscious legs bare beneath it"—his lips nuzzled her neck and he withheld more than he offered—"how could I resist?"

Her lips parted with a moan and she braced her hands on the rail.

"How indeed," she accused breathlessly, "when you know I don't have the strength to fight you off?"

He offered up a low, husky laugh. "You should never make an admission like that to a man, *mon enfant*. But why do you still think it is necessary to fight me, even after all this time?"

"Why do you," she gasped, "always think your attentions bring a woman pleasure? Is it so inconceivable to imagine a woman *not* wanting to share your lusty ways each time the urge comes upon you?"

"You mean if she, for instance, wanted to watch the sunrise instead?"

"Some people do, you know."

His body stopped moving. He withdrew himself completely and stepped back a pace, offering a formal bow. "Then by all means, I would do the gentlemanly thing and let her watch it."

Beau stood with her mouth open and her body trembling. The shock of watching him walk back inside the cabin, combined with the sudden absence of heat, eventually spurred her into following him, but by then he was standing over the washbowl, humming faintly to himself.

"What are you doing?"

"What does it look like I'm doing?" He held the sharpened edge of a knife to his cheek and started to scrape away the shadow of beard stubble. "How was the sunrise?"

Beau bit down sharply on the fleshy pulp of her lip and moved away from the gallery door. She kept a wary distance between them, not entirely believing him to have given up so easily, for it was enormously apparent he was still as aroused as she.

"I trust your hand is steady enough not to cut your throat."

He winced, having done just that, and glared at her across the room. His fingers grasped the knife tighter and he turned back to the small square of polished metal that served as a mirror, smiling grimly as he concentrated on avoiding major veins.

Beau sat petulantly in the chair behind her chart table and tapped her fingers on the wooden top. Her bare feet rustled on the papers that had been swept to the floor last night, and still keeping a glowering eye on the pirate wolf, she leaned over and started gathering them up. There were the original documents in Spanish as well as Dante's translations and as she picked them up she separated them into two piles. Other sheets had nothing but scribbling and angry black scratches of ink, and there were at least a dozen pages crumpled into balls and tossed to the floor in frustration.

"I hope," she said as she stared beligerently at the expansive waste of precious vellum, "you are not squandering *all* of my valuable paper on your scrawlings."

"When we reach Plymouth, I will buy you a thousand more sheets. And they are not scrawlings. They are diligent attempts to untangle the mind of an ambitious, bloodthirsty, ruthless fanatic who uses religion as a sword to carve an empire for himself."

Beau arched a delicate eyebrow. "Whereas we heretics of the world are more honest in our greed and ambition?"

"We don't use God as an excuse to conquer," he snapped angrily. "I have seen whole villages burned, people tortured and mutilated, all in the name of Catholic purification. These"—he pointed to the scars that crisscrossed his back—"were not given to me in an effort to make me convert. After twenty lashes I was willing to pray to anyone who would listen."

"So . . . you are a heretic in the true sense of the word?"

"You sound shocked at the notion. Dare I suppose I can have lowered myself any further in your esteem?"

Beau's brow cleared. "It would hardly be a noticeable decline."

Her sarcasm earned a caustic glance. "In that case, what shall I offer in my defense? My mother, rest her soul, was English and a devout Protestant. Father, may the devil and all his disciples be enjoying the former comte's company, made pilgrimages to Rome each year in order to wash the pope's feet. My brother owed a great deal of money to the Jews and married one to clear a debt. My own wife would have worshipped any idol, so long as it was made out of gold, but her preference was for pentacles and ram's horns and kneeling before altars draped in black."

"She worshipped the devil?"

"*Au contraire*, mam'selle. She *was* the devil and took pleasure in sacrificing men's souls."

As familiar as Beau was becoming with his body and his moods, the man himself was as much of an enigma as ever. He did not like to talk about himself. He rarely referred to his life in France and never ever spoke of his former wife without first sharpening his tongue on a curse. Thus Beau could not help herself, she had to ask. "Why on earth did you marry her?"

"Why?" Dante glared at the distorted reflection in the mirror as if it could provide the answer. "Because it was my duty, as the Comte de Tourville, to do so. Because she was beautiful. And bewitching. And because I still had a soul, possibly even a conscience then too. She made short work of both, however, and I made short work of her."

"You divorced her?"

"I would have preferred to drown her, like a stray cat, but, aye, at great expense to my pocket and what was left of my reputation I rid myself of her." He glanced speculatively at Beau's reflection before he continued. "There were children involved. Two of them: a boy and a girl. Neither of them was mine, a fact that still keeps my name prominent on the tongues of Court wags."

The admission was made altogether too casually and Beau wondered exactly how strongly he had braced himself before making it. Because he strove to give the impression his titles and responsibilities meant nothing to him at all, it probably should not have come as a shock to realize that they, like his wife, must have mattered very much at one time. The ridicule, the jokes at his expense, the general knowledge he had been cuckolded not once but twice, would have scarred his pride as deeply as any welts from a lash, and she could understand why he wore his arrogance like armor. He did not want to take the chance of being cut again.

"What did you do to her lovers?" she asked in an equally casual voice.

"The two I knew about? I shot them, then sent dear Annalise the parts of them she loved best."

The tension, the hard, piercing intensity, in his eyes remained locked on hers for another moment before he raised the blade and continued shaving.

Beau released the breath she had not been aware of holding and wondered if, by showing her his scars, he was testing her in some way? Deliberately giving her an opening so he could affirm in his own mind that all women were inherently cruel and not to be trusted? A week ago she would not have disappointed him, responding with gleeful scorn, using his humiliation as a weapon to slash at

his pride like a blade. But now . . . all she wanted to do—
and it shocked the devil out of her to admit it—was go to
him, put her arms around him, and tell him it did not
matter.

She could not do that, of course, for she would likely
be failing a test of another kind, the rules of which she
had established herself. She had been the one to insist it
could last only until they set the first foot on English soil.
Then he would be free and she would be free and they
would go their own separate ways again, with no presump-
tions, no grasping demands, no obligations of any kind.

Beau looked down at her hands. Odd, how they were
shaking.

She gave them something to do and tidied the papers
she had already tidied once. One of the sheets fell and as
she leaned over to pick it up, her eye scanned the page
filled with Dante's neat, precise script . . . the writing of an
aristocrat, not a pirate wolf, despite how hard he tried to
disassociate himself from his other life. Her own stylized
script took hours to labor over and had taken years to perfect in an effort to present the Black Swan as a scholarly
cartographer as opposed to a merchant's brat in breeches.

The irony was not lost on her as she glanced absently
down the page. He had translated harvest predictions, lists
of oats, grains, legumes, even poultry and fowl that would
be delivered to Spanish ports in the coming months. A
meaningless jumble of words, especially when her mind was
otherwise occupied.

Yet something caught her eye.

She wasn't really looking for anything, or even aware
she was absorbing the words off the page. She was too
aware of Simon Dante's broad back turned toward her,
shutting her out.

But the word *olive* was intrusive enough to break through the thickest fog of distraction.

"Why in heaven's name would they want to ship olives to Spain?" she muttered to herself. "The country is full of them now. Did you translate this correctly?" she asked in a louder voice. "It reads: 'The ship of olives will arrive in port no later than All Saints' Day.'"

He shot her the kind of glance that would have withered most men had they questioned his accuracy after so many frustrating hours of searching through an unending maze. "There are shipments of olives, peacocks, even rosaries, anticipated with great glee. Make what you will of it."

"Peacocks?" She leaned back in the chair and rubbed a hand across the nape of her neck. Jonas and Spit both claimed their napes prickled and their ballocks shriveled when something of great import was about to happen. At that particular moment Beau's neck felt raw enough to scratch and her nipples had peaked so hard, they felt like hillocks of ice.

"Simon—?"

The edge of the blade was poised just below his left ear where the flesh protecting the jugular was the thinnest. It was the first time she had called him anything other than Dante, Captain, or bastard, and he did not feel compelled to move or breathe until he determined the reason.

"Have you found something?"

"I don't know. Where are the paintings of the harbors?"

She followed the flicker of his eyes to the divided bin that held her charts. The Spanish parchments stood out from the others, and by the time she retrieved them, Dante was beside her, helping to roll them flat on the table.

Her eyes scanned the first one and did not see what she

wanted. The second offered nothing better, but the third brought a triumphant gust of air rushing past her lips.

"There," she said, stabbing a finger downward.

Dante leaned closer. The sun was not yet full in bloom and besides the shadows he had to contend with, there was the open, gaping edges of Beau's shirt. "What am I looking at?"

"Don't you know what ship this is?"

His face was level with hers as he questioned her sudden smile. A great many Spanish galleons were identifiable by their size, silhouettes, and gun batteries, especially to someone who had been plundering the Main for ten years. The galleasses were all distinguishable by the rows of oars that protruded from both sides, the thousand-ton *ratas*, Portugese carracks, and—because it was in their best interest to know—the six- to nine-hundred-ton treasure ships like the *San Pedro* were as familiar to English sea hawks as their own vessels.

The ships in all three paintings, which Dante had studied as diligently as he had studied the written documents, were nondescript and identical, with no immediately visible differences aside from the artist's attempt to give the harbor depth and dimensions; the ships in the foreground were larger, those anchored closer to shore were proportionately smaller. None showed more than a few token black gunports.

Beau looked smug. "It's the *Sancta Maria Encoronada*."

His eyebrows drew together in an undivided black slash. "How the devil do you know that?"

"Firstly—and as you've already remarked—because I have the patience to use a single-haired brush when I want special details; secondly, because I mark my charts with a black swan. It makes me tend to notice little things like trademarks and . . . peacock feathers."

Dante followed the tip of her finger to the minute detailing painted across the stern gallery of one of the galleons in the forefront. It was a tiny fan of peacock feathers, so muted and so skillfully worked into the bold rendering of the ship itself, it would be discernible only to another artist's eye—or to someone who knew what to look for. Even though he could see it now, so clearly it brought a curse to his lips, Dante was still dubious; but Beau had already turned her attention to the markings on one of the other sterns.

Her finger stabbed again. "Wheat sheaves: The *Santa Catalina*. And there . . . the *Nuestra Señora del Rosario*." She looked up. "Rosaries, for pity's sake."

"Olives?" Dante asked, scarcely daring to look.

Beau had to search the other two paintings before she found the small, delicate leaves that formed part of the cresting on the immense, fifty-gun *Napolitana*, the flagship of King Philip's navy.

"I am only guessing, but I would say your harvest predictions are a detailed accounting of what ships will be ready in what ports by a particular date," Beau said. "And if that's true"—she let the top two paintings roll themselves up again and stared at the third, the harbor Dante had previously identified—"if that's true . . . my God . . . there are at least forty, fifty ships in Cadiz alone, including half a dozen *ratas*."

Dante nodded grimly. "Any one of them capable of leading an invasion fleet."

"Then the rumors about an armada . . . ?"

"They were never rumors, *mon enfant*, they were truths the Queen chose not to believe."

"Surely she will have to believe them now?"

"Indeed she will, and she will have to strike now, strike hard and fast, while the Spaniards are gathered together like suckling pigs around a sow." He looked down at the painting and his eyes clouded with some terrible irony she did not understand. "Cadiz, by Christ. I knew it!"

His gaze flicked past her shoulder and sought the solid gold galleon resting on the corner of the table. "If I but had my *Virago*, and a dozen ships . . . *half* a dozen ships . . . I would gladly finish what we started in Veracruz. It would my greatest pleasure to make the spider king squirm and sweat out the price of his own treachery."

Beau ran her hands up his arms, inviting him to drop down onto one knee before her. "I have no doubt you would, Captain Dante. You seem to have a knack for making people squirm and sweat . . . and take the greatest pleasure doing it."

"Do I, now?" His eyes narrowed and he smoothed his palms along her inner thighs, pushing the hem of his shirt up as he did so.

"And you *usually* see a thing through to the finish when you start it."

"Usually? When have I failed?"

She moistened her lips and looked down at his hands where they rested, bronzed and bold, over the whiteness of her skin.

His smile turned softly wolfish. He coaxed her legs wider apart and ran his thumbs pensively through the feathery soft thatch of auburn curls, unfurling and exposing tender pink surfaces that were quick to glisten at his touch.

"Are you certain *you* would not prefer to finish watching the sun rise?"

Beau threaded her fingers through the glossy mane of his hair and sighed her answer as he lowered his dark head between her thighs.

She would have cause to think, only a few minutes later when the sound of shouts and running boots on the deck overhead brought a rude end to their pleasure, that perhaps she had made the wrong choice. For fifty feet above them, knuckling the disbelief out of his eyes and cursing his laxness in having drifted off to sleep, the lookout was staring aghast at a fleet of warships slung out across the horizon, coming their way.

Chapter 19

"**E**nglish," Spence announced in awe. "They're bloody English, the lot o' them. I count . . . sixteen galleons an' . . . Christ love a sinner . . . half a litter o' pinnaces holdin' in their wake. Are we at war, do ye suppose?"

McCutcheon spat over the side, but before he could offer an answer there were shuffling sounds of a commotion behind them. Both the captain and his quartermaster turned in time to greet Simon Dante, who was fastening his belt around his waist, and not two paces in his shadow, Beau, with her hair unplaited and her cheeks red as apples.

Spit snorted eloquently and caught Jonas's eye before looking back to sea. "Appears someone's up to somethin', that's a fact."

Dante clasped a hand around the shroud lines as he joined Spence by the rail. The northern sky was still a dull gray wall behind the rapidly approaching ships and their sails resembled a low crust of dirty clouds on the horizon. They were too far away to identify by ship or master, but there was no mistaking the low-charged English silhouettes.

"What do ye make o' it?" Spence asked.

Dante shook his head. "I don't know. But if England and Spain are at war, surely we would have heard some mention of it from the Flemish merchant we passed two days ago."

"True enough." Spence grunted. "On the other hand, there's too damned many sails out there for a simple venture, an' ye said yerself it took near three months o' arguin' to win a nod for yer two ships to sally on the raid to Veracruz."

"So it did. Our Gloriana would rather have her nails plucked from her fingers than part with a single coin willingly. In the end she did so only because there was the prospect of vast profits to be made if we were successful. The rest of the hawks, however, were being kept on short tethers, with the exception of Richard Grenville. She was not happy to part with him, either, but he was sent in Raleigh's place, for she did not want to lose Walter's firepower for the sake of a few colonists who needed transport to Virginia. Nonetheless, she likely withdrew her permission for Richard to sail as soon as the ink dried on the orders telling him to leave . . . just as she did mine."

To his credit Jonas kept his eyes trained on the horizon longer than either Beau or Spit McCutcheon.

"She withdrew her permission for ye to sail to Veracruz?"

"She . . . wavered in her decision. It is another affliction the Queen suffers: issuing an order with one hand, rescinding it with the other. In my case the papers refusing me leave to take my ships out of port arrived just as we cleared the harbor. The courier, poor lad, even took a tumble into the drink trying to deliver them."

Spence's barrel chest swelled on a deep breath. "A fine time to tell me there might be a price on yer head in coin other than Spanish ducats."

"I doubt Bess would go to the extreme of a warrant. And even if she did, Bloodstone has had two, maybe three weeks by now to cool her temper with gold. In fact, knowing how much oil he has on his tongue, he probably has the entire country singing his praises as a hero, with Bess herself tossing down the rose petals in his path."

Spence scowled. "Are there aught more wee details ye might have forgotten to tell me?"

"Nothing I can think of, offhand." Dante glanced past Spence's shoulder and caught Pitt's eye. "Nothing that would jeopardize the safety of this ship or crew, at any rate."

"Aye. An' that would be the *whole* crew, I'm thinkin'?"

Dante's gaze flickered back to Spence. They were both aware of Beau, who was standing nearby occupied with hastily plaiting her hair and listening to Billy Cuthbert's report on winds and currents.

"Offhand," Spence mused in a low growl, "ye might not know the boards a'tween Beau's cabin an' mine are not as stout as they seem."

"I will keep it in mind," Dante returned carefully.

"Aye. Do that." The red beard folded around a grimace. *"Helmsman!"*

Beau dropped her hands with her hair only partly tamed. "Aye, sir."

"Run up the flags. Put Aulde George front an' forward so our visitors get a good long look."

"Aye, sir."

"An' I want the word passed beam to beam, the first man who breathes a hint o' what we have in our holds, boastful or otherwise, it will be the last thing he breathes."

* * *

"She's a merchantman. English, by her flags."

The captain nodded and lowered his hand from his bright blue eyes. "A pity. We could have used some practice for our guns."

The officers gathered on the foredeck laughed on cue, knowing their leader was always at odds to fire his guns and prove himself deserving of the title the Spanish had given him.

A few who took their heroes to heart might have wished the Dragon of the Apocalypse were more imposing in appearance, including Elizabeth, who enjoyed surrounding herself with tall, handsome men in their prime. Sir Francis Drake was short and squat. His hair and abram beard flamed orange in any manner of harsh light and his eyes were positioned decidedly too close together over a sharp, pointed nose, making him look more like a basset hound than a dragon. But the common people loved him. The sailors who fought to serve under him loved him. No one doubted he was the greatest sailor in all the world, the most daring of Elizabeth's private merchant navy, the bravest and most fearsomely loyal subject of the Crown . . . including Francis Drake himself.

Captains brought their ships from all over England and anchored in Plymouth Sound, hoping they might be recruited to join Drake's elite group of fellow adventurers— sea hawks like Martin Frobisher, who had earned his just reputation for courage, resourcefulness and seamanship by leading three separate expeditions in search of a northwest passage to Cathay. John Hawkyns was another. He had been the first to challenge Spain's monopoly on the slave trade and was, more important, the treasurer of the royal navy. Walter Raleigh, Richard Grenville, Lord Howard of Effingham, John Seymore, Robert of Essex, and Sir Humphry Gilbert—they were all Drake's peers and took to heart the patent from the Queen to discover and take possession of any remote, barbarous, and heathen lands not possessed by any Christian prince or people.

The deliberate vagueness of the patent was what had attracted the sea hawks, and most had made their reputations and their fortunes sailing into "barbarous, heathen, or un-Christian" waters Spain had dominated for over a century. They had looted millions from Philip's plate fleets and were not hesitant to claim any ship, be it French, Dutch, or Portugese, in prize if it chanced to cross their paths on the open seas.

It was a wise precaution, then, for a merchant ship like the *Egret* to give no outward sign she was laden with treasure, although the scarring on her hull and the evidence of recent and ongoing repairs to her yards and rails won close attention as Drake's ship, the *Elizabeth Bonaventure*, drew into range.

Drake had signaled two of his sister ships to accompany him away from the pack, the *Golden Lion* and the *Thetis*. The former was commanded by William Borough, a dour, humorless naval officer with a gallant record of service in the Baltic. The *Thetis* was captained by Robert Flick and aboard his ship were ten companies of infantry under the leadership of Captain Anthony Platt.

The rest of the fleet hauled down sail and drifted at the alert, or took the opportunity to drill on tacking maneuvers.

Onboard the *Elizabeth Bonaventure* Drake and his second in command, Christopher Carleill, stood at the rail waiting to draw within trumpet distance of the merchant ship. A third officer, young and fresh faced, was eager to prove his worth and interrupted a murmured conversation between the two more seasoned veterans.

"Excuse me, sir, but I believe I know her. She hails from Tor Bay, near Plymouth. The *Egret*. Her master is Captain Jonas Spence."

"Is my ear supposed to tingle at the name, Mister Finnerty? I hear a thousand of them a day."

Carleill coughed into his hand and raised an eyebrow in Finnerty's direction.

"Aye, sir. Bald fellow, rather robust. Wooden leg. Beard as red as . . . er . . . well, red. He's the one with the daughter; the nasty-tempered wench who castrated a seaman named Sheepwash . . . er, well, it does not warrant what he looked like then . . . she castrated him with a butcher knife a year or so ago. He brought her up on charges but naught came of it."

Drake shook his head. "I am not familiar—"

"She is also the ship's pilot, sir," Carleill offered. "I believe you once admired one of her charts enough to commission a copy."

"*Did* I? From a *woman*? The hell you say."

"The hell I do, sir," said Carleill, whose business it was to know such things. "The mark of the Black Swan."

'Ah. Ah, yes. Betides I have the man in my eye now, though not the daughter."

"A long-legged little filly," his second remarked in a murmur. "With eyes you would not soon forget if you saw them."

Drake's hand came up again as he squinted against the glare. The *Egret* was perhaps three hundred yards off the bow quarter, carving a slow, graceful line through the water in a course that would bring the two ships briefly alongside as they passed.

"Tell me, Mister Carleill, does she look to be riding heavy to you?"

"If I am not mistaken, he deals in Indies Gold, sir. Rum-bullion. Fetches upwards of a thousand quintals a voyage."

"Is that a fact. Perhaps he'll share a tun or two with us to lighten her load." He paused and narrowed his squint. "She appears to be carrying a deal of weight in iron as well. Culverins, fore and aft, I make it, but . . . what the deuce is she mounting in her waist?"

"It looks like . . . demis, sir. Thirty pounders."

"Impossible." The blue eyes widened. "And damned impertinent for a rum merchant. Have you the trumpet handy?"

"Aye, sir, I have it here," Finnerty blurted. He fumbled at his side a moment, then raised the funnel-shaped brass speaking horn.

"Hail them, then, if you please. Identify ourselves in the name of Her Majesty the Queen and inquire if all are hale and hearty."

"Sir Francis fuckin' Drake himself." Spence gasped in awe, hearing the metallic echo roll over the water. "Where, by God's ballocks, did he come from?"

"A better question," Dante said, "might be where, by the vinegar in his own vainglorious ballocks, is he going with such beetling import?"

Spence elbowed an equally dumbfounded Spit McCutcheon. "Give them a hail, man, else he take offense an' throw us a shot to remind us of our manners."

Spit raised the speaking trumpet and gave their name and the master's name and the fact they, too, sailed loyal under the flag of Her Most Royal Majesty, Elizabeth of England.

"How long at sea?" came the hollow query.

Spence nodded and Spit advised, "Eight months by calendar, eighty by the lack o' good Devon ale!"

Spence elbowed him again and Spit defended his attempted humor with a shrug.

Sunlight glinted off the brass trumpet as it was raised again on board the *Elizabeth Bonaventure*. "Sir Francis inquires if it might be a fair trade: ale for Indies Gold?"

"Fair trade my arse," Jonas muttered, then grabbed Spit's arm. "No, bloody hell, that wasn't what I wanted repeated. Tell him . . . tell him aye, 'tis a fair trade, happily given."

Spence waved a hand in salute to reinforce his pleasure as Drake's ship slid close enough to distinguish which blot on deck bore orange hair and an orange beard. Helping to identify El Draque was the general knowledge that he always wore black on board his ship. Black doublet, black balloon breeches, black hose, black boots. That and the fact that his head and shoulders barely cleared the top rail.

Sir Francis did not return the salute. He was seen, however, to lean forward and grip the rail with both hands as the *Elizabeth Bonaventure* swept slowly along the length of the *Egret*. When they were directly abreast, he turned and snatched the hailing trumpet out of his officer's hand and lifted it to his own mouth with a shout.

"Dante? Simon Dante? Is that you, you whoreson bastard devil?"

Dante shunned the trumpet and cupped his hands around his mouth. "Aye, it's me, you pale-livered son of a bitch! And an uglier dog's face I could not have hoped to see this fine morning! Bess has finally let you off the leash, has she?"

"Let me off the leash and given me enough powder to blow you to hell and gone!"

"You're free to give it a try, if you think your balls are big enough and your wick long enough!"

Drake's answer was lost to the rush of the sea and the

booming of sails as the *Elizabeth Bonaventure* glided past and turned into the wind.

Dante laughed and lowered his hands, then caught the horrified stares from Jonas and McCutcheon, and, from up on the foredeck, a pale and open-mouthed Beau Spence.

"He is a mortal man, just like any other mortal man. He eats, drinks, and sometimes even makes the mistake of pissing into the wind like any other mortal man. If he still strikes thunder in your presence, picture him stark naked—not a pretty sight, I promise you."

No one moved. *Nothing* moved save for one of Spit McCutcheon's legs squeezing against the other.

It was Geoffrey Pitt who leaned forward and murmured at the nape of Spence's neck, "Sir Francis's second wife . . . Elizabeth Sydenham . . . is Simon's first cousin. He introduced them, as a matter of fact, and stood as groomsman at the wedding. They like to pretend they hate each other; it loosens bowels and gives them something to wager over."

"Now ye tell me," Spit bemoaned.

Chapter 20

"**M**y God!" Sir Francis exclaimed. "My good sweet God in heaven, it is you!"

He climbed the last rung of the gangway ladder and went directly to Simon Dante, his arm thrust out like a pike. Clasping Dante's hand with one of his and thumping his shoulder with the other, El Draque laughed and swore and laughed again, blinking continually as if he could not believe his eyes.

"Elizabeth wept for a week when she heard you were dead. Both of them did—my Elizabeth and England's Elizabeth. The proprietor of the Ship's Inn gave free ale the blessed day long and half the bells in London droned in mourning! Most of Newgate's brothels closed their doors as well, or draped their beds in black sheets; I'm told Bess could not even call for a cup of wine to drown her sorrows without having it watered down with tears, so distraught were her Curt ladies."

"I am flattered to know I was missed."

"Missed? Missed, by God? Where the devil have you

been? We were told you went down with all hands, somewhere off the Azores."

Dante's eyes turned a cold, flat gray. "Obviously, only part of what you were told bears truth. My *Virago* is, alas, gone, but as you can see, I am very much alive, no small thanks to Captain Spence, who happened along at the opportune moment and fished me and what remained of my crew out of the drink."

In honor of Sir Francis Drake's visit to the deck of the *Egret*, Jonas had hastily scrubbed his face and dressed in his finest. He wore a forest-green doublet with embroidered crimson stripes. The same fiery red lining showed through the slashes in his sleeves and balloon breeches. He had fought for ten full minutes with a starched neck ruff before a panicked hail from McCutcheon had cursed it back into his sea chest. He had scoured the fur from his teeth with a coarse, salted cloth, then pulled on his gloves with their padded fingertips. His boots rose above the knee and were cuffed to conceal the bulky strapping that held his wooden peg in place. His chest was thrust out as painfully proud as he could manage without the risk of putting out eyes with popping buttons.

Drake was a full head and neck shorter, but it did not stay him from walking over to the burly captain and offering his hand.

"My pleasure, Captain Spence. And my heartfelt thanks. Had this black-souled renegade truly been bested by a damned pack of Spaniards, there would have been no hope for any of us."

Christopher Carleill had accompanied Drake across on the jolly boat and, after introductions were made, offered a curious observation.

"Captain Bloodstone said he saw your ship go under."

"He must have eyes in the back of his head," Dante replied mildly.

"He has been telling the tale to whoever will listen, how the two of you were attacked by the zabras and how you courageously sacrificed your ship that he and his crew might make good their escape."

"An interesting version; you must tell me more."

Carleill was of medium build and height, no more than five and twenty years of age, but with silver threads running through the dark brown hair at his temples. He had been with Drake on several raids to the Indies, and more recently had been given command of his own small vessel, the *Scout*. He was a cautious and keen judge of character, and because he often had to play the diplomat around his commander's fiery temper, he was able to recognize when someone was saying one thing and meaning another. He had always admired Dante de Tourville's flamboyant style and nerve, something he found sorely lacking in Victor Bloodstone.

"He will undoubtedly rejoice to hear of your return from the dead," Carleill said, matching Dante's bland tone.

"As will Bess, I warrant," Drake interjected. " 'Twill be like Mary Stuart's head rolling out of the basket and reattaching itself to her neck!"

"Mary Stuart's head?" Pitt asked, in the process of having his own hand pumped and his shoulder clapped.

"Aye, the Stuart bitch. Of course—you could not know. Her head parted company with her shoulders oh . . . six weeks ago now. Nearing seven. Walsingham caught her red handed, packing secret notes in wine casks and dispatching them to a band of fellow conspirators who were—on her specific written orders—to hire assassins to kill the Queen. When he showed these to Bess, she had no choice but to brand it treason and put the witch to the axe."

"Christ Jesus," said Spence. "Has Spain heard the news?"

"We did not dally to wait until they did. Nor could the Queen afford to err on the side of caution any longer. To that end she has . . . unleashed us, as you say . . . to distress Spanish ships where we find them, capture their seaborne supplies, and to do all we can to impeach the gathering together of the King's so-called *Grande Armada Felicissima*."

"Those were your orders?" Dante asked, intrigued. "Freely given?"

"Freely on the Monday, aye. With penance on Tuesday and no doubt regret on Wednesday. But by Thursday I was already vacating Plymouth and did not look back over my shoulder to see if there were any couriers trying to catch me up. The wind commanded me away and I obeyed."

Dante exchanged a glance with Jonas Spence, for if it was true, then the captain had nothing to fear in the way of fines or rebukes for having attacked and plundered the *San Pedro de Marcos*.

"The wind appears to have commanded a good many ships to sail in your wake."

"Not so hastily as it may appear." Drake smiled. "Each ship, each captain, was chosen by me for their stoutness of heart and quickness on the guns. Among us we have nearly three hundred and fifty muzzles searching to make havoc where we may."

"You have a strike in mind?"

"Asked with such a lascivious glint in the eye, it leaves me to suspect you have somehow stumbled across the King's own itinerary."

"Not the complete plan, no. But we may have something that might interest you."

Drake's eyes narrowed. "As always, my cryptic friend, you leave me foaming with curiosity. Do I beg now or can it wait until I moisten my throat with some of this famed Indies Gold the lieutenant has been telling me about?"

Spit had anticipated needing something to wet Spence's throat and he waved a crewman forward, who bore plain pewter goblets and a jug of rum. When each man had a cup and each cup was filled, Drake offered a toast to the Queen and took a long, slow swallow, his hand on his hip, his eyes rising with the heat in his belly, until he found himself staring up at the forecastle deck.

Lucifer was standing there, his enormous black body gleaming in the sunlight.

Drake lowered his cup and dabbed a cuff across his lips. "I see you still keep company with cannibals. I am surprised he has not made a meal of you yet."

"I keep him well fed with Spaniards."

Drake's gaze wandered slightly to the left of the tattooed giant. "And that . . . must be the captain's infamous daughter? The one who signs her charts with a black swan and makes eunuchs of men who trifle with her?"

All eyes within hearing distance turned toward Beau, and she would have shrunk back against the wall of sailors behind her if Spence had not ordered her sharply down to the main deck.

"Aye! This is my daughter, Isabeau. Isabeau . . . have the honor and pleasure of making the acquaintance of Sir Francis Drake."

Beau was not certain if she should attempt a curtsy in canvas breeches or tug a forelock. She settled for doing as the men had done and thrust out her hand, first to a startled dragon, then to a smiling Christopher Carleill.

"A pleasure, my lord, Mister Carleill."

Drake pursed his lips and eyed her with renewed interest. "I am told I have one of your charts in my possession—which did you say, Mister Carleill?"

"Grand Canaria, sir. You were admiring it only the other day."

"So I was, so I was. Excellent work, Mistress Spence. You have a fine eye for detail."

"I was remarking on that very thing not an hour ago," Dante said, and looked at Spence. "She broke the King's code. It was not in the letters, after all, it was in the paintings. I could have searched for a year and not found it; Beau took one leisurely glance and made sense of it all."

"Paintings?" Drake looked askance. "You have paintings . . . of what, may I ask?"

"The King's Most Happy Fleet. The *Armada Felicissima*."

Drake leaned back in his chair, his hands betraying a slight tremor of excitement as they closed around his goblet, filled now with ale to keep his head clear. They had adjourned to Spence's cabin and were crowded around the table. The morning sun was streaming through the gallery windows, causing Sir Francis's hair to glow beyond orange. The air in the cabin was hazed with dust, thickest where the beams of sunlight poured onto the tabletop.

Drake had insisted on seeing the paintings and the documents. He had studied every last detail, and because Dante had been adamant about recognizing Beau's part in identifying the Spanish galleons, she sat by Drake's side as they went through all three pictures and made a list of the ships they decoded.

"You believe this to be the *Girona*?" he asked. "But she is a galleass and I see no evidence of oars."

"The *Girona*'s captain is the Duke of Alicante. His family crest consists of a lion, a cross, and"—Beau touched a fingertip to the carved grotesque worked into the ship's stern—"a ram's head."

Drake stared and Spence grinned.

"My father appreciates good wine," she explained. "Some of the best burgundy is produced on the Duke of Alicante's estates. His bottles bear his crest."

Sir Francis nodded slowly and looked back at the list of ships they had compiled. He himself had contributed the *San Marin,* the *Saragoza,* the *Magdalena.*

"By Christ, it is all here," he muttered. "A complete inventory of the ships gathering in Spanish ports. And for what other reason than war? Moreover, if the 'harvest' dates are correct, the King is intending a June launch." He lifted his head and scowled. "We are not sailing into these waters a day too soon. Hopefully, not a day too late either."

Dante was standing, lounging against the cabin wall. "You have the firepower, all you need do is pick your first strike with care and purpose. Do enough damage, you can set all of Spain back on its heels."

Drake looked at him expectantly. "I suppose you have the perfect target in mind?"

The pirate wolf grinned. "Cadiz."

"Cadiz? Spain's principle seaport?" Drake arched an eyebrow. "Why would you not just suggest we sail up the Tagus and attack Madrid . . . after first laying waste to Lisbon, of course?"

"Because, if they are in any way anticipating an attack, they will be anticipating it in Lisbon. Cadiz, on the other hand, is deep in their own waters." He paused and his gaze touched on Beau's golden eyes. "They will be as lax with their guard in Cadiz as they were in Veracruz."

Drake frowned and tapped his fingers on the tabletop. "An intriguing suggestion, Simon, and audacious, as usual, but we have no clear idea what defenses we would be up against."

Dante pushed aside the paintings and leaned over the table, sketching an invisible map on the wood.

"The port is shaped thus, like a funnel, with a wide outer harbor and a smaller, rounded inner harbor. The city itself straddles a detached spit of land joined to the main by a stone bridge. The defenses in the outer harbor are reasonably strong, for in order to breach the inner, a ship must first pass through this channel"—he drew a line through the neck of his invisble funnel—"and challenge the guns of the castle fortifications.

"The castle itself overlooks the channel. It was built nearly a century ago to defend the city against repeated sackings from Algerian corsairs. While not to be lightly dismissed, I suspect with this many ships in port, we would not even have to risk the guns or the shoals to make short work of the King's fleet."

"Shoals?"

"Aye, they run along the leeward side of the channel, like teeth waiting to snap at an unsuspecting keel. If I were to try to penetrate the inner harbor, I would send the pinnaces in first to sound the shoals and test the wind and currents—both of which have a tendency to lose spirit inside the harbor."

Drake was staring hard at Dante's squared jaw, the tightly compressed lips, the sudden blaze of blue in his eyes. "You never mentioned where it was you were taken," he said quietly, "when you were subjected to the auto-da-fé. May I presume it was Cadiz?"

"There was not much to do between beatings but stare out a crack in the wall of my cell and watch the harbor. I attacked it a hundred times in my mind, and each was a success."

"We need to attack it only once," Drake said. "And it would *have* to be a success."

"Given the fact you are almost as audacious as I, I cannot see how it would fail."

Drake weathered the challenge with a slow smile, but it was apparant the bait was already half taken. His eyes sparkled and his complexion was ruddy with excitement, and he stared down at the invisible map Dante had drawn as if he could already see the harbor burning, the ships in flame.

Restless now, he stood up and paced to the windows. His black satin shirt was stiff with jeweled embroidery, the sleeves of his velvet doublet were puffed and slashed, the doublet itself was padded generously to add bulk to his shoulders and dipped low in front to form a stylishly aggrandized peasecod belly. His hose, while doing little to flatter the bow in his legs, were worth more than a year's wages to a common sailor.

"Walsingham," he said, thinking aloud as he continued to contemplate the possibilities, "has suggested we concentrate our efforts on the smaller coastal ports. He thought a blockade off Cape Saint Vincent would seriously hamper the provisioning of Lisbon. He has made his suggestion in the expectations of the Spanish king choosing Alvaro de Bazan, Marquis of Santa Cruz, to admiral his fleet, despite the old warrior's age and reports of ill health.

"On the other hand, there is the Duke of Medina Sidonia, the current court favorite. Richer than Croesus, he owns half of Andalusia and covets the rest. He is neither a soldier nor a sailor, however. He spears bulls with lancets and teaches horses to caper through the air. I doubt he has even been on the deck of a ship, save once, years ago, when he went to fetch his child bride from Navarre. His duchess is more of a sailor than he, having made several voyages to the Indies to visit her father—a governor, I believe, of one of the islands. I heard some mention she was there now, for he was ailing. Or that she was on her way back, for he was dead."

Dante's face remained impassive but Pitt's turned a strangled shade of red and Spence swallowed loud enough for the sound to reverberate around the cabin. Drake was too preoccupied with his thoughts to notice the subtle increase in tension, but Carleill passed a curious eye from Pitt to Spence to Beau, who was also, suddenly, preoccupied with a scrap of paper she was folding and unfolding into a tiny square.

"Medina Sidonia would be the people's favorite," Drake decided curtly, searching for agreement from his audience, "for he would only have to snap his fingers to have fifty thousand men eager to follow him into the bowels of hell. His *palacio*, as it happens, is in Cadiz."

"In which case," Carleill observed on cue, "it would not enhance his reputation any to be defeated in his own province."

"No more than it would enhance mine," Drake countered, "to be seen acting too rashly with the Queen's ships."

"Rashness, sir, is what is demanded. The Queen will know this when it comes time to choose her admiral to champion the defense of England."

Drake smirked. "The Queen, bless her soul, has a great deal of Old Henry in her and thinks like a man when it comes to the strategies of warfare. But she is also the Queen and must think of her own position when it comes to the strategies of politics. Charles, Lord Howard of Effingham is Lord High Admiral of England, and will no doubt satisfy the needs of the Privy Council. I am, alas, only the son of a common preacher and to put me in command of men with noble blood would offend every law of nature and seigniory. On the other hand"—his smile turned conspiratorial—"we can always hope for common sense to prevail, and if I should shew the boldness to sail into Cadiz and singe the King's beard, well . . ."

"She will have no choice but to appoint you," Carleill insisted. "Noble blood be damned."

Drake bowed slightly to acknowledge Carleill's astute perception—one he shared wholeheartedly—and not by chance his gaze settled on Beau. His small, close-set eyes narrowed as he gave her doublet and breeches, her ill-fixed braid, a bemused inspection.

"I have it in my mind Bess would take to you at once, child. I half believe there are times she would forfeit her crown if she could but once fling her farthingale into the wind and climb the rigging of a ship."

Beau was not sure how to respond. Luckily she was spared the need as Drake walked brusquely back to the table.

"Mister Carleill—we shall have to call a council of war with all of the captains. If Cadiz sits well with them—and I cannot see them arguing overlong, since I have already made the decision—we shall lay in our course and sail close-hauled to the wind. A fortnight, I estimate, and we should be smelling the olive groves and camel dung."

"The, er, question of the other captains, sir . . . ?"

"Not now, Carleill."

The lieutenant glanced at Dante. "But, sir—"

"Not now." Drake fixed a smile in place and offered a casual explanation to his audience. "Borough. He likes his opinions to mean something. He also likes his pomp and ceremony and takes every care to see his enemy has a gallant opportunity to defend himself, even if it means knocking on the door and announcing our arrival. He holds no favor with surprise and stealth, the very qualities the Spaniards least expect. The very ones I admire most, unless, of course"—the bright blue eyes went to Spence—"they are

meant to impugn my own character. Did you really expect, Captain, I would be so churlish as to confiscate whatever goods you have in your holds? Goods other than Indies Gold, that is."

A slow, hot flush crept up Spence's bullish neck, and Dante interceded.

"You would confiscate the teeth out of your mother's mouth if your own were lacking. And it was on my strong advice that Jonas kept both his mouth and his cargo holds firmly shut."

"Cousin, cousin, you disappoint me."

"I also know you, and know that by nightfall you would have found some excuse to relieve us of a portion of the burden *we* relieved in good faith from a passing Spaniard."

"How did ye know?" Spence gasped, drawing the keen blue eyes—which he now suspected could see through three-foot-thick planking.

"Your hull shows signs of recent damage," Drake drawled. "And Dante de Tourville is on board. An idiot could have made the equation."

Carleill, wary of the gleam in his commander's eyes, kept his voice deliberately businesslike. "Might we know the name of the ship whose burdens you relieved? And perchance the where and when of it, lest our course be affected?"

"Six days ago, thereabout. She was a straggler, trying for Lisbon. We caught her"—Dante grinned at Spence as he quoted—"with her cod open and her pisser hanging out."

"A worthwhile exchange, I hope?"

"Worthy enough. Timely, too, for we found these paintings and letters in her master's cabin—all of which we will gladly entrust into your care in case your captains need convincing."

Drake drew a breath and laced his hands together behind his back. "And the ship?"

"The *San Pedro de Marcos*."

Carleill's head jerked around. "The *San*—? But she's—she's six hundred tons if she's an ounce!"

"She was big," Dante admitted blithely—so blithely, it sent Spence's cup to his mouth again and almost dragged Pitt's gaze up off the floor, where it had been fixed for the past five minutes.

"How hotly did she protest?" The lieutenant's voice had a catch of awe in it.

"We peppered her with over four hundred rounds before she brought down her colors."

"Yet you did not claim her as prize?"

"We did not think she stood much chance of making it to a Spanish port, let alone an English one."

Drake cleared his throat, which was suffused with a rising red tide of ill-concealed jealousy. "Her cargo?"

"Plate and bullion." Dante paused and smiled like Clarence the cat after a successful raid on the cook's stores. "Sixty thousand, thereabout. Only a rough estimate, you understand, having no guild merchant on board."

Drake shook his head, the movement barely perceptible at first, then with enough vigor to supplement the sudden bark of laughter that erupted from his throat. "You blackhearted bastard! First Veracruz, then a miraculous resurrection, then a Spanish treasure galleon. You will have the Queen appointing *you* Lord Admiral of the defense of England if you don't have a care."

There was not as much jesting behind the words as his demeanor implied and both men knew it. Drake ached for the command. He wanted it, he deserved it, the people demanded it. But unless he could accomplish something spectacular between now and June, the Queen would likely give the nod to protocol.

And if Cadiz had not been firmly fixed in his mind before, it was now, for an attack on Cadiz could prove to be his most spectacular coup yet.

"We will hold council on the *Bonaventure* tonight," Drake said crisply. "You will, of course, join us," he added, extending the invitation to include Dante and Jonas Spence.

"It will be an honor," Dante agreed.

Drake waited impatiently for Carleill to gather up the documents. With Spence scrambling out of his chair to follow them, the two men strode out of the cabin and returned topside.

As he passed, Spence plucked at Dante's sleeve and hissed, "Do ye not plan to tell him about the duchess? What if she's"—he lowered his voice to an airless whisper—"ye know . . . *the* duchess?"

"I did not mention our guest, firstly, because we have yet to determine if she is Medina Sedonia's duchess; secondly, because I have played at whist with my esteemed comrade too many times to underestimate the benefit of always holding a trump card back in case it is needed. For that matter, he rarely plays without holding one or two back himself."

"Ye think he isn't tellin' us everythin'?"

"I think he isn't telling us *something*. I just don't know what it is."

Beau did not follow the men up on deck. She went to her own cabin instead and stood on the gallery balcony to watch the famous sea hawk being rowed back to the *Elizabeth Bonaventure*. She had seen him from a distance many times before—who had passed through Plymouth and had not?—so his abbreviated appearance did not startle her. Also, she knew from the sailors' talk that he was cheerful, first to buy a round of ale, and first on his feet to defend his Queen and country with word or blade.

Something about him, however, left her with an odd sense of unease. As if he would not have been above confiscating their plunder from the *San Pedro* had Dante not been on board.

She sighed and heard voices behind her, recognizing those of Dante and Geoffrey Pitt. Pitt's was the sharpest and she surmised they must be discussing the fate of Doña Maria Antonia Piacenza and whether that was her full name or not. If not, if she was the Duke of Medina Sidonia's wife, Pitt's little duchess might just prove to be more valuable than ten shiploads of treasure and nothing would stop Drake from taking her.

The voices stopped, rather abruptly, and Dante joined her on the gallery a few angry footsteps later.

"Love," he said grimly. "Such brief pleasure for such prolonged pain; the one hardly justifies the other."

She looked at him sidelong. "Some people, I am sure, find the exchange fair."

"Some people are fools."

Beau turned her head forward again. "I gather you have asked Mister Pitt to find out if the duchess has any more titles behind her name?"

"I cannot very well ask her myself. She melts into a frightened puddle if I so much as inquire after her health."

"I was imagining that was the kind of reaction you preferred from your women. Docile, fainthearted, demurring to your every command. . . ."

He glared at her. "If it was, I wouldn't be taking you into my bed every night, now would I?"

Beau returned his stare for a long moment, then pushed

away from the rail with a curse. She gained no more than a pace or two before Dante's arm snaked out and caught her around the waist, hauling her back.

"Let me go, you insufferably arrogant—"

He kissed her hard, on the mouth, and when he did let her go, he was grinning. "You're like a keg of powder, did you know that? The smallest spark touches your fuse and *blam!* Off you go."

She wriggled and squirmed and tried to wrench herself free, but he only tightened his grip and trapped her closer against his chest.

"If you truly want me to explode, Captain—"

He laughed again and lifted her, wary of the eyes that might be watching from the *Elizabeth Bonaventure*. He carried her, still thrashing and spitting like a cat, into the cabin and closed the gallery door behind them. Turning her into the corner, he kept her pinned there with his big body even as he freed his hands to cradle her neck and tilt her mouth up to his.

She tried to bite him and he bit her back. Her gasp allowed his tongue to make short work of her defenses and within a few halfheartedly angry protests, she was all but a puddle herself.

"Bastard," she gasped when she could. "You don't play fair."

"With you? God's truth, I would not stand a chance. You would have me castrated, and without the use of a knife."

She opened her mouth to the rovings of his tongue and lips, and curled her arms around his shoulders.

"Besides," he said between suckling caresses, "I need to talk to you and I need your full attention."

"You have it," she murmured. "Talk away."

"I plan to go on the raid to Cadiz with Drake. He will

likely ask me anyway, if I have not put his nose too far out of joint, but even if he doesn't, I'm sure I can catch a ride with someone."

Beau's eyes opened and her mouth stopped moving against his. His dark head lifted, though he was careful to keep her body immobilized against the wall.

"What about the *Egret?*"

"What about her? She is going home . . . and so are you."

"Thank you very much for the dismissal, but I don't recall you being named captain."

"I don't have to be; all I need are eyes. You're carrying several tons of bullion—rather expensive ballast to toss overboard should the need arise. Your speed and maneuverability are hampered and your rudder is not as sound as it should be. You are a week, give or take, from port; your men are tired and anxious to see their families or spend their money. They have already gone through one unnecessary ordeal and survived as much through luck as anything else. It would not be fair to throw them into another conflict not of their choosing, not of their nature. You said yourself, the *Egret* is a merchantman, not a warship, and brave though her captain and crew might be—*all* of her crew," he repeated emphatically, "—Cadiz is no place for her to be. It is no place for you to be either. This is war, despite what Drake or the Queen prefers to call it, and I want you safe, Isabeau. I want you home in England, safe."

Her eyes, huge and tawny and glistening like pools of liquid gold, looked up at him without an accompanying word, and he cursed, low and soft in his throat.

"Drake would never let you come along, regardless. You heard him: he handpicked his captains and his ships. They are the fastest, the sleekest, the ones with the most firepower, and in prime fighting condition."

"Not all of them. There is at least one in as rough shape as the *Egret*, possibly even worse."

"Isabeau—"

"There is!" She pushed him away and wrenched open the gallery door. He cursed again, but obeyed her command to go out onto the balcony and, once there, to follow the outthrust point of her finger.

At first he did not see it, for there were ten or more galleons drifting in to take a position near the *Elizabeth Bonaventure*. But then a silhouette, etched into his brain like a burning brand, drew his eye and held it; held it until his lids burned and the hatred rose like acid in his blood.

It was Victor Bloodstone's ship. It was the *Talon*.

Chapter 21

Beau's jaw gaped as she heard him hiss the name. His body had gone rigid and the vast bulk of muscle across his chest and arms had turned as hard as stone. She knew this because her first reaction was to reach out and touch him.

"Are you absolutely certain? How could he have made the turnaround so quickly?"

"He could have. The greedy bastard would not miss an opportunity like this. And, yes, I am absolutely certain it is the *Talon*. I would not mistake that hull over a thousand others just like it."

"She stands a thousand yards away," Beau argued.

"She could stand two thousand. Three. I would know her guns anywhere."

Beau traced the glint of sunlight across the wide expanse of water and caught the metallic reflection off bronze muzzles. She recalled something Pitt had mentioned during an evening discussion: that he had fitted Victor Bloodstone's ship with some of the same demi-cannon he had commissioned from Marseilles specially for the *Virago*. She herself had remarked at their uniqueness, with the elegantly long snouts scrolled and embellished with gilded eagles in full wingspread.

"It does not mean Victor Bloodstone is at the helm," she said lamely.

"He is there. I can *feel* him."

Dante's eyes were a raw, angry blue, his face was a chiseled mask of rage, the squared edge of his jaw so prominent, Beau could have drawn a line by it.

"What are you going to do?" she asked in a whisper.

"What would you suggest I do? Invite him to share a tot of rum?"

"No, of course not, but—"

"But *what?*" The blazing blue eyes speared her. "What, Isabeau? Tell me what! You don't think he deserves to die? You don't think he deserves to be lashed to the shrouds and run through by every man on my crew? He ran, God damn his soul. He turned and ran like a greedy, sneaking thief in the night. He stole our food, our water, our gold, then left us to the zabras to cover his crime. Killing is too good for him. He deserves to be slashed open and his wounds packed with salt until he screams himself to an agony of madness."

"He appears to have told a different version of what happened. According to Carleill—"

"According to Carleill, he made me out to be a martyr, sacrificing my ship and crew for the sake of his scrawny neck."

"And indeed, Captain Dante, who would believe that?" His eyes narrowed dangerously, but she kept going. "Who would believe you would throw yourself in front of another ship to help buy time for a wounded comrade to make good his escape? Having seen you in battle, I would. Jonas would. Every man on board this ship would."

"You have a point to make?"

"My point," she said carefully, "is that Bloodstone has friends. Important friends, some of whom are probably here, sailing beside him. What is more, he has made you out to be the hero of the day, saving him and his crew from certain death."

"A brief reprieve, I promise you."

"I have no doubt you want to kill him—"

"With my bare hands," he interrupted with quiet ferocity.

"—but do you really think Sir Francis will allow it?"

"He will have little to say about it; this is between Bloodstone and me."

Beau bit down on her lip and looked hesitantly at the fleet of galleons, huge deadly warships bristling with purpose, entrusted with safeguarding England's future. Having met Drake, having seen the hunger in his eyes, the ambition, and the lust for power, she was not entirely convinced he would simply stand aside and let the personal grievances of two men divide his forces and jeopardize his mission.

"Why do you suppose he did not tell you Bloodstone and the *Talon* were here? He had ample opportunity to mention it."

"Maybe he *wants* me to kill the bastard."

"Maybe he does. Maybe he knows your temper well enough to predict you would run Bloodstone through the instant you set eyes on him, without troubling with explanations, without seeking the benefit of a jury. Maybe he would just let you kill him so he could be justified in throwing you in chains and hauling you back to England on a charge of cold-blooded murder."

"Why in damnation would he do that?"

"To take full credit for Cadiz?" she suggested quietly.

Dante stared at her for a long, disbelieving moment before he exploded. "He is Sir Francis Drake! He does not have to resort to throwing me in chains to protect his reputation!"

"Did you not see the look on his face when you told him about the *San Pedro de Marcos?* Did you not hear the way his teeth grated when he spoke of Veracruz? When was his last victory against the Spanish? When did he last plunder a ship or sack a city? *How many heroes can he afford to bring home to England if he is to convince the Queen he is worthy of being Lord Admiral of the Fleet?*"

Dante's mouth snapped shut. His knuckles were bleached white where he gripped the rail, rivaling the slash of his teeth as he drew his lips back in a snarl. "Can these words be from the same mouth that defended Drake as the greatest seaman and hero in the world, at the same time comparing myself to a French bull rogue who would could not sail his way out of a gale?"

Her eyes flashed hotly. "Must you remember *every* insult I threw at you?"

"You did not mean them?"

"Of course I meant them," she snapped. "At the time, I meant every word."

"Since then, of course, we've had a few good tumbles in bed and you've come to appreciate my finer points?"

Beau kept her face remarkably blank, though she could feel it stinging as if he had slapped her with the flat of his hand. She started to walk away, back into the cabin, but his hand shot out and gripped her tightly around the upper arm.

"Let me go," she said quietly.

"Isabeau—"

She looked him square in the eye. "If you want to kill Victor Bloodstone, by all means kill him; no one on this ship will stop you. Just promise me you will think about what I said. Ask yourself why Drake said nothing and if you still want to go and kill Victor Bloodstone, I will row you across myself and hold him while you plunge the knife in his heart."

She wrenched her arm out of his grasp and carried on through her cabin and out to the companionway. She did not stop or look back, not even when he cursed her on her way and sent his fist smashing into the gallery door.

A dozen feet away, on the other side of the narrow companionway, Geoffrey Pitt's fists were aching to smash something as well. He had come to Doña Maria's cabin after spending several minutes just standing outside the door, wondering what his reaction was going to be if it proved to be true that she was the wife of the Duke of Medina Sedonia. Her value as a hostage would increase immeasurably. She would be sent directly to London, where he would be lucky if he caught a glimpse of her in a Tower window.

He had not heard any sounds coming from inside the tiny cabin, not even after he had braced himself and knocked. He had knocked a second time, and when there was still no response, he had tested the latch and pushed the door open an inch or two.

Both the duchess and her duenna had been given strict instructions to remain in their cabin and out of sight—for their own good, they had been told, unless they wanted to find themselves in the hands of the Dragon of the Apocalypse. Doña Maria had wilted at the very notion of seeing Sir Francis Drake; Agnes Frosthip had vowed to confront the English pirate and lay upon his head the blame for all the evils of the world. To that end she had fortified herself with the contents of a bottle of rum and, when Geoffrey Pitt eased open the door of the cabin, was lying belly-down on the narrow cot, her arms askew, her legs drooping over the side.

Doña Maria was sitting in a straight back chair, her face as pale as candle wax, her eyelids swollen and polished as if she had been crying through most of the morning. She held a small crystal glass in her hand, and as Pitt came all the way into the cabin, she drained the last few drops of amber liquid and pushed shakily to her feet.

"Have they come for me, señor? The *soldados* who will arrest me and throw me in chains?"

"There are no *soldados*. No one has come to arrest you."

"We heard voices. Many voices. And there are many ships in El Draque's fleet, many *soldados*."

"No one has come to arrest you," he insisted quietly, closing the door behind him. "No one is taking you anywhere, not unless they go through me first."

Tears welled in her eyes and spilled over her lashes. She wept without making a sound and there was no movement other than a slight tremor in her lower lip, but the tears flowed hot and fast, streaming down her cheeks in such a quantity, they dripped off her chin and stained the rich silk of her bodice.

"They will know. They will discover the truth and come for me, and not even you, señor, will be able to stop them." She waved her hand in a futile little gesture and sobbed pitifully. "They will kill me. They will kill me for being so deceitful."

"Maria—" He moved forward, but for each step he took, she retreated an equal distance until her back was against the wall and she had nowhere to go. "I swear to you, on my soul—!"

She covered her face with her hands and her slender shoulders started to shake with sobs. "No! No! They will have me killed!"

Pitt took hold of her wrists and tried to ease her hands away from her face. "Maria, listen to me . . ."

"No! I am not Maria! I am not the Duchess of Navarre!"

Pitt's hands tightened around her wrists and he had to fight himself to keep from cursing out loud. This was the moment he had dreaded. If she wasn't the Duchess of Navarre, then she was indeed . . .

"I am only a poor maid! A poor, foolish maid, and the Dragon will kill me for the deception?"

Pitt stopped trying to force her hands and simply held her wrists as he stared down at her.

"What," he asked on a hoarse breath, "did you just say?"

She shook her head with the helplessness of it all and lowered her hands enough to look up Pitt with huge, glistening blue eyes. "It was the captain-general's idea. He ordered me to change places with Doña Maria. We were the same size and he said no one could be any the wiser. He said the duchess would be safe this way, f-from rape and from the disgrace of being held to ransom. He said—he said it was my duty to my mistress, to my country, to God, and that He would watch over me and see that no harm befell me. And—and he said even if it did, my s-soul would have earned a special place in heaven, one reserved for only the b-bravest and m-most worthy."

Pitt still stared incomprehendingly. "You are not Doña Maria Antonia Piacenza?"

"No, señor." She sobbed, weeping harder, her eyes leaking great waterfalls now at what she thought was the revulsion on Geoffrey Pitt's handsome face. "My name is Christiana and I am daughter to a humble *soldado* who served the King well. For his reward he was give a position in the royal guard, and I was allowed to tend members of the royal family."

"You are not the Duchess of Navarre? You are not the

King's niece? You are not . . . married to the Duke of Medina Sedonia?"

Her eyes blinked and splashed tears on his shirtfront. "No, señor. I am only a humble servant. And I do not know this Duke of Medina Sedonia. My mistress was the Duchess of Navarre. Her husband was old and wrinkled and beat me with his walking stick because I would not let him put his hands up my skirt."

Pitt caught the faint scent of rum-induced courage on her breath, and he wished sorely for a glass himself. The bottle was empty, however, and he settled for raking both of his hands through the thick, gold-streaked locks of his hair.

"Why . . . in God's name . . . did you not tell me this before?"

"I was afraid," she whispered.

"Of *me?*"

"Oh, señor—" She lowered her hands from her face and steepled them together over her breasts. "You are so kind and brave and noble. I thought . . . if I told you of this deception, you would—you would . . ." The words, along with her ability to speak them, came to a faltering halt.

"You thought I would do what?" he asked gently.

"I thought . . . you would hate me for making a fool of you."

She flung herself forward with a miserable little wail and burrowed against his chest. Pitt was still too stunned to react right away. There had been signs, plenty of them, but he had misread them all. The way she drew back and cringed from any discussions about herself. The way she skirted questions about her family and her life in royal circles—questions a true duchess would have flouted haughtily to a seafaring beggar the likes of him. Even the way Agnes Frosthip seemed to lose interest in her charge, abandoning her to the care of an enemy brigand, should have alerted him to the fact something was amiss. He had indeed been a fool. A blind, besotted fool.

And now she had flung herself at his mercy, expecting—what? That he would cast her aside as a cheat and a fraud?

Pitt lifted one of his hands and smoothed it tenderly over the crown of dark brown curls. He closed his eyes, savoring the softness, the silkiness, the notion of doing something he had been wanting to do since he had first seen her on board the *San Pedro de Marcos*. His other arm circled her waist and he held her as tightly as he dared without fear of crushing her.

"I should hate you," he whispered, his voice raw with emotion. "I should hate you for putting me through sheer hell for the past three weeks. Do you have any idea how difficult it has been to see you every day, speak with you every day, drown in the scent of your skin every day, knowing I could never touch you, never hold you, never . . ."

She left a great wet patch behind on his shirt as she lifted her head and stared up into the jade-green of his eyes. "I—I do not understand, señor."

Pitt swore softly and pushed his fingers into her hair, cradling the nape of her neck. He lowered his mouth to hers, explaining with a kiss what he could not form into words. The shock made her gasp and she tried to pull away, but he would not allow it. He had dreamed of it too many times, imagined it too many times, spent too many tormented nights wishing desperately he had the right to kiss her just once without the shame of his own shortcomings standing between them.

But once was simply not enough and he kissed her twice, three times, each with a bolder passion than the last. He kept his hand tangled in her hair until he was certain she would not shy away, then lowered it to the smooth curve of her throat, warming the fluttering pulsebeat he found there. She gasped again and parted her lips to his searching hunger, welcoming the gentle rolling motions of his tongue, then the deep, devouring thrusts that made her blood race and her limbs tremble with weakness.

She was still weeping. The tears were bathing their mouths and he tried once, unsuccessfully, to temper his hunger long enough to wipe away the dampness. But then their mouths came together again and her hands were reaching up around his shoulders and the tears of pain and fear became tears of unbounded joy.

"Little fool," he gasped at length. "My darling little fool—I could never hate you. Not for any reason. Could you not see I was in love with you? In love . . . from the very first moment I saw you."

Christiana, her mouth pink and swollen, buried her face in the crook of his shoulder again. "I thought . . . I hoped . . . I prayed it might be so, for I loved you, too, señor. So much so, I wept myself to sleep each night with the shame of wanting you."

Pitt was all but deafened by the sound of his heart thundering within his chest. He glanced at the bed, but Agnes Frosthip's bulky form was overflowing it, and then he felt his chest constrict with guilt that his first thought should be so base and lustful.

His second was relief. If it was true, if she was the daughter of a common soldier, it meant there were no barriers standing between them. He was free to do, say, ask, of her anything he pleased.

"Christiana . . ." He stopped a moment to taste the sweetness of her name on his lips, then released his breath on a hoarse gust. "Christiana"—he tilted her face up to his and lost himself in the depths of the huge blue eyes—

"when we get to England, I want you to stay with me. I . . . want you to marry me."

"I cannot!" She gasped, her mouth slackening with shock. "I *cannot!*"

"Why? Why, in God's name . . ." A thought came to him and sent his head crushing down onto her shoulder. "Please, please don't tell me you are married already or I swear I will sail to Spain myself and kill him."

"I am not married, señor," she cried weakly.

His lips moved around another soundless prayer of thanks and found the tender pink shell of her ear. "Geoffrey. For pity's sake, call me Geoffrey."

"I am not married, señor, but I still cannot marry you. I am a poor servant and you are an hidalgo, a lord. It would not be possible, not fitting, not proper."

Pitt might have laughed had her face, her eyes, not been filled with such solemn intensity. He did smile, however, and kissed her with enough solemnity of his own to leave her breathless and sagging in his arms. "I am no lord, my sweet. I am the son of a gunner, a lowly ironmonger whose only claim to nobility was his pride. If one of us is not worthy of the other, it would be me. Me and the sin of my own arrogance for making me always pretend I am someone I am not."

"You do not pretend," she whispered. "You *are* noble, you *are* kind, you *are* the bravest, most honorable man I have ever known."

"Then marry me, for I also love you more than any other man you ever will know."

Bright, silvery tears of joy shimmered and overflowed again, and he took them to be his answer.

"First, we will have to talk to the captains and let them know they will have no hostage to give to the Queen or anyone else. Then, as soon as the ship drops anchor, we will go ashore and find a minister—"

"A priest!" she squeaked.

Pitt laughed. "A priest, a rabbi, an Indian chief if need be. Then an inn with a very large room and a very small bed so that nothing...nothing ever comes between us again."

He sealed the promise with a kiss and she moaned her assent and eagerness into his mouth. They remained that way, locked in one another's embrace even as the captains from Drake's fleet of warships were preparing to meet for a council of war.

Chapter 22

B eau paced the width of the main deck, then walked back again. The sun was a round ball of muddy orange, low on the western horizon. Clouds were moving down from the north, vast black drifts of them bringing the distinctly metallic smell of rain. Her father stood beside the gangway hatch, eyeing the approaching storm clouds and his daughter's stormy face with equal trepidation.

Her request to accompany him to the *Elizabeth Bonaventure* had been flatly refused. She was not accustomed to being left behind in matters that concerned the *Egret*, and even though Spence agreed wholeheartedly that Dante going half cocked to a confrontation with Victor Bloodstone could well put the entire ship in jeopardy, he did not relent.

"I need ye here, daughter," he insisted in a low, rough voice. "For if aught happens over *there*, I want ye to put on all sail an' haul out o' here like as the devil were snappin' at yer heels. I've given Spit orders to put guards on the armory and powder magazine as well. The cap'n talked to his men this afternoon, but I don't trust anyone on a bellyful o' rum an' hate—not even myself."

The meeting on the *Bonaventure* had been called for eight o'clock. Spence had been ready, fidgeting awkwardly on his ill-fitting peg for an hour now. A nervous hand constantly adjusted and readjusted the stiff white neck ruff he had finally wrested into place. He had pruned his beard to a less fearsome froth of wire fuzz, which only made him look like a bald version of a portrait Beau had seen once of Queen Elizabeth's father, Henry VIII.

She swore softly and on impulse went up to him and batted his hand away from his neck ruff, straightening it herself and arranging the starched figure-eight folds.

"Be careful and look to yourself if anyone starts flinging shots about; you cannot afford to lose any more parts."

Spence chuckled and pinched her cheek, but she wasn't paying heed. Simon Dante was emerging on deck. Unlike Jonas he had not made any special efforts to dress for so auspicious an occasion, despite Spence's offer of anything suitable out of his own wardrobe. Dante wore the gleaming black silk shirt that made him look like a panther on the prowl. A wide leather belt circled his waist, notable for its glaring lack of weaponry of any kind. Not even a dagger was sheathed at his hip. No pistols, no sword, and for that, at least, Beau allowed a small sigh of relief. Walking armed onto Drake's ship might have set the stage for trouble whether it was intended or not.

Stepping out of the hatchway behind Dante were Geoffrey Pitt and Lucifer. Pitt looked grim, for he, too, had been told he was to remain on the *Egret*. Shock of hearing about the *Talon*'s presence had effectively blunted his own happy news regarding his little duchess, and save for one brief visit to Christiana's cabin, he had spent the better part of the afternoon with Dante and the men from the *Virago*.

Lucifer, standing black and enormous behind them, had his massive arms folded over his chest and his twin scimitars strapped across his back. It was obvious he *was* going with Dante and her father, and Beau did not know whether to be comforted by the thought of the Cimaroon's presence at their backs, or alarmed.

Dante had not spoken to her since the morning, and it did not look as if he was going to speak to her now. He did, however, throw an almost casual glance in her direction, one that halted whatever he was saying to Pitt in midsentence. His gaze raked over the pistols tucked into her waist and the cutlass slung crosswise in a belt over her shoulder. A subsequent quick glance around the deck found Spit McCutcheon, Billy Cuthbert, and a score more *Egret* men similarly armed, and while Beau detected a faintly mocking smile curl the corner of his mouth, he bent his head to Pitt again and finished his thought.

The jolly boat was waiting below the gangway, and with a final nod in Spence's direction Dante started for the hatch.

"Coward," Beau muttered under her breath.

He stopped. There was no earthly way he should have been able to hear her, yet she saw his big shoulders ripple with one, two, slow breaths before he turned and walked deliberately back to where she stood. His expression was stony but his eyes sparked blue with anger and before she could react, his arm snaked out and went around her waist, lifting her, crushing her hard against his chest. Conscious of the startled eyes and slack jaws surrounding them, he kissed her, full and open-mouthed, oblivious to her first furious struggles, then attentive to her half-cursed surrender.

"If you are going to call me anything, mam'selle, call me a fool."

"You *are* a fool, Simon Dante. And if you do anything foolish tonight, I will hate you for it."

"Hate me?"

"Every minute of every day."

"So I will be constantly in your thoughts?"

"Only to be hated."

"Liar."

He said the word so softly, it was almost a caress. And the way he looked at her, absorbing her into his eyes, heart, and soul, caused a hot, stinging sensation at the back of her throat.

"Please, Simon," she whispered. "Do not do anything foolish."

"I fear I already have, mam'selle." He kissed her again, tenderly and warmly, and this time, when she flung her arms around his neck and kissed him back, the men on deck grinned and slapped their thighs in approval.

He lowered her gently to the deck again and brushed the backs of his fingers across her cheek.

"We will finish this discussion later," he promised huskily. "Do not even try to hide from me and"—his gaze fell to the open V of her shirt—"wear very old clothes you have no more use for."

Drake stood by the gallery windows of the *Elizabeth Bona-venture*, surveying a great cabin that was filling slowly with the captains of his fleet. The *Bonaventure* was one of four Royal Navy ships the Queen had provided for this venture. There were four others that Drake and his business associates had contributed; a ship belonging to the Lord Admiral (a pox on his always having a finger in every pie); and eight others that a consortium of London merchants, prominent in the privateering business, had supplied, making it a fleet partly driven by patriotic necessity and partly by the quest for plunder and profit. Cadiz was the main supply port for the Spanish fleet sailing to the Indies and the amount of possible plunder should be more than enough to sway the opinions of the privateers to his cause. The Queen's men should see the strategical significance.

The idea to raid Cadiz was brilliant. Dangerous, reckless, audacious, but brilliant. Just like De Tourville himself. Drake supposed he should not have been surprised to see Simon Dante standing on the deck of the *Egret.* It was just like him to rise up from the dead, like the mythical phoenix, and appear out of nowhere as bold and daring as ever. Drake had, along with every other sea hawk in Elizabeth's fleet, declared the Frenchman insane for even dreaming up the scheme to raid Panama, and Victor Bloodstone a fool with a death wish for accompanying him. Instead, Walsingham's by-blow had sailed right into London, all flags and pennants flying. He had delivered over twenty thousand pounds of plundered Panamanian gold into the Queen's coffers and was being touted as the newest Prince of Privateers.

Hindsight excuses from the sea hawks for not having joined De Tourville on his escapade had flown in the air like feathers. Drake, whose own exploits at Cartagena and Nombre de Dios were no longer lauded as being the boldest, the most successful, raids on the New World, had become so short tempered, only his most devoted friends had not avoided him.

Now this further insult for the world's greatest sailor to endure. A merchant ship. Commanded by a one-legged, eight-fingered pirate who put his daughter in breeches and likely drank whatever profits he made . . . he had taken one of the richest prizes on the Main.

No small thanks, again, to Dante de Tourville.

Drake squeezed his fist tightly around his drinking cup,

fighting to control the surge of jealous rage that boiled through his blood. If he had any hope, any hope at all, of being named Admiral of the Fleet, he had to return to England with more than just his flags and pennants flying. He had to leave a mark on Spain and on history that England would not soon forget.

"Sir?"

Drake's head snapped around. Christopher Carleill had been standing by, discreetly guarding his admiral's privacy while the other captains gathered around the long cherrywood table, sharing drinks and conversation.

"Well? What is it?"

"Captain Bloodstone and his second have just arrived."

Drake followed Carleill's glance. He had not liked Walsingham's bastard before the raid on Veracruz, he had less cause to like or trust him now that Dante's unexpected resurrection threw suspicion on his sworn account of the pirate wolf's demise. Nor was Drake alone in his dislike of the man. None of the sea hawks tolerated Bloodstone's smug demeanor lightly, for they had all earned their positions through loyal and daring service to the Crown. Bloodstone had wormed his way into court through the belly of Walsingham's mistress. Any modest skills he displayed at the helm of a ship were generally overshadowed by his vanity, his arrogance, his undisguised ambition to further himself at Court.

It was the main reason Drake disliked him: it was like looking at himself twenty years earlier, knowing he would have rammed anyone and dragged him under his keel in order to get ahead.

"Should I, perhaps, whisper a word in his ear about our unexpected guests?" Carleill inquired.

"And spoil a happy reunion for two members of the brotherhood?" Drake smiled tightly. "I think not. I think

I prefer to let them both surprise each other. It will make for a much more interesting evening."

Victor Bloodstone was tall enough, it behooved him to bend his head to clear the low-slung lintel across the doorway. He was impeccably dressed, as always, wearing a chocolate-brown velvet doublet with satin inserts, and skintight hose that needed no padding around the hips to distract the eye from any flaws. Rings glittered on every finger— emeralds, sapphires, and diamonds mounted on thick gold bands. He wore a starched white neck ruff from which depended several long gold chains in varying styles of links. Around his waist he wore a gold-hilted dress sword and a dagger encrusted with bloodred rubies.

Cool hazel eyes surveyed the roomful of ship's masters. There was not one his equal, with the possible exception of Drake himself. He was disappointed, on the one hand, not to find himself in the austere company of Frobisher, Raleigh, or Hawkyns. On the other, there was little by way of competition. None of these petty privateers had done more than plunder a few small fishing pinnaces or sack a village or two along the coast of Spain. Penny thieves, the lot of them, hunting for their first real taste of fame.

Fame that he, Victor Bloodstone, already had. As if it had happened yesterday, he could taste the sweet triumph of sailing the *Talon* into London. Watchers had sighted her from quite a distance out and sent runners through the city, sounding the alert. Shops and houses alike had emptied, the men and women spilling onto the Queenhithe docks in a great, boisterous crowd. The *Talon*'s flags had been up, signaling a full hold, and because everyone who could walk, talk, or piss upright was aware, by then, of what her mission had been, the quayside had been so congested, there were bodies tipping off the edge and splashing into the sea.

The *Talon* and her master had been greeted, then swarmed, by a fleet of fishing boats and small harbor craft. They had acted like a bobbing, cheering escort up the Thames, their crews bartering and bickering to win bids for haulage. Coins had flashed through the air like water droplets from a fountain, for the *Talon's* crewmen had been just as eager to have ready transport for their personal bounty, hoping to keep it safe from the prying eyes of the Queen's excise men.

Those sharp-nosed, keen-eyed vultures had lost no time hastening to the docks either. It was up to them, caped in somber black like birds of prey, to make a fair accounting of any plunder taken in the Queen's name. If they were quick enough on board, they could almost get an honest tally. If they were delayed, they could hear the pocketfuls of coin and jewels walking off the ships and marvel at the remarkably rotund girth of some of the sailors who had lived months at sea on rations of salted fish and biscuits.

The *Talon* had not disappointed anyone. The crates of gold and silver bullion taken from her hold had staggered all but the most seasoned of the Queen's men—God only knew what their reaction would have been had they known he had stopped off first to unload half of her bounty into his private cache.

As it was, great roars had risen from the crowds each time a group of heroic sailors had disembarked, the greatest of all coming when Victor had appeared on deck. He had stood in the last of the afternoon's golden rays, his handsome face bronzed, his sand-colored hair streaked blond from exposure to the sun and salt air. Large hazel eyes, sensually hooded and long lashed, had sent many a gawping female swooning. He had looked magnificent. He had looked like a man who had defied all odds and sailed half-way across the world to raid the King's treasure depot.

Some of the hopefuls had continued to scan the watery horizon for a glimpse of the *Virago* and her dashing captain, Dante de Tourville. Bloodstone had known, the day they sailed out of port, that no one predicted their success in Veracruz. But Victor had gambled on Dante de Tourville's star riding high, and, by Christ, it had risen clear to the heavens. They had taken nearly four hundred thousand ducats out of the treasure house—a hundred thousand English pounds, and if not for the storm that had hammered them in the Atlantic, they would have escaped cleanly away.

Of course, if it hadn't been for the storm and the damage to Dante's ship, the opportunity would not have been handed to him to double his profits, double his fame, double his pleasure in watching the Spanish zabras send the bastard to hell where he belonged. Arrogant bloody Frenchman, always giving orders, always *telling* him the way it was going to be, always looking at him with those cold blue eyes, flaunting his noble blood.

He probably hadn't looked very noble screaming for his last breath, his mouth and lungs filling with water, his ship spiraling to the sea floor beneath him.

When word spread that the pirate wolf was dead, there was another rippling wave of swooning women and men with downcast eyes, for despite the exorbitant wagers against success, many had gathered in London, anticipating the privateers' return. Most had stared, stunned, at the *Talon*, finding it difficult, if not impossible, to believe the infamous *Virago*, her captain, and crew were gone.

Elizabeth had scarcely believed it either. She had summoned Bloodstone into her presence immediately and demanded to hear every last detail of the raid and the ensuing battle with the zabras. She had questioned him so closely, he began to suspect she was searching for some false note in his reporting of the events, which was why, in the end, he had made the Frenchman out to be a hero and a martyr. Moreover, he had done such a splendid job, she had wept—actually wept!—over the loss of the rogue. And Walsingham, the same bastard who had once slapped him halfway across a room for daring to call him "father," had swelled with pride and dared to call *him* son. He had called for the first toast and nearly wept into his cups when the Queen had rewarded Bloodstone with two fat estates in Devon. It wasn't the knighthood he wanted, but that would come. It was sure to come if he stayed close enough on Drake's heels.

Victor was smiling now as he nodded and accepted the respectful greetings of the other captains.

"You heard he took the *San Pedro de Marcos?*"

"What's that you say?" Victor's sandy eyebrows came together in a sharply demarked bridge over his nose as he caught a snatch of conversation between two captains nearby. "Who took the *San Pedro?* When?"

"Captain Jonas Spence. He is the reason we have been stopped here and summoned for a council. It seems he found some interesting intelligence on board the *San Pedro*—interesting enough to have Drake hobbling about on three legs, if you catch my meaning."

Bloodstone disdained the crudity with a slight curling of his lip. "This . . . Jonas Spence. Does anyone know him?"

In the brief consultations that followed, no one seemed to be acquainted with with the privateer personally but everyone had heard the buzz that his daughter was none other than the Black Swan.

"The cartographer? A woman, you say?"

"Ugly as the name implies, I am told, but possessed of a skilled hand, nonetheless."

"And his ship? The *Egret*? Equally ugly," avowed another voice. "I am anchored off her beam and must say, I find the notion of her taking on a Spanish carrack to be almost fantastic."

"What do you think she would carry? Ten or twelve culverins at best?"

"Closer to twenty," said the same knowledgeable neighbor. "And she's carrying demis. Big bronze teeth . . . exactly like your own, Captain Bloodstone."

The stony gaze raked over the speaker but the response came from Bloodstone's second, Horace Lamprey, an ugly brute with vicious eyes and a lip half missing. "I hardly think a mere merchant's guns could be *exactly* like Captain Bloodstone's. The *Talon*'s demis were acquired by special custom through Dante de Tourville, and there are none other like them in the *world*."

The captain who had made the comment met Lamprey's sneer. "I could swear they are similar—scrolled snouts with eagles on the barrels?"

"Impossible," Bloodstone decreed irately. "The only other guns like mine went down with the *Virago*."

"Which, of course, you say you saw go under."

Victor turned his head to acknowledge the bemused voice behind him and saw Drake, standing by a small chart table, a glass of brandy poised at his lips.

"I saw her surrounded," Bloodstone said carefully, "staggering under full cannonades from six India guards. With the damage my own ship had sustained in the fighting, I could not risk another pass to see if the last board did, indeed, go under, but I daresay no ship could have survived such a pounding as I bore witness to. I wish, with every fiber of my being, that the *Virago*, her courageous captain, and crew could have survived, but I know in my heart they did not."

Drake smiled and his bright hawk's eyes looked past Bloodstone's shoulder, fixing themselves on the shadows outside the cabin door.

"Wish for something too devoutly, too passionately, Captain Bloodstone," he murmured, "and it might surprise you by coming true."

One by one the captains turned to stare at the door. Voices tailed away and conversations ended on unfinished words and half-formed thoughts. Those unaccustomed to seeing tall, black-haired ghosts with white, wolfish smiles felt the need to vent a hastily muttered expletive before they, too, fell back and stared.

Victor Bloodstone turned slowly on his polished heel. At first he saw nothing ominous in the burly, bald-headed captain who beamed a nervous greeting through the frothed red fuzz of his beard. But then a cold chill of foreboding swept down his spine and his eyes followed a line of shadow to where a dark, gleaming ebony head was just straightening from having to duck to clear the lintel.

A moment later a breathless, choking, constricting moment later, he found himself staring into the iced, cobaltblue eyes of the recently dead and departed Simon Dante, Comte de Tourville.

Chapter 23

—⚬—

Dante kept his smile firmly in place as he walked fully into the brighter light. He advanced slowly on Victor Bloodstone, stopping only when he was close enough to smell the shock that oozed instantly to dampen the Englishman's brow. Dante's hands ached with the need to close around the stolid, patrician neck; his arms throbbed with the desire to channel all of his strength and power into squeezing, tearing, choking the life out of the treacherous thief's miserable body.

Horace Lamprey sent his hand instantly to the hilt of his sword, but a white-lipped hiss of breath from his captain stopped the action before it could be noticed by anyone other than Dante. The hazel eyes narrowed and he managed a taut "Simon."

Dante smiled. "Victor. I gather, from the look on your face, you were not forewarned?"

Bloodstone's jaw tightened. "No. I was not."

Sir Francis shrugged amiably. "For such a happy occasion I thought not to spoil the surprise."

"Where the devil have you come from?" Bloodstone asked, his eyes not wavering from Dante's.

"Kind of you to ask. And I suppose the devil would be the one to answer, but since he isn't here with us today—in his normal guise, at any rate—it falls to me to be the bearer of bad tidings."

Aware of every owlish eye rapt upon them, Bloodstone made an admirable recovery of his wits and stepped forward. "Bad tidings? I should think it is nothing less than miraculous. Allow me to be the first to . . . welcome you back to life."

Dante could hardly push away the hand Victor braced on his shoulder, though the sentiment was obvious enough in his eyes to have the intrusion swiftly withdrawn.

"The *Virago*," said Bloodstone attempting a smile. "Did she survive as well?"

"Alas, no. The zabras did their job well. She lies at the bottom of the sea."

"Then we can only thank God you do not lie there with her. But . . . how did you escape, man? The last I saw, I would have said there was no hope."

"Perhaps if you had stayed around awhile longer, you would have seen more."

A few breaths were drawn in, a few more let go on soft whistles, but otherwise, the cabin was as silent as a tomb.

"I had no steerage," Bloodstone said in a quiet, even tone. "The main was cracked, the rudder sloppy. I tried to follow our initial course of action, but the wind turned gusty and I could not bring the *Talon* about."

"I have no doubt she handled like a bitch," Dante agreed. "Especially with all that added weight on board. The barrels of food and water—?"

Lamprey cut brusquely into the conversation. "That was my doing, Captain. I did not think we should leave what few supplies we had behind to benefit the Spaniards in the event you did what damage you could and escaped. They could have used the island and our stores to refurbish and come after us."

"Indeed," Bloodstone added blithely. "I had no notion you would even be so foolhardy as to stand and fight, especially when you could see the trouble we were in. One ship against six?" He lifted his hand in an airy appeal to the logic of the other captains present. "Who would have expected it?"

"And when the wind died and your rudder was stronger, did you not think to circle back and search for survivors?"

"Frankly? No. If there were six enemy ships pounding me to splinters and the last you saw, I was leading them away so that *you might make good your escape*, would you have let the gesture go for naught and circle back—possibly to be captured and killed yourself—just so you could vanquish your conscience and say 'We searched for survivors and found none'?"

He was smooth and convincing. Logical. Reasonable. And lying through his teeth, Dante knew.

"I suppose you thought it best to take the gold out of harm's way as well?"

Bloodstone's eyes betrayed a small flicker. "After all we had gone through to steal it from the King? Would you not think it the wisest course as well?"

"The Queen was pleased? I am looking closely but see no sword imprints on your shoulder."

Bloodstone's high cheekbones warmed under a flush. "She was too distraught over the loss of her favorite Frenchman to think of aught else."

Dante offered up a wry laugh. "I can well imagine how she must have wept over my untimely demise."

Dante's apparent humor seemed to be the signal for others to relax and for one brave soul actually to join in on the exchange.

"More likely she wept over the share of her profits that went down with the *Virago*. For another twenty thousand, she would have danced on Leicester's grave."

"Twenty thousand?" Dante mused. They had easily taken six times that much; the Crown's share should have been closer to fifty. *So you not only cheated me, you arrogant bastard, you landed the* Talon *before you reached England and off-loaded some of her cargo.* "For that much I would dance on my own grave."

It was a timely jest and served to break the tension with the other captains. The shock of seeing a ghost gave way to the pleasure of seeing the pirate wolf in their midst again and the captains started to jostle forward, finding their voices all at once. Dante's back was pounded and a glass was pressed into his hand. A flood of eager questions came from all quarters and toasts were offered. Praise was heaped on the heads of the two valiant captains who had dared raid the King's treasure house at Veracruz, both of whom continued to stare steadfastly at one another, seeing and acknowledging the true way of things in each other's eyes.

It was Drake who interrupted the revelry by reminding them all of a third hero present. He hailed Spence forward and insisted he take up the story of the rescue and the attack on the *San Pedro*. He listened and cheered as enthusiastically as the others, so that one would think he was hearing the tale for the first time. But Sir Francis was nothing if not a master at manipulation, and by the time the paintings of the three Spanish harbors were produced, the men were crowding around the table, absorbing his every word, agreeing—nay, *insisting*—their first strike be against Cadiz.

Through it all Dante and Bloodstone stood in opposite

corners of the cabin. If anyone noticed that the two did
not seem overly anxious to seek out each other's company
again, it went unremarked. If anyone noticed the frequent
looks that passed across the room, laden with promises,
threats, and cutting derision, they preferred to keep their
heads bowed and their own gazes safe from accidental in-
terception.

The storm rolled over the huddled fleet like a great wet
blanket, smothering lights and sounds, pounding like angry
fists on the decks and hulls, driving all but the most stal-
wart under cover. There was no one to watch, no one to
hear his screams, no one to see the rivers of blood that
poured from Dante's knife as he stabbed Victor Bloodstone.
He used the traitor's own jeweled dagger and plunged it
into the bastard's soft underbelly, just above the pubic
bone, jerking upward on the blade until he had ripped
through the groin, stomach, chest, and eventually the
heart. All the while he was dying, Bloodstone screamed for
mercy, begged for it, but Dante only murmured the names
of the men who had died much more horrible deaths on
board the *Virago*, men who had died because of a common
thief's greed and treachery. Then he gouged the knife
deeper, giving it an added twist or taking a small but ef-
fective detour to carve out the bowels, spleen, and liver.

   Dante smiled and looked down into the celebratory cup
of brandy he had poured himself. He took a satisfied swallow, letting the most excellent liquor roll to the back of
his tongue and down his throat, warming him all the way
to his toes.

   When he looked across the cabin, Victor Bloodstone
was still standing there, talking in muted tones to his second, Horace Lamprey, and Dante had the pleasure of killing him all over again.

"Simon?"

It was Drake, with Carleill beside him, and Dante gave them his grudging attention.

"Watching the storm, were you? Hellish thing. Black as a maw out there."

Dante had only been vaguely aware of the weather and he looked now, seeing the thick white splatters hitting the gallery windows beside him.

"I thought I ought to ask formally if you would honor us with your presence at Cadiz," Drake said. "Given the nature of the hunt and your penchant for always striving to be in the hottest part of hell at any given time, I may have overstepped myself by presuming you would want to accompany us. I am reminded, however, you have just come from a particularly exhausting adventure and may feel the strain would be too much."

Dante smiled. "I think I can bear up, but I thank you for your concerns over my health. In truth"—he glanced over at Bloodstone—"I am feeling quite invigorated."

Drake followed his gaze. "I thought you might."

Dante took a sip of brandy and pushed his shoulder away from the wall. "You might have had a *thought* to warn me, Francis. You know how I dislike surprises."

"Yet you handled yourself admirably well. Victor, on the other hand, seemed a little uncomfortable."

"It *is* rather close in here," Dante mused. "So much rhetoric, so much damned zeal."

"And not one word of dissent."

"So far."

"So far," Drake agreed. "Borough will probably give me the headache with his infernal discourses on naval warfare, but the rest . . . they seem an eager lot."

"They usually are at the mention of the word *profit*."

"Do you deny the possibility that *vast* profits exist? If

nothing else, Cadiz is the warehouse for supplies that come from the Mediterranean and Baltic. Cannon from Italy, cordage, spars, sailcloth . . . even the priests who hold their court in Seville will disembark for Lisbon through Cadiz. And if we should stumble across another treasure ship or two . . . ?"

"You did seem to make that a highly likely possibility," Dante noted dryly.

"I merely suggested the *San Pedro de Marcos* would not have been sailing across the Atlantic alone."

"I also thought you skimmed rather lightly over the possibility of the King's ships fighting back. And the fact the bay can become a trap if the wind should fail."

"I saw no soft spines here tonight. They are all aware of the risks." Drake pursed his lips and took a seemingly casual step in front of Simon Dante, placing himself directly in the line of vision between the privateer and Victor Bloodstone. "He said his mainmast was damaged and his rudder too unsteady to keep the enemy engaged."

"So I heard."

Drake's eyes turned as cold and hard as two chips of broken glass. "Is that what you saw?"

"I was rather preoccupied at the time."

"I need to know I can count on every man who sails in my wake. I need to know, if an enemy is closing on my back, there will be guns there to defend me."

Dante's eyes lifted above Drake's head and fastened on Bloodstone as he took another measured sip of his brandy. "I would be inclined, in that case, to keep the *Talon* in front of you."

"Are you saying—?"

"I am saying . . . you should have a ship at your back you can depend upon to stay in the battle and not run away when his holds are full and the smoke becomes thick enough to claim convenient damages."

Drake's tongue took another stroll around his mouth, removing the sudden bad taste he had acquired. "I see. You have shown remarkable restraint, cousin."

"Haven't I, though. It must be the exalted company."

"If you care to lay a charge . . ."

"I prefer to lay a broadside, but in my own time, Francis. In my own time."

"To that end . . . have you given thought to Captain Spence's offer?"

Dante looked over to where Jonas sat surrounded by a dozen privateers quaffing ale and brandy, retelling the taking of the *San Pedro* for what was surely the tenth time. He had offered to throw his guns in with Drake's fleet, to follow them to Cadiz that he might serve God and Her Most Gracious Majesty the Queen in whatever capacity his humble talents might allow.

"I would suggest he has all the profit and glory he can handle at the moment," Dante said evenly. "He is a good man and has a stout ship under him, but I see no benefit to having him put at risk what he has already gained."

Drake pursed his lips. "He seems a proud man."

"His pride will recover the moment he sails into Plymouth Sound."

"And your most charming Black Swan? Will she recover as quickly?"

Dante blew a soft breath between his lips. "She will have no choice. She goes where the *Egret* goes."

"Nevertheless, perhaps we can soften the blow somewhat. One of our pinnaces is leaking like a sieve. We were going to send her home, but the captain would not hear of it. Now she can be given the 'task' of acting as escort to the *Egret*, and vise versa. It would be a shame, after all, to lose either ship to those barbarous French scoundrels who lurk out of Biscay. I shall put it to Captain Spence directly," he added, "couching it in terms of a personal favor to me."

"You put me in your debt," Dante said with a small bow.

"I know. And I plan to collect upon it with interest. You have knowledge of the harbor at Cadiz, you have knowledge of the defenses. With Carleill's generous permission you will also have a ship to show us the way."

The lieutenant, who had taken in the entire conversation and said nothing until now, stood a little straighter, and flushed a little darker.

"My ship, sir, is the *Scout*. She is small, but sturdy, and is currently being navigated by my brother, Edward. I have discussed the matter with him and we would consider it an honor and a privilege to relinquish command to you that you might regard her as your own until this venture is concluded. She . . . lays a spirited broadside, sir, and would be the match for any ship that might cross your path."

Dante studied the young man's tense features and wondered how much of it was an honor and how much was a direct request by Sir Francis Drake.

Carleill misinterpreted his hesitation and his coloring wavered again. "She isn't the *Virago*, I know, but—"

"No. No, Lieutenant, that isn't why I find my tongue stuck to the roof of my mouth. I am just . . ." Dante stopped, realizing Carleill had been put into a position where he might be more insulted if the offer was refused. He shook his head and smiled, extending his hand. "I am the one who is honored, Christopher, and I accept your gracious offer, with thanks."

Carleill seemed startled at the friendly use of his name, but it had the desired effect. Some of the starch came out of his face and he shook Dante's hand with something akin to comradeship.

"I have some *Virago* men on board the *Egret* who may be interested in joining me."

"Arrangements can be made for as many as choose to follow you, sir. Have you your own pilot?"

Dante's breath caught a moment. "No. No, he went down with my ship, rest his soul."

"I can promise you my brother is most capable at the helm. If it is agreeable to you, he would be . . . beside himself with the honor."

"It would be most agreeable. I thank you again."

"Well, then." Drake clapped Dante on the shoulder. "If all seems to be settled to everyone's satisfaction, I shall wend my way to Captain Spence and see if I cannot persuade him to do me this momentous favor. If you will excuse me . . . ?"

Drake strolled over to where Jonas was holding court. Carleill lingered long enough to discuss the *Scout* with Dante, but when a summons to go topside interrupted them, he excused himself, leaving Dante with a promise to introduce him properly to the ship and crew at his earliest convenience.

Dante leaned his shoulder on the wall and briefly watched the solid tattoo of rain on the gallery windows. His charming little black swan would not be thrilled at all with the notion of being summarily dismissed, regardless whether it was couched in friendly terms or not. An image of Beau standing on the afterdeck of the *Egret*, her eyes streaming from the clouds of smoke that rose from the guns, her hands raw and bleeding, her face pale with fear, came to his mind and he knew he would have to find his own way of softening the blow to her pride. He meant what he had said. He wanted her safe in England.

He wanted someone to go home to.

The thought surprised him and he narrowed his eyes against the glare of the lights reflected off the panes of glass. It had been so long since he had even thought of anywhere being home, other than the sea. His gray-cloaked accountants kept reminding him he had several in both England and France, but they had just been cold, gloomy castles in his mind's eye, full of pomp and ceremony, gilded in the rents his tenants could not afford to pay . . .

. . . Echoing with the scornful laughter of his wife throwing the proof of her infidelity in his face. Strange, but he could barely hear it now. And not at all when Beau was with him, whether she was cursing him, fighting with him, or warming his ear with the soft, rushing breaths of ecstasy.

What would Isabeau Spence make of a four-hundred-room French chateau?

The question, and its answer, brought a smile to his lips even as he tried to see past the smear of rain on the windows and find the *Egret.*

"The cocky bastard," Victor Bloodstone muttered. "He's actually grinning at me."

Horace Lamprey followed his captain's burning gaze and saw De Tourville standing by the gallery windows, staring into the reflections duplicated in the many panes.

"Blast his miserable soul to hell, why could he not have gone down with his ship?"

"Or before," Lamprey mused. "I almost had him in Veracruz, *would* have had him, if that damned Cimaroon wasn't always in his shadow."

Bloodstone looked around quickly to see if anyone was within earshot, but those who weren't discussing Cadiz were hanging off Jonas Spence's every word.

"And now he knows about the gold. He knows we

landed somewhere first and off-loaded most of the bullion before the Queen's excisemen got their sticky fingers onto it."

"Maybe that's what he's after," Lamprey suggested. "His share."

"Dante de Tourville? He's but a copper groat poorer than God Himself! What does he need with more gold? No, it's blood he's after. My blood. And he'll wait, like a vulture, circling and grinning until he thinks the time is right to strike."

"Happens, then, we should strike first," Lamprey said with a sly grin. " 'Tis a hellish dark night outside: Sir Francis is even encouraging the captains to have a care as they leave. A man could easily lose his footing, kosh himself on the head, and be over the side before he knew it. Wouldn't even hear the scream."

Bloodstone looked into the flat brown eyes of his second and, after a moment of thoughtful contemplation, nodded his compliments.

"I was thinking of leaving, myself, in a few minutes."

"Aye, sir. It would be best if Sir Francis and the others see you go."

"And best if they don't see you at all."

"Like I said, sir. It's hellish dark outside. I don't imagine a man could be seen unless he wanted to be."

Chapter 24

The rain fell in sheets. Only those who held the watch or those who enjoyed a good drenching in fresh water ventured out from under cover. All but the closest galleons were obscured behind the heavy, steady curtain of rain and then only the faint, watery blots of yellow from their stern lanterns were visible through the downpour.

Beau had retreated to her cabin. Her pistols had become wet and she had removed them hours ago. Her sword was a nuisance, slapping her thigh as she paced, so she had removed it as well. Her boots had become more of a squishing aggravation than they were worth, so when she paced, she paced barefoot.

Dante and Spence had been gone more hours than she cared to think about. Five, to be precise, and while she had no idea how long a council of war took on board a ship, the longer they were away, the more likelihood there was of trouble. Periodically, she went up on deck, thinking she could see more clearly if she stood in the rain rather than trying to peer through it. Twice she had encountered Geoffrey Pitt on the foredeck, his hands raised like visors over his eyes, his hair, clothing, body, soaked to the bone.

There was not much wind and thankfully, no lightning. Only a sodden blanket of clouds overhead and the hailing sound of billions of drops of rain striking the surface of the sea, harsh and unrelenting. Earlier, in the eerie, charged moments before the skies broke open, the *Egret*—indeed, all of the ships in Drake's fleet—had had their mastheads and yardarms bathed in the dancing, blue-white currents of Saint Elmo's Fire. Beau had seen the phenomenon only once before, and she stood in awe like the others, knowing it would have been taken as a good omen by Drake, who would undoubtedly use it to convince his captains their mission was sanctioned by God. Some of the older tars, she knew, regarded it as the touch of the devil, and in this instance, with the *Talon* lurking out in the darkness somewhere, she was not inclined to disagree.

"You should go below, you will catch your death!"

Beau jumped halfway out of her skin before she recognized Pitt climbing up behind her on the foredeck. It was the third time she had left her cabin and the third time Pitt had greeted her with almost the same warning. He looked half drowned himself. His yellow hair was plastered to his forehead and his clothes clung to his skin in dripping folds.

"It is foolish for both of us to be out here," he reiterated.

"Can you see anything at all?" she asked, ignoring the comment.

He gazed out into the blankness and shook his head. "We could be drifting into a whale's mouth and I wouldn't know it."

It wasn't the answer she had wanted to hear. Their own huge lanterns guttered and flickered and sent up enough clouds of hissing steam to turn the light opaque, but some of it glistened off the contours of her face and showed her concern.

"He will be all right," Pitt assured her. "If he were going to start his own private war, he would have done it by now. We would have heard the alarm bells or seen a sulphur flare . . . or something. Go below, Beau. I'm sure you will be the first one he comes to see when he gets back."

Beau blinked against the weight of the rain and searched his handsome face a moment. "I just . . . didn't expect to be so worried."

"None of us ever does, until it happens."

"But . . . I never *wanted* it to happen. Part of me still doesn't. Part of me just wants everything to be simple again, like it was . . . like it was before . . ." She stopped and agonized over the admission, not even absolutely sure what she was admitting.

Pitt saw her shiver and put his arm around her shoulder, drawing her against what little heat he had to spare.

"I am truly sorry, Beau, but when you love a man like Simon Dante, nothing is ever going to be simple again, believe me."

Beau looked up at him through the rain, but there was no point in arguing or denying the charge.

"Nothing?" she asked forlornly.

"Nothing. But if it is any consolation, I would say you have managed to confound the hell out of him, too, he's just too proud to admit it."

"I wouldn't be too proud to admit anything right now," she said with honest misery in her voice, "if he would just come back."

"He'll come back, I promise you."

Beau peered one last time through the driving rain and mist, then touched Pitt's arm to thank him. She was about to descend the ladder to the main deck when she saw a blur of movement near the gangway. She stood poised with one bare foot on the top rung and her hands gripping the rails, watching as something big and black swelled over the lip of the decking and rose to what seemed like monstrous proportions. It curled over and rose again and Beau was opening her mouth to scream when she caught a glimpse of light reflecting wetly off the curved blades of Lucifer's scimitars.

"Mister Pitt! They're back!"

"I'm right behind you," he said, too gentlemanly to push her off the ladder, but not too rash to vault over the rail and skid to a landing on the slippery deck below.

Lucifer grunted when Pitt arrived by his side. He was bent over, trying to haul a deadweight up the wooden steps on the hull. Beau held her breath. She covered her mouth with her hands, scarcely daring to watch as, together, the two men pulled Jonas Spence up the last two rungs and dumped him in a sprawl across the deck. Beau fell onto her knees beside him and lifted his head onto her lap. His eyes were closed and his mouth slack, but at the feel of a welcoming lap beneath him, he raised his eyelids and beamed up into the rain.

"Ay-y-y-ye, an' a jolly wee lass she were, she were; a jolly wee lass, wi' a hand up her . . . eh? Beau? Is that you, girl?"

"Father?"

"Blow my ballocks, who'd ye think it were?"

She sat back on her heels—driven back, more's the like—by the overpowering smell of spirits on his breath. "You're drunk."

"Aye, that's me, lass. Drunk an' useless." His head flopped back on her lap. "Too useless to be any good to the likes o' Drake an' his lot, so I've been told. Sendin' us home, he is. Says we'll be doin' him a favor, takin' his sick an' his sour home. Watchin' over his wee pinnace. Aye. His wee pinnace. 'At's what he has, all right. A wee pinnace fer a wee man."

Beau looked at Lucifer. "What is he talking about? What has happened?"

"What's happened," said a voice from the top of the gangway, "was that we had a hell of a time loading him into the jolly boat, and an even more hellish time finding the right damned ship." Dante sighed expressively, his breath as thick as the mist, and held out his hand. "Lend a poor, drowned sailor a helping hand, mam'selle?"

Beau surged to her feet, heedless of Spence's head bouncing down onto the deck again.

"We were worried sick about you. Pitt and I were both worried sick about you. We have been *back* and *forth*"— she punctuated both words with angry swipes of her hand—"in the *cold* and the *rain!* We have been watching and waiting and worrying about all of you. *We thought you were dead!*"

Dante pulled himself up the final few steps. "Would it please you any to know I might very well have been? Black as it is, I damned near walked into a loose spar. Lucky for me, Lucifer saw it in time and swung it back."

"Did he hit anything on the return?" Pitt asked casually.

"He may have. We had our hands too full of Spence to check." He looked at Beau. "I'm sorry if we worried you. And I'm sorry if your father is drunk, but he did not take too kindly to Sir Francis insisting he take the *Egret* home."

"I suppose you did everything in your power to argue in our favor."

"I happen to agree with him," Dante said quietly, "for the reasons I told you before. And a few other concerns I may not have mentioned."

Beau stood in the rain, trembling against the cold, her

fists clenching and unclenching as she glared at him. "Your reasons don't interest me, Captain. Neither do your heart-felt concerns."

She spun around and ran through the hatch, cursing when she stubbed her toe on a step, swearing vociferously when she slammed the door to her cabin shut behind her. She limped the length of the room twice before she thought to return to the door and slide the iron bolt into its ring, but she was a split second too late. Dante pushed his way inside like a strong wind, shedding water with every step.

"My reasons may not interest you, but you're going to hear them anyway."

She offered up an anatomically impossible retort as she presented him with her back.

Dante reached out a hand, thought better of it, and raked it through the heavy, wet waves of his hair instead. "Are you not even *interested* in knowing if I saw Victor Bloodstone or not?"

"I am assuming he was the 'spar' who hit you on deck."

"As a matter of fact, he wasn't; he was long gone by then."

"Gone?" Her head turned, barely enough to notice. "You didn't kill him?"

"No. I didn't kill him. I stood closer to him than you and I are right now—much closer, dammit—but I did not kill him. I wanted to. I did . . . in my mind . . . a dozen different times, a dozen different ways, but I kept hearing your voice in my ear saying 'don't be a fool' 'don't be a fool.' "

"You've never listened to me before."

Dante's throat worked for a moment, but the words would not come, could not come, and his hand, still threaded into his hair, started to wilt down by his side.

"Because I did not think it was possible," he said finally, "to feel anything but hatred anymore. It was all I was when I came on board this ship: hatred and revenge. It was pure and undiluted and so strong, I did not think anything that was soft or beautiful could find its way inside me again. Then tonight"—he paused to take a breath—"when I saw Bloodstone, the desire, the *need*, was still there to kill him . . . but so was the need to come back here, to feel your arms go around me and your body take me where it's soft, and beautiful"—he looked at her squared shoulders and the small white fists clenched by her sides, and his voice fell to a whisper—"and safe. And if I don't know how to say the right words anymore it's because—it's because I never thought I would *want* to say them again."

Beau's shoulders sagged and the anger drained out of her in a rush. She lifted her hand and dragged it across her cheek, pushing back a strand of wet hair that had fallen over her brow, and when she turned around, her eyes were huge and dark and glistening in the candlelight.

"I hope . . . you are not trying to tell me . . ."

"That I love you? I'm afraid I am, mam'selle. And I'm afraid I do. Very much so."

She stared at him for a long moment, then bowed her head and shook it slightly. "You can't. You just . . . can't."

He arched a genuinely curious eyebrow. "May I ask why not?"

"Because . . . it just isn't fair," she whispered. "How am I supposed to hate you when you tell me something like that?"

He closed the gap between them and framed her face between his hands. He held her that way for the short breath it took to whisper her name, then his lips were brushing her temple, her eyes, her cheeks, the corner of her mouth. The lush heat of him drew her inside, and the kiss deepened, became bruising and urgent, claiming her, branding her as his own.

"I do hate you," she gasped. "I do."

Her hands went around his shoulders and his arms brought her crushing into his embrace. Her toes came off the floor as he lifted her and he turned her in a slow circle, once, twice, before he set her down again. His hands slid up from her waist and she heard the damp rasp of tearing cloth. It was all she could do not to comment on his impatience as he growled another lame apology, but his mouth was hungry and insistent upon hers and patience of any kind became the farthest thing from her mind.

He stripped off her shirt and stripped off her breeches and his mouth followed his hands everywhere, intent upon inflaming her body with a need as urgent as his own. Blood was drumming through his temples, through his fingertips, through the raw nerve endings on his skin, but when he stood back to fling off his own clothes, her hands were already there.

She grasped the open neck of his shirt and tore it down the center seam, opening a gash all the way to his waist. She fumbled next with the buckle on his belt and cast it to the floor, then tugged at the shrunken wetness of his hose, the stubborn, clinging barrier of wool that would not budge until she broke free of his mouth and fell to her knees, peeling the recalcitrant garment down his thighs with her.

Her hands circled the iron-hard shaft of his flesh and her tongue slid over him like a hot, wet flame. Dante swore and pushed his fingers into her hair, trying, in the beginning, to hold her away, to keep her from bringing him out of his skin too soon . . . too soon . . . But her hands stroked his thighs and her lips stroked his flesh and he could only groan a warning as his whole body began to shake, to tremble. His hips began to buck against the pressure and a raw, ragged gasp broke from his throat. The heat flooded into his loins, threatening to explode, and a moment before he did, he lifted her roughly into his arms and carried her the few steps to the bed.

"And you accuse *me* of not playing fair?" he rasped.

Without preamble he buried his mouth between her thighs. Beau arched up off the bed, but he would have none of it; he kept his hands on her belly and breasts, and his tongue ravishing, plundering, pillaging, until she was hoarse from crying out and weak from the waves of pleasure so relentless and powerful, there was no stopping them, no interrupting them, not even when he rose above her and sank himself into the hot, drenching splendor.

"You need me," she whispered some time later. "You know you need me."

"I don't know any such thing," he said, his teeth clenched through a snarl.

"You don't know this Edward Carleill, you don't know what kind of a helmsman he is. For that matter you don't even know the ship, or what she is capable of doing. You need me, Simon Dante, and by God"—her mouth closed around the dark disc of his nipple and worked it until she heard him gasp out a curse—"I intend to make you admit it."

"I admit it freely, mam'selle. I need you. I need you." He twined his fingers through her hair and angled her face up to his so that there was no mistaking his meaning. "*I need you.* But not on the *Scout.* It's too dangerous."

Beau pushed herself upright and saw the quick flexing of muscles across his chest. She was straddling his thighs, he was buried hilt deep inside her, and they had been dueling over the finer points of his leaving the *Egret* long enough for both of them to be covered in a fine sheen of sweat.

"After all my father and I have done for you, how can you just let Drake send us home with a pat on the head?"

"You're going home with your holds full of plundered treasure."

"A pox," she said, sliding her hips forward, "on plundered treasure."

He swore again and rolled his head to the side. If the bed had been an inch wider, he could have easily tossed her over and reversed their positions—and then she would have learned the true meaning of torment. As it was, she kept her knees locked firmly to his hips, and braced her hands, when he made any attempt to extricate himself, on an overhead beam, pushing down as hard as he pushed up. Moreover, she was showing remarkable control. His own fault, he supposed, for bringing her to climax half a dozen times before he found himself splayed and pinned like a starfish out of water. If it weren't so unbelievably arousing, he might have become annoyed.

She cupped his chin in her hand and forced him to look at her again. "You said you thought it might have been one of Bloodstone's men who ambushed you on the *Bonaventure* tonight."

"When did I say that? I never said that."

"Then you were thinking it. And if he would dare to plan an ambush on Drake's flagship, what will he dare out in the open sea? Or in battle? Or—"

He brought her mouth down hard on his and kissed her so thoroughly, she was gasping when he let her go. Her face was flushed and her eyes were blazing with the effort it was taking to concentrate on something other than the heat beneath her.

"I will watch him very closely," he vowed.

Panting lightly, Beau combed her fingers through the springy black mat of chest hairs, molding her hands to the shape of his muscles, following each magnificently sculpted band down to his belly. She rocked her hips back and forth, testing his limits even as she tested her own, and stopped moving a shiver shy of overestimating herself.

"We could unburden some of the gold on the pinnace that is going home anyway," she said, still trying to find a way around all his manly logic.

"The pinnace is going, the *Egret* is going, and you are going. And if anyone should be unburdened, mam'selle"— his hands circled her breasts and his thumbs abraded the taut pink nipples—"it should be me, before you cause irreparable damage to the both of us."

She reached back and let her fingertips trail lightly back and forth along his thighs. She felt him tense and stretch himself farther up inside her, giving one delicious throb when her fingers danced over an area that was already acutely sensitive to every languid roll of her hips.

"So. Now I am a burden," she murmured.

He sucked in a breath and released it on a soft oath. He grasped her around the waist and forced two swift, hard strokes before she regained control and stopped him.

"You are not a burden," he promised on a gasp. "But you might become a dangerous distraction in battle. I might be inclined to worry more about you than the enemy, about what might happen if I took my eyes off you for any length of time. You have seen how fast things can go wrong in battle. You saw how close your father came to losing his other leg. Good God, Isabeau"—he brushed his hands over her breasts, her shoulders, her arms, her legs— "you cannot fault me for wanting to keep you safe and whole."

She bit back her frustration and leaned determinedly

forward, her hands braced on either side of his head, her eyes a mere inch or two from his. "No one had to keep me safe or whole before you came striding into my life, Captain, and look . . . I am all here."

His flesh throbbed in its fullness. "So you are."

"On the other hand, I have seen *you* in battle and you are reckless. You take unnecessary chances—"

"I swear I will be the soul of discretion."

"You play careless games with unfamiliar ships."

"I will stand off a thousand yards and spit my shots harmlessly into the water . . . is that what you want?"

A shiver sent her focus down to the source of all her trouble: his mouth. "I want you to trust me."

"I do."

"Completely."

"I am trying. Believe me, I am trying. But you are asking me to put aside every law of nature, society, reason, and instinct I have ever known. It might . . . take a little more time."

"How *much* more time?" she demanded.

He looked so deeply into her eyes, she thought she felt him climb inside her. "Will the rest of our lives do, do you suppose?"

Her breath came out in a rush. His hands were on her hips, manipulating them as deviously as his words manipulated her intentions. Her pleasure started to come in dark, swirling torrents and she could not have stopped it had she even been so foolishly inclined to do so. She wasn't, of course. She wasn't even sure she had won any part of the argument. Later, she would worry about reclaiming the wit to challenge him again, but for the moment, the dissolving liquid heat of the moment, it was enough to hear him cry out her name and feel the power of his shuddering ecstasy fill the last empty place in her heart.

Chapter 25

Spence appeared on deck the next morning with a head as thick as a post. His tongue was furred and he declared the foot he had left in the Indies ten years ago itched as if he were standing on a nest of red ants. He was not happy, and when Jonas Spence was not happy, he made damned sure the entire crew was not happy. Even Spit McCutcheon was acting like a cat with turpentine rubbed under his tail.

Beau had no sympathy to spare for anyone. She hadn't had but a moment's sleep all night, and naturally, that moment had come early in the morning. When she had finally startled herself awake, most of Dante's men had already transferred to the *Scout* and he probably would have happily sailed away without so much as a fare-thee-well if she hadn't come up on deck in time.

It did not matter that she had not wanted him to say good-bye, had ordered him not to, and was sullen enough when he did to send him away with less than a glowing flush of warmth and understanding coursing through his body. The heat, the passion, the poignant promises made in the dark warmth of her cabin, had vanished, leaving nothing but harsh reality in its wake. He was leaving and she was staying behind. The *rest of their lives* had taken on an ugly new meaning in the chilling gray light of dawn.

Her mood was not much improved with her first glimpse of the *Scout*.

It was a sorry-looking vessel, smaller than the *Egret*— perhaps a hundred tons in weight, with a battery of eight culverins and six sakers. It was adequate armament for a ship her size and character, but nothing near the heat Dante was accustomed to on the *Virago*—or the *Egret* since he had supplemented her weaponry with the demis. In the *Scout* he would not have much choice *but* to stand off and let the heavier guns of the six-hundred-ton *Elizabeth Bonaventure* and the five-hundred-ton *Revenge* and *Golden Lion* soften the enemy's underbelly. And for that at least, Beau felt some smug satisfaction.

But then she remembered the *Talon* was also out there, bristling with Pitt's demi-cannon, mastered by a man who would likely stop at nothing to rid himself of the specter of Dante de Tourville. Battles *were* perfect places for confusion, with all the smoke and noise and turbulence. Perfect places for a man who planned ambushes in the dark and had no qualms about abandoning fellow captains to the guns of enemy ships.

Drake's fleet was already low on the horizon. Dawn had brought their canvas out in bloom and, trusting Dante would have no difficulty making up the time, had set a course due south and turned their sails into a gray, wind-driven sky. The *Talon* had been one of the last ships to get under way, almost flaunting her presence in Dante's face. Watching her sidle past wearing her disreputable coat of sly gray paint and suit of dirty canvas, Beau could barely resist the urge to load one of the demis herself and send him off properly.

The itch to hold a gun at Dante's temple was strong too. He looked as if he hadn't slept much either—wonder of wonders. His temper was short and his jaw had a tendency to clench around every other word. For fare-thee-wells it was a pretty sorry thing also, with him doing most of the talking—and doing it fast so there was little room for argument—and Beau doing most of the glaring. Spence, McCutcheon, Cuthbert, and the better part of the *Egret*'s crew stood nearby in glum silence. There was no cheering when the last of the *Virago* men took to the jolly boats, not a single smile anywhere to be seen.

The leaky pinnace was also forced to watch the grand departure. The *Squirrel* was a small vessel of twenty tons with two masts and a row of oars as well as sail. She carried a crew of eighteen, and while there were no heavy guns aboard, there were bow and stern chasers and a row of deadly falconets mounted on each beam. They were favored by smugglers for their speed, and used by naval officers for their ability to sail quickly between warships carrying orders and relaying messages. At the moment she was nudged up to the hull of the *Egret*, her masts and rigging chattering like loose teeth in a widow's head. She looked as sound and seaworthy as any other ship in Drake's fleet, and her captain seemed happy to shout up his relief they were going home.

Spit McCutcheon's reply sent him ducking to avoid a large splatter of phlegm.

"Cheese-assed bastard. Give him to me for a month, I'll stiffen his spine."

Spence snorted and watched the jolly boat make its final crossing to the *Scout*. His eyes narrowed and his beard-parted around a curse. "Where the devil does Yarwood think he's goin'? An' Loftus?"

"They wanted to fight the Spanyards," Spit declared loudly, sending a particularily acerbic glance down to the pinnace. "An' I weren't about to stop them, they wanted to go. Whole damned crew wanted to go but they had space for only a couple o' our men. If ye'll notice the bruises on Yarwood's face, he had to beat off a dozen others just to get one o' them spaces."

Spence grunted and shook his head as the *Scout* cast off her lines and unfurled the large mainsail. It was full of trapped rainwater and showered the deck below as the canvas flapped and shook out its wrinkles.

"Sloppy work, that," Spit remarked disdainfully. "Sails are too loose, they should be trimmed tight, not luffin' away in the breeze. No wonder she nearly rammed us."

"She nearly rammed us," Beau said dryly as she joined them by the rail, "because her helmsman is an ass. If he's a day over twenty, I'll have his child."

"Bold talk for someone barely out in teats herself."

"Yes, but at least I know what I'm doing. I warrant Mister Carleill has never been out of the Channel, if even out of port. Dante"—she looked back over the side—"will probably feed him to Lucifer for an evening meal."

"Try to keep the smile off yer face when ye say that, lass," Spence advised with a snort. "Might hex the poor lad."

"I fear they may already have picked up a hex," she said quietly. "Did you see the way the *Talon* prowled past, almost like a mongrel slinking outside a butcher shop?"

"Aye. Spit had a thought for a moment, he might o' been sniffin' after us."

"Us?"

Spit leaned forward to see around Jonas's girth. "Are ye forgettin' what we have in our holds?"

"No, I'm not forgetting. But he wouldn't dare turn away from Drake and come after us; none of them would, there were too many witnesses. Besides, they'll have more than enough plunder in Cadiz."

"Aye," Spence grumbled. "Cadiz."

"Risky business, that," Spit muttered. "But God bless 'em all for havin' the ballocks to try it."

"Twenty ships against fifty? Mortal odds. They'll likely be blown out o' the water."

"Perhaps not, señor," said a quiet voice from behind them.

Spence, McCutcheon, and Beau turned as one and stared at the speaker. It took Beau a moment to recognize the little duchess (it was difficult to think of her in any other way), for she had shed her fancy gown and cumbersome farthingale. She wore what looked like one of Pitt's shirts and a pair of sailor's canvas breeches that were several sizes too big, rolled at the waist and tied securely in place with a length of jute. Her eyes were rimmed and swollen, her nose was red, and her face the color of a bleached sheet. There wasn't a curl to be found anywhere on her head; her hair had been scraped back and braided in such an obvious imitation of Beau's, it gave all three at the rail a moment's pause.

"Most of the ships in Cadiz have been commandeered by the governor of the province. They have their sails and their guns removed until such time as a Spanish crew can be provided, for fear they might sneak out of the harbor and desert the King's service."

"How the devil do you know such things, lass?" Spence demanded.

"I am but a maid, señor. The duchess and her husband

talk, and see only the walls even if I am standing beside them."

"Did you tell Pitt this?" Beau asked.

"About the ships? Yes, señora. And about the cannon and the nets they are able to string across the channel to the inner bay."

"Cannon? Nets?"

"The cannon on the castle walls, they are very old and have had to be fixed in place. They can only strike into the very center of the harbor. And the net is worked by two galleys, which can be sunk to seal off the entrance to the inner port."

"An' Drake will know all of this before he goes in to attack?" Spence asked excitedly.

Christiana lowered her eyes a moment, obviously suffering pangs of guilt, but when she raised them again, and was confronted by Beau's curious frown, they were as proud as the tilt in her chin.

"I wanted Señor Pitt to come back to me," she said simply. "I wanted him to take me with him, but this he most angrily would not do."

"A plague o' that goin' around," Spit remarked under his breath.

"He wishes to marry me and I wish to marry him, but we are not married yet and he should not be able to tell me what I may and what I may not do."

In all the time the duchess had been aboard, Beau estimated she had probably not sent more than two or three words in her direction, but she stared at her now, dumbfounded.

"She's right," Beau said, and looked at Spence. "She is absolutely right, you know."

The two pair of tiger eyes read each other's thoughts and brought a groan up from Spit's throat.

"Ahh, Jaysus. Tell me ye're not thinkin' what I think ye're thinkin'."

Spence's eyes narrowed. "I'm only thinkin'—sometimes ye have to take heed o' the flag we fly up top. That's England's flag, an' she's in trouble, an' that means, by my mind, we should be doing what we can to help, not slinkin' away with our tails tucked 'atween our legs. What say you, daughter?"

"I say it is a sad day indeed when someone tells Jonas Spence where he may and where he may not sail his ship."

Spence drew a deep breath to swell his chest. "Aye. So it would be. We'd have to put it to the whole crew. Wouldn't be right not to; they've earned the right to go home an' spend their hard-won gold."

"Then let's put it to them, and see what they say."

Part Three

Cadiz

Chapter 26

Simon Dante had early misgivings about the *Scout*.
She was designed to be light and fast, yet there was
evidence of weakness in the masts and the rudder took far
too long to ponder an order before it obeyed.

Most of the guns had given Pitt cause to suspect they
had been cannibalized off prize ships, for they were of varying calibers and quality, some bearing the stamp of an
Italian foundry, some English, some Spanish. He had insisted on testing them with live ammunition—a waste
young Carleill had strongly opposed. Pitt was not fond of
the Italian style of building their cannon in sections of
banded iron and bolting them together in the trough of a
carriage; two of these built-up culverins had obviously out-
lived their usefulness and cracked apart on the first live
shot. He was able to bastard them into one almost adequate
gun, but another of the cast-iron falconets he simply un-
bolted and let fall into the sea. Most of the powder had to
be reground to a finer consistency and brought up out of
the damp hold to dry out properly in the sun.

Still, it was a ship and Dante was in command again

and for the two weeks it took to sail around Cape Saint Vincent, he and Pitt drilled on the guns and on the rigging, startling most of the crew into becoming, if not better sailors, at least more alert sailors. At all times of the day and even in the dead of night, a sudden roll of drums would signal the men to turn to, cutlasses, muskets, and pikes in hand for boarding and hand-to-hand-combat drill. It was Lucifer who took command of these, and in the same two-week period a good many of the men were terrified into becoming able swordsmen.

In his eagerness to reach Cadiz, Drake allowed no further delays for discussions or consultations. The Queen's galleons were first to test coastal waters under their keels, and by the second to last day of April, dawn found the entire fleet lying off San Lucar de Barrameda, easily within striking distance of the Spanish port.

At noon he assembled his captains on board the *Elizabeth Bonaventure* for a final council of war and told them, in the simplest terms possible, what he wanted, what he expected from them.

"The wind is with us. The sun is behind us. And by the grace of God, we shall capture the best part of Cadiz before this night falls."

He ordered their colors struck so as to avoid early identification from any swift flyboats that might be patroling the area. He invited Dante to go over, one more time in as much detail as he could recall, the configuartion of the harbor and its defenses. An hour, no more, and the fleet was under way, the gundecks cleared for action, the ship's surgeons ready with their saws and pincers, their mortars and lint. Drummers stood ready on deck wiping beads of moisture from their upper lips, shifting nervously from foot to foot, occasionally dragging a hand down their breeches to dry the palms. Gunners readied their shot and cartridges, lit the slow fuses in their linstocks, and stood by the cannon, enjoying the silence and crystal-clear air, murmuring prayers, wondering if it would be the last glimpse of blue sky and foaming whitecaps they would see.

On board the *Scout* Dante had the dubious pleasure of watching the quartet comprised of the Queen's faster-sailing galleons stretch their lead in front of him. The *Scout* was not alone in her tardiness; many of the private vessels traveled in the same pack, including Victor Bloodstone. Whether by accident or design the *Talon* kept pace with the *Scout*, always a little to the rear and off the starboard quarter. Behind them the five remaining pinnaces struggled through the turbulence of the fleet's wake, tacking back and forth like fleas trying to avoid being capsized by the heavy waves.

Dante was on the afterdeck watching some of their antics when Pitt joined him.

"We're about as ready as we'll ever be."

Dante nodded grimly at the assessment, then his gaze went back to the horizon.

"Is it still there?"

The sun was too bright, dancing off the tops of the waves, making each pinpoint of light resemble a suit of sails. But for three days now, early in the morning and last thing at night, something had been out there, riding low on the horizon, a mere speck of white at dawn, a nagging itch at the nape of the neck throughout the night.

Dante's first thought had leaned toward a Spanish zabra or a Portugese urca bound in the same direction as their fleet. His second, supported by Carleill and considered by Pitt, was a supply boat or even a treasure ship heading for Cadiz to be refitted. In reality, it could have been any of a thousand ships that regularly passed back and forth between the gates of the Mediterranean, yet neither Pitt nor

Dante believed it for longer than it took to read the suspicion in each other's eyes.

"You don't suppose—"

"If it is," Dante had replied with quiet menace, "I will kill her myself."

Both men had looked back at the distant speck on the horizon, not wanting to believe it was possible, yet, when it was still there three days later, with no visible sign of the ship either speeding up to overtake them or falling off to veer into another port, both were more than half convinced it was the *Egret*.

"I truly will throttle her," Dante murmured, barely moving his lips. "I will close my hands around her throat and squeeze until her eyes squirt out of her head and her tongue turns black."

"Maybe it isn't them. Maybe it is, as Carleill suggests, a cautious mariner reluctant to advance on such a large fleet."

Dante stared at the green of the distant sea, then into the green of Pitt's eyes.

Neither one of them believed it for a minute.

At roughly four in the afternoon the great limestone seawall on which the town of Cadiz sat rose up from the sea, the harbor behind it bristling with a forest of masts and rigging. Heedless of William Borough's expectations of courtesy, Drake led his galleons into the bay, giving no warning of their intent until they were past the outermost spit of land. Two large galleys put out officiously from the Port of Saint Mary on the opposite side of the harbor, wanting to inquire after his business. They were shallow-draught vessels, driven by oars, and at the first thunderous volley from the *Bonaventure*'s guns, their curiosity was satisfied and they made an abrupt turnaround, stroking furiously for the shoals where they knew no galleon could follow.

Drake hoisted the Cross of St. George on his mainmast. When he ran his own pennants and standards up the lines to announce to the town of Cadiz that the Dragon of the Apocalypse had arrived, the pandemonium onshore and in the crowded harbor was visible. The streets clogged instantly with citizens running, screaming, for the safety of the Citadel. Soldiers were dispatched from the fortress in a scramble of disorganization and lined the top of the cliffs like small black spikes of hair, their presence there as useless and ineffectual as the muskets they fired or waved in the air.

Drake ordered the *Bonaventure* straight into the massed crowd of shipping anchored alongside the quays. He took a moment to admire how closely the tightly packed formations resembled the paintings Dante had removed from the *San Pedro*, and with the admiration still shining in his eyes, he gave the order to open fire. He loosed three full broadsides into their midst before sheering off. The privateers behind him did likewise before breaking off into smaller packs and attacking selected portions of the harbor. Many of the supply ships and galleons that were in Cadiz being refitted for war were indeed without sails and were hapless targets for the guns of the Queen's privateers. Some of the smaller vessels that could move cut their anchor cables and tried to bolt, but they were no match for the sea hawks, and in short order the bay was filled with smoke and noise, there were ships burning and ships sinking, few, if any, with the means or ability to answer with their guns.

A second small fleet of galleys attempted to rally and do what they could to deter the English and keep the mouth of the channel that led to the inner harbor open for escaping ships. They threw themselves at the *Elizabeth*

Bonaventure, but with the other three Royal Navy warships riding off her flanks, the galleys were dispatched, five of them in flames, the other two with shattered oars and battered courage.

Dante had managed to stay in the shadow of the *Bonaventure*, offering his support against the galleys. Wanting to give his crew confidence, he selected one of the slower ships and stalked it precariously close to the shoals, blasting away as quickly as the men could reload and fire. Through a break in the smoke he caught sight of one of the galleons making laboriously toward the mouth of the channel and he understood at once why the galleys had thrown themselves into the suicidal attack. On her foremast she flew the standard incorporating the arms of Portugal, Leon, Castile, and Naples; at the main, the crossed keys of the papacy; on the mizzen, the red-and-white ensign of Spain; and on the stern, the enormous banner with Philip's royal arms.

It was the forty-four-gun *Santa Ana*, the flagship of Philip's favored admiral, the Marquis of Santa Cruz.

Dante looked for Drake, but either the *Bonaventure* had not noticed the *rata* behind her shield of smaller vessels, or he was too preoccupied with the galleys to break free.

Once more Dante had cause to rue the inadequate firepower of the *Scout*; her guns would be no match for the enormous Spaniard. But what he could do, and what he did do, was order the helm about to put her on a direct course to intercept, hoping to delay the *rata*'s retreat into the inner harbor or at least block the deep water in the center of the channel.

"Full sail, Mister Carleill; bring us in across her bow."

They would have to look sharp if they were going to cut the *Santa Ana* off, and when there was no immediate response from the helm, he whirled around and stared at the white-faced Edward Carleill.

"Helmsman! Did you hear my order?"

"Sir . . . she'll ram us!"

"Not if you bring her in fast enough!"

"There is no room behind her. You'll drive us into the shoals!"

"Either relay my order, helmsman, or I'll bring her in myself!"

The *Santa Ana* had manned her guns. A full broadside erupted from her beam, sending shot screaming through the *Scout*'s tops, tearing sail and rigging and adding a curtain of thick smoke to further cloak her movements. She was gathering speed. Men were in her yards unreefing sail, others were on deck running out more guns, bringing her lower tier to readiness. A blast from a second broadside found a man on the *Scout*'s mizzen, sweeping him off the yard and showering the afterdeck in red droplets. Carleill looked aghast at the spatters on his mustard-colored doublet and reeled back in horror.

"Mister Carleill!"

It was no use and Dante furiously took command of the helm himself, shouting orders to the tops, spurring the men—who were themselves not accustomed to working the lines with iron shots zinging by their heads—into realigning the sails to grab the windage. His one small advantage was the momentum he had carried forward from the initial run into the harbor, and at his orders the *Scout* took a noticeable leap forward, shaking off her lethargy as if coming to realize she would have no choice with a madman at her helm.

Dante brought her streaking in, drawing heavy fire from the *Santa Ana*. Pitt returned two broadsides to each of her one, and the combined noise of their exchange finally brought Drake's attention swinging around, with the *Revenge* and *Golden Lion* following as quickly as they could break off from the galleys.

Lucifer had joined Dante on the afterdeck, summarily growling aside the man who held the tiller. He looked intently to his captain for orders and, when they came, responded without a flicker of hesitation.

Dante sheered the *Scout* across the *Santa Ana's* bow, close enough to see the sweat glistening on the faces of the Spanish gunners. The flagship had no choice but to turn off her course and, in doing so, sailed straight into the path of Drake's gunners. Together with the *Revenge* and the *Golden Lion* he started to pour round after round into the Spaniard, pounding her hull to bits, sending men, guns, sails, masts, pitching into the water. She was soon holed beneath the waterline in a dozen places and was sucked under by the weight of the sea flooding into her holds. She kept firing her guns to the last, however, with shot and flame and a cauldron of boiling steam marking her swift descent to the bottom of the bay.

Dante, meanwhile, had narrowly missed running into the rocky teeth of the shoals. He came so close, in fact, his keel scraped sand and a jagged scream of stone against wood juddered the length of the *Scout*. But he skimmed free and shook out her nerves, leaving the *Santa Ana* to Drake as he circled and set his sights on a fat-looking Levantine who was trying desperately to steal away with the clouds of smoke and cut out of the harbor, into the freedom of the open sea.

On the deck of the *Talon* Victor Bloodstone's eyes narrowed as he tried to peer through the veils of drifting smoke. He had watched the *Scout*'s run against the *Santa Ana* and he had been cheering for the huge Spanish argosy, hoping De Tourville would underestimate the speed and handling of his ship. He had wanted to see the bow of the Spaniard crush into Dante's beam, to see it shatter apart like kindling, sending the French bastard screaming into the sea of fire.

When the *Scout* had disappeared behind the galleon, there was still a hope she might smash herself against the shoals or, better yet, be caught in the crossfire from Drake and the three Royal Navy galleons.

But no. The *Scout* had emerged intact, beetling away from the confusion with hardly more damage than a few torn sails.

"The bastard is like a cat with nine lives," Bloodstone muttered. "What will it take to kill him?"

Horace Lamprey, his nose a mass of angry red scabs over a swollen and miscolored glob of crushed bone, glowered after the *Scout* and cursed her master with equal warmth. He cleared a smear of ash out of his throat and conjured a pleasant picture of the Cimaroon with stakes driven into his eyes.

"I've a few debts I'd like to repay myself," he growled. "Too bad she doesn't cut in front of us. I would not mind catching her in the crossfire."

"Maybe," Bloodstone said slowly, "we can arrange to do exactly that."

Lamprey followed Bloodstone's gaze and just caught a glimpse of the Levantine merchantman sidling away into the whirling wisps of smoke. Her sails were fully shaken out and she was gathering speed. What the encroaching dusk and the haze could not accomplish, the outer lip of the bay would surely do, hiding her from all searching eyes inside the harbor.

Trailing in her wake, stalking her like a predatory wolf, was the *Scout* with Simon Dante de Tourville at her helm.

"Bring us about, Mister Lamprey. The Levantine is far too big for one ship to take on. The captain may require our . . . assistance."

"Aye." The broken face split into a malevolent grin. "Aye, Captain, that he might."

Dante ran the length of the main deck and took the steps to the aftercastle in a single leap.

"We'll come in alongside her and try to hold the Levantine against the land," he said to Pitt. "If we can squeeze her out of the wind, we might have a chance of herding her right into the cliffs."

"Sir? Captain?"

Dante turned and saw Edward Carleill standing behind him, still gray in the face, but rigid with his own mortification.

"Sir, I don't know what happened back there. I cannot explain it, I can only promise it will not happen again. In fact, if—if I delay in following an order by so much as a blink, sir"—he fumbled to draw his sword from his belt—"you would do me a favor by running me through."

Dante studied the taut young face and could not stop himself from thinking of Beau, wishing she were there with all her stubbornness and pride.

"This . . . is my first real battle sir, and—"

Dante cursed out a breath, then tilted his head. "Stand by the rudder and be prepared to relay my orders to the letter. And you had best believe I will run you through, Carleill. Without hesitation."

Young Edward swallowed hard. He resheathed his sword, then took up his position by the tiller, his feet braced wide apart, his hands laced tightly behind his back.

Dante caught the look in Pitt's eyes. "Don't say it."

"Not a word. Not about the helmsman *or* the guns you left behind."

"She's still a woman, dammit," Dante hissed.

"It doesn't seem to bother her. Why does it bother you?"

Dante scowled. "Are your gunners ready?"

"Ready."

"Then stand by the goddamn boards, she's coming into range. Mister Carleill . . . ?"

"Aye, sir?"

"Hands to the sheets. Bring her in close and fast on a course to intercept across the bow. Same maneuver as before, only this time, let's see if we can crowd her into the reefs."

Clear of the bay, the *Scout* took the wind on her stern quarter and chased down the Levantine. Iron-gray water curled off her bow as she tacked onto a parallel course, then started leaning over degree by degree. The master of the Levantine tried frantically to put on more speed, but the *Scout* was lighter, faster. She drew alongside and loosed a full broadside, rocking the huge merchantman and driving her toward the land in a futile effort to evade. Smoke blossomed from her guns and the high-pitched wail of stone balls passed in an arc over the *Scout*'s sails, most of them bouncing harmlessly into the sea.

Dante's guns thundered and the decks shuddered as he poured another volley into the Spaniard. The *Scout* had built up too much speed, as it happened, and threatened to shoot right past the galleon, but Carleill brought her smartly to heel and veered close enough to the giant for the next broadside to bring gouts of shattered wood spraying across their own decks. An explosion, followed by a boiling black corkscrew of smoke, curled upward from the Levantine's powder magazine, and it was a mild disappointment a few minutes later to see her haul down her flags and pennants and signal her surrender.

Dante ordered the *Scout*'s sails backed so that she almost came to a halt in the water. The gunners on the larboard beam cheered and threw their caps and bandanas in the air. Those on the starboard battery started to do the same when a blast of incoming shot exploded through the rail, sending shattered timbers in a lethal spray across the deck. Two guns heaved up on their carriages, one of them crushing a man to pulp beneath the barrel when it landed. The second was torn free from its tackle and crashed through the deck boards, its nose pointing straight up to the sky.

Through the smoke and the screams of wounded men, Dante saw the *Talon* bearing down on them. He cursed and shouted a warning, most of it lost to the roar of another crushing broadside.

But Pitt had already seen her and ordered what was left of his starboard guns loaded. He shouted for the crews to fire at will even as Dante ordered the sails reset and tried to pick up the wind again.

The Levantine must have been just as surprised as the *Scout* to see another ship emerging from the clouds of smoke clogging the mouth of the bay. More so when the ship began firing on its own countryman. She was not about to be caught up in their argument, however, and veered closer into the land, leaving the two to pound each other to splinters if that was to be their intention.

It certainly appeared to be Bloodstone's, for he was standing well off, using his demis to soften the *Scout*'s hull and rigging before he moved in for the kill. Dante ordered evasive maneuvers and the privateer made a valiant attempt to obey, but she was now the one effectively trapped between the land and the open sea. Bloodstone kept pace, kept the great bronze teeth of his guns firing, chewing away at the sails, rigging, and masts, turning the sea around her into a mass of spouting fountains.

And enjoying every bloody minute.

Chapter 27

"We have to do something!" Beau shouted.

"Aye, daughter, aye. I see what's happenin' an' we're movin' as bloody fast as we can! Ye've put everythin' in the tops except the shirt on yer back!"

Beau cursed and paced the length of the *Egret*'s foredeck, her fist pounding the rail every two or three feet. It may have been the decision, unanimous, of the entire crew to bring the *Egret* around and chase after Drake's fleet. But it had been Beau's and Spence's to stay far enough back they could not be stopped and dispatched home again, their tails tucked between their legs. For two weeks they had dogged the English sea hawks, always keeping their sails barely in sight on the horizon ahead. They had only put on sail and picked up speed when the bleak thread of the Spanish coastline began to take shape.

The *Egret* had streaked in fast, pushing the miles of seawater behind them as they cut cleanly through the rolling swells. They were a good two, maybe three, hours behind the fleet when it sailed into Cadiz Bay, and as the mouth of the harbor grew closer, the dirty gray sky above it was cloaked in a massive cloud of smoke and cinder.

"He did it," Spence had muttered in awe. "Drake has set the King's bloody fleet on fire!"

"And don't think the King won't know it in short order," Beau had countered, pointing to the sudden flaring of signal fires that were coming alight, one by one, a mile or two apart along the darkening shoreline.

Then she had noticed something else ablaze, farther along the coast, well out of the harbor. Two ships were engaged, one an enormous Levantine cargo vessel, the other . . .

"Christ Jesus," she had exclaimed. She had recognized the *Scout*, looking like nothing more than a pesky hornet buzzing after a lumbering giant.

"He promised he would stand off a thousand yards," she quoted sardonically. "He vowed he would be the soul of discretion, that he would offer support, nothing else."

"Calls anythin' he's done so far discreet," McCutcheon remarked, spitting over the rail, "I'd sorely hate to see what he calls reckless."

Spence chuckled. "Ye already have. Ye saw him kiss our Beau right smack on the open deck."

Beau wasn't listening. She did not even hear the jest over the sudden loud pounding of her heart.

"Father . . . there! Another ship has come out of the harbor! It—it's the *Talon*!" She gasped and swore again. "It's Bloodstone's ship and . . . I don't even think Dante knows he's there!"

"Doubt if anyone knows he's there, what with the smoke an' all."

"*Jonas!*" Spit was leaning forward over the rail as if the few added inches gave a better view. "Look at the bastard! He's opened with all guns!"

Beau and Spence watched in horror as the *Talon*'s guns erupted in seemingly endless tongues of orange flame. They were still four or five miles out and the sound reached them as muted thuds, dampened further by the rapidly fading light. In another few minutes they would only have the throbbing glow of the burning harbor and the fire from their own guns to give the ships any kind of silhouette against the darkness.

"We have to do something!" Beau insisted.

"Aye. Spit—load the demis with fifteen-pound shot; it will carry farther. We'll fire a round as soon as Beau can pull us into position to give him a broadside. Let the bastard know someone is seein' what he's doin', at any rate."

McCutcheon sprang away, his eyes still on the two ships as he calculated speed, powder weight, and distances. Beau was half a step behind, shouting orders as she ran.

Dante could not see much of anything at all. Dusk was purpling what little clean air came on board the *Scout*, the rest was filled with smoke, flying debris, scraps of burning canvas. The mainmast was a shambles of tangled lines and broken spars. The top third was folded over and men had been sent up to hack at it with saws and cudgels to rid them of the useless drag. Every quarter knot of lost speed kept her under the *Talon*'s guns and she was already badly wounded. Most of her sheets hung from loose or broken lines; spars swung crazily with the pitch of the ship. Her hull was breached and the sea was pouring in below the waterline, almost faster than men on pumps could disgorge it. There was blood everywhere, making the decks slippery underfoot; five of Carleill's original crew had already jumped overboard, preferring to swim for shore and take their chances with the Spanish rather than remain on board and be caught in the midst of a grudge match between two madmen.

Dante's madness had a slight advantage in that the *Talon*'s gunners were nowhere near as good as his own *Virago* men, despite the fact that they were using Pitt's own demis against them. Two out of every four shots scudded harmlessly into the sea, causing a good deal of spray and chop, and a true appreciation for every one of the culverins' retorts that struck wood and bone. Pitt was keeping up a steady barrage, sharp enough and hot enough to make Bloodstone think twice about coming in too close too soon, but another ten minutes or so and it likely would not matter anyway. The *Scout*'s rudder was sloppy and she barely had enough sail to keep her moving. She was pinned as helplessly against the shoreline as the Levantine had been; the only difference being a captain who would not have struck his colors had the devil himself been spewing flame at him.

"Simon!"

Dante was manning one of the cannon. He reeled away just as the glowing tip of the linstock was applied to the touch hole and the breeching tackle jumped to absorb the recoil from the exploding shot.

"*Simon!*"

Dante swung around as the crew hauled in the gun, swabbed the barrel, shoved a fresh shot down its throat, and packed it against a new powder cartridge. Pitt was working the gun beside him, his face streaked with soot and sweat, his blond hair smeared with blood. He was pointing wildly over the side, shouting something, but Dante's ears were still ringing from the last explosion.

Dante saw nothing at first and he had to wipe his eyes to see what was causing Pitt to leap up and down like a fool and windmill his arms nearly out of their sockets. An-

gling in from upwind was another galleon, her sails full and
straining with vengeance, her guns run out, spitting thunder as she charged into the fray.

Dante could barely believe his eyes and had to blink
twice before accepting it. "By God . . . *Beau!*"

He grabbed hold of a shroud line and pulled himself up
to stand on the rail, watching as the *Egret* backed all of
her topsails and almost slid to a complete halt in the water.
In her own swirling backwash she angled her stern around
to present her full broadside, and with every man on board
the *Scout* cheering like lunatics, she fired three immense
volleys, seemingly without a break in smoke, noise, or gout-
ing sparks of flame.

Dante clenched his fist and added his own voice to
those of his men. "Bloodstone, you bloody-minded coward!
How does it feel to choke on your own treachery!" And
even though neither ship could hear him, he called to the
Egret as well. "Ahoy, Jonas, you beautiful bastard! Bring
her straight in and crucify the coward with everything
you've got!"

Spence would *have* to bring her in closer, for although
the show of support was much needed to bolster the spirits
on board the *Scout*, the *Egret* was still too far out to do
any real damage. Even so, some of the demis struck their
mark, tearing a long gash in the *Talon*'s main course and
plowing into timbers on deck.

Two more volleys and the *Egret* reset her sails, turning
bow-on to the *Talon*, running in as fast as she could gather
windage. Bloodstone seemed unconcerned. His ship blazed
with another broadside, taking out a section of the *Scout*'s
afterdeck and blowing three men into the sea.

"He obviously doesn't have much respect for Spence or
his ship," Pitt grated. "He's going to finish with us first."

"He's going to try," Dante agreed with a snarl. "But we still have a few surprises left."

"Do I want to know what they are?"

Dante grinned larcenously. "You will approve, I'm sure. Those crates of nails you found in the hold, bring them up and fill the barrels of the bow guns. Fetch up the kegs of Greek fire while you're about it and set them in the stern."

Pitt's face brightened through the grime. "I like it already."

Dante ran to the stern, where Edward Carleill stood over the tiller like a blooded hound. He looked, if anything, more terrified than before, but thus far had held to Dante's orders and executed them without so much as twitching an eyelid.

He blinked this time when Dante gave him fresh instructions and, if it was possible, went a shade paler.

"We'll need as much speed as you can give me, if it is going to succeed. Have we anything left?"

"I'll find it, sir. Count on it." He turned and ordered the men in the tops to trim the sheets, to hold them in place if necessary with their bare hands.

Dante left the rudder in Carleill's hands and ran back to the stern just as Pitt arrived carrying four small kegs filled with naphtha and sealed with a layer of tar. They would have to be within spitting distance of the *Talon* for the incendiaries to succeed, but if only one hit the target, the exploding oil would spread flames across the decks faster than anyone could think to smother them.

Getting them close enough would take just about all the *Scout* had left in her. The superior firepower of the privateer would be pounding her all the way in; their one slim hope was for the *Egret* to see what they were doing and offer Bloodstone a warm distraction.

In the meantime he kept his head low and his cannon

loaded and firing. Carleill aimed her like an arrow, straight and true, and the privateer, battered but not defeated, responded with a last burst of spirit. She gathered speed and courage and determination and threw herself at the *Talon's* guns, and from where Dante crouched by the stern falconets, he could see Victor Bloodstone standing on the foredeck, encouraging his men to shoot as fast as they could reload.

Carleill denied them as much of a target for as long as he could before he reached the point of turning. He was passing the orders, tightening the crew's grip on the tiller, when a blast from the *Talon* raked the afterdeck, shattering through timbers and flesh, sweeping the entire upper castle and everyone on it into the sea.

It gave Dante a moment's pause, staring at the gaping hole where Carleill had been standing, knowing it might have been Beau. . . . But then he had no time to think at all. The *Scout* was fifty, forty, thirty yards from the *Talon*, and with no way to turn her off her course, she was going to ram the privateer at full speed. Pitt fired the bow guns, then ordered the men back. Four lethal loads of iron nails were sprayed across the decks of the *Talon*, wreaking terrible damage, and with less than twenty yards to go, Dante lit the fuses on the stern guns . . . and fired.

Beau watched the *Scout* make her stumbling turn and start a bow-on run toward the *Talon*. She was expecting Dante to veer off at the last moment, duplicating the feat he had executed against the *San Pedro*, but something went mortally wrong. Even from three hundred yards away she could hear the screaming of timbers and the smashing of planks as the two ships collided. The hull of the *Talon* was rammed inward. The privateer staggered and reeled over, pushing a wave of water off her starboard beam. When she righted herself, the *Scout* was wedged fast amidships and Dante's men were scrambling over the side, cutlasses, pikes, and muskets in hand. Two of the four kegs of Greek fire found their marks, exploding on the *Talon*'s afterdeck in great sheets of liquid flame. The combustible ran along the rails and dripped down the sides of the hull. It fanned across the decks, rippling blue and gold and red in the darkness, running along planks and spilling hot blue fingers between the broken boards.

"Hold yer fire!" Spence shouted over the heads of his gun crews. "Or we'll hit both ships! Beau! Bring her in to grapplin' distance, we'll crowd her on the other side!"

Beau brought the *Egret* in fast and smooth. The men, led by Jonas Spence, stood ready by the boards with grappling lines and weapons. The *Talon* was still firing her guns and Spit gave them several hot replies to the insult at point-blank range, close enough to bring plumes of seawater spraying over the rails. Billy Cuthbert took men up into the shrouds with muskets and pistols and picked out their targets by the light of the fires blazing in the *Talon*'s stern.

Bedlam had erupted on the deck of the privateer. Men fought in pairs, in trios, in swarms; shadowy couples in macabre dances with swords and daggers, assuming faces and features only when heated by the glow of the flames.

Beau scanned the decks for a glimpse of Dante, but there were too many shadows twisting and writhing in confusion. She saw Pitt, a pistol in each hand, a blade glinting at his hip, swinging himself over to the deck of the *Talon* from the *Scout*. And she saw Lucifer, his twin scimitars hacking at limbs as if he were back in the Indies harvesting cane. There were dead and injured everywhere. The decks were streaked with gore.

Beau drew her cutlass, and with four *Egret* men behind

her she clambered over the boarding planks and dropped into the midst of the fighting. A shadow with a boat hook came at her from the left and she slashed without thinking, using both hands to wield the heavy sword across the man's throat. Two more shadows lunged for her and she shot one with her pistol, then used it like a club when it was spent rather than take the trouble to reload.

The carpenter, Thomas Moone, was on her left, carrying the lid from a barrel to use as a shield. He swore every time he swung his cutlass, but he did so with a practiced eye, knowing the weakest joints, the most vulnerable bones. Men charged them and more men poured over from the decks of the *Egret*, and in short order the *Talon*'s crew were throwing down their weapons and throwing up their arms, screaming for mercy.

And there was still no sight of Dante de Tourville.

He was, at that precise moment, on the only clear circle of deck space on the *Talon*. Victor Bloodstone stood across from him, panting and sweat-soaked, circling his hated enemy in a wary crouch, sword in hand, eyes blazing murder.

"Honorable to the end, Victor," Dante spat. "That is what your epitaph will read. Written in the blood of the men you sacrificed in the name of greed and ambition."

Bloodstone lunged forward with his blade. The thrust was easily put aside by Dante, though he fought with only one good arm. The other had been torn open in the impact when the two ships had collided, and dripped a steady patter of blood onto the deck.

Bloodstone retreated and circled, waiting for another opening. His enemy was big, solid with brute strength, but some of that strength was melting away. Moreover, he had seen Dante fight before and knew he had lived too long on the deck of a ship to trouble himself with the intricacies of footwork. He preferred to hack and slash, mostly to good effect, especially if his opponant had not looked into the menacing steel of his eyes before. Victor had looked—and laughed—as he did now when he executed a perfect feint and left a thin red ribbon welling across the massive chest.

"Why?" Dante snarled. "Why did you do it? Was it the gold? All for the gold?"

Bloodstone shook the sweat out of his eyes. His back was to the flames and the hated face was lit before him, burnished by the glowing heat. Farther yet, looming out of the shadows, another face, uglier than sin with a smashed nose and stealth in his mutilated smile, caused Victor to stop, to steady his blade a moment as if contemplating something profound in his answer.

"The gold? Yes, partly it was the gold. And partly . . . it was you."

"Me? What in God's name did I do to you?"

Bloodstone's lips curled in derision and he laughed, "Absolutely nothing, my dear Comte. Nothing your many righteous generations of noble blood could even begin to understand."

He nodded and Horace Lamprey raised his pistol, aiming squarely for the back of Dante's head. He pulled the trigger and the pan flashed; a fraction of a second later the gun jerked to one side as the hand holding it was impaled on the mast beside it, stuck fast by a needle-thin stiletto. The shot discharged and Dante whirled around in time to see Beau throw a second knife and reduce Lamprey's screams to a gurgled hiss.

Victor's sword flashed and Dante moved to block it. The two blades crossed and slid down to the hilt, sending a shower of sparks flying off the steel. Weapons parted and crossed again, drawing sweat and curses on both sides. The impact shuddered down their arms and Bloodstone bared his teeth in anticipation as he bore down on Dante, seeking to weaken the vulnerable left side of his body. He deliberately invited the Frenchman to lock swords again, then gave his wrist a vicious twist, bringing the blade around and up, effectively breaking the strength in Dante's arm. He saw his opening and took it, leaning back and thrusting forward, following through with a triumphant cry as he expected to feel flesh, muscle, and bone sliding the length of his sword.

But in a move that had been almost too swift to believe, Dante had anticipated the strike and pivoted—with the grace of a dancer—a full circle around and back, bringing his own blade hacking forcefully across the base of Bloodstone's spine. Bone cracked and flesh parted. The cry of triumph turned into a scream of agony as Bloodstone was split almost in half. The impact sent him crashing forward through a broken gap in the deck rail and he fell, with Dante's sword embedded in his back, into the pool of flames that were now engulfing most of the main deck.

Dante staggered to the rail and Beau rushed forward to catch him under the arm. He stared at Bloodstone's body until the flames licked greedily over it and then he looked at Beau. Her face was streaked with grime and ash, her doublet was torn at the shoulder, and a gash on her chin leaked blood down the side of her throat, but he thought he had never seen anything quite so beautiful before. Stubborn, disobedient, reckless, defiant . . . but beautiful enough to make his soul ache.

"One of these days," he gasped, "you are going to have to start doing as you're told."

Beau leaned into his chest and buried her face against his throat. "One of these days you are going to have to start trusting me."

Dante pressed his lips into the soft silk of her hair. "Yes. I know."

The flames were growing hotter. Men were shouting, running past them, leaping to the safety of the *Egret*. Pitt, Spence, and McCutcheon were calling to them, warning them they would have to cast off in the next few seconds or run the risk of the fire jumping across the ships.

Dante frowned and tucked his finger under her chin, forcing her face up to his. All of the gold and treasures in the world were right there, shimmering up at him, brimming with emotions as raw and ragged as his own.

"How much do you trust me?"

"With my life."

He glanced over at the *Egret* and murmured, "That should be just about enough."

Heedless of his injury, he scooped her up into his arms and hoisted her onto the top of the rail. He climbed up beside her and, using the shroud lines for balance, caught the length of cable Pitt swung over to them. Most of the grappling lines had been cut and the galleons had been pushed apart everywhere but at the bow. There, a single umbilical cord strained between them, and as Dante curled his arm around Beau's waist and swept them across the twenty-foot gap, Lucifer brought down one of his scimitars and chopped the two ships free.

Epilogue

⟡

Drake's fleet spent the remainder of the night burning and destroying what they could of the outer harbor of Cadiz. The next morning he took his fleet of pinnaces through the channel to the inner harbor, where he proceeded to burn seven of the King's prized galleons and a score of smaller vessels loaded to the gunwales with wine, cannon, seasoned timber, and victuals for the King's armada gathering at Lisbon. Considerable damage was done and little had been suffered, although the patience of El Draque had been sorely tested the previous evening when confronted with the sooty faces of Spence, Beau, and Simon Dante.

Victor Bloodstone's treachery, the loss of the *Talon* and the *Scout*, had caused the infamous sea hawk to glow as red as his hair. The audacity of Jonas Spence, following in their wake despite orders to take himself and his cargo safely home, caused only moderately less apoplexy, and Drake seriously contemplated confiscating the *Egret* for their impertinence. Only Dante's intervention, supported by a veiled threat of mutiny from every other captain in his fleet, prevented it.

Drake then took his small force, which now included the *Egret*, out of Cadiz two days later, leaving a pall of smoke in their wake. Over the course of the next six weeks he made good his promise to wreak havoc on smaller ports, and in doing so destroyed enough shipping and vital supplies to eventually throw the King's plans for invasion back a full year.

It was also on this homeward journey that Sir Francis happened across another of Spain's treasure galleons, the *San Felipe*. He was pleased to attack her, especially when her holds relinquished bullion, plate, and spices in such quantities as to make the plunder from the *San Pedro* seem a pittance by comparison. It was, in fact, the largest single prize ever taken by a privateering vessel, and bristling in triumph, Drake returned to England, satisfied his fame and fortune were fully restored, if not at their most rousing and inspiring level ever.

After the Queen finished counting her share of the profits, a month of celebrations were planned that she might properly thank her bold sea hawks for not only leaving the King's pride in shambles, but for infusing the royal treasury with enough funds to start building England's navy.

Beau emerged from the dressing room with a frown on her face. She was certain she was missing something. Although the three servants who had been assigned to help her bathe, powder herself, crimp and coif her hair, and dress her from the stockings up like some child too addlepated to know how to lace a garter, she was convinced a crucial article of clothing had been forgotten.

"Simon—?" She had her head bowed when she came into the salon, concentrating on the combined task of eas-

ing the wide wings of the farthingale through the doorway
and not tripping over the wide hoops and multiple under-
skirts that kept snagging her toes. "You know more about
these things than I do. Would you not say something is
amiss here?"

She looked up and saw a stranger standing by the window. "Oh! Excuse me, I thought you were . . ."

Dante turned around. He had been waiting in the salon
exactly two hours, the interminable ticking of the ormolu
clock relieved only now and then when he heard a muffled
string of blasphemies make its way through the door of the
inner chamber. Pitt had kept him company the first hour,
but a summons from his dark-eyed little duchess had sent
him scurrying to his own apartments. Geoffrey Pitt had not
waited to return to England to marry Christiana Villa-
nueva. There had been a Catholic priest on board the *San
Felipe* who had agreed, for the sake of the soul of one of
Spain's daughters, to wed them. They certainly hadn't
waited for much else, either, for Pitt had come today, full
of the news he was going to be a father.

Spence, likewise, had blustered about the delicate furnishings of the salon like a whale out of water. He had lost
another finger and half an ear in the fight with the *Talon*,
and had declared his intention to take his profits and build
a small fleet of merchant ships that *other* captains might
take out at risk to life and limb. He and Spit McCutcheon
would take to the helm for pleasure only. Or when his
supplies of rumbullion threatened to run perilously low.

McCutcheon had also been outfitted to attend the
Queen's presence. He had been scrubbed, shaved, and clad
in a new suit of clothes that made him look like a colorful
marionette. Dante could only imagine how Beau would fare
in the transition. He had seen the maids and the armloads
of frilly clothing go into the dressing room. He had also

seen the maids stumble out hours later, their necks clammy with sweat, their caps askew, and their shoulders sagging with exhaustion.

Now she was out and the suspense was at an end. He turned when she called his name, and for a second or two the glare from the window remained too bright on his eyes to see much more than a dark blur.

"Excuse me, I thought—I thought you were my husband," Beau said, her voice trailing off to a whisper. She stopped dead in her tracks and stared at the tall, elegant figure who stood in front of the twenty-foot-high mullioned window, certain her eyes were playing tricks on her.

It was their first full day in London, the first time she had seen him not at a dockyard helping Spence supervise the repairs on the *Egret* or cloistered in a stuffy warehouse haggling with guild merchants over the sale of the cargo. He had waited to the last minute to come to his house in London, despite a flurry of dispatches from Drake and the Queen. He had used the excuse of a fever to delay their leavetaking from Plymouth, but the only heat he suffered from was doctored quite adequately in Beau's arms.

Reluctantly he had come to London and even more reluctantly he had left their bed this morning to be attended by a barber, a valet, a tailor; all in anticipation of being received, fêted, and berated by the Queen. To the latter he had already weathered a storm of letters regarding his insolence in marrying someone not of noble or even elevated birth. To each of those he had simply sent back a card embossed with the De Tourville coat of arms and a very large fleur-de-lis, expressing the regrets of the Comte and Comtesse that his fever was still too high to permit travel.

Spence had expected warrants any day. Dante had sim-

ply made love to his new wife and gone about his business
at the shipyards.

And now here they were, a half hour's coach ride to
the Queen's audience chamber, and Beau felt as if she
ought to curtsy to *him*. Dante's hair had been trimmed to
within an inch of ebony perfection, his jaw scraped clean
of the rough fur she had come to appreciate in more ways
than one. He wore a white satin shirt beneath a midnight-
blue velvet doublet, edged and banded in gold, with a row
of jewel-encrusted buttons glittering down the front closure. The narrowest of embroidered collar and cuffs stood
out in breathtaking contrast to the deeply tanned color of
his face and hands, while his legs—long and thewed like
iron—were cased in hose the same rich blue as his doublet.
His shoes were made of the finest, softest leather, buckled
in pure gold. The dress sword he wore at his hip was
sheathed in a bejeweled buckler, the hilt an elaborate
weave of scrolls and curlicues.

He looked, for the first time ever, like a member of the
royal French aristocracy, like the urbane and elegant
Comte de Tourville. His only obstinate act of rebellion was
the wink of gold prominent in his earlobe.

He walked slowly forward, his approach drawing even
more air out of Beau's lungs, if that were possible.

His eyes were as blue as the sky as he made a deliberate,
measured perusal of her hair, her gown, even the tiny rows
of pearls that ornamented her belt. He had chosen the
gown himself—everything, in fact, from the sheer silk
drawers and corselet to the wheel-shaped farthingale with
its descending layers of wire hoops. Her sleeves had enough
rich cloth in them to fashion two normal shipboard shirts.
The bodice was flat and rigid, narrowing past a surprisingly
small waistline, dipping to an elongated V to exaggerate
the flaring velvet skirts. All was in the deepest, purest

black, seeded with black pearls and glittering jets. Her hair
was a puff of soft auburn curls around her face, then pulled
back into a coif and decorated with tiny clusters of jewels.
Around her neck she wore ropes of De Tourville diamonds,
so dazzling against the dusky hue of her complexion, it
would make the Court's eyes water with envy. On her finger she wore another de Tourville heirloom, an enormous
pearl circled by more diamonds, reputed to have once belonged to a Plantagenet princess.

Dante could think of no one more suited to wear it.

"*Mon cygne noir magnifique,*" he murmured, his voice
husky enough to allow a little color to leak back into her
face. "I never imagined you could look so beautiful . . . with
or without your breeches on."

"You are just saying that to be kind."

"My dear Comtesse"—he advanced closer and took
both her hands in his, kissing each palm before he spread
her arms wide and let his silvery eyes feast on all her splendor—"a blade at my throat could not make me be *kind* to
anyone in my present mood. But it warms me to know Bess
will be so envious, she will undoubtedly banish us from
Court for a very long time."

"Because of me?" Beau gasped.

"*Thanks* to you, my love. Moreover, her ladies will suffer
to remove all of the mirrors from her sight so as not to
allow too harsh a comparison to her wrinkled skin and
painted white complexion. The courtiers will all be
springing out of their codpieces like schoolboys. I will be
forced to defend my claim a thousand times ere this night
is over."

Beau laughed and curled her arms around his shoulders,
coming to him in an irreverent crush of silk and velvet.
"Be silent, fool. Or put your mouth to better use."

"Gladly." He bowed his head, kissing her with a lusty

vengeance that left her lips redder than any rouge wash could have done.

When he released her, she continued to stare up at him, her eyes so round and compellingly flecked with gold, he laughed and kissed her again. "Here? Now? What of all the hard work your maids have done?"

"I would not give it a moment's thought," she breathed honestly.

"Well"—he gave her a husbandly peck on the cheek— "I would. Once I come out of this stuffed peacock's costume, I stay out of it."

Beau grinned. "I would not—"

"—Give it a moment's thought, yes. I know. And if that is the case, I shall have to occupy your mind with other things. What were you asking me when you came into the room? You thought something was missing?"

She stood back and ran her fingers over her bodice. The cut was so snug, her breasts compressed so flat, there seemed to be far too much plumping of flesh over the squared edge of the neckline. "I tried pulling up the ruff of my corselet and down the strands of the necklace, but there still seems to be too much of me to cover."

Dante tried not to smile. "It is the French cut, I will admit, and probably too scandalous for a court of English Protestants."

"Then why did you put me in it?"

He feathered a fingertip over the mounds of tender flesh. "So I can ease my boredom over the next few hours by imagining the pleasure of taking you out of it."

"And in the meantime? If I bend over?"

"If you bend over, mam'selle," he murmured. "The Court will be more than simply scandalized."

The suddenly very young and not very assured Comtesse Isabeau de Tourville sighed and pressed her cheek against his broad shoulder. "I wish we were a thousand miles away, with a deck beneath our feet and canvas over our heads."

Dante wrapped his arms around her briefly, then straightened with a smile. "Perhaps I can make your evening a little easier to bear by giving you your gift now."

"Gift? What gift?"

He kissed her on the tip of her nose and led her to the window. "You have to understand she isn't quite finished. Pitt still has to put in her teeth and Lucifer has to do something with rooster gizzards that I'm not altogether certain you want to know."

Beau frowned and looked out the window. Dante's London house sat on the banks of the Thames, giving him a mariner's view of the busy river. Lying at anchor in the deeper water midcourse was a new galleon, so closely resembling the golden replica of the *Virago*, it sent a small shiver down Beau's spine. There had been some slight changes made in the design. Her lines were cleaner, her castles almost level with the main deck, allowing space for an extra sail on the mizzen and fore.

"I had ordered her keel laid before we left for Veracruz," he explained softly. "I just hadn't thought of a name for her yet."

Beau followed the gracious sweep of her bow and found the carved figurehead beneath. It was a woman's head, as shockingly familiar as the one she saw in the mirror each morning, but below, it was the body of a swan with her wings outspread to catch the wind.

"My other magnificent *Black Swan*," he said. "Do you like her?"

"Like her?" Beau whispered. "She looks . . . like she could fly."

"Indeed, mam'selle, I am told she can . . . with a firm enough hand to guide her." He waited until the large golden eyes turned to him before he added, "You once told me you would not marry a man who tried to take you away from the sea. How do you feel about having married one selfish enough to want you as much for your skills at the helm as for your skills at rescuing him from his own foolish pride?"

Beau opened her mouth to reply but words, for once, failed her.

They did not fail the Queen, however, when she was in receipt an hour later of another note embossed with the De Tourville coat of arms. It seemed the comte's fever had returned with a vengeance, and, as he advised His Most Gracious Majesty, it would not be safe for either him or his wife to attend Court until all risk of a relapse was out of his system.

The Four of Hearts Checklist

Books by Marsha Canham:
__STRAIGHT FOR THE HEART
__IN THE SHADOW OF MIDNIGHT
__UNDER THE DESERT MOON
__THROUGH A DARK MIST

Books by Jill Gregory:
__WHEN THE HEART BECKONS
__DAISIES IN THE WIND
__FOREVER AFTER
__CHERISHED

Books by Joan Johnston:
__MAVERICK HEART
__THE INHERITANCE
__OUTLAW'S BRIDE
__KID CALHOUN
__THE BAREFOOT BRIDE
__SWEETWATER SEDUCTION

Dell